LAMBS OF GOD

R I V E R H E A D   B O O K S

a member of Penguin Putnam Inc.

New York

1 9 9 8

Lambs of God

Marele Day

Riverhead Books
a member of
Penguin Putnam Inc.
200 Madison Avenue
New York, NY 10016

Published simultaneously in Canada

Library of Congress Cataloging-in-Publication Data

Day, Marele.
Lambs of God / Marele Day.
p. cm.
ISBN 1-57322-079-5
I. Title.
PR9619.3.D382L3 1998 97-38602 CIP
823—dc21

Printed in the United States of America
1 3 5 7 9 10 8 6 4 2

This book is printed on acid-free paper. ♾

Book design by Marysarah Quinn

ACKNOWLEDGMENTS

I would like to thank my indefatigable agents Elaine Markson and Jerry Kalajian; editor Cindy Spiegel; George Mannix, Julian Miller, and Michael Witts for casting careful eyes over the novel in manuscript form; and especially Susie Rourke, who heard every bleat.

It was soft. Soft and silky as a mouse's ear. More like a soft little quivering animal than a sprig of sage. Sister Iphigenia rubbed the leaves once more, vigorously this time to release their volatile oils, then dropped them into the teapot. She briefly sniffed her fingers, then wiped them down the front of her woolen vest. The nuns had long ago dispensed with formal habits.

Sister Iphigenia sat in the cloister, in strips of bright light alternating with deep shadow. If she had looked up she would have seen the ribbed vaulting arching over her like the skeleton of an immense dinosaur. But Sister Iphigenia was otherwise occupied. She was watching the fire in the courtyard, watching for the jet of steam from the kettle. Somewhere behind her was the rasping noise of Sister Margarita scrubbing the Eucharist table. Soon, both she and Sister Carla would leave off their tasks and join her in the courtyard. Today was Haircut Day.

None of this accounted for Iphigenia's sudden alertness. Beyond the smell of sage, the heavy odor of her own body, the cold ashy smell of stone, the lanolin of sheep everywhere, her nose picked up an unfamiliar scent. Far away and faint, it was barely more than a whisper. A small but regular disturbance.

It was there and then it was not, it was there and then it was not. Like the inhalation and exhalation of breath.

The kettle hissed and spattered water onto the coals. Iphigenia pulled her weight up off the bench. She went into the courtyard, lifted the heavy kettle, and poured boiling water over the leaves in the pot. The fresh antiseptic smell of sage was pleasant and it did seem to keep insects and vermin away.

On Haircut Day they washed each other's hair and cut it. Then they'd tease out the strands, card and spin it, just as they did with the sheep's fleece. On Shearing Day the sheep would have their turn. The sisters always did their own fleece first, to set a good example.

The sheep wandered wherever they liked. In the fields, through the cloisters, in the monastery chapel their bleating would resound, echoing up an ovine hymn to God. In addition to the ritual Shearing Day the nuns collected wool throughout the year. Bits of fleece caught in bushes, on the statue of our Blessed Virgin, or in the crevices of the stonework where the sheep brushed past.

They wandered all over the monastery but did not stray. There was plenty of sweet grass in summer, enough to get them through the winter as well. They didn't shy away from the sisters. The flock of nuns and the flock of sheep had been together for so long that the sheep, if they had enough brains to consider the matter at all, thought of the nuns as part of the flock rather than shepherds. So that on Shearing Day they would meekly allow themselves to be sheared, one side, then the other till big lumps of fleece flopped softly to the ground, the greasy woolly outer layer protecting the fine soft fibers close to the skin.

Occasionally a ram would break out of the routine and run

rampant. Till the nuns found it and slaughtered it for their table. One ram to a flock was quite enough. More than one and trouble started.

The scrubbing stopped. Iphigenia heard the clank of the bucket and sluicing of water down the drain. Then into the full sunlight came Sister Margarita, her pink hands still wet and dripping, her face flushed with God's work.

Iphigenia's nose was jutting into the air.

"What?" asked Sister Margarita, drying her hands on her woolly skirt. This had been a great favorite, one of the first pieces in which they had incorporated dyed wool. They had boiled up nettles and steeped the wool to produce a lush green. Then they had knitted a landscape. The nettle-green grass, the white wool of lambs dotted in amongst it. This was before they had started on more complex themes. The grass in the landscape had faded to a dull olive green and Margarita had started wearing it as a skirt. It had grown thin in the front where Margarita knelt on it and a couple of holes had developed which gave a glimpse of her strong sturdy legs.

"Smell with no name. Distant."

Sister Margarita sniffed the air, taking it in in tiny bursts, then staying very still and letting the grains of odor float into the nasal cavity. She smelled tallow, traces of blood, pollen, the aroma of the sage tea brewing in the courtyard, the pervasive smell of sheep. All these smells had names.

She shook her head. But because she couldn't smell it didn't mean it wasn't there. Her nose was becoming myopic. Unless a breeze carried them directly to her, distant smells had ceased to exist for Sister Margarita.

"Vinegar, pear, leather," prompted Iphigenia.

"Sheep knocked over a bottle?" suggested Margarita.

Any further discussion of the smell was waylaid by the appearance of Sister Carla. She was younger than the others, and her wild and woolly hair was still black and lustrous. There were twigs, leaves, and other debris in it. She dumped a basket of hair on the table, hair that had been collected from the sisters' brushes throughout the year. A whole basketful. Nestled in the hair was a pair of scissors, not quite concealing three shining drops of blood.

Sister Iphigenia looked at her sharply. "Accident," Sister Carla explained, avoiding Iphigenia's eyes.

"Never mind," consoled Sister Margarita. "Turns a lovely russet."

The three nuns were gathered in the courtyard. In the courtyard they were closer to the Lord. Four walls with an infinite canopy of sky. Besides, in the chapel they never knew when another fragment of roof might fall on their heads.

This Haircut Day it was Sister Margarita's turn to go first. She leaned over the wash trough and let the sisters cleanse her hair with the tepid sage liquid, the words they murmured every year on this day trickling into her ears. Then they sat her in a chair, her hands resting in her faded green lap. Sister Iphigenia surrounded her with a sheet to collect the hair while Sister Carla approached with the scissors.

Sister Margarita listened for the crisp decisive snip. The sound of sharpened scissors so close to her ears always took her back to the first time she had been shorn. There had been other novices with her that day, silently looking at one another, not speaking, full of expectancy and a need to be brave. Margarita remembered the carpet of hair on the floor when the job was finished. The modest browns, tawny reds plush as foxes' tails, black hair shiny as raven wings. And her own, as light and golden as a halo.

Sister Iphigenia watched the clumps of gray fall onto the sheet. It was stronger now, the smell in the distance, and no longer intermittent. Sister Carla was intent on her task, Sister Margarita had her eyes closed. Iphigenia moved her nose around, going through a catalogue of smells trying to identify it. Vinegar, pear, leather. And something else, yeasty but not the yeast of bread or wine. Her nose hovered, brought each element into synthesis. She recognized it now. It was a smell that she knew but had almost forgotten. It was the smell of a man.

Sister Carla lay hidden in the long grass. She'd been there practically the whole of the drowsy afternoon, skirt up, belly bare to the sun. She'd done this as a child, lain on the ground and looked up at the sky. It may have been only once, it may have been many times and her memory, for the sake of convenience, had gathered all those times in and skeined them into one. What she remembered about it then was the way the leaves cut patterns into the sky, the way a breath of wind would move the leaves and enlarge a space for the sun to fill her eyes with a shimmering that spread and faded out every other detail of the picture. She couldn't remember how the child was lying, what she was wearing, only the pattern of leaves and the sudden strength of sun. The child would most certainly not have had this round belly with sprigs of hair at the base of it. Carla closed her eyes. When she saw her belly she imagined a sand dune with tufty grass growing round it.

What was that, the shadow passing so suddenly in front of her? Had she called down Jesus at last? A falling leaf? Her eyes blinked open and looked. A spider. Making a web. She was hanging there, suspended animation. Carla moved her head ever so slightly and saw the sun's glint on a single thread of silk. The drop thread. Carla looked farther up for the bridge line. She found the most likely place, where two branches arched toward each other, but the thread, if it was there, was invisible. The spider was directly above Carla now, pulling silk out of her own fat abdomen. She continued her journey down the drop thread, looking for an anchor.

Carla hardly felt the spider at all as she anchored in Carla's sticky tufts of hair. Carla moved her head farther to the side and saw that the first three threads made a big capital Y. The spider continued, spinning other threads, returning to the center, and soon the framework was complete. It shimmered in the tiny breeze, a display of iridescence. Ever so carefully Carla arced her head forward a little and blew her own tiny breeze onto the web. But the spider hardly even noticed. She worked on undisturbed, making a small central spiral to lock the spokes into position, then spun a temporary spiral all the way to the extremities of the web. Back she came to the center, took up the temporary web, and replaced it with the sticky one. The spider disappeared, leaving Carla anchored to her web.

Odd that the spider should be doing her spinning in the drowsy afternoon, not as they usually do, at night. Carla crept her fingers down the length of her belly and with a sharp chop at the air broke the anchor thread. The web floated free. Weakened, but not destroyed. She pulled her skirt down, shutting her body off from the last of the sun. Time for Vespers. She stood up and made her way back.

The evening meal had been cleared away, scraps buried. On the table were wool and hair from last year's harvest, all washed, spun, dyed, and skeined. The fresh crop of hair lay in a basket ready to be put through the same process. Sister Margarita sometimes wondered whether it wouldn't be altogether simpler if they just started knitting the hair directly from the head. They could leave the needles eternally in place and knit another row when the hair was long enough. The pain suffered by sleeping on knitting needles could be offered up for the sins of the world.

They were about to begin. The knitting pattern was laid out on the table, the pieces that they were working on individually in front of each nun, needles side by side, their points buried in a ball of wool.

Carla reached out for a skein of red wool, the size of a rat. It wasn't really red, though that's what they called it. They had boiled it up with beetroot to produce, unexpectedly, a bright shade of orange. Still, it was closer to red than the wool dyed in blood.

Fully aware that Iphigenia was giving her one of her looks,

she picked the skein up, turned it over, and examined some invisible detail of it. Taking her time, taking her time. At the very instant that Iphigenia took in a mouthful of breath to chastise her, Carla put the wool down and piously placed her hands together, one over the other, at the edge of the table. Iphigenia released the wasted mouthful of breath. With their eyes closed the sisters began:

Athena thought: " 'Tis well to praise what others do:
But let me earn the praise I give, nor see
Too cheaply scorned my own divinity."
And as she pondered thus, her mind was bent
To plan Arachne's punishment—
Her Lydian rival, who was said to claim
Of all who worked in wool the foremost name.

On they went, setting forth once again on the story that ended with Arachne being transformed into a spider. They mouthed the words over prayer-poised hands, over the work awaiting them. Arachne and Athena, the litany they used to get the rhythm of the knitting going. The pattern of the story was deeply etched in their minds, any one word from it would evoke the whole. Nevertheless, they liked to say each word and every word, one after the other, a reminder that the whole was composed of thousands and thousands of stitches.

It wasn't just the meaning of the words, it was the rhythm and the rhyme. The comfort of knowing when they got to the end of each line there would be the echo of the line before. And the tantalizing suggestion of the line yet to come. In less than ten lines the nuns were knitting, their voices trailing off as their hands took up the rhythm.

In celebration of Haircut Day a fat cake sat waiting to be eaten—gritty millet, cooked soft and slowly till it held together, flavored with lavender flowers. As they ate the cake they allowed themselves a little conversation.

"Agnes Paul has a big belly," announced Margarita.

"Spring," said Iphigenia.

"Father John," smirked Carla.

Though the Agnes sisters went about their business in their own way and trod their own invisible tracks, they all had names—of former members of the community who had finally joined with Christ. The monastery was so vast that it made the nuns feel more numerous to imagine that the souls of the departed returned to them as sheep. Strangely enough the sheep, as much as sheep had any traces of individuality, took on the characteristics of the sister they were named for.

While each of the ewes had her own name, the ram was always called Father John. Father John wasn't a priest who had been part of the community but it was a name that seemed to fit. There had been a succession of priest-confessors, even the Bishop visited the monastery once. A long time ago.

The sheep were asleep somewhere, lying wherever they happened to be standing when night pressed them down. Occasionally through their talk the women heard a snuffle, like a sequence of wet rubber rings. Sheep-dreams of other lives, of rounding up herds of wildebeests on sun-bright plains, standing on a rocky outcrop like a goat, queen of the realm.

"Father John," repeated Margarita. She admired his horns, as beautiful as coiled rope. But sometimes in his docile brown eyes she thought she caught glimpses of a wilder creature prowling around. She was glad that the soft woolly body stopped it from getting out.

"Margarita," Iphigenia said softly but firmly.

Margarita swallowed the last pappy bit of cake in her mouth and stood up, rattling the heavy earthenware cups on the table. Her feet were firmly planted on the ground, her hands resting on the curve of her belly, one on top of the other. She felt comfortable and composed.

"Beauty and the Beast," she announced. And on the night of Haircut Day, this is the story that Sister Margarita told:

"Once upon a time there was a merchant. Since the death of his wife from consumption his pretty young daughter had become his only treasure. He had promised her that when his ship came in she could have anything she desired—gold from the Indies, a bolt of silk, rare saffron. But all the girl wanted was a single white rose. He went to the port and waited. But alas, there was a terrible storm and the ship foundered.

"On the way home, he got lost. He trudged through the snow and came across the gates to a big house. Before he had time to knock, the gates opened. He took the path to a great door, a path lined with snow-laden bushes. The door opened and some invisible force ushered him in.

"There was a blazing fire to warm him, some slices of meat on a gold plate, and red wine in a beautiful crystal decanter. He availed himself of this hospitality and, feeling much better, left the house. As he walked down the path he noticed for the first time that the bushes bore splendid white roses. How strange that they were flowering in the depths of winter. Though he had no bounty to bring home he could still grant Beauty her wish. He picked an armful of the plush white roses and in so doing, pricked his hand on a thorn. Three drops of blood fell onto the virgin snow.

"Suddenly, a hideous beast sprung from nowhere, a beast wearing a crimson smoking jacket. 'Ingrate,' bellowed the beast. 'Stealing my beloved roses!' He lapped up the blood on the snow.

"The merchant cowered. 'I'm sorry, Sir,' he began.

" 'I am the Beast and you will address me so.'

" 'I'm sorry, Beast, they are for my daughter, my precious Beauty.'

" 'Send her here and I will spare your life.'

"And so Beauty came to stay with the Beast. She wore her mother's wedding ring. 'Take this, my dearest, and may God and his angels protect you,' her mother had said on her deathbed the year before. Beauty was frightened at first, even though the Beast kept his distance. He fed her and clothed her but if he went to lay his head in her lap, she held the ring up and he backed away.

"Beauty lived there for many months, her every need taken care of, her mother's ring protecting her. She wandered in his garden among flowers of every hue. After the first fall of snow the white roses started to bloom. It was nearly a year now since her father had given her away and in all that time not one word had she heard from him. When Christmas came, the table was laden with sumptuous foods but Beauty was too crestfallen to touch a single crumb.

"The Beast was eating pudding with his paws when suddenly he stopped and sniffed the air. The door opened and in walked her father! Beauty ran to his arms. So delighted was she to see him, she did not notice at first that he carted behind him an enormous chest.

" 'Good evening, Beast,' he said. He looked miraculously well, rosy-cheeked, dressed in a long coat with fur trimming to keep out the cold. 'I have worked hard,' he said. He opened the chest and in it Beauty and the Beast saw gold from the Indies, bolts of silk, rare saffron, and a myriad of other treasures. 'I suppose your unfortunate appearance prevents you from traveling abroad,' her father said to the Beast, 'so I have brought the world to you.'

"The merchant was pleased to see that the shiny, sparkling yellow things in the chest mesmerized the Beast. He pushed the chest closer to him. The Beast picked up pawfuls of jewels, caught his claws on the silk. 'Yours,' said the merchant, 'in return for Beauty.'

"The Beast stood on his hind legs, straightened his smoking jacket, and bared his claws and teeth to the man. 'You also have three drops of my blood,' said the merchant. It was to this blood that the man was appealing. The Beast's head lolled to one side, it circled around, as one might circle a brandy balloon to release more of the flavor. Slowly his head bowed and the merchant realized that the Beast was acquiescing to his proposal.

"When the Beast lifted his head again the strangest thing happened. His ears grew small, the hair fell away from his face and hands, his forelimbs turned into arms. He had become a man. He saw now that Beauty was hardly more than a child, far too young to be mistress of his house. He shook hands with the man and Beauty left with her father. They all lived happily ever after."

This was Margarita's version of Beauty and the Beast. There was another version but she didn't like it. So she added a bit here and there, cast on a few stitches, cast off a few others. At points in the storytelling Margarita changed her voice. She growled when she spoke the Beast's words, made the merchant stutter with fear, boom with confidence when he came back with the chest. And she did not remain standing in the same position that she had adopted when she announced the title of her story. She took a little step back when the Beast reared up, moved her hands to show how enormous the treasure chest was. A couple of times she had to scratch her leg.

Iphigenia's nose was jutting into the air again.

"What?" said Margarita.

Iphigenia realized with a start that the story was over. "Bed," she said.

On cold winter's nights they all lay down together, huddling in the warmth of each others' bodies like the sheep did. On very cold winter's nights they would even lie down with the sheep. But it was spring now and they were each in their own cell on a narrow strip of bed. Sheepskins underneath their backs and at least the smells and liquids were their own. Margarita felt the slow creaks of her body when she lay down on the ground, and the even slower creaks as she stood up again. The weight of years pressed down on her, as if her body already recognized its final resting place and wanted to nestle in it.

So Margarita did not lie on the ground to ask the Lord's forgiveness for what she was about to do, she simply lay on the bed. Forgiveness had been asked for many times in the past, and Margarita no longer expected bolts of lightning to strike her down, but still she did it. Then she took out the hair.

That plait of dead hair, from her girlhood self, still shone bright and gold while the hair supposedly alive on her head was now gray and wiry. She had hung onto it all these years, the hair that had been cut from her head when she was accepted into the community. She had managed to find and keep this part of it. She hung onto it like a rope, the one remaining thread of her girlhood.

She stroked its sleekness, arranged the plait into different shapes. Tonight, the night of Haircut Day, she would be bold. She'd keep it with her till morning. She coiled the plait around and placed the golden hair back on her head, wearing it like a crown.

She thought the story had gone well, though she wondered at the end when she saw Iphigenia's nose jutting into the air whether she had got a bit of it wrong.

She picked up a book. It fell open where it always did, at the picture of The Knitting Madonna, a black-and-white reprint of an altar piece. The print was dark and somber but there were lines of white, Our Lady's halo, the embroidery of her robe, the curls of an onlooker, the collar and halo of the Infant, that Margarita imagined must be painted in gold. The Virgin Mary wasn't knitting in rows as the nuns had done this evening, she had four needles in the garment, knitting the stitches around the neck.

The Infant had a book open in front of him and was resting his chin on his hand. His face was turned to look up at the attendant who was holding a wooden cross taller than himself. It was hard to tell whether Our Lady was looking at her knitting or at the Infant, one being in line with the other in the composition of the painting. The ball of wool that threaded onto the needles lay in a wicker basket. The haloes of both Madonna and Child were ornate and had patterns worked into the edges, like the stand-up collars or headpieces of medieval women. Margarita knew these were the artist's embellishment. The haloes of

Madonna and Child were pure circles of light, with no need of ornamentation.

She blew the candle out, let the book flop shut, and slept on the golden plait of her girlhood, breathing in the tallow of the extinguished candle.

Sugar and spice and all things nice. Majestic Zeus, Neptune with his tall trident—the gods in their glory. The motifs in Athena's weaving. And Arachne's? Sticks and snails and puppy dogs' tails. The gods in their bestiality—Leda beneath the swan, Neptune the bull ravishing the Aeolian maid. As Carla worked on the garment, words and images swam by like gold-flecked fish.

Her escapecoat was made from many things, wool, hair, the silk of spider web carefully spun and rolled so many times between her fingers that its stickiness was no longer a trap for her. But it trapped other things. It had the same lacy construction as the spider's webs she'd watched being made, knitted on needles so fine they were barely thicker than a single strand of hair. It was now long enough for her to put over her head and reach to the ground. It was her capsule, her escape. She could put on the coat and disappear. No one would find her inside it, it was a world of her own creation. There were petals knitted into the fabric, grasses, butterfly wings, scars and injuries she had received, pieces of cloud, wings of angels, colored glass from the monastery windows that had fallen out.

The monastery was the only world Carla knew. The grounds were big enough to romp in, everything was here—food, shelter, companionship, the sisters, the sheep, the courtyard flooded with the light of the Lord. There was everything here, except being elsewhere.

The escapecoat had started with some slight from Sister Iphigenia, an admonishment for one of Carla's many peccadilloes. Instead of washing away the sins, asking forgiveness, and removing them from her existence once penance had been done, Sister Carla started saving them. Knitting them, with her own fingers, into this garment that grew into her escapecoat. And as it grew she wove into it not just peccadilloes but anything she took a fancy to. It was a tower she locked herself into, a gown she wore like a bride, it was her castle and her queenly robe, the web of her doing and undoing, the thread from the tight ball in her belly that filled her cell when she took it out at night to admire and to work on. Her magnum opus.

On the bed was the piece of hair that her blood had dripped onto this morning, already turning a lovely shade of russet. It was part of last year's harvest and she could no longer tell whose hair it was. She hoped it was Iphigenia's.

Margarita, if she noticed the bloodied hair was no longer in the basket, wouldn't say anything. She'd probably assume it had faded, or that it had never been there in the first place and her mind was playing tricks. Margarita would never think to come and look in Carla's cell. Iphigenia might, if she had a mind to do it. But she would never find the place where Carla hid her secret web. More in Iphigenia's line would be to give Carla a look or ask her directly. If she did ask, Carla would look mystified or say it was one of the sheep. Carla could feel the first quivers of laughter. One of the sheep. One of the sheep taking hair from the nuns. After all the years of nuns taking wool from the sheep.

Carla sat on her bed shaking with laughter, feeling the little squeaks and creaks of the bed as she did so. She bit her lip hard, told herself, as Iphigenia might, that this was no laughing matter. She stood up, a little more composed, as if her life depended on not laughing. She kissed the blood on the hair and worked the piece into the garment. It was a hastily done job tonight but there was night after night to come back to it. She admired it briefly, folded the garment into a triangle no bigger than her hand, and hid it away. Then she let go with it—peals of laughter that hit the walls and bounced off the stones, peals that turned to helpless cackles, the only sound in the midst of night. Then the laughter died down and in the silence came the answering shriek of a lone nightjar, thinking it had found its familiar.

Iphigenia heard it and it wasn't the first time. Usually she simply grunted and rolled over in her sleep. But tonight she wasn't asleep, nor paying much attention to what came in through her ears. She was lying on her back, her nose subtly sniffing the air. Not taking great draughts of it, just gently tugging it up, trying to get the measure of it. It was quieter now than it had been, the smell that she'd noticed on and off through the day. At one point there'd been a big rush of it, the rush of odor of an animal panting, the sour smell of fear tensing its body.

She remembered the precise moment this had happened. It was during Margarita's story. Right at the point where the Beast stood on its hind legs and bared its teeth and claws to the man. Iphigenia thought at first that perhaps she had imagined the smell, that it was the Beast in the story. But she had heard this story many times and never smelled the Beast. This was a real smell, in her nose, not her mind.

It was definitely the yeasty, custardy smell of a man. Boot

polish, metal, hair oil, a petroleum kind of smell, she was distinguishing all these. When she got the rush of odor the smell had become a stench. He was afraid, sweating. The smell came higgledy-piggledy. He was stumbling, going round in circles. The rush had lasted till the merchant and the Beast had shaken hands. Then it had subsided. But still she'd kept her nose out, waiting for more. She checked all the rooms in the monastery, the cloisters, fields, all the way to the brambles. He was in the faint salty tang coming from outside, still far away but within range.

Iphigenia's eyes opened wide in the blackness of her cell as she realized—she was no longer thinking of it as just a smell. She had attached it to a body and was calling it "he." And now came another odor, a brew of anticipation, disquiet, wariness. The smell her own body gave off when she sensed a storm approaching.

She calmed her breath, closed her eyes, and concentrated. The regular emanation of an animal at rest. He was sleeping. She lay there, her nose standing vigil. Perhaps it would blow over, stabilize, or peter out before it got here. She imagined her nose as the center of a huge circle, a field of sensation. She marked the distance from the center that she perceived the man and his smell to be. She would check later for any change. Perhaps by morning it would have gone away and she wouldn't have to burden the others with it. She nuzzled into the comforting lanolin of the bedclothes, snuffled a prayer into her vest, and tried to go to sleep. It would not be the first burden Iphigenia carried on her own.

"Kill a lamb. Eucharist."

Sister Iphigenia made the announcement straight after Matins.

Margarita was perplexed. "But . . . not till after Shearing Day. Scares the sheep."

Iphigenia showed her square yellow teeth. "Short memories. Agnes Paul is with child. Others. There will be more lambs. If it please you, Margarita."

It was all very well for Iphigenia to give the orders but it was Margarita who had to do it. Part of her chores. She had come in as a lay sister, with no dowry. The sheep trusted the docile Margarita, she could lure them into the chapel, then click. Imagine a finger making a straight line across your throat, left to right.

"Bottle of wine?" Margarita suggested an alternative. Wine was perfectly acceptable for the Eucharist.

"Tonight. With the roast."

Wine and roast meat. "Is it Sunday?"

Mostly the nuns ate plants but on occasion they treated themselves to a nice leg of lamb or a chop. The sheep ate the grass and the nuns ate the sheep. Living things ate other living things in order to stay alive. The sun, the air, rain, and earth were absorbed by simpler life forms and transmuted into sustenance for the more complex. Everything was food for something else and when eaten, became part of the creature that had consumed it. God in his wisdom had made the world thus.

The nuns did live frugally, in a material sense. When things ran out, or were too hard to make, they simply rid themselves of the need for them. They had lamb's meat, milk, blood, and wool, they had vegetables, herbs and fruits, tallow. They had books in the library. They had clothes on their backs, they had their simple pleasures.

Sister Margarita was at her task. Carla and Iphigenia sat in the courtyard and stared into the middle distance. Through their ears floated the coaxing bleats of Sister Margarita as she sung an unsuspecting lamb to the slaughter. Carla seemed a bit fidgety but Iphigenia was sure she hadn't noticed the smell. It was much stronger now, closer, coming in regular waves, in and out like breathing.

Its nervous little feet made a scraping, scuffling sound on the floor of the chapel, then they heard the bleating cries to its mother. Iphigenia breathed deeply as she smelled its fear then the warm mineral scent of its blood. She and Carla mouthed the words for the Killing ceremony, thanking their sister for visiting and letting her know she was now free to leave the little lamby body which they would honor and take unto themselves. Then they wished the soul God's speed and safe journey.

They used to all stand as witness to the slaughter of a lamb, the separation of head from body to let out the soul. But the more sisters in attendance, the more fearful the lamb became, even though the sisters were praying. Out of respect for the little creature, they averted their eyes from the actual killing and let it be alone with Margarita. Also, the less fearful the lamb, the more tender the meat.

Margarita came out into the sunlight, the deed done. She had blood on her woolly apron and on her sleeves. It had been an effort lifting the carcass up to the hook. She whisked a fly away from her face, leaving a smear of the lamb's blood on her cheek. Iphigenia and Carla smiled at her as she emerged, the encouraging, congratulatory smile grown-ups give children when they've done something especially brave.

Margarita's normally beatific face wore a scowl. It was all right for Iphigenia and Carla, they didn't have to wash up after the deed. But they would treat her with respect for hours afterward, she had that to look forward to. It didn't, however, make up for the betrayal she felt toward Agnes Teresa and the others in the flock. The sheep treated her as one of their own and like Judas she betrayed them. Year after year. At least it kept her humble, she thought as she scrubbed her hands at the trough, living this ongoing guilt. So easy to succumb to the sin of pride when you just sat out in the courtyard congratulating yourself because you didn't assist in the killing, didn't even witness it.

They entered the cool striped shade of the chapel, Iphigenia holding bread in her blood-free hands. They made the sign of the cross before the lamb hanging above the Eucharist table, dressed in a fine cloth so that it could drip blood without being interrupted by flying insects and other forms of life that like to fasten themselves to the corpses of the newly dead.

So much blood from one small lamb. Iphigenia broke off a chunk of bread, then divided it roughly into three portions.

Margarita lit the candles and Carla distributed blood from the sacramental vessel into bowls. The blood was still warm. Delicious. She wanted to dip her finger in and lick it straight away, but then that would end the thrill of anticipation.

"Who eats my flesh, and drinks my blood enjoys eternal life, and I will raise him up on the last day. My flesh is real food, my blood is real drink. He who eats my flesh and drinks my blood, lives continually in me and I in him."

They spoke the words in unison, though there had been no perceptible signal given to start or to finish. They knelt, heads lifted upward to the patches of sky through the roof, to the eternal life all around them.

The juices of Carla's mouth moistened the dry bread balanced on her tongue. She cast her eyes down to the vessel of blood cupped in her hands. There were days when her belly was filled with blood. A bright flood of it, with chunks as fleshy as liver. In the dark mirror of blood she saw her own eye in the center of the vessel. Through the eye her gaze seemed to penetrate, till she was looking at a reflection of her secret self. Though Iphigenia and Margarita were now beyond the days of blood perhaps they also paused before drinking, catching sight of their eyes in this cup. Carla lifted the vessel to her lips, careful not to disturb the surface, careful to keep her gaze steady. Her eye looked back at her all the way, till she tilted the vessel and her reflection dissolved in the taste of warm blood.

Wonderful. Nothing to do all afternoon and roast for dinner. Carla lay in the grass looking up at the sky, this time through the net of spider web. It was still there, decorated like Carla's escapecoat with the occasional jeweled insect fixed into its warp and weft. But the spider was nowhere to be seen. A bubble of gas rumbled up from her stomach and exited out her mouth. She chomped her lips, snaffling the aftertaste of the Eucharist. She felt pleasantly sated after this morning's offering.

Carla liked blood. She liked the taste, the smell, and the color. She liked the clots of it on Christ's hands and feet, the crown of drops hanging from his crown of thorns. It was so hard to dye wool this shade of red, so hard to get a true red. Even real blood when it faded was no longer blood red. Even in the Bible the red was starting to fade. The *Children's Bible* she had looked at many times, its pictures smeared with the blood of martyrs and saints. The Roman soldiers had shields and swords, and great flourishing helmets with red feathers in them. Athena also had a shield and a sword and a helmet, all made of gold.

Carla felt too lazy and comfortable to think about pictures in books. The afternoon sun was playing on her belly, shafts of it penetrating her skin. This was how the Virgin Mary had become impregnated with the Son of God. Right through her like sunlight through a window. Without even moving a finger, without helping even a tiny little bit, her body stirred. Carla could feel warmth flush into her cheeks, her own warmth, and see orange light filtering through the thin membrane of eyelid. It was as if just beneath the skin her body held clusters of buds, all of them clamoring for the teasing fingers of sun. "Kindle me with the bliss of Your burning love. Let me be Your servant, and teach me to love You and make me serve You, loving Lord, so that Your love alone be ever all my delight, my thought and my longing."

Carla waited for God's reply. She could hear birds twittering, movement in the canopy of leaves as the birds went about their business. A downy feather floated down, avoiding the web, and came to rest on her belly. Spring. New lambs, baby birds. Everything bursting forth again.

Into all the familiar sounds of this sunny afternoon came another. The sound of an animal pushing its way through undergrowth, the scrape and crackle, twigs snapping. Probably Agnes Teresa looking for her lamb, perhaps smelling its blood on Carla's outgoing breath. Carla closed her mouth to keep the smell in.

The animal came crashing through. "Damn!" Carla sat bolt upright. "Damn, damn, damn," the voice repeated in a low grumble.

Carla rolled over and peered through the grass. It was a creature with four legs, shaking its head from side to side. Before her very eyes it stood up. On two legs. Miraculous! It was dressed in black from head to foot with a white band of collar around its neck. There was a scratch of blood on its cheek. It wiped it off and looked at the streak of red as if it had never seen blood before. Carla remained crouched in the grass, still as stone despite the gonging of bells in her head. It wiped its hand clean, then took out a folded sheet of paper from its pocket. It was too far away for Carla to see the detail. It looked at the paper, then looked around, as if trying to get its bearings. It started to walk, in the direction of where the monastery gates used to be, before they disappeared in the vegetation. Carla eased herself away, breaking the spider's web, oblivious to the stickiness wrapping itself around her head. She stood up. Then she ran and ran and ran.

Though the youngest and fittest of the three, Carla was panting and out of breath when she burst into the courtyard where Margarita and Iphigenia were butchering the meat. Margarita stopped in midstream, as if she'd seen an apparition, cleaver up ready to separate the ribs into cutlets, eyes open wide to this sight in front of her.

Carla wanted to speak but her lungs were too greedily siphoning off all the air, in and out like bellows, for any of it to pass over her vocal cords to shape words. Margarita lay down her cleaver and went to Carla.

"What, child?"

Carla was holding one hand against her chest and wildly gesticulating with the other. "Fa . . . Fa . . . Father John," she blurted out.

"Horns stuck in brambles?" asked Margarita with concern.

She shook her head vigorously, her chest still heaving. "In black. With white . . ." She drew her thumb and forefinger about a collar-width apart around her neck.

Sister Iphigenia looked up. "A man," she said, bringing her chopper down on the bony part of the lamb's leg. "A priest."

The other two stared at her, puzzled. She may as well have said a giraffe, it seemed so extraordinary. More extraordinary was the fact that Iphigenia showed no surprise, almost as if she'd been expecting it.

"This is a monastery. Entirely normal that a priest come."

It was not entirely normal, they hadn't had any sort of visitor for years.

"Did you know? Was there . . . a letter?" asked Margarita. The idea of a letter after all this time was outlandish. Even more outlandish was that one could arrive without them all knowing about it. But one extraordinary thing could surely only be explained by another extraordinary thing.

"No letter," said Iphigenia. "Our guest shall eat meat, roast potatoes, cheese."

"Nettles, turnips," said Margarita, trying to gain some ground and status with Carla, who was the first to see him, and Iphigenia, who must surely have had a premonition.

"Nuns' food. Priests eat well." Iphigenia turned to Carla. "Where?"

Carla explained. It was quite close to the outer wall although that was hidden from view by the brambles and other vegetation that had gradually engulfed it over the years.

"And then?"

Carla explained the direction he'd taken and told Iphigenia about the paper he was looking at.

"Hmm," pondered Iphigenia. "Map. He is looking for the path."

The path was now covered in brambles. "Won't find us?" suggested Margarita, not sure whether she wanted to be found.

"Hide?" suggested Carla, as if it might be a game.

"We will prepare for him. Then we will wait."

Perhaps it was the smell of the roast that led the man to the courtyard because he was there well before nightfall. They watched for his coming. Sitting back to back, each of them facing a different direction so they would not miss him. Carla saw him first—stopping every now and then, wiping his forehead, pulling the chafing collar away from his neck, swatting away little insects trying to sup off his sweat.

They watched as the chapel and cloisters came into his line of vision, the astonished look on his face when he saw the plume of smoke from the fire curling up into the sky like a genie. His moment of hesitation, then his quickened, determined step.

He approached from the west and warily entered the cloisters. He looked around, at the walls, the roof, the arches. The bleating of a sheep rose into the still air. He stood alert, waited. Agnes Teresa emerged from the chapel and entered the courtyard. She nuzzled into Sister Margarita's skirt, smelling her lamb on Margarita's body. She seemed to pay no heed to the smell of the leg roasting in the oven.

As he started on his journey down the cloister the three nuns turned to face him. A panoply of smells spurted from him. The pungent accord of acetone, petroleum, rich redolent tobacco, stale meaty sweat, drops of urine, spicy apple, a faint whiff of frankincense. Tiny darts of nervousness in a booming elemental mustiness. Iphigenia was drenched in the tidal wave of his odor.

They stood up as he came out of the striped shade into the sunlight. He was a young man, thin. Dressed in black, as Carla had described. There were still spots of bright shiny polish on his shoes even though they had gathered a bit of mud and dirt. His face and hands were scratched, his trousers were torn at the knee but in spite of it all they maintained a crisp crease down the front.

"Father John, I presume?"

"Father Ignatius, actually. And you . . . ?" His voice trailed off.

"Sister Iphigenia. And Sister Margarita and Sister Carla."

He looked at them in utter disbelief. "Sisters! I didn't expect. Actually, I was led to believe that the property was uninhabited. Had the Devil's own job locating it."

A tiny suspension in the rhythm of the nuns' breathing.

Devil. It was many years since this word had been uttered in the monastery.

"Cup of tea?" invited Iphigenia. The nuns resumed their breathing.

"Why yes, that would be delightful. I've got some mineral water back in the car but I didn't think to bring it with me. I didn't expect—"

"Car?" said Carla. It was part of her name.

"Yes, the car. Seems to be stuck, I'm afraid. I couldn't call anyone, the battery on the mobile phone has run down." From his trouser pocket he produced a black rectangle with rows of numbers on it. He whipped up the short antenna and gave the nuns a demonstration of how it wouldn't work.

A telephone? It did not look like one.

"Where's the cord?"

"Cordless," he said, stretching his hands open and waving them around like a magician demonstrating to his audience that there were no strings attached. "Battery operated. But it needs recharging. I should have brought the spare up with me, always best to be prepared," he babbled on. "Do you have a power point? Electricity?"

The sun had dropped from the sky and outside the walls night was gathering. As if called by some invisible shepherd, the rest of the sheep entered the courtyard, bleating occasionally, filling it with their lanolin smell.

"Do you have a flock?" asked Iphigenia.

"Flock?" At first he seemed not to understand, then it dawned on him. "No," he said. "I'm not a parish priest, I am the Bishop's secretary." He smiled grandly.

Iphigenia was tiring of the conversation, of the listening and the doing. Her tongue felt thick in her mouth, as if not used to making these awkward shapes. Telling a story was different. That was like finding the end of the yarn, seeing the way it was wound in the skein, and then just pulling to unwind it. She wondered whether it wouldn't have been better to have hidden after all.

"Vespers," announced Iphigenia, to end the conversation. "Father John?"

"Ignatius. Father Ignatius," he corrected her. "I'd be pleased to lead you in Vespers."

He walked piously toward the chapel, displaying his knowledge of the layout of the monastery.

One or two confused sheep started following him, but the nuns remained exactly where they were, eyelids lowered, lips moving, chests rising and falling as they breathed the Holy Spirit in and out.

"Ahem," he cleared his throat. "The chapel?"

Calmly they opened their eyes. Without any further discussion of the matter the three rose and entered the chapel.

The last rays of the setting sun seeped through the holes, through the windows. The warm red hues surrounding them gave the impression that they were inside the body of a large benign animal. The bloodstained Eucharist table only added to the effect. Preparing to lead them in Vespers, the priest rested his hand on the table and discovered a purple-red stickiness.

"Wine?" he suggested.

"The blood of Our Lord, Jesus Christ, through which we have eternal life," said Sister Iphigenia.

Sister Margarita felt that somehow Iphigenia had said too much but couldn't quite put her finger on it. Nevertheless, the words appeared to placate the priest. He brought his blood-sticky hands together in prayer and began intoning. He did not raise his eyes to the hook above the Eucharist table from which the lamb had hung just a few hours ago. It had been a very unusual day, reflected Margarita, and it wasn't over yet.

"Why is he here?" whispered Margarita as they prepared the evening meal.

Iphigenia surveyed the dinner table. A plate, a cup, a knife for each person. And one fork each. Was that enough? Priests came for lunch or afternoon tea with the abbess but they never stayed for dinner. Iphigenia's memory threw up a picture of bright shiny forks in a special box lined with plush blue velvet. But the forks on the table had been found in a bundle at the back of a drawer. The tarnish remained, despite a vigorous rubbing on the nuns' woolly aprons. "He will tell us. Or we will find out. Meat on his plate first."

He had washed the stickiness from his face and hands, smoothed his hair close to his head. He was sitting waiting to be served.

After the ordeal of getting here, Ignatius was prepared for anything. The sight of the smoke had filled him with both relief and apprehension. He knew he was too far away from the car to make it back before nightfall but who might he find at the source of the smoke? Gypsies? Hunters? He had quickly intoned a psalm and with the strength of the Lord's rod and staff comforting him, had continued. He certainly hadn't expected three old women dressed in a motley collection of woolly rags. At first he thought they were Gypsy women who had taken up camp in the monastery and wondered whether there were menfolk about somewhere, sons or brothers more suspicious of strangers than the women appeared to be. He was sitting at their table now but

he was not entirely comfortable. Things could easily turn nasty. He felt like one of the mission priests in deepest darkest Africa.

They were unkempt, practically savages. Their teeth were yellow, their skin lined and leathery. They wore no shoes. Everything about them suggested that they let nature just take its course. Except the close-cropped hair. It gave them an odd monkish look.

They brought the food to the table. The one with the dark glittering eyes and black hair sat down opposite him. Carla. Younger than the other two, she stared blatantly, expectantly. The tall one, Iphigenia, the one who had first greeted him, had a nervous twitching nose. Her eyes were clouded with cataracts. The shortest of the three, Margarita, had hefty arms and double chins.

The smell of the roast lamb and roast potatoes made Ignatius realize how truly ravenous he was. He hadn't eaten a proper meal since yesterday's breakfast. He'd brought an apple from the car but that was hardly a meal.

They bowed their heads for grace, their soft whispers scattered in the boom of his voice. Carla picked up a slab of meat and took big chunky bites out of it, the juices and fat running down her hand and disappearing into the pad of her woolly sleeve. Margarita picked up a potato, the callused thick pads of her fingers immune to the heat of it. Iphigenia speared a piece of marinated cheese with her knife and gulped it down.

Despite his hunger, Ignatius proceeded at a more civilized pace. He cut off a small piece of potato, a small piece of meat, assembled them on the prongs of the fork, and popped the lot into his mouth. The one with the slab of meat watched, fascinated. He stopped, chin long, teeth apart inside his closed mouth. Self-conscious now with her eyes on him.

She picked up her fork and copied his movements. When she got the fork to her mouth she bit down on it. She made a face, threw the fork to the ground, and went back to using her hands.

Ignatius resumed chewing. He tried to begin a conversation but all he got in return were grunts. They were like pigs at a swill trough, tearing off chunks of food, swallowing almost without chewing, as if they were in some kind of competition to see who could finish first.

It was the one who had previously done most of the talking, such as it was, who won the competition. Sister Iphigenia. She pushed her plate to the middle of the table and fetched the kettle from the fire. She threw some leaves into a teapot, then poured in the steaming water. Carla was now licking the palm of her hand, looking across the tops of her fingers at him. Margarita was gnawing on the end of the leg.

The arrival of the teapot on the table seemed to be some sort of signal. The plates were whisked away, even his own, though there was still a good piece of fatty meat on it that he had been saving till last. A tea the color of swamp water was slopped into thick ceramic cups. Grimy hands were wiped down grimy garments and baskets of knitting were brought out. A ball of greasy wool and a pair of needles were held out in front of him.

"Knit, Father John?"

Father Ignatius, his mind shouted out. How many times did he have to repeat this? "No thanks," he said politely, as if they'd offered him a biscuit.

"Story?"

"A story?" he repeated.

"You must know stories," Sister Iphigenia insisted.

"My turn for a story," Carla reminded her sisters.

"We have a guest," Iphigenia quietly chided her.

"No, no, go ahead. Ladies first," he said, almost choking on the word "ladies." "You can show me how it's done."

The women placed their hands together on the edge of the table and started a whispering murmur that he took for prayer. He bowed his head, with no prayer of his own, one eye half open waiting to see what would happen next.

Carla stood up. "Briar Rose," she announced.

"There was once a king and queen who had been married for many years. At long last a daughter was born to them and they called her Briar Rose."

He watched the women pick up their knitting and start looping the wool around their fingers, working the needle in and out of the stitches. "At her baptism they decided to hold a great celebration. There were thirteen Wise Women in the realm but the king and queen had only twelve gold plates so they decided not to ask the thirteenth. But she came anyway. Uninvited," Carla added ominously.

He settled back in his chair and sipped the tea which he found to be pleasantly aromatic. He recognized this story, though under a different name—"Sleeping Beauty." And they weren't wise women, they were fairy godmothers. Glossing over these details, he relaxed and let himself be carried on the rhythms.

"At the feast each of the Wise Women conferred on the baby princess their gifts. The thirteenth Wise Woman came out of the shadows, causing a ripple to pass through the assembly. 'My gift is the greatest of them all,' she said, her voice cracking like lightning. 'On her thirteenth birthday the child will prick herself with a spindle and die.' There was a great cavernous gasp from the assembly, led by the king."

Carla went on with the story, about how the king decreed

that every spindle in the realm and every object that could draw blood be destroyed. As Carla took the girl on her journey up to the attic which housed the old woman and the fateful spindle, Ignatius had a vague feeling that something had been omitted, but he was entranced by the story now and didn't want her to stop. This tatty woman in front of him, who had previously barely been able to grunt out one syllable, was now transformed into a creature of eloquence and fluency. The knitters knitted on, looking up occasionally when they came to the end of a row, or reaching for new wool.

"There had been something itching Briar Rose that day, the day that she decided to explore a part of the castle she had never explored before. She went right up as far as the steps would go till she came to an old wooden door. She reached out to push it but before her hand made contact the door opened. 'Come in,' said the voice of an old woman who was sitting spinning. The curious girl entered and as soon as she stepped over the threshold she discovered that she was bleeding. She thought it very odd because she hadn't touched anything, and the blood wasn't coming from her hand. She entered the room and the door closed forever behind her. Then the thirteenth Wise Woman, for it was she who was spinning the fabric of life, explained to the woman newly emerged from the girl, the mystery of the body that bleeds but is not wounded. And she lived happily ever after." Carla sat down, feeling very satisfied and accomplished.

Had she not been so preoccupied with the storytelling she would have noticed him starting to fidget.

"No, no," he protested, "she pricks her finger on the spindle and falls asleep for a hundred years, after which she is woken by the kiss of a handsome prince."

They looked at him, taken aback.

Margarita put down her work and waved a needle at him. "Have you seen a spindle? No sharper than this knitting needle. Devil's own job drawing blood with that!"

For a moment he thought she was going to jab him with it but Margarita fell back into silence, shaken by her own outburst.

"No doubt you are right," he conceded, "about actual spindles. But the one in the story is purely symbolic."

Carla watched the to and fro with excitement, waiting for what would happen next.

The time had come to put his foot down. He had to set these people right. It may only have been a children's fairy tale but if they couldn't get a childlike thing right what hope was there?

He stood up, pushing the chair back with his strong calves. "Sleeping Beauty," he said with emphasis to let them know that was its proper name, "Sleeping Beauty pricked her finger on a spindle and fell asleep for a hundred years. The prince hacks his way through the brambles, finds the princess in her castle, and kisses her back to life whereupon they marry and live happily ever after. End of story."

Margarita's mouth dropped open but it was Iphigenia who spoke. "Yes, Father," Iphigenia said, "you are quite right."

Of course he was right, he didn't need to be told by the likes of her. He had the weight of history behind him, thousands and thousands of years. Nevertheless, before he sat down, he felt something shift underfoot, the feeling he'd had as a child at the beach when the tide was going out.

Margarita lay rigid, gripping the sides of the bed. The room was spinning, she felt as if she was lying on a raft in a dark stormy sea. The darkness swirled around her, it hummed in her ears. Her heart was fluttering in her chest like a bird caught in a trap. Her whole being was trying to cope with the avalanche of events, the shadows of which were now flying around the room like dark, angular angels. Unbound, out of proportion, grotesque.

The priest was floating, horizontal, black and white like a reproduction in a book, his trousers crisp as knives, his collar gleaming around his neck like a fallen halo. The lamb hanging on the hook, dripping blood onto the Eucharist table, Agnes Teresa bumping into the man, bleating for her lamb. And out of the wide-open mouth of the man, in letters bright as scimitars, came the word "Devil."

Despite the enormity of everything else, that was the worst of it. Never in all her time as a nun had Margarita uttered that word. It was a word exorcised from her vocabulary. And there it was, escaping across the threshold of her lips like a thief leaving a house. Something from long ago had spun loose in Margarita tonight, broken free and was giddying around her.

Margarita closed her eyes but still she could see the floating figures. She crept one hand up to her crucifix, holding it to her like a breastplate. "Put on the whole armor of God, that ye may be able to stand against the wiles of the devil. Above all, taking the shield of faith, wherewith ye shall be able to quench all the fiery darts of the wicked. And for me, that utterance may be given unto me, that I may open my mouth boldly, to make known the mystery of the Gospel." But it was Margarita who had opened her mouth boldly. "The Devil's own job drawing blood with that!" As if the Devil's job was hard. It was not. The Devil's job was easy. It was the Lord's job that was hard.

Whose work had Margarita been doing when she had slaughtered the lamb today? She had killed it to glorify her Lord yet she had caused the death of one of His creatures. She could still see the little lamb's eye looking at her as she held it to slash its throat. Its little eye that God had placed at the side of its face so it could see what was creeping up behind. Lambs were prey. Hunting beasts had eyes in the front of their faces, to see the thing they stalked. Margarita's eyes were in the front. She shared her origins with wolves, foxes, and tigers, powerful muscular creatures, yet Margarita felt more like a sheep. She would be a sheep one day, an Agnes sister.

She liked her wooliness, she liked the routine. She had no room for new things and new people, even if they were priests. Her head was aching and there was a sour taste in her mouth. Perhaps the wine had soured in the bottle, so rarely did they drink it.

The floating figures dissolved into the fading night as the first thin tendrils of day entered the high window in Margarita's cell. The crucifix under her hand was warm and glowing. Its warmth entered her heart and calmed her. He was just a minor interruption. He would leave soon. Silence would close over the visitor and he would never be mentioned again.

It was so exciting! Nothing like this had ever happened, not in her whole life! Not a sheep, not a nun, not a bird, not a spider. Not a saint, not a statue. A man of flesh and blood! His teeth were white, he was thin as a stick of licorice, his skin was smooth like Jesus', he was not wrinkled and rumpled like Margarita and Iphigenia. He was young. It was a long time since Carla had seen young.

First he had the form of a four-legged creature. In two blinks of an eye the beast of the earth became a man and walked, looked at his piece of paper and came forth to meet them. "And the Lord God planted a garden eastward in Eden; and there he put the man whom he had formed."

She knew straightaway it wasn't a sheep. It was more like a dog, a lean black dog, but it didn't bark, bark, bark. "Damn, damn, damn." Carla would never forget it. She said the words over to herself, growling them the way he had, feeling her mouth open to let out the middle of the word, her lips coming together again to close off the sound. Now, lying on her bed, eyes wide open to the pinpoints of stars, the circle of moon, her body surging with excitement, Carla decided to weave him into the escapecoat. But later. Iphigenia thought herself so smart, so clever, showing no surprise, as if she knew he was coming all along. But it was Carla to whom God had first revealed Father John. He was hers.

Carla rolled off the bed and down on all fours. Around her tiny room she went, saying, "Damn, damn, damn," to the floor, her eyes bright as night owls. Then she stood up, the way he had done, wiped imaginary blood from her face, and held her hand up in the darkness to smell it.

She let her body go soft and fell lightly to the floor like a baby. She'd done this lots of times, it hardly hurt at all. Babies didn't hurt themselves when they fell this way, it was just the surprise that made them cry. Carla didn't cry, she wasn't a baby. She lay there on her side for a moment, one leg over the other, one eye looking out at the night, one cheek against the stone worn smooth over the years by the wash of her body.

She was ready now. She lifted the stone, took out the escapecoat, and spread it out around her. She had a tiny piece of meat from his fork. Under her fingernail a crust of blood she had salvaged from the trough where he had cleaned his scratches. She blended the two, molding with her fingers. She picked up the threads of the coat and worked the new element in. In the warmth of her hands it seemed to come to life and grow. Bigger and bigger. She caressed its contours, teased a detail out, blended other pieces together. Then it was done. She looked upon her creation.

He had the gentle eyes of Jesus, the skin, the face of suffering, and the wounds of Christ. Out of his mouth came the words that had changed the story, "She pricks her finger on the spindle and falls asleep for a hundred years, after which she is woken by the kiss of a handsome prince."

Carla slipped into the escapecoat. She swirled it around so that the image hovered above her. "My Prince, my Savior," prayed Carla, lifting her arms and pressing him to her. She kissed those flimsy, gauzy lips. "Wake me from my sleep and lift me unto Your Rapture," she whispered into his mouth. She kissed the lips again but the Lord remained silent and immobile. It didn't matter, she would try again another night. The girl in

Father John's story had waited a hundred years. Sister Carla would wait a thousand for her Lord. He would come one day, it was prophesied. Or Carla would go to him. She took the coat off, folded it small, then put it back in the little hole under the stone. Carla liked to bury things. Bury and dig them up again.

Though she had smelled him coming it still hadn't prepared Sister Iphigenia for his actual arrival. He had not stumbled in by accident—he had a map. It had been so long since someone had come that Iphigenia had largely forgotten about life outside. The monastery was Iphigenia's world. It was filled with the light of the Lord in the day and His darkness at night. The stars in the sky were His eternal vigilance and the earth the provider of His bounty. "And there shall be in no wise enter into it any thing that defileth, neither whatsoever abomination, or maketh a lie; but they which are written in the Lamb's book of life."

What was his purpose here? Was he an emissary of the Lord or a thing that defileth or maketh a lie? Priests are from the Lord but this one had said Devil. Sister Iphigenia sniffed the air. The smell of fear entered her nose but it wasn't the man. It was Margarita. She smelled strongly like an animal caught in a bramble—confused, afraid, wondering how it got there and whether it was going to get out.

Iphigenia watched the steady rhythm of her breast rising and falling, feeling the passage of air in and out of her nostrils. Solid as a rock. A slight queasiness in the stomach, that was all, probably on account of the meat being too fresh and the wine too old.

An unexpected burp rumbled up. The sour taste of it stung the back of her throat. A bit of heartburn, a bit of queasiness, it was to be expected at her age. What had he said? He thought the monastery was uninhabited. Perhaps he was on holiday or on retreat. He'd said monastery in a peculiar fashion. It had sounded like property.

The feeling of queasiness had now diminished in favor of a small headache that intermittently stabbed at a precise point on her left temple. It was the thinking. It was trying to leap from what she knew to what she didn't know, could only guess at. She wasn't used to it. For years she had known every detail of her life, the slow turn of the seasons, budding, flowering, withering, dying, green shoots of grass being eaten by the sheep, digested, excreted into clusters of pellets to fertilize more grass, more sheep. And so it went on as the Lord made it so.

She turned her nose in the direction of the priest. He'd said he was so tired he could sleep on a clothesline. The nuns had no clothesline, leaving their clothes out to dry on bushes on the rare occasions they washed them. They made up a bed for him with fresh straw and a woolly blanket. He insisted on blocking off the door so that the sheep couldn't wander in. His smell came in a regular pulse. Sleeping like a baby. Breathing in the monastery air and subtly altering it in his breathing out.

The nuns are in the courtyard praying when Ignatius enters. He pauses for a moment, contemplating.

"Where two or three of you gather to pray in my name, there you will find me," said Jesus. Ignatius watches them mouth their prayers, sacred passwords to the Kingdom within, a country of infinite riches to the pilgrim. Their heads are bowed, the words spoken into their hearts, he sees the breath falling damply on their chests. Into the silence shapes are cut and the Spirit solidifies into form. Three hermit nuns, the perfect image of mystic Christianity.

The twitter of an early-morning bird interrupts his reverie. Such a pretty little tableau, reflects Ignatius before going about his business.

God doesn't have their full undivided attention this morning. The nuns feel the gaze of the man on their backs, the low slanted rays of the sun invading the courtyard like arrows.

Under the familiar liturgies, Sister Iphigenia is trying to decide a course of action. Or non-action. Today is Shearing Day.

Should they proceed as normal or should they entertain their guest? A priest has never stayed overnight. They came with the tide and went back with the tide.

Iphigenia knew he had entered the courtyard but he did not kneel down with them. In the crisp morning he smells warm and vigorous, like a puppy dog after sleep. There is an odd chemical smell too. Like faded ink. His clothes are not made of wool.

There was a stirring of leaves as he entered the chapel. Carla, closest to the entrance, saw him go in and disappear, melding into the darkness as if his cloth was made from its fabric. In half shadow herself, she observed him move about, from pools of shadow to light, according to where the holes and gaps were. He stood squinting up at the sky, hand up like a visor, protecting his vision from the bright light of God. He moved into the shadow, hands on hips, looking upward, surveying the roof, the holes, the swallows nesting in the vaulting. Bats had made a home there too, sleeping like vampires now that the day had arrived. A white dart shot from heaven and landed with a splodge down the sleeve of his jacket. "Damn," he said and bent down for a leaf to wipe it off.

The nuns' mouths stopped in mid-phrase at the word. It gonged out of the chapel, sonorous as a tolling bell. Carla's eyes quickly returned to her hands, one curved over the other. As if to make up for the sudden suspension, their lips started moving in double time, the prayer engraved on their hearts now manifest in breathy whispers.

He was running his hand over the face of the Virgin Mary. Our Blessed Lady who had, like a miracle, sprouted vegetation from the accumulation of leaf mold and bird droppings on her head. A halo of green vines, in emulation of her Son's crown of thorns. He pulled at it, to clear the profane from the sacred.

The vine had taken root in the statue. He tried again but it did not yield. He yanked more firmly and this time pulled away not only the vine but the top of the statue's head, all in one piece. His attempts to restore Our Lady to a more civilized, dignified state had resulted in a grotesque clumsy scalping. He looked with horror at the growth in his hand as if it was a lump of living flesh, and quickly replaced it, tamping it down as best he could. Then he brushed his hands together, wiping away the stain of earth.

The nuns finished their Matins and stood up, Carla venturing right to the doorway and looking in. When he became aware of their presence he headed back outside. "Well," he said, clapping his hands together decisively, "needs a bit of work."

They didn't quite know why he made this statement. Was he here to do repairs?

"Well," said Carla, clapping her hands in imitation.

Nettle tea was poured into cups, bread was torn apart, and chunks of cheese cut with a knife. The nuns ate in silence, their jaws rotating. The sheep had already started breakfast, in fact it was difficult to tell where one meal finished and the next one started with the Agnes sisters. For them life was one long meal. Birds twittering, the soft tearing of grass, the occasional thud as the knife sliced through the cheese and hit the table—it was a fine spring morning.

It unsettled him a little, the eyes watching, the silence. "And what's on the agenda?" he asked. The three mouths stopped chewing. A cud of wet bread dropped from Margarita's mouth. He cleared his throat and tried again. "What is the routine for today?"

"Shearing Day," announced Iphigenia. The chewing resumed.

"Perhaps I can help?" he offered, although he really wasn't all that keen on touching animals.

The nuns looked at him blankly.

Ignatius took their hesitancy for reluctance. He would have to tread carefully, he didn't want to get them offside. He had barely crossed the causeway onto the island when the car had gotten stuck. He needed a hand to shift it, although he felt a little embarrassed having to ask three old women to help him. It wasn't exactly a picnic walking up and down that hill. Or getting through all that gorse and the brambles surrounding the monastery. He wondered how they came in and out. Perhaps they didn't. He seemed to remember that it had been an enclosed order.

He had tried to phone the Bishop as soon as he'd woken up. The mobile had crackled a bit, then cut out. Still, it was better than last night when there'd been no action at all. He could go back to the car and recharge but he did need a bit more time here. Better to get the assessment done in one go. He didn't fancy going down to the car and coming back up. It wasn't just the climb, he doubted he'd be able to find his way in again. He'd already spent one night out in the open, going round in circles before realizing the futility of trying to continue in the dark. He'd waited till daylight but it wasn't much better. Even with a map he'd only stumbled in by chance.

He remembered one of his uncles leaving batteries in a warm place to revive them. Perhaps that would work. All he needed was enough power for one phone call. He looked up at the sun, then around the courtyard. He walked over to a flagstone, felt its warmth, and laid the battery down.

When he stood up he found the three of them standing right behind him. "Solar power," he joked. There was no response.

"I'll just walk around, I won't interfere. Let me know if I can give you a hand."

Like Easter, Shearing Day wasn't on the same day each year. The liturgical calendar was overlaid with the turning of the seasons. Shearing was done in the spring, after the cold of winter, when the wool had risen, the yellow greasy wool of last year's growth lifted by the new white wool underneath.

The best time was on the morning of a fine day, when the fleece was dry and the sheep's stomachs relatively empty. Despite the gentle nature of the shearing, the experience did produce a frisson of stress in the sheep, especially if it was the first time. And the way sheep's memories are it was always the first time. Occasionally, an Agnes sister would bring up her meal from one of the four separate stomachs that processed her food, a pungent-smelling green sauce, and usually, as it happened, over the hand of the shearer, in a warm runny stream which left a stain.

The three nuns came round behind the flock, Margarita in the middle, Carla and Iphigenia taking care of the flanks. They walked very slowly, calling the lambs to them. "Kiri, kiri." As they approached they chanted in quavering voices resembling baas. "Lambs of God, oh blessed lambs of God, meek and mild. Blessed Shepherd, blessed Shepherd, suffer the little lambs to come unto Thee."

Ignatius followed. Despite the nuns' lumpy bodies, they glided along as if they were standing still and the landscape was moving behind them, gracefully through the grass like clouds through the sky. Their voices were good. The sounds rolled resonantly out over the fields. The nuns chanted chords in a way that the ear was pleased, not only by the ensemble but by the quality of each individual voice. Carla's soprano, the bright crystal clarity of a prepubescent boy as she now rounded one side of the flock. The basso of Iphigenia, moving the flock from behind, and Margarita with her fine tenor. They would be perfect in the choir. It was only in spontaneous speech that their words came out in grunts. They rarely had a conversation with each other. Perhaps, he reflected, they were shy or uneasy in his presence. Tongue-tied.

Three sheep were now inside the enclosure, the rest of the flock milling around, the ones inside and the ones outside baaing to each other, keeping auditory contact across the barrier of the fence like prisoners on visiting day. One sheep was encouraged into the courtyard. The nuns took up positions like sentinels, Iphigenia blocking the entrance to the chapel, Carla near the holding pen, Margarita with her shears, ready but unobtrusive.

All the time the nuns kept chanting but now the words changed. "Lambs of God, oh blessed lambs of God, meek and mild, stand in the light and let the servant of God unclothe you, shed the old that the new may be blessed and sanctified in the Lord's name." Then an "amen" echoed through the world. And soon the ovine baas came into harmony with the nuns' voices as one voice accords to the other, the music of the spheres. Oh, how inadequate, how paltry, was this word to describe the sound emanating from these servants of the Lord. Not the cursory amen that the congregation said at mass, a thanks-be-to-God that mass was over and they could go home and relax. No. It was an infinite resonance that might endlessly circumnavigate the globe, gathering itself unto itself with each round like the hosts of peoples standing up to be counted, each individual voice joining the multitude to become one. It was a sound that could at the same time charm birds from the trees, sheep into courtyards, cause granite to vibrate, calm the savage beast. It was the A-M-E-N that God might have uttered after creating the world, bringing forth the multitude of things, the sound billowing from His mouth when He woke on the seventh day and saw that it was good. That He could rest. Amen.

The sound died down, the sole sheep in the courtyard transfixed, as if hypnotized. It was easy for Margarita to put her arm around Agnes Teresa's head, leaning her back slightly and to the right. With the other hand she clipped the wool from the sheep's belly, the muscles in her arm twitching to life as she gripped and relaxed, squeezed together the blades of the shears. Then she did the hind legs. Agnes Teresa sunk blissfully back into Margarita, into her woolly clothes. Two woolly bodies, the larger arched over the smaller as in a dance or the act of fornication.

Margarita worked down one side of the body with short clips, then cleared the wool from her partner's back. Placing Agnes Teresa's head between her knees, she clipped the wool from the head and shoulders. Then she pulled the sheep over and completed the remaining side. Finished. She gave Agnes Teresa a friendly little scratch on the head, a pat on her rump. The sheep trotted off, hesitant at first, then with a spring in her step, light and airy having sloughed off last year's old and matted pelt.

Iphigenia came forward, swept the breakfast crumbs off the table, then spread the fleece and rolled it up tightly, starting at the rear.

With each successive sheep Margarita felt better. The topsy-turvy night, the unpleasantness of being tossed about like a cork on the ocean had retreated and everything had settled. She immersed herself in the salty tang of hard work, flicking her tongue up to the beads of sweat and smacking her lips. The breeze played lightly around her head bent to the task, God blowing his cooling breath on the delicate nape of her neck. She became one with the sheep, with all of Creation, with the growing grass, the growing wool, the growing hair, the nurturing, benign Beneficence.

Four down. Time for a break. Margarita joined her sisters for a cup of tea, chunky fingers around thick ceramic mugs, lanolin unctuous on her hands, the smell of sheep and sage intertwining.

The visitor was bending down, searching for something. Like the sheep looking for their fleeces, mused Margarita. During the shearing, she had almost forgotten about him. Now she saw him again, distorted by the veil of steam rising from the cups. He walked over to the table, scratching the pinpoints of black which had sprouted around his jaw. It made a rasping sound.

"Did one of you move the battery?" he asked. The three of them sat in front of his looming presence. "It was over there in the sun." He gestured in the direction.

"No," said Iphigenia, feeling obliged to speak on their behalf.

Ignatius discovered that the battery wasn't the only thing missing. He looked around for the mobile. He had left it on the table. Perhaps it had been inadvertently rolled up with the pelts. He started feeling them. The fleece was unpleasant to the touch, greasy and sticky at the same time. He especially didn't like it when his hand came across a lumpy bit. "The phone," he said, trying to explain what he was doing. It couldn't have been the shearer, he had watched her working all morning, she'd never left her post. His eyes bounced from Iphigenia to Carla, backward and forward, a game of Ping-Pong. He couldn't very well search them or start pulling the place apart but he wanted to get to the bottom of this.

"Sheep?" Iphigenia suggested the next time his eyes swung in her direction.

He sat down with a slump. He was overreacting. He must stay calm and alert, make sure his behavior was appropriate. Insinuating that the nuns were responsible, it was uncalled for. A cup of tea would put a perspective on things. It probably was only a sheep. Dislodged the battery and nudged it into the grass. The phone too.

The tea was bitter and astringent. Ignatius smacked his lips back and ran his tongue over his teeth. They felt furry and he remembered he hadn't cleaned them, nor had he shaved. He would have preferred a cup of coffee but it didn't appear to be in their repertoire. The thought of coffee naturally led to cigarettes. He felt his jacket. Yes! A packet in the inside pocket. It was crumpled, as were the remaining cigarettes, but hopefully they were salvageable. He tapped the packet on the table, as if to make the cigarettes stand to attention. Using two fingers he slid a cigarette out. Bent but not broken. He straightened it, then flipped it to his lips. Every move he made was watched intently. "Oh, excuse me, would you like one?" He offered the packet around.

Somehow it was not the question that should have been asked. It was an attempt at politeness but it fell short of its mark. Margarita and Iphigenia had not seen smoking for years but they knew what it was. Margarita's father had smoked. What he said in the company of strangers was, "Do you mind?" She saw him again, sitting in the big leather chair, occasionally dabbing ash into the glass ashtray on the wide arm of the chair, her mother knitting or mending a basket of socks, Margarita and her brother sitting on the floor, the whole family listening to the wireless in its walnut casing, listening to serials. Margarita leaning against the chair taking in the smoke and leather, the brown comforting smell of Daddy. "No," said Margarita, surprised by the loudness of her own voice.

Ignatius took out his lighter, tried it a couple of times, shrugged his shoulders, more for the benefit of his audience than anything else, put the lighter back in his pocket, and reached into the fire for a smoldering twig. The cigarette finally alight, he inhaled its calming smoke, felt a slight dizziness, then relaxed.

It was a picture-book day; a china-blue sky, tufts of cloud sprinkled over it, a mirror image of the ground with the stray tufts of wool caught in the grass sprouting from the cracks between the paving stones. Though the breeze here was slight and whimsical the movement of clouds across the sky told of a strong high wind. Mingled with the smell of the smoke was the tang of the sea. Who could have imagined the existence of this little oasis? From one side of the island, if you looked up from sea level to the forbidding cliff, all you saw was a bank of brambles. From the other, more hospitable side facing the mainland, the hilltop blocked any view of the monastery.

He looked at the tableau framed in the archways—white sheep, noses in the grass, some patches more verdant than others. It was a pity he'd left the camera in the car, it was exactly the idyllic scene one sees in tourist brochures. The high walls, the barrier of brambles that had sprung up over the decades had acted as a windbreak and created a veritable Eden here. He thought of how he had broken through those barriers, how he would bring this place to life again.

The smoke from the cigarette recalled the coil of smoke from the fire. How surprised he'd been to find three women living in the ruins, themselves sinking back into nature along with the architecture. He'd come along just in the nick of time. He snorted, forcing jets of smoke out of his nostrils.

"Dragon!" It was Carla, staring, eyes glittering, nostrils flared.

"Oh. Yes," he said, acknowledging her comment with a flourish of his cigarette hand. She continued staring, wanting more. The other two were waiting, mildly amused. Ah well, he thought, no harm in it; showing off was only a minor sin, and this time it was for a greater good. He inhaled the smoke with deliberation, held it in for a second, then made a little fish mouth and sent out a volley of smoke rings. Oh, and wasn't Carla delighted! Yes, the rings had been impressive.

Carla reached for the cigarette, wanting to join in the game, have a try herself. Ignatius hesitated, he didn't really want her slobbering on his cigarette. On the other hand, he felt that with the perfect harmony of this moment he had broken through an invisible barrier of brambles and he didn't want them springing up again. The cigarette was almost finished anyway.

He handed it over. Carla, the perfect imitator, held it between her fingers the way he had, then brought it to her lips while he nodded encouragement. She poised, as if about to jump off a cliff, then drew in a deep sucking breath. An instant of surprise, a coughing and spluttering, then she crushed the cigarette in her hand as if it were an insect that had stung her. When she recovered from her surprise Carla started laughing, the remaining traces of smoke wisping out of her nose and mouth. Then they all started laughing, the bleating sheep as well, till everything was drowned in an avalanche of laughter.

In the late afternoon when the sheep were resting, the three nuns and the priest went collecting tufts of wool. These weren't the best locks, they were used for stuffing pillows and the like. Nothing was wasted.

Bending, stooping. The thorn hidden in the fleece. Sweet penance, love's labors. Sheep big and bold as lions, ranging round their rocky home, fleeces were manes, brilliant as the sun. Psyche moved among the sleeping lions fearlessly, gathering swatches from every bramble, every stone, every crack and crevice where the lion-sheep might leave traces of their golden fleece.

When she did this task Carla imagined she was Psyche. Gathering the fleece of ferocious sheep was one of the tasks Venus made Psyche do. She also made her sort a big mound of wheat, barley, millet, peas, and beans into separate piles, gather water from a dangerous spring on a mountaintop, go into the underworld and fill a box with Persephone's beauty. And all because her son, the God of Love, took Psyche as his bride.

Psyche waited on a high lofty mountain. "The voice of my beloved! Behold, he cometh leaping upon the mountains, skipping upon the hills." The wind came for Psyche, gathered her up and transported her to the palace of the God of Love. Then the God of Love laid her down on a bed of flowers and enfolded her in his wings. "Behold, thou art fair, my love; behold, thou art fair; thou hast dove's eyes within thy locks; thy hair is as a flock of goats."

A buttercup! Such delight. Carla bent and plucked it from its grassy bed. A rich velvety cup, saturated with sun. She popped it in her pocket with the locks of fleece. She looked forward to finding it later when she did Psyche's task of sorting. Carla didn't like Venus much. Such a jealous and spiteful mother, she was more like a witch. Much nicer was the Blessed Virgin. She knew the nuns were the brides of her Son, Jesus, but she never went into a spiteful rage. In the chapel, the Blessed Virgin always smiled down on them. She listened when you prayed and didn't mind anything that you did.

Carla harvested another fleecy lock from a thorny bush. Jesus and the Blessed Virgin, St. Anne, the saints, the hierarchy of angels, the apostles, disciples, all were God's creations. They were there when Carla prayed and chanted, they were in the air she breathed. They were forever stories, with no beginning and no end. Venus was like Arachne and Briar Rose, knitting stories. Once-upon-a-time stories, that had a pattern, a beginning and an end. They were made-up stories. Like the knitting. You started with thread and needles and you made something up. A blanket, a garment. Something that had form and substance, something you could touch and feel, put on and take off.

Carla had a pocketful of locks now, Margarita and Iphigenia were already making their way back to the courtyard. Psyche's task was complete. Only the man kept on. Though he had the same smooth skin as Jesus, Carla didn't think he was the Savior who would come. That Savior would drop from the sky like an angel, not start off on all fours. Carla looked behind. He was on all fours now. He appeared to be sniffing the ground.

He had deliberately dawdled, held back from the group. Ignatius reflected that the nuns, seen at a distance, looked like clumps of wool themselves, moved by a slow breeze, stopping where the wool had caught, plucking it from a fold in the mantle of Our Lady, from her feet, bending to pick it out of a broken edge of stone. Sometimes swirls of it lay on the green grass like fairy rings.

Though he felt resistance give way in the moment of shared laughter, a genuine sharing of Christian love and fellowship, he couldn't shake that niggling feeling that they knew more than they were letting on. He couldn't even begin to guess what possible use an inoperative mobile phone could be to them. Although it didn't completely allay his doubts and suspicions, lack of logical motive turned him to other explanations. Perhaps it was one of those things that mysteriously disappear and then just as mysteriously reappear. As he bent to gather wool he kept his eye out. In the course of his search he examined a lot of sheep droppings, small hard beads compacted into longer shapes which at first glance looked deceptively promising.

He flicked a squashed poo pellet off his trousers. Foolish, he supposed, not to have changed before climbing up to the monastery. He had picked the car up, thrown his holiday gear in the trunk, and driven straight down from the presbytery. The clerical dress served as a sort of passport, especially in the country where priests were held in higher esteem than they currently were in the city. Twice he'd gotten lost on the unmarked country roads and had been forced to stop and ask directions. He had been received most cordially, given scones at one house and a glass of whisky at the other. He knew it was because he was wearing the clothes of a priest.

The grounds were vast, he had already ascertained that from the acreage, and had at one time supported a large self-sustaining community. The land was good, there was a supply of fresh water. The buildings were in a shocking state but he was confident that the medieval flavor could be faithfully restored. He had discovered quite a number of valuable relics: gold chalices, some interesting statuary, antique books, illuminated manuscripts.

He would recommend 4WD access, a helipad, and a marina. He felt sure he could present the women with an attractive alternative. There were no problems that money couldn't solve. A very pleasant place altogether—sunshine, clean air, the great outdoors—he was beginning to feel as if he were on holiday himself, despite his cramped quarters and his unexpected companions. By the end of the afternoon he had a pocketful of wool. But that was all.

Boiled nettles and swedes. They came steaming out of the pot and onto the plates. A faint murmur of grace, then the nuns' hands scooping them up to their mouths, slurping in the pap of green, biting chunks off the ochre-colored swedes, the steam condensing into tiny drops of moisture that dribbled down their chins, to be wiped off, although not always, by the backs of hands and grubby sleeves.

He might have had a laugh with them, he might have mucked in and helped them with the chores, much as he disliked the odor of sheep building up in his throat like catarrh. Things had been pleasant enough but, Lord Almighty! They snuffled, they slopped, they gurgled, and at the end of it all they belched. Even pigs didn't belch, though not having spent a lot of time with pigs he couldn't be sure.

No ablutions before dinner, they shoved food into their mouths with hands that had spent the day sorting through fleeces, picking off stale, encrusted sheep feces. "Dags" is what they called them.

His mouth fixed into a determined slit. In Rome one didn't always have to do as the Romans. If one had a better, more hygienic and civilized way of doing things, perhaps one could teach the Romans a thing or two. As the Romans, in fact, had taught the world.

"Excuse me," he said during a lull in the slurps, "would you have a fork?" He knew very well they had forks, they'd been on the table the first night. The nuns, although at the moment he was finding it more and more difficult to think of them as such, had even made desultory attempts to use them.

"Fork," repeated Carla, letting a mouthful of green drop onto the table. She ran off and returned with a fork.

He plucked it out of her fist, like an arrow from a quiver. It was encrusted with bits of food and gritty with dirt. Was it the fork he had used or the one she had thrown on the ground? That had been in her mouth. When he took out his handkerchief to wipe it clean they stopped eating and watched intently, as if expecting him to perform a magic trick.

He was quite conscious of the way he placed his fingers around the fork and observed that it was very similar to holding a pen. He brought the edge of the fork down into a piece of swede, cleaving it in two, slowly, deliberately, showing them how it was done.

He speared a cold flaccid lump and popped it into his mouth, smiling and nodding as if savoring deliciously cooked meat. In the privacy of his mouth, his tongue squashed it against his palate, rounded it up into a soft glob, then swallowed. He repeated this process several times. When he'd finished his meal, he lay the fork neatly across the plate.

"I was wondering," he began, "I was wondering if you could give me a hand with the car in the morning. I'm sure the four of us could budge it. If I had the mobile I could get someone from the mainland to come over but . . ." He shrugged and lifted his palms up. It was a pity about the phone but he could call the

Bishop from the nearest garage, then his holiday would begin in earnest. The nuns were looking at him blankly. "An outing would be nice, wouldn't it?" he went on. "You could make a day of it. There's a nice little beach down there. We could have a picnic. I've got some scones in the car, biscuits."

It slowly started to dawn. He wanted them to go out.

> We command by this present constitution, whose validity is eternal and can never be questioned, that all nuns, collectively and individually, present and to come, of whatsoever order of religion, in whatever part of the world they may be, shall henceforth remain in their monasteries in perpetual enclosure.

"We are enclosed." Margarita finally found her tongue.

They ate like pigs, they walked around dressed like God knows what, surely they weren't going to stand on ceremony on the matter of enclosure.

Iphigenia pulled herself up to her full height, lifted her head so that she looked down on him. "Why are you here?" she asked.

"To do an assessment," he said.

"To what purpose?"

It would be easy just to leave without saying anything, to let the Bishop notify them officially. But that was the coward's way.

"How would you like soft beds, sheets, complete plumbing with running hot water?"

Iphigenia could feel herself turning to stone. He came dressed like a priest but he did not behave as a priest. He had blasphemed in their house, he had tried to engage them in idle chat at mealtimes, he had suggested they go outside for a picnic. And now he was offering them worldly comforts.

He looked from one to the other. The only one showing a

glimmer of interest was Carla. "Clean clothes," he said, "good food, shops, companionship, an on-duty nurse."

"A nurse?" asked Margarita.

"Forgive me for saying so, but you're getting to an age, well . . . it's just in case, you understand. You can live out your old age in comfort. No more nettles and swedes. You can have beds with proper mattresses, roofs that don't leak. Everything here needs fixing."

"We don't need a nurse," said Margarita. "And nothing needs fixing." It was enough trying to cope with him, she didn't want nurses and builders here as well. Their life wouldn't be their own. Nettles and swedes were appropriate fare—nourishing without overexciting the appetite.

"Retirement homes are very enlightened nowadays," he said. "They're just like village living. You have your independence and you are part of a community as well."

It would have been simpler if the place had been unoccupied as they had all assumed. Now certain steps needed to be taken. Relocation of the nuns was one of them. Of course their presence here didn't alter the overall plan. The property ultimately belonged to the diocese, to do with as the Bishop saw fit. There was no question of them staying, the three of them in these vast grounds, it was a criminal waste of real estate. They could build housing for four hundred on this property. Not that the Church intended building housing for the poor. The rich too needed spiritual sustenance, a place of retreat from the pressures of their lives.

Now Iphigenia understood. He didn't want to improve their life, he wanted to shut it down.

"You want us to leave." The words were almost spat out.

"You can't very well stay here."

"But we have been very well staying here," Iphigenia pointed out.

"It's too big for the three of you to manage."

"But the sheep. They need to graze. What do you have in mind for them?"

Relocating the women was one thing but he doubted there was a house that would take sheep. It would be a nightmare just trying to get them down the hill. "Probably be best to slaughter them. We would arrange for you to have the meat, of course."

Iphigenia stood up violently, pushing the table and rattling the plates. "You have been received into our community, you have been our guest. And now you want us to slaughter the Agnes sisters?" She leaned so close into his face he could feel her breath. "Begone!" she shouted as if she were exorcising the Devil.

Then it was Iphigenia who was begone, taking herself off to her cell. Margarita looked anxiously around, felt the huge gap Iphigenia's sudden departure had made. She stood up, waving her hand in front of her face as if to clear the air, then she too hurried off to the security of her cell.

Carla grinned merrily. Iphigenia rattling the table, Iphigenia rattled. Carla had never seen the like. And all the talk the man had brought. She had so much to think about, so much material for the escapecoat. The man leaned toward her, a conciliatory gesture but Carla too was moving away, giving him a little wave as she went.

Ignatius sat there alone at a table that wasn't his. Oh dear. He knew it would be a big change for them but he hadn't anticipated quite such a violent reaction. Perhaps he had overdone it a bit, perhaps it hadn't been altogether necessary to mention slaughtering the sheep.

Iphigenia leaned against the door of her cell breathing heavily. It wouldn't happen. It simply wouldn't happen. They would not be moved from their home. As for the wholesale slaughter of the Agnes sisters, the annihilation of the flock, it was unthinkable. It was one thing making a ritual offering to God, but as for doing it for the sake of expediency!

The man was a fool, a toad, an insensitive; bombastic, impolite, a dandy, a blunderer. Iphigenia went through a whole string of insults trying to ward him off, the expulsion of air like sobs, as if his announcement had gotten stuck in her throat and she was trying to dislodge it.

He was not a creature that had strayed innocently into their midst; he had come with purpose and intention. His initial darts of nervousness had disappeared and self-importance had taken their place. She remembered the previous visits of priests, when the flagstones and tables had to be scrubbed extra clean, when the abbess and novice mistress moved more quickly, felt their wimples, checked that their veils were perfectly in place, when "best behavior" rippled through the convent body. The abbess would show the priest around, and he would smile assuredly and let his gaze sweep across the sea of faces, not looking at any one in particular but seeing them en masse.

Afterward, the priest and abbess in conversation, she with her head bent, he looking at some records or listening to a request, writing it down in a little notebook, finishing with a flourishing full stop that bounced the pen off the page, then tucking the notebook away in his pocket and never referring to it again.

Iphigenia couldn't remember when the priestly visits had ceased. Before or after the last abbess had gone to God? It must have been before, the numbers were already dwindling in the time of the last abbess. Iphigenia, Margarita, Carla, and the handful of others who remained let the days go by without officially electing a replacement. The daily round continued, the months turned to years without an election.

She missed the last abbess. For the first time in many years Iphigenia wanted to seek the advice and counsel of a higher human authority. The abbess was strict but unwavering in her ability to listen to the members of her flock. While she rarely gave the very practical advice that would solve the immediate problem, after a moment of silent prayer with her the supplicant felt her burden lighten.

As the years went by it fell to Iphigenia to make decisions on the rare occasion a decision had to be made.

It was impossible. They could not leave and go to another place. Under the pads of her fingers she felt the comfort of the old timber, worn smooth by the years and by her touch; the slight ridge and density of a knot in the wood. She ran her hand along the wall, felt the rougher texture of stone. She had rubbed up against this stone to relieve the annoyance of an itch, the minuscule creatures she was host to, like a bear rubbing its back against a rough-barked tree. Bathing was an extravagance, the community had lived and worked and slept in their habits until they had become a second skin.

It was more than an itch that Iphigenia had now and it would take more than the old stones to relieve it. She wrapped the woolly blanket around herself and moved to the window, standing in the shaft of cold night, the walls so thick that the window space made a cube of air. Had anyone been wandering outside they would have seen Iphigenia framed in the glassless window, a proud face with a band of worry encircling the eyes like a blindfold. Iphigenia's eyes were staring into midair. Out there were the archways yawning like mouths and the sleeping sheep, but Iphigenia was staring at fog. If there was any movement it floated through her field of vision untracked.

There was a disturbance, a screech, a flutter, a night bird killing its prey, tearing a rent into the Great Silence.

Iphigenia's eyelids came down, a film of moisture to relieve the dryness of her eyes. God was far away and silent. Iphigenia needed the community. She unlatched the door and went outside, drifting silently along the cloisters. The moon was waning, almost half of it obscured by shadow. She came out into the field. Now that the bird was sated, night had folded over it like lava, pressing everything in its wash to sleep.

Except for Iphigenia. A wakeful shepherd watching her flock by night. Watching for the wolf that might enter their midst and steal a lamb away. She squatted down amongst the rise and fall of newly thin bodies. The sheep shifted a little, like sleeping children rolling over and making room for another. She lay down with them, curved her body into the sleeping Agnes Teresa, a troubled child seeking the warm solace of the mother. Agnes Teresa, whose fleece warmed Iphigenia, whose lamb had so recently been sacrificed.

Teresa snuffled, chomped her jaws in sleep, the dreams of prancing across the sunlit plains momentarily suspended. Instinctively Teresa took this lamb unto herself, the coarse curly head lying on her softly heaving body. The night hung low over Iphigenia, the jagged stars like splinters of ice. If she opened her mouth they would drop right in. Under her ear Teresa's body was warm and rhythmic, oblivious as were all the other members of the flock to the pronouncement of their slaughter.

Iphigenia sat up, the sheep around her like a flowing white skirt. She saw their bellies and throats exposed and vulnerable even though their ovine instincts herded them together. There were no predators in these pastures, except for the occasional swooping bird searching for nesting material. She put her arms out and stroked those within reach. No wolves entered here. Unless they entered slyly and with maps.

They murmured and twitched, taking her outpouring love into their dreams. Iphigenia stood up, her mouth determined and set, her nostrils flared, glittering eyes reflecting the ice of stars. What a snorting irony that a lamb had been slaughtered in preparation for his coming. The guilt of error hung above Iphigenia like the carcass dripping over the altar, as if somehow in offering the lamb she herself had given him the idea for slaughter.

The darkness was thinning. Iphigenia stepped carefully over the sleeping bodies, went back along the cloisters into the chapel. Margarita and Carla were already there, on their knees in front of the Blessed Virgin who looked beatifically down on them, the tangle of vines sprouting from her head not quite covering the crack left by the priest's handiwork. The faces of Carla and Margarita were firmly pressed into the stone of her garment, like frightened children hiding in their mother's skirts. They did not turn at the sound of Iphigenia's feet padding across the stones and sprigs of grass, but they made way for her when she came to take her place among them. They pressed prayers and urgencies into the gown of the Queen of Heaven, kneeling in unison like on nights of vigilance before an important feast day.

And this is the way he found them. The three nuns kneeling in a semicircle, locked together in holy trinity.

He was not totally oblivious to the fact that something was awry. He had not slept soundly. There had been movement in the night, a disturbed atmosphere. He needed to get back to a proper bed, not this meager straw offering. He had seen more comfortable beds in prison. He was sleeping in his clothes, which never pleased him, he needed a shave, and his teeth were furry. Running his finger along them made a squeaking sound but didn't really clean away the grime. Stupid to have left all his gear in the car. But then he hadn't expected to spend more than a few hours on the property. He was feeling decidedly uncomfortable now. He wanted to leave as soon as possible. If he couldn't get the car going by himself he'd walk over to the mainland and get help. If he had to wait for the tide, he'd wait by the car. From his vantage point in the doorway it looked as if the Virgin Mary had cloned herself. The three of them, heads bowed, around the base of the statue like smaller bulbs forming around the parent one. If they had heard him they showed no signs of recognition. He would wait till their prayers ended before he said good-bye. But it seemed the prayer would never end. Even when it did they remained there, silent, immutable as the statue herself.

What he wants is for them to disappear, to have never been

here in the first place. But he cannot in all good faith continue treating this as *terra inoccupata.* He must deal with their presence and their removal as efficiently as possible. Difficult to onsell the property with tenants and besides, the old women have to see the nonsense of them remaining here. He will let them say their prayers, he will have a cup of tea, and then he will be off. He won't mention the slaughter of the lambs. He will assure the nuns that they will be cared for and their wishes taken into consideration. And then things will proceed.

Forever and forever has existed the pattern of light and dark, the earth rolling through day and night. Come to the mount and ye shall be washed in the light of the Lord. It was morning now but they could not start the day. They kept their eyes closed, trying to make him disappear. He had ripped a gash in the silk of their lives. He was not a slow nibbling moth fraying the fabric away, but a quick precise snip of scissors. Through their thin papery eyelids they noticed a lightening of the atmosphere when he vacated his post at the door. But he hadn't gone far. They prayed for guidance, a sign, their whispered prayers rustling like leaves in the chapel.

And a sign would come, before the morning was out.

The hiss of steam, the acrid woody smell of wet ashes. Their eyes sprang open.

Light streamed into the chapel through all the orifices, awakening everything. Even the Queen of Heaven wore a sudden look of surprise, as if she'd just woken from a long sleep to discover them kneeling at her robe.

"Damn." A sharp intake of breath, then, "Damn, damn, damn!"

How could he? How could he let the blasphemy enter the sanctity of the chapel? Margarita looked across to St. Anne, Mother of Mary, Holy Grandmother of Christ. Wise Sibyl who had foreseen the Birth and had raised her daughter to be the Savior's mother, teaching her from the Book in which the Child's destiny was written. Her kindliness was wrinkled with disapproval.

Even Carla was taken aback. Carla who normally delighted in disruption, who herself had taken scissors and snipped threads, who held her breath in surprised pleasure when she first heard the word coming from the four-legged creature in the brambles, knew that it should never enter the ears of the Blessed Virgin or the Blessed Grandmother. She glanced at them quickly, hoping their stone veils muffled the sound.

The nuns hastily wound up their long vigil and marched into the courtyard. He was flicking his hand back and forward trying to cool it. The kettle was on the ground and there was white steam hissing off the coals.

"I'm sorry," he said, truly sorry and annoyed that he had to apologize to them. "I was just trying to make a cup of tea before I went. I'm afraid I may have put your fire out."

Iphigenia looked straight through him, marched over to the fire, and got down on the ground. She sniffed around for the aroma of salvageable wood, gathered up unburned twigs from the periphery of the fire, and made a little pile on top of the remaining embers. She rounded her mouth till the opening was no bigger than a pea, then sent into the smolder of red a flow of air so gentle it would not disturb the flame of a candle. The red grew rounder, fuller. Then there was a glimmer of flame. She coaxed it up. When she knew that the twigs had caught she put on branches, filled her cheeks, and blew gusts of breath into the fire till the flames sang and danced merrily off the blackening wood.

Benign fire was a constant companion. They gazed at it in the long winter nights and drew stories from it. It warmed their bodies and kindled their imagination. There were cities and castles in the embers, forests; fairies and monsters leaped out of the flames, wicked stepmothers and beasts.

When the fire was safely at its full strength, she let loose and blasted the full force of her rage and fury. The flames licking hungrily along the twigs and branches now swept through Iphigenia's vision like the conflagrations of history. This was the fire that burned midwives and saints, Joan and the other staked martyrs, scourged the heathen, witches and warlocks, the hellfire grave of the sinner, bereft of eternal rest.

Ignatius stood with his burned hand under his jacket, for warmth, comfort, and to keep his injury out of their sight. His throat was parched. He hadn't eaten or drunk anything since the meal last night. He was a little shaky and wanted to sit down but felt awkward about joining them at the table without being asked. He felt relieved that they'd gotten the fire going again. Relieved and useless. Uselessness was not a feeling he enjoyed. "Well done," he said. If nothing else he could still mete out praise.

Iphigenia could see him through the waves of heat rising from the fire. Even with her clouded vision she could see. And she could smell. He had arrived with intention and he was departing with intention. He might leave but he wouldn't leave them alone. He would put out more than their fire if he wasn't stopped.

"A cup of tea," she announced. "Carla, fetch some salve for our guest and a special tea." He started to demur but Iphigenia took no notice. "A nice big cup of stay-at-home."

Carla could hardly believe her ears.

Away she went, trying to hide her glee. There were lots of special teas, some dried and stored, others freshly growing in the garden and Carla's secret places. There were plants that kept insects away, plants that made you remember, that made you forget, plants that eased delivery of lambs, that aborted them, plants that soothed the body and soul, plants that made you run like a rabbit. And there was stay-at-home.

Stay-at-home had spiky serrated leaves. It had a different name in the pharmacopoeia, but Carla liked to give each plant her own special name. Stay-at-home grew slowly, one small spurt of growth a year and its flower, in the winter, resembled a rose. Its petals were pale green, almost white.

How wonderful that he had burned his hand. Carla knew the sensation of burns, of cuts, the scratch of brambles as she ran through them seeking the passion of Christ. She knew the lightness of mind afterward. Sometimes she even fainted. She recalled the sick in the stomach, the buzzing in her ears, a galaxy of dark stars pricking her vision, all preludes to the final fall into complete and utter black. Then she would wake up on the floor. This happened easily in the days when young Carla got her first blood. How wondrous to discover blood trailing from her like the miracle of saints. Then she grew stronger and she had to do a lot to induce the fainting: starve herself, make incisions to let the blood out. All with careful secrecy because the sisters did not like Carla's miracles. In the end she had grown bored. Miracles were a lot of trouble and there were other ways to be flooded in God's ecstasy.

Carla often made up mixtures and potions but rarely did she have a chance to test their efficacy. And fancy Iphigenia suggesting! She took a good pinch of stay-at-home, then crushed some lavender flowers into it to disguise its bitter taste. Carla hummed a little nursery tune as she went about her work. Occasionally a word popped out of her mouth—roam, home, bread, dead. She sniffed the mixture and added a tiny bit more stay-at-home. It was done.

And now for the salve. Carla opened the corner cupboard where she kept her salve herbs, laid out like an apothecary's cabinet. It hadn't always been like this. In Carla's childhood this room was the bakehouse. She would sit on a wooden stool, helping Sister Cook peel vegetables, Sister Cook with her sleeves rolled up, arms speckled brown and glistening with sweat. Sister Cook had watery eyes and more than one chin. Friar Tuck. One of Robin Hood's band of merry men. Carla thought of the sisters as her band of merry men.

Carla remembered the dark cupboard of her childhood, the cupboard in the corner. Corners were places thick with whispers, urgencies, brown dusty things. Spiders built webs in corners. Motes of dust which had danced golden in the late-afternoon light went there to die.

The cupboard was used for the game of bread-in-the-oven. Usually it was Carla who suggested it but sometimes the nuns themselves initiated the game. "Ho there, Carla, time to play bread-in-the-oven." And into the cupboard she went. The nuns wanted to play this game even when Carla wasn't in the kitchen and they had to come and fetch her specially. Carla did think it was a bit strange because she noticed that whenever this happened, special preparations were going on, a time when the nuns would surely be too busy for games. Cloths on tables, flowers in vases, brass polished. A quickened beat, a flurry in the slow daily round of the sisters. They popped her in and shut the cupboard door. It was very quiet and there was no sound at all except for a buzzing in her ears. Nothing to see save the swirl of dark formless souls and nothing to feel but the damp settling on her. She liked it in there, it was small and quiet, like having a special friend. When she thought she was cooked she knocked on the door for Sister Cook to let her out.

But one time no one came. She banged and banged till her knuckles were raw. She was frantic, she knew what happened to bread if you left it too long. It burned. Burned till it was black as death. Black and smoking. The cupboard became hot with her panting breath. She was in Hell, she could feel the tongues of fire lapping at her.

The hard cupboard walls melted in the heat, became red, spongy, and wet, she was in a boiling sea. Her eyes squashed shut, body curled up like a worm, the tiny hands banging but no sound coming. She wanted to scream but was unable to do a simple thing like bring her lips apart.

Then the expulsion began, her whole body urgent with movement, bursting to be free. Crawling, swimming, pushing against the spongy dark walls. Finally she passed through. She was out. With a shock she felt cold dry air. She took in a breathful of it and gave it back in a scream.

And then there was light. A thousand pinpricks of it in the firmament. Huge hands wiping pulp, stickiness from her face and body, cleaning her tiny eyes. She followed an ancient path, the map of it deep within her, till her tiny mouth latched onto the scent of milk and coaxed out its warm sweet fluid. The beached mother body on which she lay rose and fell in great waves, gentle respite from its labors. Mary and her Child.

No midwives, no wise men beneath the myriad stars, just the watchful eye of the beasts of the earth.

Later, years later, when Carla had come back to look for the thing that had happened to her in the cupboard, she found it had become an innocuous place. A small tidy cupboard with no hidden panels, no trapdoor, the walls quite solid and not a bit spongy. It was hardly big enough for a cat to crawl into, let alone a child. Nevertheless, she had smoked it out with slow-burning leaves to expel any residue of her dark brown episode.

The pot was boiling merrily when Carla arrived back in the courtyard, unctuous green salve in one hand and special tea in the other. A few sheep had idled by. Iphigenia and Margarita were sitting at the table, the man standing to the side with his hand still under his jacket. The Three Bears. Carla, Iphigenia, and Margarita were the three bears and now they had a Goldilocks. He had wandered into their forest while they were away at prayer. He had tried the porridge but it was too hot and he had burned his hand. He had broken something, not a chair, but he had broken something. And he was about to run away and leave the damage. But the story didn't say what happened next. How the bears went after Goldilocks and ate her, because bears do eat little girls who wander into their forest.

"Let me mend your hand," said Carla in her sweetest voice.

"I will fetch the water," sung Iphigenia.

"And I will fetch the cloth," said Margarita.

"No, it's perfectly all right," he protested, "I don't think it will blister. Just a bit of redness, that's all."

He brought his hand out of his jacket and turned it over and back to show it still worked. "Better to be safe," said Margarita.

"For your long journey," said Iphigenia.

"Come. Sit," said Carla.

It was a storm in a teacup, but it was the way of old women to fuss. Still, if it made them feel better, the least Ignatius could do was oblige. He sat.

He watched the pouring of water for tea, watched the unction being applied to his hand. It made him feel drowsy, a pleasurable drowsiness he felt at the barber's when all he had to do was lean back and let Rodney massage his head.

They wrapped his hand up snugly and although he felt soothed, it was as if the hand didn't belong to him.

Carla poured the tea into a mug and held it up to his lips. A sharp whiff of something as the steam hit his nostrils, then it was lost in a cloud of lavender.

"Thank you, I can manage." They were going a little overboard treating him like an invalid. It wasn't as if he couldn't use his free hand to pick up the mug. Still, he reflected, it was fortuitous the way things had turned out. All this fussing over him, it meant they would be parting on good terms. He could put up with it for fifteen minutes. The gesture made him feel magnanimous. He sipped his tea.

"Bread," said Margarita, who looked the picture of health. Strange he hadn't noticed it before. Her round beady eyes bright as newly minted coins, her cheeks red and shiny as apples.

He took the offered bread but instead of eating it he put it in his pocket. He rationalized this unusual action by reminding himself that he needed something to sustain him on the long walk down to the car.

"Apple?" coaxed Margarita. Now her head looked more like a pumpkin, a Halloween pumpkin. She was holding an apple in front of him. So he hadn't been mistaken before, there had been apples. But this wasn't red and shiny like her cheeks. It was a wizened winter apple. When he bit into it, it tasted sweet and mellow as an autumn afternoon.

Then he felt stuffy. He pulled at his collar. He needed to go outside, to get some fresh air. He couldn't really understand why, he already was outdoors. He needed more, he needed to stand on a rocky outcrop and have a gale-force wind in his face. His hand lay on the table wrapped in its swaddling. He seemed not to be able to move it. He would leave it behind if necessary. Stomach cramps now and an excess of saliva. A gob of it hit the table like a tear. Oh God, he was dribbling. "Shock . . . burn . . . drink plenty of fluids." The three faces, Halloween pumpkins with cut-out mouths, the words spitting out like pips.

His mouth tasted bitter, he lurched, his hand sprang off the table and the poultice fell away. He lunged toward the air through the archway, then up came the apple, tasting on its return journey like bad cider. Then he heard the ringing and saw Carla's dark stars of ecstasy. But he was sick, very sick, and ecstasy was the last thing on his mind.

His head was aching, his mouth was dry, and everything was far too bright. He had the world's worst hangover. He closed his eyes in the vain hope that when he opened them again he would find himself back at the presbytery. But he wasn't. The three were still there, standing by the bed like nurses.

"Fell . . ."

"And hit your head . . ."

"Vinegar and brown paper."

Did they really say that or was he hallucinating? He opened his eyes wide, needing to stay alert. How had he gone from a simple burn to being bedridden? Was this his body's way of telling him to slow down? He thought all that listening to your body business was a lot of mumbo jumbo. But perhaps this excursion, the uncomfortable beds, lack of decent food, had taken more of a toll than he realized. Thus weakened, the shock of what had been a superficial burn had a greater effect. He remembered his own father falling off a ladder, getting up complaining of nothing more than a slight bump on the head, then having to be rushed to hospital with a concussion.

He looked around the room. It was not the same one as before. It was larger, there was a wicker chair in the corner with a neat pile of garments on it, pictures of saints on the walls, and the bed, though not the springy mattress with fresh crisp sheets he had at the presbytery, was at least softer than the straw-covered ironing board of a bed he'd slept on the last couple of nights. He was lying on layer upon layer of sheepskins. On top of the bed, covering him, was a blanket with colored patterns knitted into it. A Bible scene at first glance.

He felt his burned hand. Or rather, he didn't feel it. The redness had cleared and it was no longer tender to the touch. Miraculously it had healed. The nuns' folk remedy had worked, at least on the hand. Pity it wasn't strong enough to stave off the consequences of shock. His stomach was cramped and his head overcome with waves of pain. He felt as if he'd spent the night in a threshing machine.

Margarita pressed a bowl to his lips, tilting it so that the liquid moistened them. His tongue came out and gathered the liquid in. It tasted like clear water though his taste buds were not at their most objective and neither were his critical faculties. But his instincts were strong, his body needed water. He brought his hands up to replace Margarita's, tilting the bowl up farther and farther till eventually it obscured his face completely.

So hungry was he for the bowl, so greedily did he slurp at the water that it trickled onto his chin, his neck, and right the way down; a sensation that he remained unaware of till he felt the cold furrow extend as far as his navel. He quickly put his hands under the cover and felt for his clothes but all he came across was his goosepimply flesh. He gulped. He was in a nun's cell, the cell of the abbess judging by the size of it, and he was naked. He looked wildly around the room. The garments neatly piled on the chair were his.

He was grateful for feeling so poorly, otherwise his embarrassment would have been even more acute. It was all so preposterous. He sank lower under the blanket as if that would hide his nakedness, but of course it was too late. They had undressed him. They had looked, they had seen and they may have even . . . He felt his genitals shriveling up, trying to hide at the mere thought. He found small comfort in the fact that they were old women. He'd heard that the older ones often make the lewder jokes.

He felt weak, helpless, and humiliated, the way he had as a young seminarian when he'd had his appendix removed. The nurse was young and buxom, freckles smattered across her nose and cheeks, a cheery smile and dimpled arms, a country girl fed on milk and potatoes. She had come to shave him, drawn a curtain round the bed and asked him to pull down his pajama trousers. "Now then," she'd said, "don't be embarrassed on my account, I've done this millions of times." She was too young to have done it millions of times. Was it really necessary to verbalize the embarrassment? His penis had shriveled up so small on that occasion that it was lost in the tangle of hair.

Till her hand brushed against his groin. Then the curious penis popped out. The warmth of her through the surgical glove excited him. Her warm rubber touch. He looked to the ceiling, glued his eyes there during the whole procedure and tried to quell the rising sap with furious prayer. "Thy rod and thy staff," one of his favorite invocations, had to be quickly dismissed. In fact he had started several familiar prayers with their words of strong, fatherly support and dismissed them all, finally deciding to direct his will at the fly spots on the ceiling and hope for the best.

He knew it wasn't working when he felt his stiffened member find the girl's hand, as if it had an inbuilt radar device for searching its target. He flinched back from it, his face reddening. "It's only natural. At least you're normal," she said, as if that was a consolation. Of course it was natural, of course he was normal, he didn't need to be reassured of that. Normal but without the liberties of a normal man.

The Church was ablaze with the celibacy issue and while he wasn't an active participant, he stood, as a matter of principle, for Progress. The Church had to look to its own future if it was not to become a moribund institution. Hence the economic rationalism, hence the sale of properties. As for where he personally stood or what he had to gain from the celibacy issue he wasn't sure. He had entered the seminary as a young man with a bright future in mathematics, a gift that he'd dedicated to the Church. He was sure that, had he chosen the path of the family man, he would have found a good woman willing to share it with him. It would be quite nice to have a family. He saw himself at the head of the table, the youngsters' heads bowed in grace, all washed and polished, the wife ladling out soup. He couldn't see her face but saw quite clearly her delicate long-fingered hands.

But he had chosen otherwise. He had never felt all that comfortable with girls. They called him names. He was mortified when the girls from the neighboring school tipped his cap, and he had shied away instead of taking part in the good-natured banter, the rough and tumble. He could never quite tell whether they were genuinely interested when they gave him difficult mathematical problems to solve or whether they were nudging each other behind his back.

Sexual release at his own hand was not the issue. It had not sent him blind, nor even remotely dimmed his sight. At times he was quite elaborate, stroking different parts of his body first before taking the matter in hand. No, as far as he understood it, the issue at the heart of celibacy was intimacy. How could you fully give yourself to God if there was another?

"Better?" asked Iphigenia. Their guest appeared to be smiling.

"Thank you," he said. He was feeling a little brighter than when he'd first awoken but he didn't think he was yet ready to travel. He could put up with their ministrations for another day, then he would be off.

"Margarita will watch over you tonight," announced Iphigenia.

Watch over him? As if he was dying? He didn't need that. "I'll be fine," he assured them.

"In case you need anything," said Margarita. "I'll sit in the corner."

He was hardly in a position to argue. Still, it was only for one night. It wasn't as if he had a chronic illness. A bit of rest and he'd be fine. Night. It was early morning when he burned his hand, now it was night. But which night? He was an organized man who could account for every minute of his day. Now there was a gap. He had stopped and time had gone on without him. He needed to catch up.

"What time is it?" he asked.

"Storytime," replied Margarita.

He didn't want a story. "My clothes," he demanded.

"We'll wash them. Nice and fresh for your journey."

"But what if . . . what if I need . . ." He couldn't bear to bring himself to discuss bodily functions with them.

"Margarita will provide."

"Pot," whispered Margarita into his ear.

Oh, the humiliation of it. Not even a bottle as he'd had in the hospital. A pot. Like a child.

"Lying comfortably?" said Margarita. "Good. Once upon a time there was . . ."

What a day, what a day, what a day! There had never been such a day! Carla didn't know where to start. She should have started at the beginning, with the disruption to prayers and the burned hand, the tiny thing that had set the rest in motion. But she could tell herself the beginning later. Right now she wanted to go over the most exciting bits. Ah, but which? Was it seeing the effect of the potion or was it the other thing? Oh, it was the other thing.

The disrobing. She said the word slowly, succulently, feeling the movement of her tongue, the place where her lips came together and parted again, the final syllable of the word that vibrated in her throat. It was delicious. It was the best. She would discipline herself. Put disrobing away and save it for later.

His eyes had rolled up as if he was trying to look into his brain. Margarita had stuck her sausage fingers in, righted them, and pulled the eyelids down. So his eyes wouldn't dry out. And so he wouldn't look like he was dead. Carla had held her breath when he fell over and didn't get up again. Was it too much stay-at-home? She had given the mixture to a ram once to stop him roaming. She simply doubled the dose, assuming that the man was twice the size of a ram, but perhaps he wasn't. Iphigenia and Margarita hadn't looked at Carla or admonished her when they marched over to pick him up, she hadn't made a mistake.

The nuns had waited till he had fallen before they moved from the table, waited till he'd lurched and flayed around, as if he were a dangerous, unpredictable animal who might turn on them if they got in his way. They watched. And when he'd finally fallen in a lump and the curious sheep came to sniff him, they finished off their tea and attended to him.

The abbess's room had been shut for many years. It was not the abbess's office, they would never put him in there. They swung the door backward and forward a few times to push out the smell of mustiness, piled together the skins of all the rams that had been slaughtered over the years, and brought out one of the blankets. Around the edges were scenes from the life of Jesus and in the middle a panel of the Lord as the Good Shepherd, surrounded by His flock. It was a soothing comforting blanket that would make him feel safe and secure when he awoke from his long sleep.

It wasn't till they had heaved the body onto the skins that they saw the threads of vomit on his clothes. Iphigenia of course had noticed the curdled smell of it, they'd all noticed it, and were quite happy to leave it there. It was only vomit. But it was not fitting to have this smell in the abbess's cell.

"Off with his clothes."

Carla thrilled at the prospect with the anticipation she felt on Shearing Day. Because things would be revealed. How different the sheep looked without their woolly coats. She liked the way shearing exposed the parts you didn't normally see, unless you quietly crawled through the grass with them and looked up. But fully coated, all you saw was curly wool, matted together with mud and grass and shit. When Margarita held the sheep up, creases and folds and other things were revealed. Carla didn't know exactly what she would see but she was very keen to see it. The thrill crept enticingly through her whole body.

Margarita and Iphigenia moved in on him. They were familiar with the task of laying out departed sisters, preparing the bodies for burial, for them to be planted in the ground like seeds.

Margarita's strong beefy arms propped him up while Iphigenia slipped the jacket off. The collar came off next. There was a gurgle in his throat and he seemed to breathe more easily.

"Carla. Shoes."

Though Carla was never allowed to be present when priests came, once she hid in the brambles and saw one. Not all of him, only the shoes. The shoes were talking to the abbess. Rocking backward and forward, heel to toe, heel to toe. They were black with a pattern of holes on the front and laces tied with bows.

Iphigenia and Margarita were busy with his shirt. Carla put her hand out to touch the bow. She pulled and tugged and worried it. She had tied and untied bows, had endlessly made cat's cradles with wool in her childhood games, but try as she might her nimble fingers would not untie the man's knots.

"Can't."

"Scissors."

She ran off to get them.

Iphigenia and Margarita worked on the trousers. There were clasps at the waist that were easy enough to undo but hidden beneath the vertical flap from the waistband to where the garment split in two weren't buttons but a cold metal thing with a set of interlocking teeth straight as a railway track. Zip. There was a tiny handle to it which they pulled and miraculously it traveled down the track, parting it as it went. Then it stopped, caught on something on the other side, the shirt or undergarment. Try as they might they could not loosen it.

Carla hurried back with the scissors, glad to see that Iphigenia and Margarita were no further advanced than when she left. She did not want to miss one single bit. She snipped at the knots in the laces and the shoes loosened, almost seemed to breathe a sigh of relief. She slipped them off his feet, releasing an odor of old cheese. It didn't take long for the smell to drift up to Iphigenia. She turned from her own task to see Carla sniffing the feet with delight.

"Scissors," she said, holding her hand out like a surgeon.

Carla handed up the scissors. Snip, snip went Iphigenia. She tugged and pulled and the hindrance disappeared. The trousers divided smoothly. Margarita lifted the body and Iphigenia pulled the trousers down past the buttocks.

"Pull the legs," Iphigenia instructed Carla.

Carla wrenched at the man's legs, almost toppling him off the bed.

"Trousers."

Carla latched onto the trouser legs, one in each hand, and pulled. They slid off as easily as a snake's skin.

Underneath he had fleece, just like them. Sparse black curls of hair on skin as pale as a fish. And he was wearing another, shorter pair of trousers, without legs. Tight around the hips and across the mound in front. Iphigenia and Margarita took off this undergarment. He was disrobed.

They stood there looking at the naked body, as if they themselves, with their efforts and exertions, had created it. Frankenstein admiring his creation as it lay inert, before the bolts of electricity that would jolt it to life and make it run amok.

An entirely new creature! Carla opened her eyes as wide as they would go to take it all in. Instead of floppy breasts he had flat cherry mouths with tufts of black hair around them. A dark brown crinkly spot on his side. A line of hair like the metal track Iphigenia and Margarita had wrestled with, which descended from his navel into the bulrushes of black hair between his legs. And there nestled in the bulrushes was Baby Moses, a flaccid little sleeping thing curled up like a white worm. Such a dear little baby thing.

The man's leg twitched, like sheep twitch in their dreams, and Carla shrank back. Iphigenia pulled the blanket up over him. Margarita neatly folded his clothes and put them on the chair. Then the three nuns stood in vigil, waiting for him to awaken.

Iphigenia and Carla had gone to their cells. Margarita sat on the chair and watched. He was sleeping now, completely motionless. He didn't even appear to be breathing. Margarita used to watch her father sleeping, when he was full of the drink. Sleeping in the leather chair, mouth open, head back and snoring. Sometimes there was a cigarette in his hand. She would watch the ash grow longer and longer and when it dropped, she would catch it. One day he was going to burn the house down.

They had been such a happy family when her mother was alive. Then everything changed. Her father took to drinking, playing cards. For the company, he said. There were fights with Margarita's brother over the drinking and one night her father hit him. Her brother disappeared for days and when he came back he announced he was emigrating. "Walk out of this house and you walk out for good," her father shouted. Her brother just smiled. He kissed Margarita on the forehead and promised he would write. If he had written, the letters had never reached her.

Now all the father had was Margarita. She had to attend to him, to get drinks for his friends, prepare them food. The cigarette smell that she had loved on her father, she grew to hate. The men talked of bawdy women in front of her and when the bud of her own womanhood began to open, their eyes fixed on her body like grasping hands. Her father was proud of his hospitality.

Sometimes he won at cards but often he lost, even in his own house. One day he called her from her room, told her to put on her special dress, there was a visitor. Margarita put on her white dress with its blue ribbons. She stood at the mirror, slowly combing her long golden hair. The rumble of conversation—men's conversation—wafted up to her, the occasional laugh at a shared joke, the smell of cigars.

She stood at the top of the stairs and looked down into the study. In the frame of the doorway she saw the man. He had a bushy black mustache and when he laughed his lips were shiny with spittle. He had a gold chain and a watch and his waistcoat strained against his corpulence. A suit of good quality, white shirt and gold cufflinks. The hands coming out of the cuffs were black with hairs.

He looked up and smiled, showing her the gap between his teeth. She wanted to retreat into her room. "Come," he invited her. She could not refuse. Down the stairs she went, sinking lower and lower with each step. Her father introduced him, a business associate. She knew his face, one of the card players. "He wants you to stay with him for a while. You will do some chores, light housework. But it will be a holiday for you. He has a nice big house in the country, with a lovely garden. You'd like that, wouldn't you?"

"Yes, Father." Then Margarita understood that she was being sold.

Iphigenia lay with her nose jutting into the air. He would not be going anywhere tonight but it was as well to have him watched. The sight of him helpless on the abbess's bed made her see God's purpose in bringing him here. It was to minister to him, to bring him into the fold. A priest who had strayed, not only into their pastures but strayed from the Church. He was a young man who had been tempted by worldly comforts. Invoked the name of the Devil and blasphemed. He had spoken of slaughter and sinned against the community. "Unless ye come as a child, ye shall not enter the Kingdom of Heaven." They had to make him as a child again, teach him the way of salvation. It was a test. Iphigenia sighed. She thought all the testing was over with. One more, in her twilight years?

There were practical matters to attend to. Who else knew he had come here? Would others follow? Would he be missed? Perhaps answers would be found in his car.

The breath surged in Iphigenia's throat. The car was outside.

She had not been outside the walls for many many years. Even in enclosure there were times to go out. Not for a frivolous picnic but for something important such as a death in the family. Iphigenia had not been allowed to attend Grandmother's funeral. But she had been out.

Iphigenia was a young nun when the extern, Sister Assumpta, had slipped on wet flagstones and broken her leg. It was the extern sister who ran errands on the rare occasion the community needed something from the world. Even then, they never crossed the strip of tidal sand.

This was an emergency, they needed help quickly. Somebody had to go to the village and fetch the bonesetter. The abbess nominated Iphigenia. She was nimble and fleet-footed, the best to negotiate the treacherous path.

The abbess had spoken to the priest about the path many a time, especially when he and his party arrived huffing and puffing, even though they'd ridden on donkeys. He always said yes, indeed, what was needed was a road. But the priest came less and less frequently and the road never came at all.

Iphigenia hitched her skirts up and down the hill she went, agile as a mountain goat. It was summer, the air hummed with insects and sunlight, there was the gurgle of springs and brooks. She scooped up water when she got thirsty, happily munched on the cress growing in crevices. From afar she saw the village, a cluster of houses, some gray stone, others painted white, the fishermen's boats in the cove bobbing in the lull of water like matchstick toys.

But the place was practically deserted. "Good day to you, Sister," said one of those who had remained. A young man with eyes black as plums, brown hands threading knots into the rope, over and down, across and through. She explained that the community needed the bonesetter. "He's over on the mainland, for Midsummer. Big celebration in the tavern. I'll warrant he'll have a few bones to set by the morning," said the young man with a grin on his face. Iphigenia looked across to the village on the other side. She could just make out the public house. Music and merrymaking floated over the water so clearly she felt as if she could reach out and touch it. But it was at least a mile away. The tide was in and the strand submerged. Iphigenia gazed into the distance.

"Could you telephone, please?"

"I can try," said the young man, "but as you can hear, they're making a fearful racket. The seals won't have anything to worry about," he joked.

"The seals?"

"On Midsummer Night they come ashore, lured by the music. They shed their skins and become human. If you can capture their skin they can never go back and must stay with you forever."

He stepped out of his boat. His shirtsleeves were rolled up and his waistcoat unbuttoned. Around his neck a glint of gold caught Iphigenia's eye. She followed it down to the small gold cross nestled inside his shirt like a little bird. He went to the public phone, turned the handle a few times to get the operator. They exchanged a few friendly words, then she connected him to the tavern.

"Hello, Jack? They're wanting the bonesetter at the monastery. Can you find him for me?"

He hung on for a long time. He heard a lot of noise, a lot of laughter, and eventually the phone was hung up, no doubt by some soul doing a good turn and correcting a carelessness. The young man looked at Iphigenia apologetically. "I'm going over myself directly. I can take you."

It was very, very late when Iphigenia returned that night. Without the bonesetter. The nuns were in the chapel praying, prayers that were answered by Sister Barbara's announcement that Iphigenia had returned safely. It was Midsummer in the world and the village was deserted. She'd gone over to the mainland. She'd asked many people if they had seen the bonesetter. She couldn't find him. She had left a message for him at the public house. She had to wait for the tide to walk back. That's why she had taken so long. That's why her garments were wet.

Although the community was overjoyed to have their sister back, the abbess was less than pleased with Iphigenia's adventure. She wanted every tiny detail of Iphigenia's time away from the monastery, whom she had seen, whom she had spoken to. How her garments had become so wet. But Iphigenia was unwavering. She repeated and repeated the story many times. She had learned it so well that even years later, whenever she saw poor Assumpta limping on a leg that had never properly mended itself, and when the other thing happened, this was the story she told herself about Midsummer Night.

Iphigenia drew out the priest's map. She unfolded and smoothed it out but still the creases remained, cutting it like a cross. In the top right-hand corner was a north-pointing compass. A heavy black line marked the perimeter of the monastery, a shape trying for circularity but interrupted by angles where the terrain had to be taken into consideration. The entrance was on the western side, away from the mainland so the path spiraled around the mountain rather than going straight up. The village was marked by a cluster of buildings, homes of the fisherfolk who had gradually drifted over to the mainland. In the center of the grounds was the chapel, the two wings of transepts stretched out at right angles to the nave. Iphigenia recognized the adjacent cloisters and dormitories. Other wings were unmarked. From the gatehouse a neat path had been drawn leading straight to the chapel, sculptured trees on either side of the path, and on the south-facing side, gardens delineated by neat rows of vegetables that appeared to be cabbages. There was also a garden of crosses where the human bodies of the nuns lay.

Iphigenia never thought of looking at the monastery in this way, as if hovering above it. It was God's view. She closed her eyes and tried to imagine the monastery the way it was on the map. Yes, beneath the brambles and bushes that had grown up, around the buildings sinking into the ground, the sagging ceilings and cracked walls she supposed, yes, she could see the mapmaker's boundaries. But there were no nuns in this picture, and no sheep.

. . .

Iphigenia woke with a jolt, the map across her breast and the sun already risen. She was late for Lauds. She hurried along to the chapel where Carla was kneeling in prayer. Kneeling in prayer but studying a beetle crawling across the floor in front of her. Iphigenia fell into rank beside her. She did not admonish herself too much for her lateness. The lapse was understandable. There had been two nights with little sleep, the first a night of prayer so intense that blood had almost burst through their pores. And then last night, saying Compline by the man's bedside, waiting for him to awake and all of them still awake when the Great Silence fell on the house.

Lauds were over quickly as Iphigenia remembered Margarita was still with the man. She and Carla hurried along to the abbess's cell to see their sister asleep on the chair in the corner, her head slumped to her chest. He was also sleeping, like a baby, undisturbed by Margarita's snuffles and snores.

It was midmorning when Ignatius awoke feeling so much the better for his long sleep. There'd been a dream, a faint memory of children lost in the woods. He tried to track it down but it disappeared in front of him. The old crone in the corner had gone and the three nuns were once again beside him, with tea, bread, and cheese. His bladder was full, as it always was first thing in the morning, but his initial impulse to leap out of bed was quelled by the realization that he was still naked.

"Can I have my clothes back?" he demanded, as if he were in control of the situation.

"Need mending."

"Need mending?" First it was washing and now it was mending.

"A tear. When we removed them."

If it wasn't bad enough to be lying naked under the covers they had to remind him of how he came to be in that state. He fell back into the pillows. "I need to go outside."

"Go outside?"

"I need to urinate."

"But the pot," said Margarita, somewhat affronted that he had passed the pot by.

"I'm feeling perfectly well, I am not an invalid," he assured them. "Now, if you'll just return my clothes." He stared severely down the line of nuns. He was not to be trifled with.

Iphigenia broke the thickening silence. "Blanket."

It was better than nothing. He sighed. They did not move. Was it too much to ask that they wait outside? Apparently. He gathered the blanket about himself, swiveled around and placed his feet on the floor, quite pleased with the maneuver since at no time had he exposed any part of his body. The floor wasn't as cold as he expected. He looked down to see that he still had his socks on. Why had they left the socks, he mused cynically, when they had been so thorough with everything else?

They moved aside to let him pass, Carla in the middle holding the breakfast tray. The bread they'd heated up on the fire had grown cold now but its warm aroma still hung in the air. A little wobbly on his feet, a little encumbered by the blanket, he managed to walk out of the room and down the corridor.

The padding of large feet told him he had not made the journey alone. He turned. There they were, the three of them, following him like a train of anxious children.

"Well?" he challenged them.

"In case you fall."

Oh, he'd had enough of this. "For God's sake, I'm only going for a piss!" he shouted at them.

They jumped back. He continued on his way, leaving his voice behind, a flame-thrower keeping them at bay. Finally he felt grass pricking through his socks. He was outside.

The urge to urinate had returned in full force, after momentarily subsiding in his efforts just to get to a place where he could actually do it. He could not see them but he felt their eyes watching him from somewhere. He kept his back to the building, held the blanket with one hand, and urinated gloriously. He splashed his socks but ah, he was feeling almost human again. He stood there long after he had finished, enjoying the crisp morning, the bleat of lambs, the swirl of sunlight, and the chirp of birds. An idyll. What a location.

"Father . . ."

The voice seemed far away but it was a form of address he responded to. He turned back to face the buildings. There they were, much as he had left them, offering the breakfast tray. Trusting and innocent as lambs themselves. Humility and self-effacement in the service of the Lord. He softened. Perhaps he had been too harsh, the very peculiar circumstances in which he found himself had affected his judgment and his temper. It would be churlish of him not to accept bread from the handmaidens of the Lord.

He followed them to the table in the courtyard. Well, one more day. His clothes would be mended and he would be off. His stomach took hungrily to the food and drink, with no ill effects this time. His hand was perfectly well, as if nothing had ever happened to it. Nevertheless, he took pains to steer clear of the fire.

Sorting and picking. They sat at the table in the courtyard, dealing with one pelt at a time, plunging their hands into it, picking up clumps of fleece, enjoying the feel of lanolin and suint. The work was done in silence, the actions dedicated to God, leaving minds free to be absorbed in contemplation. They picked out seeds and other debris that might interfere with the processing of the wool—the carding, teasing, spinning, and finally knitting. Some of the imperfections they left, to add texture and interest to the finished work.

Iphigenia found the priest's smell much more agreeable now that it was surrounded by their own woolen blanket instead of that damp inky odor. Though the smell in no way resembled them, the blackness of his clerical garb, the white collar, made Iphigenia think of their habits. She recalled the bodice with the long sleeves, the underskirt with the big pocket in front. They had kept this pocket in their later homespun clothes, so practical for carrying all manner of things. Then came the scapular, the tunic that covered the robe, right to the ground. And in pure, pure white the headdress with the wimple wrapped round the head under the veil. Bodice, scapular, wimple, veil. Iphigenia rolled the words around in her mouth. A string of old beads spooled around a life that had weathered as they had weathered, by a running down of things, by clocks that stopped ticking and were never fixed, by a discipline whose crisp defined edges started to blur, by spiritual sustenance that came from the earth as much as the heavens. By sisters who had stepped out of bodies as worn and threadbare as their clothes and were resurrected as frolicking lambs.

Now it was Agnes Teresa's fleece on the table. Iphigenia remembered life under the rule of the first abbess, when Sister Teresa had momentarily let her singing soar above the choir to reveal a voice like an angel's. Then Teresa lying prostrate in the cloisters, arms out like a crucifix; the nuns on their way to Compline, walking by as if she wasn't there, forbidden to cast their eyes down and acknowledge her presence.

The black-robed sisters whose bodies lay under the grass and whose souls hovered in the living community filed through Iphigenia's memory. She saw the mass of them assembled at prayer, a black night sea, heads bowed, the ripple across the surface, the white capped waves as they lifted their heads and rose, the swift flow of them on the way to chapel, the clack and swish of rosary beads as they answered the bell, the call of the Divine Shepherd reaching with His crook of faith to haul them into His loving care.

She saw individual faces, young, old, fat, thin. The sea-blue eyes of Sister Hilary, the wispy hairs on the chin of the sacristan, the abbess, face lined like the grain in polished timber. Faces alive in memory and shining with God's love and the sweat of daily toil. All cloaked in similarity, to annihilate the individual self, a work continued in prayer and the discipline of bells. Iphigenia herself in that tide of nuns, her secret self hidden beneath the anonymous robes.

A waft of lanolin, suint, the nutty flurry of small seeds invaded her nostrils as the last fleece was spread out. The dead returned to their realm and Iphigenia found herself gazing at Carla methodically sorting the debris into neat little piles. She was mouthing verses over them, and had kept aside a yellow buttercup petal.

Margarita smiled indulgently at the neat little piles—burrs, bits of bracken, seeds, miscellany. It was Margarita who had found the mewling child, red and angry, tiny fists punching the air, reaching out to God. Just inside the heavy gate, wrapped in a blanket, surrounded by straw.

Margarita used to imagine that the prayers cascading from her mouth were lifted by the wind to be carried to those most in need, landing on their doorsteps not unlike the appearance of wee Carla. Up till then the world for which she prayed, the sick and needy, was an abstraction. Behind the heavy gates and grilles, with little contact or news from outside, it was hard not to think of the world as such. When Carla arrived the sick and needy became flesh.

Of course, what her origins were they could only privately reflect on. Carla was a gift from God, an infant given to them to tend and care for as they would for the Lord Himself. She was Christ among them, a holy pure innocence, no matter in what mysterious way God had placed her here. They fed the infant on watered-down ewe's milk, took turns watching over her at night. The abbess and the body of sisters waited for a sign from outside concerning the child but no sign came. No one came to fetch her or inquire after her. Eventually there was a christening and Carla entered into their holy community.

Margarita looked at the visitor, sitting there wrapped in a blanket like baby Carla had been. Both had turned up unexpectedly, in an extraordinary way, a test to her Christian charity. It had been easy with the sweet defenseless Carla, the little body struggling to be free of its swaddling. But he was different. It didn't seem right that he should join in, to enter so easily into a life hard earned.

Three days went by, a round of prayers, chores, stories, and knitting, and still his clothes were left unmended. He had even offered to do it himself, not that he knew how to mend. Soon Ignatius began to see that the clothes would not be coming back.

The only way he could escape was to steal away and leave his clothes behind. Leave everything behind. He would have to be clever and choose his moment well. They took turns sitting with him through the night. "In case you need anything," they said. What he first thought of as misguided beneficence now took on a more sinister shadow. The nuns had become wardens.

By day, if he strayed too far from the courtyard, one or other of them would miraculously appear by his side, asking if he needed anything. Apart from everything else, if he didn't get away soon they would kill him with kindness.

He would go at night, a night of no moon. He would feel a lot better once he was outside the monastery. If he could find the gate, climb over the wall, he would be safe from them. The nuns wouldn't come after him once he was outside. He had seen their reaction, they wouldn't break enclosure. Would they?

Though getting out of the monastery was his first priority he had to think about the rest. Even if the nuns did not follow, he was not looking forward to the journey back. The way up had been bad enough. Then he had only really stumbled in by accident. But finding his way down at night, no map and no light . . . The leeward side of the island had safe havens but on the windward side insatiable waves crashed against black forbidding rocks. He could easily fall.

He no longer had the passport of his clerical clothes to give him immediate, unquestioned assistance. He couldn't very well walk naked across to the mainland. The car keys were with his clothes and the trunk of the car, with his holiday gear, was locked. He could not believe that he would ever find himself cursing his own efficiency and attention to detail. He was somehow going to have to break into the car, smash something. Damage property.

First, he had to get out.

He was more clever than he imagined. He didn't need a complete night of no moon, he only needed darkness till he was out of the monastery. Then the heavens could light up like New Year's Eve. All the better to find his way down the hill.

The nuns had just brought in his dinner. The idea hit him with such a bolt that he quickly transferred his attention from the square of night framed in the window to one of the pictures on the wall, in case any of them noticed. The picture was of a maiden with very long hair which covered her in modesty. Her hands were joined in prayer. Six angels with feathery wings bore her aloft. "Saint Mary Magdalene. Tilman Riemenscheider, limewood, fifteenth century." It was the tall one, Iphigenia.

She sounded like a museum guide. "Magdalene in her ecstasy, repenting of her sins and stripped of her finery." He peered at it appreciatively, then abruptly sat back. Beneath those tresses Magdalene had curly fleece and furry thighs.

He gobbled up his nettles and turnips, trying to move things along. He told a story and then Carla insisted on telling one. It vaguely resembled "The Three Bears" but something unpleasant happened to Goldilocks in the end. All the time she was telling the story he kept his eyes closed. She had by far the sweetest voice and if he blocked out the matted hair and devouring eyes he could imagine the voice belonging to an angel in a flowing gown, hair the color of gold tumbling down into the snowy white feathers of wings. When she had come to her version of the ending his impulse was to protest. But he brought his mind to the more important task. Everything must appear harmonious. He must be lulled to sleep by the sweet voice, the rhythms and repetitions of the tale.

Carla and Iphigenia picked up their knitting and bid him goodnight. That meant it was Margarita who would be minding him. Excellent. She slept heavily and made noises that would provide cover for any he might make. He sighed dreamily in his feigned sleep. As he did, he recalled the story that he had told them. On the surface it was a standard rendition of "Little Red Riding Hood"—he was Granny sick in bed and they were Red Riding Hood triplets. Except that Ignatius had entered the story with the cunning of the wolf. He needed things. He asked for some strands of good strong wool so that he could arrange it on his head and simulate Granny's hair. They were delighted with this detail and clapped their hands like children.

"Oh what big eyes you have," they said, playing the game, furiously clicking their needles.

"All the better to see you with," squeaked the wolf in a falsetto of Granny.

"And oh, what big ears you have."

"All the better to hear you with, my dears."

"And oh, what a big mouth you have."

"All the better to eat you up."

But the wolf did not attempt to leap out of bed and devour them. He finished the story with a cough, said he was feeling tired and thought perhaps he should go to sleep. Upon which Carla pleaded for one more story, oh just one, she would tell it softly and sweetly and it wouldn't take long.

"Very well, my dear." He smiled, showing his teeth.

The clicking of knitting needles stopped and the room was quiet. Margarita grunted a few prayers, then arranged herself in the chair for the night. With his eyes closed, other senses were heightened. He heard a soft muffling as she arranged her blanket, the squeak of the wicker chair as she searched for a comfortable position. Heard the whoosh of air as she blew out the candle and waited for the tallow smell that followed. He felt the breeze from a draft on his left cheek. He smelled the damp in the walls, the mustiness imbued with a faint smell of incense that must have pervaded the whole place at one time. Heard the tiny sounds outside—crickets in the grass, a bleating that finally wound down into silence.

Heaviness descended on him. He focused on all these things because in the Great Silence he had to stay awake. Alert. In the preceding days, he had reconnoitered as best he could under the watchful eyes of his captors. He tried to impose the map onto his visual recollection. He knew the layout of the buildings quite well from his initial exploration. Although, he reminded himself, he had appraised it as a piece of real estate, not as a place from which he would have to escape.

The thicket of bushes and brambles must once have been the shrub-lined path leading from the entrance up to the cluster of buildings. Now it was more like a forest. How much easier it would be if the bushes still resembled those neatly clipped clumps on the map, the path clearly marked and the gates wide open. But ah, perhaps there still was a path through the forest and when he entered, he would find it. He had to be careful to take the right direction. Although on the map the monastery faced west, the nuns' lives faced south, following the daily passage of the sun. Their gardens were on the south side, as was the cemetery, a grassy patch through which the sheep grazed, working their way around the obstacle course of crosses. Their table in the courtyard was arranged so that when they sat at it they faced south. It was the natural direction any of them would walk when they stepped outside the courtyard.

But Ignatius would go west. He had found a way in, he would find a way out. He would like to have taken some tools, weapons, a knife perhaps, but he couldn't risk the delay in wandering around looking for things. And then he thought of it. Something right in this room. The pot. It was brilliant, an excuse and a protection. If Margarita woke he could say he needed to urinate. And wouldn't she be pleased he was using it at last? Yes, he was going to use it—as a shield to forge his way through the brambles.

He listened for the sleep rhythms from the corner, the old woman's wheezy breath, her snuffles and snores. There was not another sound in the world. Under the blanket he felt for the lengths of wool that had been Granny's hair. He pulled one of the sheepskins out from under him and laid it on top, then picked up the ends of the skin he was lying on and tied it to the top one with the wool. Sheepskin front and back, the woolly side out.

Without a sound he lifted the blanket and swung his socked feet to the floor. Shoes would be a better protection on his journey down the mountain but they would make a noise along the cloisters. Considering the option, as if he had a choice in the matter.

He dropped on all fours, silently as a cat landing, and retrieved the pot. The old woman snorted and chomped in her sleep. He stayed there, still as a table. Satisfied that she would not wake, he stood up. Too suddenly and not mindful of his new clothes. The sheepskin tunic slipped and dropped to his knees. Damn. She snorted and chomped again, rolled her head from side to side. She grunted. Ignatius stood stock-still, tensed, the pot in his hand. He realized for the first time that he was prepared to knock her unconscious, should it come to that. She was old, it wouldn't take much. He watched, her head etched in the dark light coming through the window.

She did not stir. He hitched up his dress, he would secure it later when he was out. He moved gingerly past her, never taking his eyes off her face. Which was not the most sensible place to be looking, as it turned out. In passing, his sheepskin brushed—ever so lightly but nevertheless brushed—and caught her blanket, the one wool adhering to the other for a fraction of a second, then dropping it just as swiftly. But enough to dislodge it. The blanket slipped down her arm. "What big eyes you have," she slurred sleepily. He froze, his heart thundering. He waited for a shout, a movement, but nothing else came. Would the night air on her arm wake her up? His hand reached out.

Should he adjust her blanket or not? He decided not. "All the better to see you with, my dear." It was only a whisper but he could barely believe it had come out of his mouth.

He went into the corridor. It was fortunate that the abbess's room was at the head of the block of cells. Of forty or more cells only three were occupied. Though initially he had surveyed them with the eyes of a property assessor he was still a priest and did not feel comfortable entering those occupied cells. As a fugitive he wanted to stay as far away from them as possible.

Through the cloisters and out into the courtyard, their sleeping fire a soft red glow just enough to keep going till morning, a thin drift of smoke ascending into the night air. He skirted the courtyard, past the holding pen, and came out onto the grass. In front of him were the white mounds of sheep scattered among the small crosses of the cemetery.

The monastery was vast and silent. He realized as he stood listening for sounds of awakening from within the house that he was saying good-bye. A twinge of regret that this would be the last time he'd see it like this, that he would be the last person seeing it like this. This brought with it a quivering surge of power, because Ignatius had already laid a vision of the future on the property stretched before him. He was the explorer who had discovered this virgin territory and it would never be the same again. In forging his way in he had produced the crack which tore asunder the past and future.

He hitched up his sheep clothing, adjusting the skins so they fitted better and allowed movement without coming undone. Each step he took was careful, measured, alert. Like the creature whose skins he wore he cast his awareness behind him, in the direction of possible predators. Though dressed comically in animal skins and carrying an enamel pot, he felt more exhilarated than he had ever felt in his life. He was free and roaming, alone, moving through the night, lord of all he surveyed.

He headed in the direction he took to be west and soon found the thickening bushes. He dropped to the ground and discovered the best way through was to crawl. It was slower but safer. His posture and his clothing accorded perfectly. At first he held the pot in one hand but the three-legged movement was awkward so he put the pot on his head, butting against undergrowth to make his way through. There was a movement in the bushes, a sudden squawk and the flapping of feathers as the night bird flew away. Ignatius stopped perfectly still, waiting for repercussions. The squawk faded and silence descended like velvet. He pressed on.

If it had been the squawk alone that had wakened her, Iphigenia probably would have turned, pulled the blanket up farther, and gone back to sleep. One lone sheep moving away from the flock. Smelled like ram. Something wasn't quite right. Her nose made tiny searching movements, nostrils quivering. Ram, but something more. Urine? Vinegar? An old smell, only faintly alive.

In one rolling movement the blanket was tossed aside and her feet found the floor. She put her cloak around her shoulders and hurried down the corridor to the abbess's room.

Iphigenia could tell by the shadows and creases that the bed was empty. She shook Margarita by the shoulder.

"He's gone."

"Gone?" Margarita's eyes were open but it wasn't till she peered at the empty bed and noticed the pot was missing that she said, "To urinate. Pot's gone."

She'd made the observation but she couldn't quite get the sense of it. He went outside to urinate. Why did he take the pot?

Iphigenia's hand was feeling the bed. "Sheepskins gone too. Get Carla."

It was all wrong. Iphigenia had come into the room and announced to Margarita that he was gone. Margarita was guarding him, it should have been she who had sounded the alarm. It should not have happened at all. He had slipped away, tricked her.

Iphigenia paced up and down in front of the fire. The smell was in the brambles to the west. It had slowed but it was still moving. She could have gone after him by herself, tracked him down with her nose but then what? Could she fall on him in the brambles and wrestle him? Iphigenia held a stick in the fire and watched it jump into flames.

Margarita came back with Carla and the three stood hunched by the fire.

"Stray sheep, Carla. In the brambles."

They followed the trail of scent he had left behind. They stepped out of the courtyard as he had done, stopped and looked over the flock nestled in the graves of dead sisters as he had done. Then as one body, they turned toward the west, Iphigenia in the middle with her radar nose, Carla and Margarita flanking her, their night cloaks billowing out like bats' wings.

They glided along in formation the way they did when rounding up the sheep, until they came to the brambles. He was still in there, moving slowly. They crossed to the northern side, less sun and less overgrown. Had he deliberately chosen the brambles thinking that it would be more difficult to root him out?

The nuns started up the chant. They hummed till a wave of

sound spread through the air and on that wave they cast their words. "Lamb of God, oh blessed lamb of God, meek and mild, stand in the light and let the servants of God unclothe thee. Shed the old that the new may be blessed and sanctified in the Lord's name." They kept up the humming as they advanced toward the brambles.

Ignatius stopped. His pot hat was vibrating with sound, humming like a top. He took the hat off but still it was hard to discern exactly where the sound was coming from. Whispers from all directions. Sounds and sweet airs. The voices were heavenly, a flight of angels to coax him out of the brambles.

Iphigenia smelled the softening of tension as their voices reached his ear and entered into his spirit. Perhaps after all he would come meekly as a lamb. There was a chorus of bleats and baas as the sheep arose and answered the call.

He pulled the pot down over his ears till it hurt. But still the sound snaked in. He crashed on through the undergrowth, losing the upper skin as he did so. No time to adjust it. He kept blindly on, his faith in the west and hope of the gateway, the gateway that on the map was open. Spiky fingers and thorns tore at his flesh. He could smell blood.

Quite clearly now, yes, Iphigenia had pinpointed him. The blood, the smell of fear and urgency. They continued chanting, bringing the sheep with them in their wake. He was thrashing wildly, the voices closing in on him, his trail quite clear.

"Carla."

Suddenly the singing stopped. Then he heard the sound of crashing in the thicket. A big animal, coming steadfastly toward him. He expected the baying of hounds. He must not listen, he must not think about what is behind him. He must go on with his faith, with faith that the opening is there. Eyes blink in the darkness, eyes of creatures big as night. He goes on, no longer feeling the spiky fingers as they reach out and grab his flesh. Then, miraculously, it is there. The opening! He throws himself into it, down, down he plunges, a scream tearing out of his body like a rat deserting a sinking ship as he flies through the night.

This time they secured him good and proper. Margarita said that for penance she would maintain an eternal vigil and never drop off to sleep, keep a stone tied to her chest so that when her head rolled forward it would wake her up. The visitor needed to be punished too, for tricking her, but Margarita kept this thought to herself. Iphigenia said that a vigil was not necessary. They needed to deal with the matter once and for all. Then return to the routine of their lives.

Iphigenia had thought about it for days and she knew it was the right thing. After prayers the next morning she made her announcement. "We are going outside."

"Outside?"

"The car. There may be things," said Iphigenia.

Carla was wide-eyed, breath suspended. It was so quiet she could hear her own heart beating. She had never been outside, though once she had caught a glimpse of it.

The ditch he had fallen into was one of Carla's childhood ditches, much shallower than fear and panic had led him to believe as he fell through the air toward it. Carla had dug it in her games, scuffling the earth behind her like a dog. She found pebbles and a tiny shell that had become a treasure for a while. She kept on digging, hoping for more. She scraped and scratched with her fingers, with sticks, with spoons spirited away from the kitchen.

When she had made a nice round hollow, she lay down and rested from her labors. Sister Cook said it was good for children to rest and be still. Even God took a rest. She especially said this when she was busy and Carla asked her too many questions.

After her rest Carla got up, moved on, and made some more hollows. As she pulled back the brambles to make the digging easier she discovered a big pair of doors, old timber doors the same color as the brambles that grew over them, vertical planks with a diagonal one on each. What was on the other side? she wondered. A metal chain was looped through the handles. At the bottom of the chain hung a square of metal that had a slit in it like a keyhole. Little Carla's eyes grew round with excitement. She searched all over, on the ground and in the bushes, but there was no key to be found.

She tugged at the chain but the square of metal would not release it. She looked up. Too high and nothing to get a foothold on. She tried the diagonal plank but her leg slipped down and she got a bruise. Then she knew just the right solution. Under. She got down on the ground again, started burrowing. She scraped with her fingers and dug with the spoon till she was able to put her finger between the ground and the door. She dug some more, her tongue stuck in the corner of her mouth, her face fierce with concentration.

Then she lay her head on the ground and put her eye to the space. Straightaway she felt the draft of wind, sharp and narrow as if a spark from the fire had hit her eye. She turned her head away, blinked several times, heard the whistle of the wind under the door. When she was brave enough she tried again. All she could see was blue. Blue space, howling with wind. Perhaps if she went a bit farther she would see more. She could crawl through the space between the ground and a door, she knew how to do it. Once she'd watched a rat make itself very flat, disappear under the cupboard, and never be seen again.

Carla looked out with her one eye on the ground. There was nothing out there but space. She had come to the edge of the world. The walls and these heavy locked doors were there so that Carla and the nuns and the sheep wouldn't fall off. Carla stared out. She knew she could do what the rat did but she wouldn't do it. She didn't want to fall off the edge of the world and never be seen again.

"Not going," announced Margarita.

"Not going?" All Iphigenia could do was repeat it stupidly. There had never been a mutiny before.

Margarita's toes were dug into the ground, her fingers wrapped around the edge of the table like bird's claws around a perch.

"This is our home." She had taken vows. She had chosen the cloistered world. She was not agile, she did not like adventure.

"But we will come back," argued Iphigenia. "Back before nightfall." One day more, that's all it would be, then they would pick up the stitches of their life and knit it back together again.

Perhaps Margarita should stay. The way might be treacherous and they couldn't afford an accident. There was no bonesetter to fetch now.

"And what will you do?" asked Iphigenia.

Margarita wished now that she hadn't blurted it out so abruptly. She didn't want to go but she didn't want to be here without them either.

"Pray. I will pray."

Carla and Iphigenia started making preparations. Margarita

put bread in a basket, cheese and some apples. She felt the separation intensely, as if they had already gone.

Before they were even out of the courtyard Margarita called, "Wait!" Iphigenia and Carla were her community. She had to go with them. She started making her way across the courtyard.

"Wait!" mimicked Carla. She ran off and came back with a stick. Assumpta's walking stick. She gave it to Margarita. They were all pleased she was coming. Whatever waited for them out there, they would face together.

And so in the late morning the three set out, going as far as they could through the grass and then entering the thicket at the last moment. Fortunately in his thrashing about the man had cleared a path for them. But not quite up to the doors. A number of ditches and diggings remained from Carla's childhood, she was surprised to see so many. She led her nuns around and through them, so much easier in the light of day. And there she was once again, in front of the doors.

Iphigenia started tearing at the brambles, pulling them aside. Margarita joined in, using Assumpta's stick. Then Carla saw the old chain and its metal lock, yanked at it, and it came away in her hand, bringing with it a section of the door. The wind of the outside world whistled through the gap. Carla lowered her eyes to protect them and saw the brown stain of rust on her hand. She rubbed at it. She tossed the chain aside and helped the others with the door. Though the brambles were strong, the doors were frail and weathered. There were soft tearing noises of the wood falling away, the hiss and crack of brambles. They had made an opening big enough to pass through.

The three of them stood on the threshold of descent. For the first time in her life Carla had a clear view of the outside. It was sky. The same sky they had above the monastery, and when you looked at it you saw the transparent squiggles that Carla imagined were souls going up to Heaven. So many souls out here! Then she saw the other blue, the darkly rippled blue, an ocean of it, and seabirds squawking and swooping toward it. Carla was pleased that under their feet the ground was solid. Dark green vegetation rolled down, down to the rippled sea and the white crash of it against jagged rocks.

She felt dizzy, the dizzy ecstasy of fainting. The white crash, the deep blue. All she had to do was lean forward and fall.

He was in a dream where he couldn't move, where his effort strained to no avail though his will was tremendous. Sweat streamed from every pore, his mind was a sea of agitation, huge looming waves and giddy whirlpools, yet still the message of movement was not getting through. In his mind he knew he could do it; swim oceans, leap over continents, but his legs wouldn't move an inch. His body was a weight, an anchor, holding him back. It was inert, moribund. This was no place for the breath of life to be. If he could not move his flesh and his bones he would leave them behind. On the next breath he would break through the taut membrane of skin and send his soul soaring to Heaven. He gathered everything about him, his memories, his prayers, the things he had yet to do, waited till he could hold the breath no longer, then burst through.

It was only a dull gasp but enough to wake him. But was he awake? Or had he simply shifted gears and entered another register of dreaming? The darkness had gone, there was an immensity of light, too bright for his eyes. He was staring into the sun. He snapped his eyes shut. He had been crawling through undergrowth, he had panicked, hit the ground, and twisted his ankle. Then he had blacked out.

He was awake, alive, but still his body was in great torpor. His arms had disappeared and his legs were covered with a heavy sheet. He tried to shift it but couldn't. He gasped again, an involuntary prayer this time that it was all a dream. But it wasn't, it wasn't. He started weeping, shuddering and weeping, when he saw what had become of him. It was not his body anymore, he was in the body of a stranger. Every hair on the body had been shaved. The penis lay exposed, a slump weak, helpless thing, and below that . . . He couldn't stop looking, even though he was drowning in waves of revulsion. They had plastered his legs together, from crotch to toes. Bandaged like a mummy. He was a merman with a plaster cast for a tail.

The sun was high in the sky, bleaching the color out of it when Margarita sat down on a warm rock.

"Sext."

It was time for midday prayers. Besides, Margarita needed a rest. Her breath was short and her chest heaving but she was faring better than she had expected. The salty tang of air, its brisk uninhibited movement, had cut through some of the congestion in her lungs. By the time they had finished their silent prayers her breath had returned to normal.

They still had a fair way to go. The ground around them was covered in gorse, dark green and prickly, softened by sprigs of yellow flowers. On the rocks were mossy lichen and other growths that looked like miniature forests. They had seen no footprints, snapped branches, no sign left by the visitor. There was no sign of human life at all. This was the world before the creation of women and men, of secular life and sin. It was the day when the spirit of God moved upon the face of the waters, the day when God made fowl that flew above the earth in the open firmament of Heaven. The seabirds wheeled and dipped in the gathering air, screeched their long and lonely calls. So crisply white—wisps of wool caught up in the wind. Margarita breathed it in.

Carla stared at the curly hairs on Margarita's legs. Mary Magdalene had come to an island, just like this one, the nuns had told her, and performed miracles. She had saved a child from dying of hunger by making its mother's corpse produce milk. Carla would like to have seen that.

On the whole, she was a bit disappointed. Oh, it was wonderful seeing so much sky, but they had sky at the monastery. She liked the sea but it looked a bit like the sky too. She had expected more. She liked all the things that grew, the little clumps of sea-pinks with the tough narrow leaves of windswept places, loved their rosy carmine buds and the more delicate shade of pink of the open flowers. But where were all the things of the world? The cities of gold, of salt, the Tower of Babel? Where were the poor and needy? The people, red and yellow, black and white, all precious in His sight? She had very much been looking forward to seeing the world but when they had finally caught sight of it across the water it was just more land.

Still, it was a wonderful adventure. She had angels in her pocket and she had a task to do. Every so often, she attached a fleecy angel to a bush or stuck one in the crevice of a rock. She had left six so far. They made a path that the nuns could put down and pick up so that when their outing was over they would leave no trace.

Iphigenia remembered the hillside of Midsummer Day, the gurgle of brooks, the granite outcrops, buzz of bees in the honey-scented gorse. A memory so vivid, so indelibly set. But everything looked different. Where was the spiral path that had wound round the island like a long apple peel?

They drank water and tore chunks off the loaf of bread. Iphigenia looked at Assumpta's walking stick propped up against the rock. Grandmother had had a stick, a very fine stick with a brass handle. And she had picnics. On the lawn. The ladies wore hats and everyone was in their finery. After a cold collation the tablecloths were whisked away and the adults would play croquet. When somebody executed a difficult shot, the ladies clapped their hands and the men said, "Good show." While the adults played, Iphigenia would lie on the perfectly clipped grass, propped on her elbows, staring at Grandmother in her big chair with a high back, just like a throne. She was always buttoned right up to the collar and her hair pulled back into a stiff white chignon. Despite the stiffness of her clothes and hair, her head was in perpetual motion, swaying from side to side involuntarily, as if she was always saying no. Iphigenia was fascinated by everything about Grandmother, especially the swaying head, and the hands. The prominent veins—which Iphigenia took to be the roots of her fingers—reached all the way back to the old woman's wrist. On the grass, Iphigenia would examine her own hand, crook it over the way Grandmother held the walking stick, but she saw no veins in her smooth little child hand.

She had veins now. Her hands looked older than Grandmother's, rough-skinned, her fingers blunt. Grandmother's skin was smooth, almost transparent. She often wore gloves. Iphigenia supposed her face was old and lined as well. There were no mirrors in the monastery. She had never seen her old woman face.

Iphigenia looked at Carla's face. Handsome, with a sweep of black eyelashes, a straight nose, full lips. There was still the child's innocent cunning, but wrinkles fanned out from the eyes. The lines disappeared in the fullness of the cheeks, then reemerged to take up position around her mouth. There were one or two curly hairs on her chin.

"What?" said Carla, as if she was being accused of doing something wrong.

Iphigenia felt a tiny silver dagger stab her heart.

"Enough rest," she announced.

Iphigenia felt sure they had descended far enough to have come to the village but she couldn't see any signs of it. They had heard that the fishermen had gone across the water to the mainland. Perhaps the village had gone as well. Washed away by the sea, and relics of it stranded on the shore. The sea had given the island relics too, salvage from shipwrecks. A golden eagle, gold doubloons, figureheads of ladies and gentlemen, of saints, eternally leaning forward as if they were about to fall. Sailors too came ashore from shipwrecks, walking out of the sea. Sometimes they stayed and gave the island babies with bright skins from other climes. The island also had babies from sailors who didn't stay.

Iphigenia knew about the golden eagle and other relics because some of them found their final resting place in the monastery. It was best these gifts from the sea were given back to God. Once the fishermen trawled up a crucifix. What fate might befall someone who hoarded a relic from a dead ship? Would the sea stretch out its icy fingers and claim a life in reciprocity? On the other hand, occasionally a lone fisherman would come across a relic and say naught about it. He could sell it on another island and the sea wouldn't be any the wiser. It wasn't as if he were stealing from her. If it was tossed up on shore the sea had no further use for it, did she?

Apparently a coconut had once washed ashore, a gift from the tropics. So rare and exotic was it that the islanders never broke into it to drink the milk or eat the flesh. It sat among them when they gathered and they told stories of how it happened to end up here, an orphan kidnapped by pirates from the jewel-encrusted land of a king and queen pining for their golden child who was never seen again.

There was the sea's own debris too—clumps of seaweed, kelp, and bladderwrack, dumped high on the sand like beached whales—that had missed the outgoing tide and could never get back. It was transformed into a land life, lay the winter on the villagers' gardens, and when its salt was gone, planted out with crops.

From the rhythmic crash of the sea on rocks and the dance of spray arose a strange singing. It echoed everywhere. Unknown creatures calling to one another. Iphigenia's nose was twitching uncontrollably. A salty sea smell, but there was an oiliness too. Not the solid fat of lanolin, of the sheep, it was more the oiliness of seabirds. But it was not the song of birds.

Carla picked up the sound and echoed it back. They came to a narrow passage where the cliff curved round. They took small careful steps, watching where they put their feet.

"Angel!" said Carla when they had rounded the corner. The angel was made of stone. A pair of gulls perched on her back, ready to take off.

It was the Wailing Woman. Iphigenia remembered what the islanders called her. Leaning toward the sea, watching and waiting for a husband and son who would never return, scanning the horizon for them, her huge tears dropping into the ocean. Rain, wind, and sun had washed over her and eventually she had turned to stone. The Wailing Woman overlooked the village, they would come to it soon.

Or what was left of it. They had wandered into it without properly realizing. The roofs had blown away, windows looked like empty eyes. But it was not uninhabited. There was rustling and flapping, the ruins wriggled with movement. At the approach of these three new creatures, heads popped up from everywhere, looked curiously, then scampered into the sea, mothers and babies, the little ones scurrying after the big ones.

The village had become a seal colony.

Carla ran down among them, delighted by their smooth round heads with snub noses, faces like bears, and whiskers like cats. One brushed right by her and she felt the roughness of that sleek body, raspy as a cat's tongue. Another one came and looked at her curiously. She tried to pat it but it flop, flopped into the water. They took off as she chased after them, all heading for the safety of the sea.

Carla laughed and laughed, mimicking their movements, flopping along. She lay down on her belly, making her limbs rubbery, stretching her fingers and discovering the tiny webs between them. All she had to do was inch herself up a little more, then plop! Over the edge and her head, round and cropped from Haircut Day, would be bobbing along with theirs.

"Carla." Iphigenia was calling her back.

Margarita was propped up against a wall, the buzzing of bees diving into the flowers making a soft halo of sound around her. It was difficult not to give in to the pleasant drowsiness. The walls held in heat and beamed it out so that the abandoned houses provided a haven. Spring flowers of every hue grew here, not just the gorse that had claimed the rest of the island. The droopy heads of purple and pink fuchsia, dogrose climbing up the stones, perfect shiny little buttercups in protected corners, pink clover and lamb's lettuce.

There were no people, no curtains in the windows. Iphigenia walked through the ruins to the cove. No boats, no music, no fisherboy with eyes as dark as plums. Gone. All that was left was a rusting anchor wedged in the sand, a crumpled lobster pot, some bottles, a wisp of net so flimsy that when Iphigenia touched it, it dissolved into dust.

Margarita leaned on the walking stick and pulled herself up. They were not here to enjoy themselves. Beyond the wall she had a clear view of the mainland. But all she could see on the shore was a small square of building.

It was the public house. Margarita remembered when she first came here, waiting outside the tavern with her fellow novices, Assumpta and Sister Cook, waiting for the low tide so they could walk across to their final home. It was a blustery day with the feel of snow in the air. The locals, nice people, invited them in for a glass of port. For the stomach, they said, for the warmth. But the sisters said no, they would wait outside. The priest went in, however. "Just for the one, mind you." Margarita remembered the cheery cheeks of that priest, his white hair. "Come in," he said, dispensing permission, "a hot lemonade, perhaps." But no, Margarita did not want to go. There were men in the public house, men who played cards and smelled of cigarettes and pipes. Men with white teeth and handsome black mustaches, gold chains across their portliness. Margarita wanted a life that was too hard and cold for these things.

"Car?" Iphigenia put the word into Margarita's line of vision.

"No."

Iphigenia called Carla back from the seals once again. He had driven across, but where was the car? The three nuns spread out, extending their collective sight.

They hadn't gone far when Iphigenia felt her face flush. The smell of metal was strong. But it was Carla who saw it. A big glistening thing, black and glossy as a knight's steed. It had fat wheels that gave the vehicle solidity, despite the fact that it was leaning at a precarious angle and one of the wheels was wedged in a crevice between rocks as black and glistening as the car itself.

It was completely black, even the windows. Carla peered in. There was someone inside. She brought her hand forward to touch the dark face but found she could not touch the flesh, only the glass.

Now she understood why the Lord had said, "Touch me not," to his beloved Magdalene of the fleecy legs. Because in the garden when he had appeared to Magdalene he had already turned into Jesus of the stained-glass window, bright and luminous but cold and hard to the touch.

Now Carla understood the miracle of the Resurrection. She gazed at it in awe.

"It's . . ." Iphigenia wondered whether to leave Carla with her vision. "It's a reflection, it's yourself," she finally said. This was not to become a special thing. There would be no miracles surrounding the car.

Carla knew it was a reflection, she had seen her face before, in pots and pans, the blades of knives. But those had always been distorted. In the dark glass she had found her most perfect reflection.

She turned her head this way and that, examining herself from every aspect.

Iphigenia felt the pull of temptation. To look, to see her own dark image. As well as the window there was a small mirror jutting out from the side of the car. Iphigenia was so close. She would only have to take one more step.

But it was a vanity and already she could see how Carla was taken with it. Iphigenia pulled out the keys they had found with the priest's clothes.

"Keyhole, Carla."

Carla looked while Iphigenia sorted through the keys for the one most likely to open the car. Carla did not find anything that looked like a keyhole but she did find something. A small circle, and in the middle of the circle was a tiny panel. She poked her finger in. The panel moved.

All of a sudden there was a high-pitched whirring. The car had become an animal, protecting its territory with a terrible screech. The nuns pulled back, hands over ears. From behind a rock they watched but the car didn't move. The screeching went on and on, hurting their heads from the inside and drowning everything else out. They kept watching, but the car remained perfectly inert. Sound appeared to be its only defense.

After a while, they approached the car and began trying keys till they found one that slipped in smoothly. With a small click the door opened.

The screeching faltered and grew weaker, as if the animal had given up. Nevertheless, they proceeded with caution, sniffing around, in case it had another trick in store. Inside was a dashboard beyond comprehension. There were clocks and wheels and numbers, a pulsing red light, tiny icons. The whole interior of the car was black. Grandmother's car was white and very long. It had a running board but Taylor wouldn't start the car till Iphigenia was sitting in the back seat like a lady.

In the space between the two front seats was a short stick

with a shiny black knob decorated with white lines. There was a tray of coins and the smell of stale cigarettes. On the far seat was a shiny transparent folder, with a book and some other things.

Iphigenia tried to retrieve the folder but the car was tilted at such an angle that she couldn't reach. She didn't want to climb in, afraid that her weight would upset the precarious balance.

Margarita had an idea. She held the walking stick by one end and thrust it into the car. She managed to hook the handle around the folder and pull it carefully toward her. When the folder was close enough to pick up, she handed it to Iphigenia. It was slow, she had to repeat the process several times, but in this way she retrieved everything except the coins. Margarita was very pleased with herself. Now they could go home.

Not quite. "Glove compartment," said Iphigenia. Grandmother often kept important things in the glove compartment. It would have to be approached from the other side. There was a narrow ledge but not much room to maneuver. If they could get the window open, they could reach a hand in without putting too much weight on the car.

Taylor's car had a handle for winding down the window but this one didn't seem to have such a handle.

"Excuse me." It was Margarita, this time holding the stick like a jousting knight. She leaned into the car and tilted her lance at the passenger window. The glass shattered. Margarita could not believe how good she felt. She thrust again and again, till the window was just a frame.

Iphigenia edged her way around to the passenger's side. Gingerly she put her hand in and opened the glove compartment. Inside was a cardboard box with a soft piece of paper sticking out of it. She put it in her pocket. There was a battery, the same as the other one. By the time she had finished, the entire contents of the glove compartment were in her pocket.

Now there was only one thing left to do. The car was already leaning toward its final destiny. They just had to give it a helping hand.

Six weathered hands with yellowy nails edged with dirt, veins bulging from the effort. If Iphigenia had known it was wedged so securely she would have had no qualms about climbing into the car.

There was a movement, a slight one, not enough to send the car over. They rested from their labors, then tried again. It started to give.

Suddenly the car was in motion, the wheels were coming up, the big black rutted wheels. Carla could see the underbelly of the car, its intestines. They stood back and let it continue of its own accord. Over it went, crashing a chunk off the ledge on its way. It dropped through the air, the door flying open. It hit the sea with a big crashing noise. The waters parted to receive it. White foam danced up and then the sea closed over the shiny black car as if it had never been.

Carla stood mesmerized. In the gap that the car opened up she had seen something else. She stood in the howling wind. Seabirds squawked, the seals dived under. Beneath her feet was the pattern the wheels of the car had made. She bent down and touched the miniature furrows and ridges. She found it very easy, with one sweep of her hand, to erase these traces. She would not so easily be able to erase the memory of her own dark face beneath the surface of the water.

It was late in the day by the time they had dispatched the car. The soft grass inside the village walls looked inviting, but Iphigenia had said . . . back before nightfall. The words tolling over them like a bell.

They had eaten all the bread and apples, drunk most of the water. They picked a few leaves of lamb's lettuce for sustenance and set off, out of the village and up the hill again. When they reached the Wailing Woman they turned for one last look. There, in the ebb of the tide, was the sandbar.

Carla was entranced by the bright and shining thing joining them to the mainland. All day it had remained hidden and now it was showing itself, like the legendary submerged islands that appear only once in a hundred years, islands over the horizon, to which warriors and knights sail when their quest is done.

Carla scanned the sea, looking for the place where the car had entered but the only interruption to its rippled golden surface was the bob of seal heads. She gave them a little wave.

The three pushed on up the hill. Iphigenia felt every step. The urgency for getting back to the monastery had left her, she had no impetus of her own and was dragged along in the wake of Carla and Margarita. Night came down, squeezing the golden mist into a thin bright line of horizon.

By the time Carla had retrieved Uriel, the third tufty angel, they felt the wind change. Darkness rolled in across an ever-darkening sky, sheets of gray drifting like smoke, and finally they saw needles of rain pockmarking the sea. They hastened along but could not avoid the incoming storm. After the cold moist wind came hard rain. They felt the heavy drops, one, two, then too many to count. There was nowhere to shelter, they had to go on. Progress was slowed because now the rocks were slippery. They prayed for safe deliverance, wet, sloppy prayers, hissing with rain.

A standing stone loomed up before them. They sat down, pulled their vests over their bent heads, and continued praying. Though Carla loved the rain, loved the drops splishing and splashing and making rivers on her, she was worried about the angels. What if, despite her careful twining, the remaining tufts of wool had blown away or dissolved in the rain? How would they find their way back? She knew every inch of the monastery but she didn't know out here. Everything around was black and wet and windy.

Carla wondered if Psyche got scared when she was out on the mountain, alone and shuddering in the darkness, with only faith as a shield and garment. But her Lord did deliver her, wrapped in his wings and his sweet murmurings. She lived in his house yet never could she see his face or ask his name. Carla and the nuns dwelt in the house of the Lord, their prayers kisses on an invisible mouth.

It didn't seem so windy now. Carla lifted her head out of her vest and stole a glance at these sisters who had received the yoke of the Lord and bore His burden, sweet and light. They looked small and bedraggled. As a child, sisters would sit Carla on their shoulders and run with her. She would like to sit Margarita and Iphigenia on her shoulders, carry them through the storm, but she didn't know the way.

The wind had dropped but the cold rain continued, hissing and splattering. It fell onto the spikes of gorse, descended in a slab down the standing stone, and ran in rivulets around them. They were wet through now, their faces shiny with rain. They couldn't get any wetter by walking.

Just beyond the standing stone they found another of their angels clinging to the bushes, too sodden and bedraggled for the wind to have blown it anywhere. There remained only Gabriel. They kept climbing, the rain a constant companion.

They retrieved Gabriel near the bank of brambles. Now all the angels were safely back in Carla's pocket. Up they went. Where was the threshold on which they had stood this morning, so long ago? There was no moon or stars to light the way and they could barely see each other in the thickening gloom.

They felt their way along, Carla in front, Iphigenia in the middle, and Margarita at the rear, holding onto each other's vests, strung together like mountain climbers.

The storm eased, the rain dwindling to drops instead of sheets. Margarita began thrashing the brambles with her stick. Iphigenia breathed heavily, her feet numb with cold despite the sharp edges of rocks, the prickly gorse. The rain dwindled even further till there was nothing but the drip of water on leaves. A star appeared in the sky, then another and another. The storm was over.

The brambles took on shapes, thick black holes of darkness, etched tangles of branches, dark hearts of leaves. Margarita kept poking and prodding till she found what appeared to be a tunnel.

"Carla."

Carla felt her way in and found biscuity pieces of door. Strange how already the brambles had started to close over. Carla cleared a path for them and the three nuns reentered the monastery.

A bright fresh day greeted Iphigenia what seemed only minutes after her head had touched the pillow. She was under a pile of blankets. She could feel the slight scratch of the rough wool but there was something wrong. She saw the shaft of sun from the window, she could hear the birds and the sheep, she saw the texture of the stone wall and the heavy door but it was as if she was looking at a picture. She had lost a dimension. Then she realized what it was—she'd lost smell.

She tried to throw off the weight of blankets but found her body wrapped in a shroud of pain. It was not so bad if she lay perfectly still but the slightest movement brought her in contact with the pain. Her mouth was open and dry and when she tried to swallow, her throat convulsed. She heard Margarita's wheezy breath and realized it was her own.

She struggled out of bed, her feet tender on the stone floor. They were scratched, with crusts of blood on them. She stood in the sunlight absorbing its warmth, then hobbled her way down the corridor, wrapped in her aches and pains, her body bent trying to comfort itself.

Margarita and Carla were already in the chapel when Iphigenia sneezed her arrival. There was a small interruption to the rhythm, then the murmuring continued. Iphigenia wiped her nose on her sleeve. Though it was a clear day, she was surrounded by fog. She gazed at the everlasting candle in St. Anne's corner, imagining it burning away this fog.

When Matins were over Iphigenia found she could not stand up again. She grunted and heaved, bent and put her hands on the floor, tried to put her foot flat but it was too painful.

They helped her up and led her into the courtyard. Iphigenia groaned. The fire was just about out. Her sisters gathered small bits and pieces, and larger, thicker branches from the stack of firewood. They piled it up in a pyramid under the kettle. Then they left it to Iphigenia. Margarita watched and Carla went off to get sick herbs.

With a great deal of effort Iphigenia got down to the fire. She blew on it in her accustomed manner, she huffed and puffed. But no bright genie of flame shot up from the smolder.

Margarita looked at her solemnly, trying to hide her dismay. She had suffered no discomfort from the outing, she felt remarkably well. But they had broken enclosure, broken the vows of centuries. God was displeased and this was the sign. He had made Iphigenia's fire-breath cold and moist.

Iphigenia turned her head, coughed, and tried again, but the fire remained inert. Iphigenia was sick. Would she die? Would God take away all her breath? *Domine miserere peccatrice*, Margarita prayed silently. Was it a sin to not want Iphigenia to die? Death of a sister was a joyous occasion. Their lives were a continual waiting to be lifted up to the presence of the Lord. What if there was only Margarita? Could she do all the chores, maintain the rituals, tell the stories with only herself as audience, sing the sheep in on Shearing Day, keep the fire going? Could she be the whole community and live in the terrible loneliness?

She didn't want to take over the lighting of the fire; Iphigenia had to succeed at it. Nevertheless, the Lord wouldn't mind if Margarita helped just a little. She went away and brought back a sheet of the soft pretty paper they had found in the car. Perhaps the Lord would look kindly on priest's paper. She gave it to Iphigenia to try but it smoked away to nothing and drifted up to the sky.

Iphigenia had lost her fire power. She had lost her smell. She could see Margarita and the sheep in the courtyard but beyond it were just splotches of color with no defined edges. She had no defined edges herself, as if the rain had leached out her strength. Like a sick sheep she wanted to go away and lie in a quiet dark place.

He had cried for a long time, the silent inward sobbing of Christ on Calvary. The tin pot, his excuse and his protection, was nearby, a mocking reminder of his thwarted escape. It was full of water. Beside it were some crusts of bread. He saw bars and rails, and realized he was in the holding pen.

Though he lay like a huge pale fish on a shore gasping for air, he had one fish eye turned toward the events in the courtyard. Stripped of all human dignity, stripped of everything, clothes, even body hair, shivering with cold, he had eventually discovered animal cunning.

He had first thought that they were deliberately absenting themselves, as a form of torture, but when he saw the apricot-colored tissue come out he realized that they had gone down to the car. If they had brought that back they had probably brought other things. They had no doubt taken the keys from his jacket. He wondered how they had coped with the car alarm. He hoped it had frightened the shit out of them.

He watched the feeble attempt the tall one made to get the fire going. She coughed and spluttered and breathed onto it but nothing happened. There had been a storm last night. He knew what a tearing wind there'd been outside and they were caught up in it. They couldn't get their fire going. Good. The tall one had caught a cold by the look of it. Good. He was feeling the worst he'd ever felt in his life but he was young and resilient. They were old. Perhaps they would all catch her cold and die.

He could get in the car and fetch a doctor, go to a chemist and buy some aspirin. All they had to do was give him back his clothes, his keys, and let him out. He'd be back the same day. He would promise. Would they go for it? The tall one was their strength. With her sick the others would be easy to persuade. He would wait a few days, watch her get sicker, watch them fret. Then he would make his offer.

She got clumsily down on the ground again, like a slow elephant at a circus, going through the pantomime of trying to breathe fire into that inert, damp wood. She'd gotten it going before but now her powers were defunct. He hoped she was feeling as humiliated now as he had then.

The fat one came back with a book this time. A handsome maroon leather cover with gold lettering. She tore a page out of it, then snapped the book shut. It was a missal. They were going to use a page of the missal as a fire starter. He almost shouted out in protest at the sacrilege.

There were stacks of missals in the library, the nuns didn't need them. They knew the words off by heart. Burning books was a Church tradition. Nevertheless, when it had become necessary they had thought carefully about which books to burn.

Those of which there was only one copy would be the last to go. Books that were rare, books that were relics, illuminated manuscripts. But missals, there were so many of them. They would burn, the words turn into smoke and drift back to God.

They had started burning books around the time of the death of Sister Scholastica. Scholastica had died on a gray Good Friday. They had not lit the stove because for the forty days of Lent they ate cold food. On Sunday when they had buried Scholastica and rejoiced in the Resurrection of the Lord and life everlasting, and the first crocuses poked their heads out of the grass, they found there was no paper to light the fire to prepare the Resurrection meal. Not a scrap.

Somehow, transmuting paper words into smoke seemed an entirely appropriate way of signaling to the Lord that the spirit of Scholastica, the librarian, was on its way. They had chosen a couple of pages, put a candle to them, and repeated the prayers as they burned. The fire scoured the pages and gave off a bluish tinge. Whether the Lord was pleased to receive this communion or whether from other causes, the paschal lamb, eaten with tinned apricots, a gift from the village, tasted particularly good that year.

Quite a pile of missals remained from sisters who had no further use of them. Margarita gave the book to Iphigenia. When it caught fire, Margarita would send her own prayer up to Heaven. A prayer of thanks for her safe passage down and up the mountain. She looked at the walking stick propped against the table, perfectly intact despite the damage it had done to the car. It had given her strength and durability. Assumpta had lived into very old age with the stick, despite the leg that never set properly. Perhaps Iphigenia's illness was an individual, not a collective, punishment. Margarita remembered that night they had spent in the chapel praying for Iphigenia's safe return, Assumpta lying in pain waiting for the bonesetter.

Still Iphigenia could not get the fire going. She heaved herself up from the ground, refusing help, and limped into the chapel. She came out again with a candle lit from the everlasting one, her hand up protecting its flame, carrying it steadily like one of Hestia's vestal virgins. She scrunched up pages from the missal, placed them under the twigs, then held the candle to them. This time she did not blow on the fire at all. The paper caught and flames danced gaily. Soon the thicker branches gave off their slow sustained flame and the water in the kettle began to rumble. Iphigenia smiled weakly. She had finally gotten the fire going, but it had taken her last drop of energy.

"Damn," muttered Ignatius.

Her foot was throbbing badly. This time she had to accept help to get up. Margarita rubbed Iphigenia's cold hands while Carla threw sage leaves into the pot and added a drop of cider vinegar to Iphigenia's mug. She had also brought wine from the cellar which she would heat and season with the sick herbs to make Iphigenia sweat. Iphigenia lifted her foot to Carla.

"Sore."

Carla gently balanced the foot on her knee. Never before had she touched Iphigenia's foot. She saw the gash in the leathery sole. She moved her fingers over it and felt a sudden sharpness. She held the foot to the light. A piece of the car had lodged itself in Iphigenia's foot. Carla pulled out the glistening shard of glass and held it up for them to see. While Margarita poured the tea, Carla put her punctured finger to her mouth and sucked the blood that had mingled with Iphigenia's.

Sage. Their favorite and most useful tea. Iphigenia felt her body loosen as she imbibed. She placed her face over the steam and breathed it, feeling its heat prick her nose and eyes yet still not smelling. She felt separated from everything, as if she was behind a glass wall. On the other side of the glass she saw Margarita's square fat fingers bringing the mug up to her face, Carla preparing the wine, sheep wandering in and out of the tableau.

"Gargle," said Carla, nudging the potion in front of Iphigenia. Iphigenia was staring into nowhere.

Carla gently took Iphigenia's hands and placed them round the bowl, her own on Iphigenia's like protective shells. She could have forced the bowl up, could have made Iphigenia spill it and say, "Clumsy child, Iphigenia. Look what you've done." Many times Carla had done this in her games, spilled something and pretended Iphigenia had done it. "Clumsy child, Iphigenia!" But now Iphigenia was sick. She was the poor and needy of the world.

Iphigenia was not oblivious to Carla's ministrations. She felt how gently the child had removed the splinter from her foot. She felt the rim of the mug against her lip and the liquid enter her mouth. Iphigenia tilted her head back and gargled, like Carla had shown her, the bubbles of air tickling the back of her throat.

Carla seemed pleased with the noise Iphigenia was making. She made a spitting motion, indicating the next step. But Iphigenia was enjoying the game. She gargled some more, watching Carla pretend to spit two or three times before she finally brought the liquid into her mouth again and spat it as far as she could. She gargled a few more times, then swallowed the rest of the mixture.

When Carla had taken the bowl away, Margarita wrapped her up in a blanket, bringing it right up to her chin. Although

Iphigenia still felt foggy and her head drooped she was touched by the efforts her sisters were making. After the vinegar gargle came the mulled wine. She drank it down and with each swallow, her throat eased. She just needed to sit quietly in the sun, sweat out the rain and get her smell back. And she had to absorb into her illness the care of the community. That was the duty of the patient. Sometimes as a child, Carla would make special treats for the community. Little cakes made of mud with sprinklings of flowers on top. The nuns would declare them delicious and pretend to munch. In the glow of Carla's mulled wine, Iphigenia recalled those times. Now she didn't have to pretend.

She did not want to be put to bed, she said when asked, she wanted to be here. With them. Carla and Margarita went to fetch one of the high-backed chairs reserved for visiting priests, some pillows, and another blanket. They installed Iphigenia on her throne. Arranged the pillows around her, put her feet up on the bench, covered the whole with the other blanket, and tucked her in. She felt like Grandmother, except that Grandmother would never sit with her feet up and Iphigenia's head didn't sway. She actually checked herself, looking at a detail of the blanket and making sure her vision didn't waver.

She was feeling very warm and sweaty under all the layers of coverings. It was a fine bright day, everything sparkling after the rain, with just the right amount of breeze. Seabirds wheeled through the sky far above, and closer, small brown birds chirped in the apple trees.

"Washing Day," she croaked.

Margarita filled the trough with water that had collected that night in buckets and pans, while Carla got the bag of sorted fleeces and brought over what was to be washed. Some fleece they left unwashed, so that although rougher, it retained more of its waterproofing lanolin.

Washing softened and brightened the wool. They had a piece of soap in a wire cage with a handle attached. Margarita moved it vigorously about in the water. The suds came easily in the soft rainwater. Carla tipped in the creamy fleece and they started working their fingers in it to loosen the dirt, working with the grain of the wool, not across it, careful not to mat it, preparing it for spinning.

Iphigenia watched, eyelids heavy, ready to fall asleep at any minute, her head nodding to her chest.

The sun shining, the birds singing, sheep in the grass, women at their washing, it was a picture of bucolic bliss. What about him, was he invisible? Couldn't any of them see the human being caged like an animal, hands tied behind his back, legs in a plaster cast, every hair of his head and body missing? Was this part of the pastoral idyll?

At least the first time he had passed out he had woken to find the three of them standing there staring at him. Oh, how he wished for that now. He would not have believed it but he craved the company of his captors. He opened his mouth as wide as he could and produced a heart-rending scream. He was not a stone or a blade of grass. He was flesh and blood, the same as them.

Iphigenia's head lurched up and her eyes opened at the disturbance. Margarita and Carla turned lazily from the trough and looked. The scream wound down to a quiet whimper. As there appeared to be nothing further, they went back to their tasks.

A bank of white fleeces hung on the bushes drying by the

time Carla and Margarita felt that their cold fingers needed the warmth of a cup of tea. They pressed their hands against cheeks which had grown rosy from work and went back to Iphigenia and the fire.

Iphigenia was asleep, head resting against a pillow, breathing through her mouth and snoring. A thin line of spittle had dried white on her chin like a scar. She did not stir when Margarita and Carla joined her. Carla put her cool hand on Iphigenia's moist hot forehead. The sick herbs were working.

It was time for Sext. There at the table they said their prayers softly, punctuated by Iphigenia's snores. When they had finished, Carla dipped her finger in the remaining tea in the pot and wet Iphigenia's dry lips with it, her teeth and her tongue. She added a branch to the fire.

While Carla continued with the washing Margarita made a quick unleavened bread. They went about their tasks wordlessly. Words were for prayers, chants, and stories. In the silence they could carry on eternal adoration of the Lord.

He watched. Looking for hints, trying to determine what they had in store for him. Were they going to keep him here forever, torture him? He watched the way they fussed over the one sitting on her throne snoring grotesquely. How vulnerable she was. Asleep, mouth open, limbs tethered beneath the coverings. He was sick, too. He had his legs in plaster. He had spent the night on straw stinking of sheep shit and his own urine. Why weren't they fussing over him?

As a priest he had spoken of the resilience of the human spirit, of those crippled by war and famine, prisoners of conscience who had suffered unbearable torture and had never lost faith. It was easy to give out those lofty words, to pray for the victims in his crisp neat collar, knowing he'd soon be enjoying a glass of wine with the Sunday roast. And now he was one of those wretched creatures. He had never imagined, never really imagined, that he and the unfortunate belonged to the same species.

The fat one worked away, slapping a lump of dough into shape, using the tea from the pot the young one had stuck her finger in to moisten it. Disgusting. She oiled the pan, patted the dough down in it, then put it on the fire. With her hands she swept the flour off the table, wiped the floury hands down her vest, then blew the residue onto the grass.

The other one walked past, giving him a look that was hard to discern. It was certainly more than curiosity and lasted too long to be furtive. She had a small basket of what appeared to be black wool. She carefully placed it onto a thin cloth, wrapped the cloth around like a plum pudding, then sluiced it in the water. Doing this with one hand and looking at him at the same time. He couldn't turn from her gaze even though he felt a sharp prickly sensation, like thousands of tiny needles, all over him.

She squeezed excess water out of the bundle, then placed it in the basket and opened up the cloth again. Why in the basket instead of on the bushes with the other wool? Black sheep, he giggled with an unwanted hysteria. Had to be kept away from the rest of the flock. She tilted the basket toward him.

It wasn't wool, it was hair. His hair. He wanted to curl up into a little ball but it was impossible. He couldn't even bend his legs.

She put the basket down in front of the fat one. They stroked the hair, picked pieces of it up. He was horrified but he could not look away. Even though the hair was no longer attached to him he felt violated at every stroke. They turned the hairs around, looking at the gloss. Examining the quality.

His eyelids came down closing the image off. They had his hair, they had his body. But he would keep his mind and spirit from them as long as he could. He would think of saints and martyrs, those who had undergone every humiliation, and he would dwell with them.

Carla left the basket of hair at one end of the table and went to get some apple chutney for lunch. Margarita tested the bread in the pan to see if it was done. Satisfied, she turned it out on the table.

The mellow roundness of freshly cooked bread and the sharp stink of sweat woke Iphigenia. Everything seemed to have more depth, definition. Smell. She could smell. She moved an arm. Tender but no longer cramped. She brought it out from under the blanket and rested her hand in her lap. Her mouth was parched and dry, an irony considering that her body was a lather of sweat. She did a sucking motion with her mouth to get some saliva going. Margarita poured hot water straight from the kettle and gave it to Iphigenia to sip. Ah, much better.

Iphigenia felt as if she'd woken from a sleep of a hundred years instead of the few hours it must have been. She was not completely recovered, her head twinged every now and then, her throat still felt lumpy, but the aches and pains had been sweated out. Best of all she could smell. She was out of the fog and part of the community again. She brought her other hand out from under the blanket, placed them together, and with her sisters bowed her head for grace.

The abbess's room was lit with oil lamps and candles that cast long looming shadows on the walls. The basket of car relics sat on the abbess's bed almost glowing with a life of its own.

The nuns were going through the relics, sorting them into piles the way Carla sorted debris from fleeces. They would discard nothing they had brought up from the car, but they knew already that not everything was useful. The papers in the pretty box were just playthings. They had examined the lighter fluid more than once, and without really knowing what it was, understood that it was important. Likewise with the battery.

While Iphigenia examined the contents of the folder, Margarita and Carla browsed through a book of maps. It was very colorful—black, red, or yellow lines traversing green countryside. There were tiny squares of towns, inverted v's for mountains, circles of lakes, crosses that denoted places of worship, churches and monasteries. They turned a page and came across a thin length of ribbon, similar to ribbons they used to mark their place in the Bible. This page was a map of the coastline, with islands scattered out from it like crumbs from a loaf of bread. Some of the islands had names, others were just ragged green shapes in the blue. Was their island one of these? What was it called? The monastery was St. Agnes, but if they ever knew the name of the island it had long been forgotten.

Carla and Margarita turned to another book, *Negotiation Skills*. It was difficult to read, almost as if it was written in a foreign language.

"Connoisseur Resorts." It was Iphigenia. Carla and Margarita gave up on *Negotiation Skills* and gathered around. Iphigenia didn't look up from the pamphlet she was poring over, seemingly unaware that she had spoken at all.

The pamphlet was shiny with lots of pictures. In one picture was a blue pool with people drinking colored drinks and floating on buoyant mattresses. They were all wearing glasses, black as the car windows. In another picture people were seated at a big table, with candles along it. There was plush red carpet on the floor, tapestries on the wall, and ornate decorations on the ceiling. It looked like a palace. In a third picture, some men were in a field poised with sticks. Croquet. No, it was another game. Golf.

"The ultimate away-from-it-all," read Iphigenia. "Discretion and privacy. Luxury accommodation for private individuals or groups . . . Medieval fortresses, castles, manor houses." She turned the pamphlet over a few times. Nothing was left unread. Carla picked it up, examined the pictures closely, while Iphigenia went on to the next thing. A list of names. Connoisseur Resorts Hotel Marketing Group had a circle around it. She put the list aside too. The next item was a map, the same map of the monastery they had retrieved from the man's pocket. But drawings of other things had been superimposed on it. The courtyard had been made into a blue square, and the chapel was different. Iphigenia's mouth set hard.

Carla and Margarita looked at Iphigenia, waiting for her to tell.

"He wants to turn our home into these pictures."

Carla grinned broadly. She liked the picture of the table with the candles on it, the blood-red carpet underneath. But Iphigenia did not grin, and neither did Margarita. "The pictures are nice," Carla defended herself.

"But we are not in them. In such a place we will not exist."

Carla started peering at the people around the table. Some of them had their heads turned and you couldn't see their faces properly. They could very well be Carla and Margarita and Iphigenia.

"He said we would have to go to a place with a nurse, he said they would slaughter the Agnes sisters. Remember, Carla. The story of King Henry the Eighth, dissolution of the monasteries. All destroyed. All sold to the world."

"But God is the king of us."

"God is the king of us. But the Bishop is the king of the monastery. And he has sent the man here."

Carla arranged her own relics from the journey outside. Now she had another—the shard of black glass, as sharp as a crucifixion nail. She played her finger on it, tapping with enough pressure to feel the sharp point but not enough to pierce the skin the way it had pierced Iphigenia's. Iphigenia didn't even know she had brought this relic up with her. It had been in her body, nestled in her flesh and blood. Carla held its blackness up against the night, then buried it in a special place all of its own. It might tear and break the fabric of the escapecoat.

It was very late, the Great Silence had descended hours

ago. She had lain there while the sliver of moon passed by her window and still sleep did not come.

In turn she held up a sprig of sea-pink, a yellow gorse flower, and a shell. The shell was the shape of an ear. She pressed it against her ear and heard a faraway windy sound. She pulled the shell away and looked at it. How could it make the noise of the sea? She listened again. In the shell she heard the echo of the creatures' song. She saw their smooth round heads and lovely whiskers, their great rubbery flippers. Carla flapped her forearms up and down, and sang their song until she grew tired. But not tired enough.

With the shell still in her hand, she went outside. Sometimes when she was little and couldn't sleep she would creep into one of the nuns' cells. As she grew bigger they did not like it and said she must find comfort in the Lord.

Down past the arches of the cloisters she went, holding the shell, singing the seal song, humming, mouth closed so that the sound stayed in her head and did not escape. She passed the glow of embers in the courtyard. And then she saw the fish. She stopped the singing, she pulled the sea sound away from her ear but the fish did not disappear.

Quietly she crept up. She saw his glassy eye. He was breathing in short spurts. "Kiri," she called softly but he did not respond. She unlatched the gate to the holding pen. He did not move. But the glassy eye did not stop looking. She went in and put the shell to his ear. The head turned abruptly as if trying to flick off a fly. She got down, her skirt rustling the straw.

She was very close to him. His white skin was covered in tiny black dots, minute grains of sand. When she patted him it had the raspy feel of the sea creatures.

"Sleep?"

He observed the Great Silence. Carla would have liked to observe it too but her thoughts were chattering. When she went to the sisters at night, they sometimes broke the Great Silence to tell her a story, to pray with her until she fell asleep.

"Story?"

Still he observed the Great Silence.

She lay down beside him, curving into his back. He was cold so she pulled him closer to warm him. He wriggled violently but after some gentle patting, he gave up, like a little bird or insect does eventually if you hold it firmly.

She would tell him a story. But which one? Something he would like. She lay there feeling the movement of his breath, then she decided. She didn't have all the story but she knew when she started the rest would come. She fingered the shell.

Resting her other hand on his tummy so that he was snug and warm, she began.

"Once upon a time there was a beautiful princess. One day she set off with her lords and ladies for a land across the sea but there was a storm, a terrible storm, and the ship foundered. The sea closed over the ship without a trace. The people were not dead, only sleeping, waiting to be delivered up. By and by, a prince came along on a big black chariot. And do you know what happened?" She started rubbing his tummy, his cold and prickly tummy. And then, oh, she felt Baby Moses. Poor little abandoned Baby, with not even the bulrushes to keep him warm. She would not abandon him, she would love him and hug him as the sisters had done for Baby Carla.

"The prince's big black chariot parted a way in the sea, just like Moses stretching out his hand and dividing the waters." She stretched her hand and closed her fingers around Baby Moses. "He would deliver them to the promised land where they would drink colored drinks, and eat at a table with a carpet the color of blood." She hugged Baby Moses with her hand. "And then . . ."

And then a miraculous thing happened. Right there in her hand Baby Moses started to grow up. He kept his soft baby skin but inside he grew solid and hard as a lamb's leg.

It was unspeakable, he could barely believe it was happening. It wasn't enough that she breathed her clammy story into the back of his neck. She was now playing with him.

Soul of Christ, sanctify me
Body of Christ, save me
O good Jesus, hide me within Thy wounds . . .

He thought he had reached the place where all dignity had disappeared, where he could not get lower, but still they had managed to find a way. He tried to feel Christ's thorns pricking his own head, feel the nails through his own hands and feet, the sword in his side, to have heroic pain instead of this. He was in the wilderness. God had deserted him, left him with no weapons to fend for himself, not even control over his own body.

She kept on and on with her stupid story, the parting sea and carpets of blood. Though God had deserted him it seemed the hunger of the flesh had not. It did not matter that the hand belonged to this mad she-creature, it had the softness and surety of the nurse. He reviled them both. He reviled all temptresses, the embodiment of flesh and carnality. Of all that must be denied and abhorred by a spirit dedicated to the Lord. The phlegm, bile, rheum, the lowliness of being born between woman's shit and piss. He dredged up St. Augustine on woman's vile venality, St. John Chrysostom, but none of it prevented tumescence.

She wasn't even using the firm quick rhythm of his own grip, it was simply the soft warmth of her encompassing hand. Oh, he could resist no longer. He let fly with it, words so corrosive they scoured his own soul.

"The curse God pronounced on your sex weighs still on the world. You are the Devil's gateway, you desecrated the fatal tree, you first betrayed the law of God, you who softened up with your cajoling words the man against whom the Devil could not prevail by force. The image of God, the man Adam, you broke him, it was child's play to you. You deserved death, and it was the Son of God who had to die!"

His mouth screamed it out, all the rage, all the indignity that had been visited upon him and yet he knew not how he mouthed those words with such eloquence, the words that had come to him across the millennia of history.

When he was spent he lay there sobbing, exhausted and limp. In the soft cooing with which he tried to comfort himself, he heard the chorus of sheep, a bleating that sounded remarkably like his own.

Then all around him was still, the great cold blanket of night pressed down on him and he was once more alone. The woman was gone. At which precise moment she had shrunk away from him he couldn't tell.

Iphigenia woke with the noise. A banshee. She had never heard the like. The outburst had started up the sheep, then there was quiet sobbing, and then there was nothing.

After Carla had gone to her cell Iphigenia and Margarita had discussed. "He has strayed, that is why he wants to make our religious house a secular one. God has sent him here so that we can minister to him. If he cannot be persuaded with our ministering, others will come." Margarita did not think the Lord had sent him to be ministered to. "We must try," said Iphigenia.

It was time. They did not want an uncontrollable wild thing on their hands, that terrible screeching creature. Yes, tomorrow was time. They would bring him in, start him on the edges of their company. She did not know whether Carla had provoked the beastly howl but she thought she detected the scent of a frightened Carla scurrying back along the corridor.

Remarkably, Ignatius thought when he opened his eyes to misty sunlight, he had survived the night. As he had not eaten anything he had not defecated. He thanked God for this small mercy and asked for faith to get him through this ordeal for which there was no name. He prayed for humility, for release from pride. He gave himself utterly to the Lord for His will to be done.

He could hear the hissing of water and the scrape of mugs on the wooden slab of table. Sheep grazed around him, giving no indication they had been disturbed by the events of the night. No one did. The chair from the day before had been brought out again but the tall one was not sitting in it. Blankets and cushions were piled on the chair. Something had changed.

"Good morning," said the tall one. "How is your ankle?" As if he were a patient in hospital. How was his ankle? Lord Almighty, he didn't need to be covered in plaster just to protect his ankle.

They came into the pen, all three of them. The one from last night held back a little, avoiding his eye. He would have said she looked sheepish but the word was bereft of normal meaning in this gathering. The other two stood him up and brushed the debris off. They untied his arms, then tied them up again, this time in front of him, smiling, as if they were doing him a favor. He became a limp doll, letting them do what they would. He could not sink any further.

His encased legs were resting on the bench, cushions around his head, blankets tucked in, bound hands resting in his lap. Propped up like a dowager queen. He watched them pour tea, then place a mug of it in front of him.

How in Heaven's name did they think he was going to lean over and pick it up, trussed up as he was like a Christmas turkey? He looked at them dully. He would accept and receive but he would not initiate. He would be as indifferent to them as they had appeared to be to him. Though he had undergone humiliation and degradation beyond all imagination, he had to admit that they were not gloating tormentors. They had left him alone to his pain and suffering. Until the succubus in the night. Lying with him, teasing and tempting. Tormenting him with her story and her blasphemous hand.

Perhaps she had been sent to bring him to utter degradation, to test his humanity. Out in the wilderness he had been through a rite of passage. Now he was being accepted back into the tribe.

When he made no movement toward the mug, Iphigenia pushed it within his reach. He looked at it, looked at them watching him, then he fanned his fingers around it, felt its nourishing warmth.

They drank their tea, inviting him with their actions to drink his. He had lost track of when he had last eaten or drunk, but now he felt acutely his hunger and his thirst.

Perhaps he had had an accident and broken both legs. He had a fever and the rest was a hallucination. He had been ill, had a few bad dreams, and now he was sitting in a chair convalescing. A convalescent with his hands bound together.

He guided the mug up, trying to stop his hands from shaking, trying to disregard the ache in his arms. The mug finally arrived at his mouth. He breathed in the refreshing aroma, then took his first sip. His body felt like a big empty well, he could feel the trickle of tea going all the way down. He took another sip and held it, aware now of how bad his own mouth tasted. The tea lacked the minty freshness of toothpaste but it was pleasantly sharp and invigorating.

In the loneliness of the holding pen he had wanted to die. He had not partaken of the water and crusts they'd left for him, had refused his body any sustenance, wanting the Lord to take him as quickly as possible. But he was alive. Out of the pen and sitting in the warm sun drinking tea. God obviously had other plans for him.

The tea finished, they brought out baskets of fleece. There were natural colors of creamy white, dark gray, and brown. There were also soft greens, yellow, blue. Perhaps after all he had imagined that basket of black, the basket of his own hair. But he had none on his body, they must have done something with it.

Next they brought out a spinning wheel and a basket of sticks with knobs, and other things. The fat one sat at the spinning wheel, the young one stood near her, and the tall one sat at the table.

"Spinning wheel," said the fat one.

"Spindle," said the young one.

"Cards," said the tall one, holding up what looked like two square wire brushes. She placed them on the table, then went over to a grazing sheep.

"Wool," she said, touching its back. "Shearing, sorting, washing, carding, combing, spinning." She mimed the actions.

He watched them grab chunks of fleece and set to work.

"Cards," said the tall one once again, holding up the brushes. Having shown him the tools, she sat down. He was being initiated into the secrets of the tribe. It was like one of those morning television shows where they show children how to make things out of egg cartons and other kitchen litter. "One card on lap, wires pointing up. One card in hand, wires pointed down." She demonstrated. "Place fleece on card." She did so. "Brush the free card," she said, indicating the one in her hand, "from top to handle, top to handle." She repeated the words as she repeated the gesture, brushing the one against the other, teasing the fleece till the fibers lay straight. "Teasing." From the basket of knickknacks she held up a dull purple ball covered in stiff, hooked spines. "Fuller's teasel flower, used by the spinsters of old." She replaced it and went back to her wire brushes.

Ignatius listened intently. There might be an exam, to see how much he had learned. He tried to memorize her actions, like memorizing a catechism.

"Brush deeply." She did so, transferring the fleece from one brush to the other. "And again." Transferred it back to the original brush. "Sheep fleece," she said as if it wasn't obvious what was on the brushes. She took a hank of textured gray and placed it on the brushes with the fleece. "Our fleece." She repeated the brushing and transferring process several times.

All the while the others were in the background spinning, one at the wheel, the other twisting, spinning the yarn around the stick in a steady regular rhythm, providing a background to the speaking part.

"Rolag," she announced with a flourish. She held the fleece on her lap card with one hand, then used the wooden edge of the other brush to tuck up the loose ends of the fleece under her thumb. Next, she placed the wires of the upper brush on top of the folded fleece and rolled it off the brush. It looked like a sausage. She handed this to the young one, who started to work it into her thread.

Ignatius assumed that in handing it over, she was handing over the microphone, so to speak, but in fact she went on. She walked over to the one at the spinning wheel.

"Leonardo da Vinci," announced Iphigenia. "Leonardo da Vinci designed a wheel that twisted fibers and wound yarn onto a spool. But this wheel was not produced till 1530." Then she sat down and the fat one took over.

"Flywheel." Margarita pointed to it. "Spindle, bobbin, spindle shaft, pulley, treadle." Then she started up again, her foot rhythmically on the treadle, feeding the fleece through. The fleece, like a hank of fairy floss, being transformed into spun yarn.

That was it. She didn't finish with a flourish, she simply stopped speaking. Her foot continued working the treadle, her hand feeding fiber into the twist. She had spoken her part and withdrew into the background of the tableau.

That left only one.

He looked away, not wanting to catch her eye. He could hear the whirr of the spinning wheel, the soft chomp of the wire brushes. She remained silent. Perhaps she was waiting for him, the way teachers at school waited till they had the full and undivided attention of the whole class. In this school, Ignatius was the class. He felt compelled to look.

If she'd been waiting for him to pay attention, it wasn't obvious. Her eyes were focused entirely on the short distance, not on him at all. Holding the sausage of fleece up, fanning the fibers out, then twisting them with the lower hand into yarn. Ignatius followed the line of the thread down to where it was gathering on the rotating spindle.

" 'What manner of thing is that, twisting and twirling so giddily?' asked Briar Rose, for indeed it was a drop spindle the woman in the tiny room was working." She kept on fanning, kept on twisting, one hand feeding the material into the other.

Carla stopped, remembering how on the first night he'd gotten cross with their version of Briar Rose. She hadn't meant to frighten him last night but a terrible wind had come out of his mouth and smitten her.

"But this is not the story I have for you today. Today we will hear the story of the first spinners. Look at the picture." Perhaps this would please him, a story with pictures.

He looked around expectantly.

"It is a place of softly curving walls, dark and grained. Perhaps the hollow of a great tree trunk or a cave in the earth or under the sea."

Oh no, she was going to resume her story of the night before. This was all sport. Only it was worse now, she was going to humiliate him in front of the others.

"There are rocks and pools, and in the background is a tiny doorway open to the light of the world. The walls are etched in darkness but the light shines brightly on the thread the spinsters hold between them. From time to time they touch the spindle to keep it twirling. Some say they are the trinity, not separate but three faces of the one. Lachesis who sings the past, Clotho the present, and Atropos the future. One holds the distaff, one the spindle, and one the scissors. And one is young, and one is old, and one is between."

She kept her distance, seemed entirely occupied with the spinning of the fleece. He relaxed a little, lulled by her rhythms.

"Souls between one life and another come before the spinsters to be given the measure of their lot. The soul about to enter a new body is greeted thus, 'Ye may each choose your own lot but the choice is irrevocable. Choose carefully.' Then the soul enters the anteroom where every condition of life is present: rich and poor, animals, ferns, princes and paupers, happiness and bereavement. Some are guided by memories of their former life so that musicians choose to become birds with the sweetest of song. Some men become beasts."

He felt it like a little arrow aimed directly at him, but her face was placid, absorbed. It was as if he no longer existed.

"Some eagerly choose the riches of greatest sovereignty, not looking closely enough at this lot to discover they might be destined to devour their own children. The wise soul reflects and remembers. Ulysses, heartsick from his wanderings, chose a quiet simple life of contemplation in a place visited by few."

Mesmerized by the twisting and turning of thread, he did not at first realize that she had stopped. He wanted more.

The story had stopped but the rhythm of work went on. He could hear the wheel, the brush of the cards.

"Then," she took up the story again. Not the end, merely an interval. Waiting for the next piece of the story to come down the thread, feeling her way along. "Once the lot is chosen, the soul passes into the chamber of the Fates who spin the lot into a cocoon around the soul. Lachesis gives fiber so that the soul's destiny can be fulfilled. Clotho turns the spindle to confirm the choice, and Atropos twists the thread to make it unbreakable.

When the allocated portion of life has been spun, the thread is snipped off."

Again she paused, but still it was not the end. "Then the soul wades into water, lies down and sleeps in the Sea of Forgetfulness. By and by a disturbance will part the waters, a great ship foundering or even a disturbance as small as a fish jumping. And through the gap in the sea the souls will come. And the water will send up a shower of stars and the souls will rise on them and be scattered upon the face of the earth. Then they will awake from their long sleep and will find themselves in the place, and the tight cocoon they have slept in will begin to unwind."

She was at the end of her story, at the end of her roll of fleece. Yet she continued twisting. Ignatius sat very still, as if he had been spun into a cocoon as well. She gathered the finished wool and pulled it off the spindle. The whirring of the wheel wound down and came to a halt. They started to pack up.

He was released from their thrall. What should he do, clap?

They took the finished work, the baskets and the paraphernalia, all the props of performance, inside and came out again with lunch. Bread, chutney, and green leaves. Ploughman's lunch, he thought wryly. He had no idea what the leaves were, some sort of weed, no doubt. Yet his mouth watered at the sight of it all.

He bowed his head in grace and then he ate with them, shoveling the food in, spilling it down his front, snuffling and snorting and slurping with as much gusto as his companions.

They had brought him in. To a smaller room than the one from which he had escaped. There was a high window with a slit of evening light but no extra security. With legs in plaster and hands tied it was no longer necessary.

On the wall was a huge drawing the size of a blanket. A bucolic scene in the middle—three shepherds surrounded by a tight flock of sheep. Apple trees, a couple of white birds interrupting the flow of blue sky. There were rough tangled strokes at the edge like brambles, and inside that, a border of individual scenes too small for him to make out. As they lay him on the bed, bringing him closer to it, he saw that the whole was crisscrossed with fine vertical and horizontal lines like graph paper. Thousands of tiny squares and in each one a tiny cross. It was a knitting pattern, each cross in the grid representing a stitch.

The tall one placed herself in front of it. "The knitted piece tells a story, a fabric stitched from the thread of language, an artifact bright with meaning. It holds the memory of learned stitches, the inventiveness of imagination, and the cables and ribs of the knitters' own lives. Islands, sheep, religion are only some of the themes running through it."

Compared to this morning's demonstration of carding, it sounded somewhat stilted, as if lifted straight out of an encyclopedia. Carding. A new word. Ignatius smiled to himself. What a lot of new things he was learning.

"Although the exact origins of the craft are still to be unearthed, early fragments of interlocked fabric have been discovered in Arabia. It would be reasonable to assume that knitting originated in fishing communities, knitting being so similar to knotting and the meshing of nets. By the thirteenth century, wool, the growing, processing, and trading in it, had become such a profitable industry that British ships traveled in convoys to guard against piracy. Knitting was such a highly regarded craft in the Elizabethan Age that the apprentice was required to spend six years traveling to learn the techniques. For his final examination he had to knit a cap, a shirt, a pair of stockings, and a carpet. When machines took over in the world, hand-knitting was relegated to an interesting and therapeutic hobby."

Ah yes, performing much better now. More confident, more fluency. Seven out of ten at least.

"But on the islands and outposts the craft stayed alive. Though the basic shape of the gansey, traditional garment of island fisherfolk, is the same everywhere, stitches and patterns vary from island to island. It is said that when a fisherman drowns the island he comes from can be identified by the pattern of his gansey. This notion may have little basis in fact because fisherfolk visit many places in their travels, learn new stitches. A certain amount of borrowing goes on. Nevertheless, distinctive patterns and stitches came to be associated with particular islands. The cable knitting characteristic of the Aran Isles is thought to have been inspired by Celtic crosses. Cables and ribbing also provide thickness and warmth against the biting winds."

She paused again, as if waiting for the next bit to tick its way into her memory.

"Knitting is not limited to the functional. In the long cold Shetland Island nights lace knitting developed. So fine and beautiful is the work that a shawl the size of a table can be passed through a wedding ring." As if to demonstrate, she made a circle with her thumb and forefinger and pulled air through it.

The fat one added a little more detail. "Shetland sheep aren't sheared, they're plucked. When new fleece grows, old wool comes out easily. Plucked wool has a lovely long staple."

The tall one took up again. "The shawls are knitted on needles thin as wires, employing stitches such as shell, print o' the wave, fern. A most ethereal and rarefied example of the craft, producing a gossamer with the delicacy and strength of spider web." At this, the young one sat up abruptly. The tall one gave her a look. "In former times it was nuns who knitted or embroidered the sacerdotal vestments of bishops and priests. The lambs which provided the wool for these vestments were ceremonially blessed on the feast day of St. Agnes."

That was it. A hesitant beginning but when she hit her stride quite authoritative. Ignatius smiled benignly, the way his uncles smiled when Ignatius and his sister had to do recitations for them after Sunday dinner.

It looked like the lecture was to be followed by a demonstration. The nuns had their needles with them and the baskets of spun wool. Everything was there on the small table—needles, wool, and scissors—laid out with the precision of surgical instruments.

They placed their hands together, lowered their eyes, and

began to chant. Automatically Ignatius also bowed his head and lowered his eyes. His hands were already together. Bound.

He listened carefully, assuming that now they had included him, he was expected to join in their prayers. It took him a while to realize that these were not holy words they were chanting. He caught the odd word here and there. Arachne, Athena. It was not a prayer he was familiar with.

The chant ended and they picked up their knitting. Again he scanned the baskets for his own hair, but didn't see it. Had they already knitted it up or were they saving it? He wondered if when they started looping and poking needles through, he would feel it.

They fell silent, the needles poised in their hands.

"Story," they instructed.

Ah, good. Something for him to do. But what to tell, what would the ladies like tonight? He remembered the last time he had lain on the bed and told the little company a story. How clever he had felt then. Now he had to win back cleverness, a long strong thread of it to carry him out of here.

The nuns waited impatiently, as if he was stopping them from getting on with their work. Carla idly rolled a ball of yellow wool across the table, watched it unravel, then rolled it back up again. And this gave him the idea.

"Once there was a king who lost his way in the forest. It was near nightfall and he had begun to despair, when he came upon an old woman. She promised to show him the way out if he would marry her daughter. The daughter was comely and the king thought he had struck a good bargain indeed. But, ah, once out of the forest she turned into a witch. Now the king had thirteen children—twelve sons and a beautiful daughter—from a previous marriage. Fearing they might come to some harm from their witch mother, he told his servant to hide them away in the forest. A different forest," Ignatius added.

"One day the new queen, suspicious of her husband's frequent absences, went through his things and found a ball of magic wool. She let the wool unravel and followed where it led—straight to the children. Thinking that the wool announced a visit from their father, the boys ran out to greet him. But alas. The witch mother pulled white shirts over their heads and they turned into swans. They looked at their snowy pouting breasts, the yellow webs of their feet, lifted their great wings, and flew into the sky. The thirteenth child, the daughter, was saved this fate because she was in the little cabin preparing supper.

"When it was ready she called them. But they didn't come. She called again. Where were they? She searched and searched all through the forest but they had vanished into thin air.

"As the third day reddened into night, twelve beautiful swans flapped down to earth beside the princess. When they landed, their webs became feet again, their wings folded down into arms, and she recognized her brothers.

" 'Haste,' they greeted her, 'we are men but for these few minutes of the day. Our stepmother has cast a spell on us.'

"The princess wrung her hands. 'Tell me, oh tell me, what I must do to break the spell.'

"The brothers cooed among themselves, looking everywhere but at their sister.

" 'Tell me what I must do!' she implored.

"Then the eldest brother spoke. 'It is too much to ask.'

"The sun was barely visible above the horizon, the princess even more urgent, aware of how short a time they had to speak and willing to do anything. 'Nothing is too much. Tell me. Speak.'

" 'That is just it,' demurred the eldest brother. 'You must not speak. You must weave twelve shirts of nettles, one for each of us. And you must not speak till all twelve are completed and we are restored to men.' Even as he spoke the other brothers were turning into swans.

" 'I will do it,' she whispered up to the sky as they flew away."

Ignatius continued with the story of "The Twelve Swans" and of the sister who for years toiled in silence. "Even when she in turn married a king, and her mother-in-law accused her of witchcraft and put a drop of blood on the girl's dress to trick the king into believing she had murdered her own child she kept silent, sewing and sewing her secret shirts. 'She shall be burned at the stake,' the king pronounced sadly, all the while imploring his beloved queen to speak and save her life. But the queen did not.

"As she was led to the fire there was the beating of wings and twelve swans swooped down to free their sister. When they descended she threw the shirts over them and instantly twelve princes stood guard around her, including the youngest prince who, because the girl did not have time to complete the last shirt, had a wing in place of an arm.

"Freed from her vow, the queen could now speak. She told the king about the spell and how she was innocent of the dreadful deeds of which his mother accused her. Instead of his wife, it was his mother who was put to the fire. Then the king, the queen, and all her brothers lived happily ever after."

Ignatius stopped, surprised that he had come to the end of the tale. Surprised too that he had filled it with such detail. After a while it seemed to flow off his tongue. It had been a long time since he had heard the story and he did not realize that he remembered it so well. Perhaps he had invented some of it, not remembered it at all.

He was also surprised to see how much knitting they had done. At some point the story had taken over and he had become oblivious to time. The clickety-click of the knitting needles had become the clip-clop of horses entering the forest. He flew like a bird with the princes, felt the welts the nettles made on the princess's skin, her anguish at the overwhelming task.

Now he was out again and the needles were still. The room was full of silence, of things suspended, being absorbed, digested. They pursed their lips, nodded slowly, as if he had presented a learned dissertation and they had found his argument convincing. What had they heard in the story and what were they judging?

From the idle roll of a ball of wool had come a story of regaining human shape. But who would make for him the shirt that would break the spell of the plaster cast?

Though he had finished the story it had not gone away. He had conjured it up and it sat in the room like a hologram. When he looked at it from one angle he saw swans. If he tilted it a little the swans became men again. And the women in the story—beautiful from one angle, vengeful and witchy from another. Daughters turning into wives and mothers; mothers and wives into wicked witches and old hags.

And yet it was mothers who passed these stories on, mothers and grandmothers. The soothing comfort of the rhythms, as soothing as a cradle being gently rocked. And though the world is wicked, my son, I am always here. To kiss you goodnight and tuck you into the blanket of happily ever after.

He looked at the three of them, childless grandmothers sitting by the fire knitting, harmless as his own grandmother knitting in front of the television. And yet they had trapped him. In their sticky web.

On the table was a basket of green that hadn't been there before. Nettles. He had a very strange feeling in the pit of his stomach.

"Knit?"

His mother had shown him a way of knitting when he was a child. Not with needles but with an old-fashioned wooden cotton reel with four small hammered nails marking the corners of a square. She started it off for him, lowering a length of wool through the hole in the middle of the reel, then winding wool around the nails to make a fence. Then she showed him how to loop the underneath wool over the nail. He tried it a few times, Mother keeping a gentle eye on him and smoothing over his initial mistakes. Then, joy of joys, a thin knitted snake appeared through the bottom of the cotton reel. Oh, he would make one so long that he could coil it around and around to make a mat that covered the whole floor. He had races with his sister to see whose snake was the longest. He used all the different-colored scraps of wool and eagerly watched as a new color came through.

He had only enough snake to make a drink coaster by the time he lost interest. His sister, on the other hand, went on and on, trailing her snake from room to room, as if it was a pet. He pretended he didn't care. It was girls' stuff anyway.

"Not really," he said.

"Time to learn," said Iphigenia. She and Margarita stood up. Iphigenia came over to the man and loosened the binds around his wrists. It was a good start. He rubbed circulation back into his wrists, wiggled his fingers.

Outside it had started to rain. He could hear the different

rhythms of it, heavy then soft. The sound of it on the roof, the splash as it ran off, the change in pitch as the buckets began to fill. He imagined the rain falling through the holes in the roof of the chapel, watering the vegetation growing out of the head of the Blessed Virgin, cascading down her garment. At least in here there were no drips and though the window had no glass the wall was too thick for the rain to splash in.

Margarita gave the demonstration, picked up a ball of gray wool and a pair of needles thick as skewers from a Sunday roast. "Left hand like this," she said, holding up the needle with the cast-on stitches. "Needle through stitch, loop around needle, pull first stitch over." He watched as the stitches were gradually transferred to the needle in her right hand. "Plain. Later comes purl. Plain and purl together make stocking stitch. More tension and spring and gives a nice finish."

She completed one row, then another, working slowly and deliberately. But not the way Miss Black or his mother showed him things. She didn't seem to care whether he was learning or not. It was just a chore. She dropped the knitting in front of him.

"You."

The wool had an odd texture, the color an exact match for her hair. A cold clammy shiver overcame him, as if she was breathing on his body. He tried to concentrate, think of something positive. At least his hands were free. He pushed out his elbows, trying to give himself more room. He stuck the needle through the first stitch. And now? It had looked so easy. But which way did the loop go? And why wouldn't the stitch come off smoothly? He tugged and tugged at the knitting, bringing three stitches off the needle at once.

Margarita gave an exasperated sigh.

He wondered whether free hands were worth this humiliation. With a calculator or a keyboard his fingers were so agile. What was stopping them now? He looked at her hands, dry and tough like animal paws. Thick yellow fingernails. Yet they could work a row of knitting in no time.

He tried again, but all he managed to do was pull the existing stitches off the needle.

He could have cried with frustration.

He knew this feeling. Six years old again and learning to write. The board was a pattern of p's and b's and words: pop, bob, bib, pip. Miss Black, the lay teacher, had ruled lines on the board and told stories about how the letters got their shapes. In his writing book "p" and "b" were outlined in dots. He held his pencil as if he was going to stab someone with it and traced over the dots.

Miss Black came around looking at everyone's work. She changed his grip, putting his little fingers into the right position. "Good," she said. Her voice was like honey on toast. She moved on, bending over the next child. As soon as he went to trace over the next letter, the pencil slipped. Of course his fingers had forgotten Miss Black's intricate arrangement and returned to the stabbing position. To try to keep control of the pencil, he pressed heavily, so heavily in fact that the pencil point snapped off and he dug a hole in the page.

"Damn."

He was in such a cloud of red fury that he did not know the room had been shocked into stillness. When it cleared enough for him to see, he saw Miss Black glowering at him, her pretty eyes as black as coals.

"Stand up."

He obeyed. Even in a standing position he felt remarkably

tiny. So tiny he could not even hear what Miss Black was saying but he knew she was cross. Very. Not a pretend cross, a real cross. He kept staring at her black belt with its large gold buckle as bright and gleaming as a fireman's. Her perfume and beration mingled with his shame and he felt a strange tingling sensation as she shouted at him, her pointy bullet breasts hovering over his head, a feeling that would remain unnamed for years.

Now, instead of Miss Black it was Margarita who loomed over him. The lesson had been to no avail. Resigned, he held the knitting out to her. She went to take it but instead gasped and shrunk away. She hastened back to the table, picked up other knitting, and tried to lose herself in it.

Ignatius was mystified.

Iphigenia and Carla exchanged glances. "I will show," Carla announced.

She moved over to him and, after a moment's hesitation, put her hands around his, the soft round curve she used for holding baby birds. Then she placed his fingers into position and together, double-handed, they knitted a whole row.

She let him try for himself. He poked the needle through a stitch, wound the wool around. She nodded encouragement. She made a movement with her hand indicating he should loop the stitch over. He did it.

He did it. Without stretching the wool or losing the stitch. He wanted to smile, but he kept his head down. It was just menial knitting, it wasn't as if he'd discovered relativity. Nevertheless, he was pleased to accept her praise. "Good," she said in a voice that sounded just like Miss Black's.

It was Carla who wore the smile of pride as she rejoined her sisters at the table. She wanted Margarita to look and see that he had learned, that he was knitting all by himself. But Margarita appeared not to want to look. "Story?" suggested Carla, trying to get Margarita out of her mood. Margarita took no notice. "Beauty?" said Carla, reminding Margarita of the story she always liked to tell.

Margarita stopped. "Beast, Beast, clip your nails. You will scratch your lovely furniture. You . . ."

Ignatius heard a noise, a chair being scraped, but kept on, the work under his hands absorbing all his concentration.

Then he too became aware that everything had gone quiet. He looked up and saw the gap that Margarita had left. Perhaps he had somehow offended her. Good.

Iphigenia sensed the man's knowingness. "Enough," she said. It was the tone a diner might use to a waiter ladling out soup. "For tonight."

They started packing up. "I will practice," he offered when they came for his knitting. They took it away and without saying a word, bound his wrists.

It popped out. The thing that had broken loose in Margarita had now found its way to the surface. She lay in the Great Silence, the Knitting Madonna on her chest, so stiff and straight on her narrow bed that it might have been a coffin. Her eyes were riveted to the ceiling. In between the bones of timber, cobwebs, and other things she saw the chandelier, its pendants set hard and bright as tears.

Beauty did not go to the Beast's house, the Beast came and fetched her. "Beauty, my Beauty," he said. He played his tongue out so his cherry-red lips became moist and shiny, touched his mustache as he looked at her, running his fingers over it, curling it up at the ends like a suggestive smile. He had a name, a tawny name, but she had willed it out of her consciousness.

"Beauty, my Beauty." The house was brown in her memory, with an upstairs and downstairs. The third step creaked and the corridor at the top was lit by gas lamps converted to electricity. Brass fittings on the walls with delicate glass hats. The garden had nothing in it except a few hard bushes. The house was in the country on its own, about an hour's drive in the horse and buggy from the train station. There were two or three cars in the train station town but a horse and buggy were better suited to the country roads.

"It will be an adventure for you," promised her father with a pasty smile. "A trip to the country. Imagine that. You can make up some lunch and take it with you."

Standing in the kitchen of her father's house in her best white dress with the blue sash, preparing thick slices of bread with pickled onion and ham.

"No need," said the man with the black mustache. "We can stop at a tavern on the way and have a hot dinner. Grilled kidneys, a nice stew. What do you say?"

The two men looked at her expectantly. She noticed her father's shirt fraying at the cuffs and a few gray hairs around his knuckles. He wore the same air of bravado he wore when trying to bluff at cards.

"Will you come too, Father?"

"Oh no no no no no no no," he said. "I have my affairs to attend to."

He had not attended to his affairs in months. When he did venture out he would be gone for hours, all night sometimes, and in the early morning she would hear him come in, hear him knock things over, crash. On those nights she would stay very still and quiet.

The visits of the men to the house became more and more frequent. She would put out the ashtrays, serve them wine, sit in the kitchen and listen as the room filled with their smoky conversation and leery jokes. The man with the black mustache and cherry-red lips would often be there. When they played cards his jacket would be off and his sleeves held up by gold armbands that rippled like metal snakes. He clasped a cigar between his teeth, even when he was talking. When she entered the room with a new carafe of wine, beckoned by her father's bell or, later in the evening, his rough shout, the man would wiggle the cigar at her. He was not the worst of them.

The day he came for her there was a lot of talking. When they saw her at the top of the stairs he showed her his cherry-red smile, then Father shut the door, the dark timber door. She had crept down and listened but she could hear only voices, not words. Every so often her father's voice would be raised, then imploring, and when she put her eye to the keyhole she saw the visitor sitting in the lounge chair and her father passing in and out of the keyhole view. Pacing the floor, running his fingers through his hair, then turning as if he'd suddenly had a good idea. But the man shook his head and stood firm. The man was in charge and her father only a visitor. Her father came toward the door and she shrunk back so as not to be seen.

When she looked again the man was holding his hand out for her father to shake. She would never forget that hand. It had clipped black hairs on it, and the nails were buffed and manicured like a woman's.

Margarita had seen that hand again tonight.

She closed her eyes but the hand did not disappear. Instead, the rest came into view. He had horns now and a cavernous mouth, he was going to eat her up. Long curling tongue, red and glistening. Run, Beauty, run. Run, run as fast as you can. Down the corridor, out into the open. There was a wall of fire.

Margarita lay on the coffin bed, wet with fear and sweat, as if a hand was reaching into her rib cage for her heart, a little bird wildly flapping about bruising itself. She gasped. She had scrunched the Madonna up into a little ball. When her heart subsided she smoothed the picture out again. Margarita held it to her breast, trying to take into herself the Madonna's forgiveness and charity. She was having visions. Perhaps it was indigestion. When she closed her eyes again she saw that below the horns and the cavernous mouth was the collar of a priest.

Margarita got out of bed and knelt on the cold hard floor. Her jaw was hurting, she'd been clenching her teeth. Give me the strength to forgive, to accept with Christian charity. And if vengeance be Thine, oh Lord, let me be worthy. Let me be Thy sword, Thy vessel, oh Lord.

It was the gap left by Margarita that gave him the idea that they could be worked on one by one. A gap that he could make wide enough to slip through. Iphigenia, Margarita, Carla. In his mind he saw them as a collectivity—the nuns, the women, the three—but they were not all the same. They had always presented a united front but tonight for the first time he saw dissension. He rather suspected that he was the cause of it. How pleasing. Because then he could play them off, one against the other. Divide and conquer. It had worked for the British Empire. He rolled the thought around in his brain, sucking at it every now and then like a lozenge.

The power of the community resided in Iphigenia. They followed her lead. But Margarita had taken it upon herself to get up and walk out of the knitting circle. He could work at this fraying edge.

His legs beneath the plaster were excruciatingly itchy. His nails were growing but he doubted they'd grow long enough for him to reach in and scratch. His hair was growing back too. Judging by the scratchiness of his beard it must be close to a week since they'd put him in plaster. He must have been missed by now. He only had the Land Rover for ten days, the car rental company must have phoned the presbytery to see why the car hadn't been returned. The presbytery would ring his sister, she would tell them that he hadn't arrived. She'd be worried. Ignatius was punctual, reliable. If he was delayed for some reason he would have phoned. If he was able to phone.

Would they alert the police, send a search party? Or just assume that he was yet another priest who had gone AWOL, like Brother Terry. Thirty years in the order, then one Christmas he failed to appear. There was no word of him till eighteen months later when he sent a postcard from Canada, apologizing for any inconvenience and announcing that he was living in a gay relationship with Denis, the handyman who had fixed up their guttering.

Say someone had notified the police, say someone had come looking. But Ignatius had no way of knowing. He felt lonely and abandoned, two emotions that beckoned him dangerously. If he went down either of these tracks he'd be lost. He veered away.

The tall one. Iphigenia. If not officially Mother Superior then at least de facto. Iphigenia seemed to be the most worldly wise. She would probably have made a superb matron or school principal. Somewhere in her background lurked the maintenance of a stiff upper lip. He wondered how her vocation had come to her, how she had ended up in a place like this.

Ignatius had felt genuinely called. He remembered the precise moment that God had breathed on him. It was at the age of fourteen, in a math class with Brother Carmody. He had spoken to the brother afterward as if he had somehow played a part in it. He and Michael Duigan were invited for afternoon tea. Fat scones and soda bread with Mrs. Tilley's homemade jam and lashings of cream. He hesitated at first, having heard things about boys who were invited by the brothers, but nothing like that happened.

It was explained to him that he could begin now if he wished. "God knows," said Brother Carmody, "fewer and fewer are joining and the Church needs talented boys like yourself. You will be the new breed," he said, putting his hands on the boy's shoulders. "But perhaps it is better to wait a few years, to know something of the world first. Girls," he said. "You may wish to marry, serve God in that way." He did not need to add that the purest, most committed way of serving God was through the priesthood. As for getting married, it was the furthest thing from the boy's mind. He could barely bring himself to sit next to a girl, let alone marry one. Nevertheless, he had waited a few years and though he never forgot the breath of God in the math class, by his late teens he was seeing the Church as a career, as other boys from school had joined the Army or Air Force.

If there was one among them who could possibly be reasoned with, be pragmatic, it was Iphigenia. Lying there in the darkness, he examined the possibilities. He had to demonstrate that he had the community's interests at heart. He could show his usefulness, offer to do repairs, perhaps bring in materials from the mainland. No, not a good idea. His legs itched enormously, if only he could get at them. All he could do was bash them up and down on the bed, hardly the relief he sought.

He came back to Margarita of the pumpkin face. She smelled. They all smelled but she had the odors of a fat woman, sweats and secretions fermenting in the folds of flesh. To Margarita he was an unwanted guest. He had to show her that he understood, that it pained him to interrupt their life. It hadn't helped her resentment of him, he supposed, that his thwarted attempt at escape had taken place on her watch. He wondered if he hadn't deliberately chosen the night of her watch, the way a wolf singles out the weak member of the herd.

Damn, his legs were itchy. He'd have to make up some story about why he was delayed, why he hadn't phoned, but there'd be plenty of time for that while he was driving back to the mainland. He had to escape, report his recommendations regarding the property. They were going to be relocated, whether they liked it or not.

Ignatius had a particular degree of dedication to this project. It was he who had come across details of the forgotten monastery in among the files and papers. It was he who had suggested selling, subject to inspection and suitability. The monastery was too remote to be turned into a school or hospital. It was Ignatius who hit upon the idea of an exclusive resort, who saw remoteness as its biggest drawcard. A few companies were already offering such places. Refurbished castles in areas away from the public gaze, staffed with the best chefs. Pheasant and woodcock on the menu, the freshest seafood. Seaweed-fed lamb.

He could see it now. A runway on the mainland for private jets, a permanent causeway that didn't depend on the tide. Away from it all, the location its own security. Ideal for sensitive meetings, political and commercial. Preliminary talks concerning the reunification of East and West Germany had been held in such a place. The Bishop loved the idea when Ignatius told him. "Negotiations over a couple of bottles of Courvoisier, walking up grouse to clench the deal, a round of golf. It has potential, Ignatius."

How could his legs be so itchy? Perhaps he was getting sores, cankers. He knew that once sold he would have no official role to play in the development of the site but he liked to think about it. God knows, he had plenty of time to think now. Perhaps they would take some of his suggestions on board.

He could see himself brokering, negotiating with prospective buyers. Connoisseur Resorts, that was his first choice. The sale of this monastery was his project and he would see it through to the end. Perhaps he could convince them to keep him on as some sort of advisor. First, he had to get this plaster off and his hands untied.

Someone was in the room, he could feel it.

"Problems?" The Mother Superior.

Ignatius stopped his thoughts right there. He was prickling all over. Even though the hairs were still short he felt them standing on end, his follicles reacting, putting his body on alert. Was she a mind-reader? He could make out the shape of her now. The dull light etched her features like a woodcarving, hollowing out the eye sockets.

"Problems?"

"Thumping."

"Oh," he said, realizing. What big ears you have, Grandmama. "My legs are very itchy." Then he had a better idea. "I may have an infection under there." She looked at him, her eyes like owls. "Perhaps a doctor should take a look," he suggested innocently. She remained silent, as if listening for something, then left as quietly as she had come.

Now his legs were really itchy, he imagined sweat caught down there, fermenting. It would drive him mad if he kept thinking about it. The third nun. Carla. She turned and whirled in his imagination, temptress, idiot, wild thing, child in a middle-aged body. A voice so sweet that if he closed his eyes he saw visions of angels. Yet she would forever be associated with his night of ultimate debasement.

But that was finished with. He was indoors now and lying on a bed. How quickly a roof and a bed changes the beast into a man again. A man who, instead of lying helpless with the weight of his despair upon him, was now riding on top of it, plotting and planning. It was a dream, all that, he told himself, a nightmare brought on by hunger and despair. His beastly nature had risen and used his eloquent tongue to speak its piece. He always imagined the Devil as having an eloquent tongue. No horns or tail, the Devil went about as an urbane man with well-shaped eyebrows and a flash of gold tooth.

Or perhaps when it suited, the Devil slipped into the body of a teasing, tempting woman. In his mind he saw her, looking out at him from between her fingers. She was certainly the shapeliest of the three. He imagined the outlines beneath all that wool. Then another detail. He flicked it out of his mind but it swam back in again. The feet. Horny and hoofy they were, like the others, but between Carla's toes grew curious little webs.

The eye of God is in the grass, round and perfect, smooth as the surface of jelly. It is a dark-brown eye, with a black center. A black circular aperture which allows light to enter. Like glass. "The light of the body is the eye: if therefore thine eye be single, thy whole body shall be full of light."

When Carla looks up at the sky this hole gets very, very tiny. But still the light floods in. So hungry is her eye for equilibrium, for some darkness in that white shining that it compensates by producing blinks of black suns.

Right now Carla is lying belly down, head on her outstretched arm, and her God eye is close to the ground, the line of vision crisscrossed with spokes of grass. She focuses on a single blade, the ridges of fiber along its length, its tip a slightly paler shade of green. And hanging deliciously, pregnantly, pendulously from it a drop of water. Soft jelly egg. It is striated with curves of green, the one blade having become many. Beneath her body thousands of blades are flattening themselves into the earth, the minuscule creatures that dwell in the grass emitting fear-smelling panic.

She reaches her finger out to the sac of water, feels the slight coolness as it makes contact, then slowly, ever slowly, draws her finger away, the water adhering to it, changing shape, making a bridge between blade and finger. Just a fraction more. Then it happens. Plop. She never sees the exact instant when it divides and becomes two, it always happens in a blink. Now there is one drop on her finger and one on the blade. She flicks the water away and mates the tip of her finger with the tip of the blade. Feels its little tickle. Sweet young grass, the sort the sheep love best. There is other grass whose blade can quickly cut you.

"Blade?" repeated Carla when she first heard the word describe grass. "Like knives?"

"Yes, my child," replied Sister Cook, her forearms dusted with flour, a little dab on her cheek.

"Why?"

"It just is," sighed Sister Cook. "Run along and play."

Carla ran along and played. Into the grass where the big clumps were. She pulled off a piece of grass and tried to cut her hair with it but it didn't work. "Cut," she said crossly, reminding it of its function. She tried it on a beetle, she tried on a worm. "Cut, blade, cut." But it wouldn't. "Naughty, blade, naughty," she said, hitting it. Then the miraculous happened. Her fingers somehow caught the blades of grass and in the upsweep from her hitting she found they had sliced very sharply, very neatly. Lines of blood welled out and slowly trickled down. So bright, so red! It had not hurt at all. She brought her fingers up and poked her tongue out to lick at the blood, its full meaty taste.

She ran back to the kitchen. "Blade, Sister Cook, blade." Holding up her hand in triumph, eyes shining brightly.

Sister Cook had just put the last batch of bread in the oven and was drinking water from a mug. She looked with alarm at the little girl offering up her dripping fingers. Then she relaxed. A couple of minor cuts. The child hardly seemed distressed by it. "You should be more careful," she said, hands crossed in front of her, looking a long way down her nose at Carla. Then softening, "Why don't you come back after Sext, there'll be some rolls to take out of the oven, all hot and crusty."

"But if thine eye is evil, thy whole body shall be full of darkness." The Bible is also flattening the blades of grass down to the earth. Carla likes the way when the Bible is open, a tunnel appears between the spine and where all the pages are stitched together. When she puts her finger into this space it feels cozy and snug, fits just like the finger of a glove. She also likes the smell of the print and the way when you hold one page up to the light you can see the words on the other side. Words backwards.

Sometimes Carla likes to read like this, through the page with the light shining on the words on the back. She only does this when she is alone with God, she thinks her sisters would frown if they knew. It might be the way the Devil reads the Bible. "Behold, I send you forth as sheep in the midst of wolves: be ye therefore wise as serpents, and harmless as doves. But beware of men: for they will deliver you up to the councils and they will scourge you in their synagogues."

He smiled at her today, while they were eating their silent breakfast, when he brought his tethered hands up to drink his tea. His teeth were very white in his face, his cheeks sucked in. They turned into crinkles when he smiled.

He had scourged her in the holding pen where she had gone full of longing and empty of sleep. He couldn't sleep either. He was alone and cold. She had started to hold him and tell him a little story to send him off to sleep, a story about his picture people, but wrath had rained out of his mouth and words as burning as dragon breath.

In the dew-moist grass with the twittering birds and God's light shining all around, she no longer feels the fire in her face. It is something that happened a long time ago, on the other side of sleep.

Red and yellow, black and white, all are precious in His sight. He was a black-and-white one. His lovely white merman tail was getting dirty and his body was sprouting black. As Carla had drunk her breakfast tea she looked at each and every one of those hairs.

Once, some time ago, they had found a little hedgehog on the kitchen step. The sisters wanted to call it Carla because it had been put on the step by God. "Just like you," they said. But Carla's little brow had furrowed in consternation. She liked the creature well enough but she did not want to share her name with it. She thought she might have to share her soul with it as well, that it would take it and bury it in the ground. She would never get it back from such a prickly thing. But the hedgehog had disappeared before she could tame it and it never did get a proper name.

Carla felt guilty, it was mean not letting it have her name. The hedgehog was unbaptized and could never go to Heaven. Instead, the poor little thing floated around in Limbo with the curled-up dead babies.

Carla thought about when she put her hands around his for the knitting. He'd done a secret to Margarita to make her scurry away but he hadn't done it to Carla. He'd let Carla show him. He would let her tame him too. She would start with the hairs. She moved a little way toward him. Just a tiny tiny way, you wouldn't even notice. Then a bit more. She put her hand out and touched them. Oh, prickly little quills just like the hedgehog. He didn't flinch or anything. He smiled. She wanted to touch more but she put her hand back in her lap. You have to do taming slowly.

Carla's outstretched hand plucked at a piece of grass and pulled it up by the roots. White roots sliding out of the sweet black soil. She dragged herself along and peered down into the chute left behind. The eye of God sees everything. She had uprooted a giant tree, it squeaked and sighed on releasing its hold on the earth. It would be like an earthquake down there, every living thing on the alert. Soil mites, armored hippopotamuses, gigantic ants with gigantic heads, long-haired antennae scanning for danger.

Carla had her eye over the hole, looking right down into the dark soil world. An ant crawled out. Carla could easily imagine the world of an ant. The forests of grass loaded with water bombs ready to drop. She banged her hand on the ground. Ants loved it when she did this. All the little soil mites getting disoriented and moving toward the surface. A big breakfast for ants. If a single ant comes across such a feast, she doesn't chomp away and eat all of it herself. Like Carla, the ant is part of a community. The ant has a good mouthful, then lowers her hindquarters and makes a smell trail to bring the other ants to the breakfast table.

Carla watched the ant approaching the immense mountain range of her outstretched hand. The other hand was pressing the seashell to her ear. Listening to its faraway sound, she recognized a pattern in it, notes held and repeated like prayer or lamb song. Perhaps it was the murmuring of souls in the Sea of Forgetfulness. She let the music wheel through her without holding onto any of it.

She pulled out another blade of grass and this time an earthworm sprung to life. She felt its slippery jelly body as it wriggled and twisted into impossible contorts. Carla had tried to do this herself but she couldn't loop her body the way the naked wet earthworm could. The earthworm burrowed down into the moist rich earth, avoiding the drying sun that would bake its body to the consistency of leather.

The little white worm in his rich dark home reminded Carla of Baby Moses in the bulrushes. Unlike the worm that wriggles and loops in her hand, trying to jump back into the earth, Baby Moses worm grew strong and thick as if it had a bone inside it. Carla would like to see that again. Miraculous. She would have to do more taming first. She tingled with the pleasure of it, of seeing something change before her very eyes. Carla was a bit disappointed to find that when she dug into the earth, it was much the same as it appeared on the surface. Dense with itself. She would like to scratch the surface and find a cavern. She would like the earth to be an egg, a smooth dry surface with a wet slippery surprise inside.

She stirred her finger around in the loose soil where the worm went. Once in her excavations she did find something. It was dark and folded. At first it looked like a thickening of the earth. But she was able to pull it up and open it out. It made a dull tearing sound. It was a gray blanket. In parts it was so frail that it crumbled into the soil at her touch. She found it near the bushes and it was very odd to be there. When she opened it up there was less soil and more blanket, the inside of it protected by folds. It was stained and discolored a darker rusty tone. Blood.

She rolled over, bored with the earth, and lay with her eyes closed listening to the shell. It had become her favorite thing and she carried it everywhere. Not only did it make sound but Carla could use it as a cutter, like the one Sister Cook had to make pastry shapes. One Easter, Sister Cook made little men out of the dough. Carla put raisins for their eyes and three down their front for buttons. They baked the little men in the oven and on Easter Sunday the nuns all ate them.

She pressed the shell into her arm to make intersecting curves, put it back to her ear and watched the marks fade away.

Cla . . . cla . . . cla . . . cla . . . cla . . . A different sound in her ear now. Louder and louder it gets till she can hear it even in the ear without the shell. Something creeps over the sun. She opens her eyes and stares straight at it.

He heard it coming long before he saw it. He was sitting in the courtyard, tail propped up, hands tethered. His offer to help with the chores had gone unheeded.

The three nuns had spent the morning picking up sheep droppings in the courtyard, then Carla went off to gather them from farther afield. Margarita and Iphigenia were now in the chapel. He had grown used to the smell of the droppings, it was not like dog or human feces, there was something fresh and earthy about it. He idly wondered whether the feces of vegetarians smelled fresh like this. It must have rained lightly during the night because the grass was wet and the sheep poo soft and slippery.

If it had been him, he would have waited for a dry day when it was easier to handle. But they said it was better for the garden this way. Seep into the soil better wet. They would lay it on, let it settle before planting. They had seed potatoes from last year. The man had offered to help with the digging. "Digging on Digging Day," they said.

Ignatius presumed that the feces he deposited in the pot

eventually ended up being mixed in with the sheep feces. Not that he had contributed a great deal during his stay so far. His body had reacted to its extreme stress with constipation, in an attempt to hold everything in and not disintegrate. He looked at the mounting pile in the holding pen. He felt much more at ease dwelling on sheep droppings than his own.

Every so often they would come out of the chapel, empty their front pockets onto the pile, and go back in again. He sat with his eyes closed, absorbing the sun, straining to overhear any conversation emanating from the chapel, especially conversation that pertained to him and his predicament. They remained taciturn as ever. He heard the occasional echoing bleat, the scraping against stone, an occasional grunt from the nuns as they bent over or straightened themselves up.

The noise began as a faint mechanical ripple in his field of hearing, then it solidified. Cla . . . cla . . . cla . . . cla . . . cla . . . His heart leapt in his chest, his eyes sprung open, and there it was. A small black speck in the sky wheeling closer and closer. They were coming for him. Oh yes, this was it. The island wasn't under a regular flight path, he'd seen nothing but birds in the sky all the time he'd been here. They had to be coming for him. He wanted to shout, wave a big colored flag, send up a flare. I'm here, I'm here. He could hardly contain himself.

But of course he wasn't the only one who had heard the approaching rumble. The poo-gatherers were in the courtyard now and looking into the sky. Margarita gave the man a long swipe with her eyes as if he were personally responsible for the disturbance. And of course he was, oh joy, he was.

Although his heart was leaping skyward, although his mind was already up there with the chopper, airlifted to safety, arms and legs free and all his troubles down here minuscule and toy-like, nothing on the ground had changed. He was in the same position in which the nuns had left him. He could not pick up anything and wave it, he could not move. And what was the point of calling out? They'd never hear him.

The chopper was still far away but circling closer. Iphigenia had her hand up, shading her eyes from the sun, straining to see. Her nose was twitching like a rabbit's. Margarita was trying to calm the sheep who were baaing nervously.

"The chapel," Iphigenia announced decisively.

They carried him into the chapel and plopped him down in front of St. Anne.

"Sheep."

While Margarita started the lamb chant to herd the sheep into the chapel, Iphigenia hid the red glow of fire under a bucket.

"Carla." Iphigenia and Margarita looked frantically around for her. "Carla."

Their call was answered by feet pounding into the courtyard. Carla looked wildly at Iphigenia and Margarita, her finger jabbing the sky. The three scurried into the chapel as if it was an air-raid shelter.

The helicopter was overhead now and very loud. They could feel the floor vibrating. A piece of tile shook loose and dropped, breaking its fall on the head of St. Anne. There was a collective gasp and everyone started praying. "Deliver us."

"Deliver us, oh deliver us," prayed Ignatius earnestly.

Every so often the chopper came into view in the circle of sky. The sheep bleated restlessly while the humans, hands together in prayer, watched the machine pass in and out of view.

"Lord, make it land," prayed Ignatius, "make it land. Come and have a closer look." He could think of plenty of places for it to land, the fields, the courtyard even. Were there signs of life outside? Smoke from the fire, had they seen Carla running, the sheep being rounded up? What a pity there were no brightly colored hanks of wool hanging out to dry. Ignatius saw it the way it would look from the sky. A circle of brambles, monastery ruins, nothing they wouldn't have known about already. It would look abandoned, deserted.

Eventually the helicopter stopped appearing through the holes in the roof and soon the sound started to fade. He was shuddering with frustration. Come back, come back. God had offered His hand but Ignatius couldn't grab hold of it. Just out of reach.

The car! That's what they'd be looking for! The car wedged in the rocks. "Oh please God, let them find the car. Let them land and have a closer look. Let them know I came this far. Make them look for me." His eyes were tightly shut now and he was sniffing in gulps of air. He would not let them see him cry, he would not let them see how much he wanted salvation.

It was fainter and fainter. It had descended. They were landing on the beach. They were examining the car. They would see that the car hadn't simply been abandoned, that things were missing. They would assume he had gone somewhere and start looking for him on foot. First the abandoned houses near the beach, around the rocks. The nuns must have left tracks the night they went out. Even though it had rained, there must be some sign. They would assume he'd made his way to the monastery, they would come back, they would find a way in. That's what he would do, he would land, he would go over every inch of the place, pull it apart stone by stone looking for himself.

It had been a long time since the helicopter had faded into nothing and still the little gathering remained in the chapel, waiting for the all clear. No one spoke, even the lambs had stopped bleating, hushed into the atmosphere of silence. The nuns were kneeling in the attitude of prayer and the fishtailed man was propped up against the statue. He looked up at the grandmother of the Lord. If it hadn't been for her the tile would have hit him on the head. One thing he could be thankful for.

Bang! They all jumped. There was a loud rolling rattle of metal on the flagstones. The sheep ran hither and thither, bumping into each other, while the nuns crossed their hands over their hearts. Ignatius held his breath, hoping against hope that it had something to do with the helicopter.

Iphigenia relaxed, let out a little laugh of relief. "Bucket." There was a collective expulsion of air, a shifting of weight, an easing of the suspension in the chapel. They waited a bit but all they could hear outside were the birds twittering.

"Cla . . ." A shy cautious attempt. Carla glanced around the chapel, then up at the circle of sky. She stood up. "Cla . . ." She spread out her arms and turned, taking little shuffling steps. "Cla . . . cla . . . cla . . . cla . . . cla . . ." Bolder and bolder.

Iphigenia stood at the doorway. All was calm. She went out into the courtyard, lifted her face to the sun, and turned around, a slow version of Carla. The intrusion was gone. She checked for strangeness, something they might have left behind, the smell of more men, but all she got was a slight whiff of the fuel that had drifted down. That and the rich heady mixture of fear and relief from the chapel.

They had surrounded themselves with a mist of prayer so that the helicopter wouldn't find them. It had gone now and they were safe. The Agnes sisters started to file out of the chapel to return to their task of grazing. Iphigenia had not expected a helicopter. If they were to come, she had expected it would be the way he had come—by car. Such an extraordinary sight. Like a big dragonfly.

She had seen a helicopter only once before. The wind of it made the grass go flat. She and Grandmother had been playing cards, Iphigenia fixing up the ones that Grandmother's wobbling hand was shifting out of place. Grandmother looked through the lace-bordered windows, her head shaking as if already she disapproved. "Taylor," she commanded, "ask him what the blazes he thinks he's doing."

"Yes, Madam," said Taylor.

She picked up a card from the pile on the green baize table, knocking the rest of them askew again. It was the card she wanted. "Gin," she announced, spilling her hand down in front of her.

But Iphigenia had lost interest in the cards and had climbed up on the window seat. A man was coming toward the house. He had a white scarf around his neck, the tail of which hung over his shoulder, and glass eyes on his forehead bulging like a fly's.

"What in blazes do you think you're doing?" Taylor asked from the portico.

Before Iphigenia's very eyes a remarkable thing happened. He shed his skin like a snake. Took off his leather jacket and goggly eyes and underneath was a gentleman wearing a dinner jacket and a black bow tie. A little white collar stood up from it. He fished a card out of a pocket. "Reginald Ketteridge. Here for Nancy's bash." He showed Taylor the invitation.

"He's lost," said Grandmother. "It's the Fuller girl's engagement do. Make tea."

Taylor brought the gentleman in. At Grandmother's request, he sat down. Grandmother was at the same time exasperated at his foolishness for getting lost and blasé, as if young men in helicopters dropped in all the time.

"You're going to be late," she informed him, "you had better telephone. Taylor?"

Iphigenia watched Taylor dial the number and inform the Fullers that one of their guests, a lost one, wished to speak to them. The phone was cream and gold and on the dial was a cameo of a lady who turned catherine wheels when you dialed a number. Iphigenia loved the sound the phone made when you replaced the receiver. She did this over and over again, just to hear the ding. Until Taylor warned her off. "The telephone is not a toy," she said, pushing "not" and "toy" out in front of the other words.

Taylor handed the phone to the gentleman. "Reginald Ketteridge," he said into it, smoothing his slick hair behind his ear, putting his hand in his pocket, turning his back to carry on the conversation.

Reginald Ketteridge's helicopter was gray with a red nose. The helicopter that had intruded into the monastery sky was black and shiny, as was the man's car. Iphigenia wondered if shiny and black were the way of all machinery in the world now.

They wouldn't find it, the car. It was too far under the water.

And up here? What would they see from the sky? No nuns, no sheep, no smoke. No man. Just brambles and crumbling buildings. Ruins. Rocks and crumbling statues. They were living in ruins, like the seals in the village.

The last lamb bleated out of the chapel, then Margarita appeared at the door. It had been an ordeal. She picked up the bucket. Ruined. She walked past Iphigenia without saying a word.

Iphigenia attended to the fire. From a helicopter, the monastery might look like an abandoned ruin but it was their home. This was consecrated ground. She would never let it become a holiday resort. Never.

No story, no knitting. They had put him to bed and gone off to huddle. Hubble bubble, toil and trouble, today's most unusual occurrence was certainly one to stir the cauldron.

Ignatius was done with feeling disappointed, he couldn't afford to let his spirit fade away. Yes! The world outside the brambles still existed and had come looking for him. If he'd been able to he would have rubbed his hands together with glee. He had to focus on this rather than the fact that they had not found him. They'd see the car. They'd come back with a ground crew. Hope surrounded him like a halo.

He congratulated himself on not shouting out, a reflex action that would have provided immediate relief but remained ultimately futile. At the time he was motivated by pride, despite the anguish he felt at seeing his chance slip away. But now he saw the cunning of it.

"He behaved as we did," argued Iphigenia. Discussion had been a long time absent from their lives, it came slow and without the finesse and eloquence of stories. They were unpracticed. There had never been anything to discuss, no ideas, nothing new to deal with. Once they had taken vows their lives were preordained, mapped out before them. Idle chat was an indulgence. It is in contemplative silence that one communes with the Lord.

Sometimes a phrase came out already formed, surprising them, as if it had been there all the time like an old piece of machinery that still worked, just needed a hand to give the wheel a bit of a turn. Other times they groped around, sorting through words as if they were pieces of a puzzle higgledy-piggledy in a box, trying out pieces to see if they fitted.

Margarita was no more astonished by the appearance of the helicopter than she had been by Iphigenia's first announcement that they had a visitor. Even when the tile dropped on St. Anne's head she was hardly surprised. She had already reached the limit of her astonishment, used it all up. As long as he was here nasty things would happen. The tile wasn't the only thing. Bits and pieces of their life were dropping down all around them.

"I told you he would bring others." Why weren't they knitting tonight? Margarita would have liked some knitting to burrow into, one furious stitch after the other.

"They have come and gone. No harm has been done."

No harm done? Was Iphigenia blind? Had that cold affected her judgment as well as her smell? The thorn so sharp in Margarita's side had obviously found a more accommodating home in Iphigenia's.

"They did not find him, they will keep looking."

"Perhaps, but not here. There are many places he could have gotten lost on the way. An accident."

Indeed, an accident. A very good idea.

They were nuns. It was not right for him to be living in their midst, living as one of them. It was not the same as when Carla had come to them. There had been discussion then, when Margarita found the bundle on the doorstep. What should they do with the foundling? Though she was a gift from God, was it fitting that she be brought up in the harsh monastic life? They prayed over her, they discussed. And they decided to keep her till someone came to claim her. It wasn't till this decision was made and they unwrapped her from her swaddling that they found the webs between her tiny toes. No one would be coming to claim the child. There were legends on the island about selkies, about the wild dark mer people, with hair like trailing seaweed. Better that she wear the Church around her neck like an amulet.

It was one thing to take in a little baby, it was another to take in a grown man. The candles burned steadily. An insect landed and hissed in the wax. Iphigenia saw the fact that he didn't signal his presence to the helicopter as proof that they were persuading him. Margarita thought he was more cunning than that. Iphigenia wanted to give him back his legs.

"If you give him legs he will run," said Margarita.

"We must trust in the Lord."

They had trusted in the Lord before. He had not prevented him from trying to escape. On her watch.

"But He did prevent him from succeeding."

Margarita sat staring at the shadows cast by the candles.

"*Caritas*," Iphigenia appealed in her softest voice. Iphigenia had not been all that keen on putting him into a cast, yet she saw the necessity of properly securing him. It had been Margarita's idea to use the plaster. They had gotten plaster, among other supplies, after the bonesetter incident. Even after all this time and dear Assumpta long dead, Iphigenia still carried the burden of her sister's limp.

"Let us not pass judgment. The time it takes to make him a garment. Give him this. A garment of our design, with his hair knitted into it. A garment to make him ours. If he has caused no trouble by the time the garment is ready, we give him back his legs."

"And if he causes trouble?"

Iphigenia demurred, the bow of her head almost imperceptible. Then it would be Margarita who could decide.

He woke with a start. There was a thickness in the darkness around his bed.

"What do you want?" he demanded, trying to keep the intrusion at bay till he shook the remaining sleep off him and assessed the situation. His heart was thumping and he could feel his forehead crawling with sweat. She was here again. The darkness remained impassive.

"Soon," she said. "Soon the bandages will come off."

She offered this news and waited for him to take it. As his eyes grew accustomed to the darkness, he could see the silhouette of her, like an outcrop of rock he remembered from a childhood holiday. The family had rented a lonely cottage on a headland. Nearby, standing stones jutted out of the sea. They were called the Apostles or the Disciples, he couldn't remember which. But he remembered being woken by the wind knocking against the window and when he had gathered up the courage to investigate he saw a sight he was not prepared for. The Apostles had come to life, silhouetted against the fast-moving sea, backed by moonlight, casting vast shadows. It was as if he had seen something he shouldn't have seen. And now he knew why his parents hushed him at night and told him to go to sleep. Because the night belonged to other creatures.

It was Iphigenia who stood at the window, the slice of moon casting her long shadow over him. "Soon?" he repeated. A little hope, a little inquiry for more information, wary of showing a surfeit that might reverse the decision. Because obviously a decision had been made.

"When the garment is finished."

"A day or so? A week?" he suggested.

She stood implacably by the window.

"When the garment is finished," she repeated.

There was a suspension, as if she was about to say something else, a holding of breath in her throat. He heard it release and she seemed to deflate. She eased herself out of the room, the darkness rolling in like fog to fill the space she'd left behind.

Doing and undoing. Penelope and her embroidery. The work of the day undone at night. Margarita had agreed with her voice but not with her heart. That would take longer. It was not so bad during the day, she had chores, communal prayers to keep her mind occupied. The Light filled the courtyard. But at night. Margarita held the Bible to her, afraid to extinguish the candle. The Beast lurked. She had conjured him up but she could not make him disappear. He was there in the darkness, thickening, taking on substance.

The Holy Bible. She would like to wrap herself in it, for its words to become her flesh. To feel their strength, their solace. Eternal and unchanging.

Caritas. Margarita held the candle up closer, turning the page to the somber light. "Charity suffereth long, and is kind; charity envieth not; charity vaunteth not itself, is not puffed up. Doth not behave unseemly, seeketh not her own, is not easily provoked, thinketh no evil. And now abideth faith, hope, and charity, these three; but the greatest of these is charity."

She would try. Given enough time he would reveal his true nature. Then Iphigenia would see that some beasts do not turn into men and an accident is the only way.

"Though your sins be as scarlet, they shall be as white as snow; though they be red like crimson, they shall be as wool . . . if ye refuse and rebel, ye shall be devoured with the sword; for the mouth of the Lord hath spoken it . . . Ah, I will ease me of my adversaries, and avenge me of mine enemies . . . And the destruction of the transgressors and of the sinners shall be together, and they that forsake the Lord shall be consumed."

Margarita lay with her hand on Isaiah, the candle lighting but a small circle in the musty darkness. It was hard to stay vigilant every night, she could feel herself descending into sleep. A dark plain spread out in front of her, a desert with the distant bumps of sand dunes. She descended farther, warm and drowsy. A rider appeared, a shifting spot before her eyes, closer and closer he came like a ball of wind. She could smell the blistering sand flurrying up from his steed. She was not afraid, she would sink deeper into the sand and avoid the hooves as he rode over her. The farther she sank, the hotter it got.

Margarita's eyes sprang open as she smelled it and felt it. The candle was overturned, the Bible burning. Instinctively she brought her hand down on it, sending smoke and black papery ash into the air. She coughed and spluttered, righted the candle. It was still alight.

When she had recovered she inspected the damage. There was a circle burned in the middle of one page. The page underneath was scorched but the words were still there. Only the passage about vengeance had been burned away. This verily was a sign from God. A sign that vengeance would blacken her soul if she fed the flame.

Despite the flare of danger, despite the fact that the bed could have become her funeral pyre, Margarita felt relieved. The Lord had shown her the way. Even though vengeance might flare up inside her she must be charitable, she must be like St. Joan and endure the flame, let the Lord lift her spirit out of it. If she was to be the sword of the Lord she was to be the sword of Christian love and charity, a sword tempered by the fire of vengeance.

She would spend the rest of the night prostrate on the floor, hardening her resolve. Margarita's eyes burned brightly in her face, her cheeks flushed. She felt the striving for purity, for tempering the body into a vessel of goodness, that she had felt as a young nun. She prostrated herself. She repeated and repeated the words of charity, humbled herself before the Lord.

She was still prostrate when first light awoke her, a trail of saliva on the floor. She lay there, afraid to put her body through the moves necessary to stand up, unwilling to pass yet again through the gauntlet of pain. She heard the cry of the first birds. The darkness lifted. It was Prime. She had to go to the chapel and pray. She would pray with her sisters, do her chores, contemplate the Light of the Lord. She would do her best to ignore the visitor.

She wiped her chin and prepared to stand up. It was every bit as painful as she expected it to be.

It was between Nones and Vespers. Carla was off somewhere, Margarita was in the chapel praying. She seemed to pray a lot lately. Iphigenia was walking around the cloisters, in and out of the yellow afternoon.

This had been a religious house for centuries; it had an everlasting life unbound by temporality. There was a round of days and nights, light and dark, sun and moon. They had lost track of the secular days, the months, even what decade it was. There was a round of years marked by holy days, by Easter and Christmas. Easter was the first full moon after the spring equinox, Christmas in the low ebb of winter solstice, Shearing Day when the new wool pushed the old wool out. They went to chapel and chanted the canonical hours in the same way they went to sleep. Taking in the play of light, the movement of the sun across the sky, the moon, changes in temperature, moisture, the air on their skin. Instinctively knowing when it was time.

She stepped out into the courtyard. Iphigenia could hear the steady murmur of Margarita's prayers, the occasional ovine bleat. Though it was a round of days not everything came round again. Iphigenia's bleeding had stopped and never returned. Her sight had dimmed and her smell increased. The Agnes sisters would never return in human form. Tiles fell down but did not fly up to the roof again. And some days she felt better than others.

Now they had a priest who didn't come and go but stayed. Iphigenia knew that Margarita resented the priest in their midst but it was not the first time that both sexes lived together in a religious house. In the great double monasteries of medieval times lay brothers worked in the fields and priests ministered to the nuns. Such monasteries were ruled by abbesses. There were rich and powerful abbesses then, who owned lands, conferred with kings, sent knights into battle.

If they had an abbess now, what would she do? Would she gather everyone up and hide in the chapel? Or would she have been prepared for the intruder and stood her ground? Would she have said, "Rubbish, young man. If your Bishop thinks he can turn this monastery into some kind of holiday hotel he has another think coming."

Perhaps they needed more than prayers and a persuading garment.

Iphigenia cast her mind back to their first encounter with the priest. At the time they had been shocked, taken aback by his invocation of the Devil. "Had the Devil's own job locating it." But now Iphigenia remembered the rest of what he said. "Actually, I was led to believe that the property was uninhabited." He had come assuming there was no one here. But then he talked about the retirement home. That didn't come from the Bishop, he had made that up himself. Being inhabited, by a religious community, must make a difference.

Would the abbess have been able to stop it merely with the tone of her voice or were there other ways? The sisters knew only prayer and chores and contemplation of the Lord. But the abbess knew other things, rules and regulations, duties and privileges. Consecrated ground had to be deconsecrated. There had to be a . . . procedure.

For the first time in many years Iphigenia found herself standing outside the door to the abbess's office. Even now, long after the last abbess had died, none of them ever came to this part of the monastery. The abbess's room, where they'd first put the priest, was different. In her cell the abbess was a nun, like the rest of them. But in the office she discussed the affairs of the monastery with the outside world, with priests and Church dignitaries. This was the place where rules and regulations were made. And to which nuns came to be admonished when those rules were broken. It was to this room that Iphigenia was summoned when she returned without the bonesetter.

Iphigenia stood looking at the grain in the timber, reluctant to put her hand to it. It was to such a door that Briar Rose had come. Did she too hesitate before crossing the threshold? Iphigenia pushed the door.

The entire room was furred in dust, like an old gray mouse, and there were spider webs everywhere. Hanging from the ceiling, the shelves, the abbess's desk. The Blessed Virgin in the alcove had been spun into a cocoon.

The room had no smell. Everything was still, suspended, covered in a shroud of sleep. No leaves rustled, nothing scurried away at the opening of the door. Iphigenia stepped in, dust flurrying up into her nose even though she trod cautiously. She made her way along the wall of books, peering at the titles. So many books, their ribbed spines identical. Iphigenia remembered staring at that wall of books staunch and unmoving while the abbess circled, question after question, coming round to the same ones, time after time. "Was it altogether necessary to go over to the mainland? What would your grandmother say? What would the Bishop say? And what, Sister Iphigenia, would God say?" And then the silence when the questioning finished. But it was not the end.

Iphigenia lifted the veil of cobweb and pulled a tome from the shelf, *Canon Law Governing Communities of Sisters.* Mustiness escaped like a moth. She read:

> In what manner may a religious institute, papal or diocesan, be suppressed or become extinct?
>
> (1) by the egress of all its members
> (2) by the death of all its members
> (3) by uniting with another religious institute
> (4) by act of legitimate authority.
>
> If the suppression is on account of the egress or death of all its members, one hundred years must pass after the egress or death of the last of its members before the suppression becomes a legal fact. Suppression by union with another religious institute or by act of legitimate authority can be brought about only by the Holy See.

Not every word was comprehensible to Iphigenia but she understood the solemn and irrevocable tone. Extinction. As if they were animals who had been hunted or had died off because the world had changed and they hadn't changed with it. But they were not dead. Here in the rocks and stones of the monastery was eternal life. The vows they had taken were forever and timeless.

The community had not died nor joined with another religious institute, nor did they intend to do so. Egress. It sounded like a bird. They had gone out, but only for one day. What was an act of legitimate authority?

She turned a page, holding the book steady. Warmed by her hand its faint leather smell began to come through.

What is to be done with the property of a suppressed institute?

> All temporal goods, both movable and immovable, belonging to a religious institute are Church property. Therefore in case of suppression of an institute its property may not be divided among its members; nor may the members divert it to other pious or charitable works, even though they should have the consent of the Bishop of the diocese to do so. Neither may the Bishop claim it or any part thereof for his diocese; but the entire property is subject to the disposition of the Holy See.

What did this mean? What would happen to the Blessed Virgin and the stained-glass saints? They couldn't be diverted and they certainly couldn't stay in a holiday resort. The words were like a secret code. Iphigenia felt like a young child again, hearing the words her grandmother used when the solicitor came to visit.

The solicitor sat in the study with his back upright and his briefcase on his lap, as if he was afraid to put it down anywhere. Taylor would often be in the room, Grandmother's friend and confidante as well as her housekeeper. When the solicitor was there it reminded Iphigenia of the grown-up games of bridge where special words were used. Grandmother used special words with the solicitor—settlement, estate, my affairs, titles, deeds. Property. That was one of Grandmother's words too. She remembered Grandmother telling the solicitor about the Fullers, who bought some property, a wedding gift for Nancy, only to find that the sharefarmers adjacent were driving their horse and cart right through the middle of it. Well, the Fullers went to see them, told them they were trespassing. And the sharefarmers told the Fullers they had right of carriageway. They had sought legal advice. Can you imagine, Mr. Banks!

Banks. That was the solicitor's name. "You can always bank on Mr. Banks," said Grandmother as she sliced open an envelope with the carved ivory letter-opener. Iphigenia remembered the beautiful copperplate letterhead on the solicitor's correspondence. Iphigenia would say this word under her breath, "correspondence," as if it had special powers. It was much more ponderous than "letter." She imagined old Mr. Banks was ponderous. Iphigenia was too young to remember old Mr. Banks but she did remember young Mr. Banks, his briefcase with the gold latches that snapped open and shut. He was a snappy kind of man, too, brisk and bright in his movements. Iphigenia imagined that the priest in their safekeeping would have a briefcase like that in the outside world. He would also use these heavy, weighty words.

"Mrs. Featheringale here. There is a matter I wish to discuss with you," Grandmother would say on the telephone. Then Mr. Banks would come. After his visit, Iphigenia played solicitors. She would get a case from the cupboard and sit at the table. "This correspondence requires your signature." Then snap open the case and take out imaginary correspondence. Once she persuaded Betty, the youngest of the Fuller girls, to be the solicitor but she didn't do it properly. When Betty snapped open the case she said, "It's full of forks."

"Hand me the correspondence," Iphigenia prompted.

"But we'll get into trouble. It's your grandmother's best cutlery."

"She lets me. Hand me the correspondence." But Betty wasn't keen. At the Fuller house they were never allowed to play with grown-up things, they had to play either in Betty's room or out in the garden.

But at Grandmother's, Iphigenia could wander in and out at will. Because Iphigenia was Grandmother's pet, like white fluffy Puddles who died of old age. She thought dying of old age must take a long time but it didn't. One day Puddles was dead. Iphigenia had seen foxes and ducks that were dead. They had been killed by hunters and there was always blood on them. But Puddles just lay on the kitchen floor, extremely still.

"It is the hand of God," said Grandmother. "It is sad for us but God wants Puddles to be with Him now." Grandmother wiped her eyes with the edge of her lace handkerchief. Barney dug a hole with his big spade and his big boots and laid the body to rest.

For days afterward Iphigenia kept looking at the sky, looking all around her. Who would be next—Grandmother? She fretted and even wet the bed. She knew Taylor would scold but she couldn't help it.

At night she left the candle burning and tried not to fall asleep in case God was sneaking around in the dark. But she would fall asleep and then wake with a start. The candle would be out and Iphigenia swallowing blackness—what if God was coming for her? She wanted to run to Grandmother's room but was so frightened she could not even let out a scream for help.

Iphigenia's behavior did not go unnoticed in the household and Taylor proposed that they send for Dr. Foley. This scared Iphigenia even more because often when the doctor came people died. Grandmother said, "Nonsense, the child is just going through a phase."

Grandmother began to stay with Iphigenia at night and eventually Iphigenia told her what the matter was. Grandmother was quiet for a while, the hint of a smile settling into the corners of her mouth. Then she reached her arms out and Iphigenia snuggled into her embrace, sinking into her lavender smell and soft papery skin.

"God was probably lonely and wanted Puddles for His pet. God won't be taking a crusty old lady like me, and He won't be taking you, not if I have anything to say about it," she said in her voice that meant business. She squeezed Iphigenia tighter to her, squashing the child's nose in the wool of her crocheted bedjacket, bouncing her wobbly chin on the top of Iphigenia's head. They said a prayer together.

In the morning Iphigenia was no longer afraid of God's invisible hand. Never ever again afraid of God. Because in her prayer she had told God that when she was old enough she would go and stay in His house. What she didn't tell God was that if she lived in His house she could keep an eye on Him and He wouldn't be able to sneak up unawares.

To seal the pact, she thought a small offering appropriate. She went to Grandmother's dressing room and pulled the fox fur from its hanger. It had a head on one end and paws on the other, and smelled of mothballs. It must have been a fox that had also died of old age because there was no blood.

In the misty morning she went to the shed and got out Barney's spade, careful not to disturb any of the other spick-

and-span tools. She thought about opening up Puddles's burying place—as God had already received one animal through that channel He might take another—but she was afraid of what she might see. She found a separate place and started digging the way Barney did, putting her foot on the spade and pushing down on it. It was a lot harder than it looked, she was even having trouble breaking through the grass. So she decided to bury the fox in the rose garden because the earth had already been dug over and the ground was softer. It took her a while but she managed. The hole didn't have to be as big as Puddles's because the fox had no bones or insides, just a shiny satin lining.

It was not till Christmas that anything was said about the disappearance of the fox and by then Iphigenia had forgotten all about it. "I can't imagine what's become of it," Grandmother said to Taylor. "I've probably left it somewhere and can't remember. Oh well, at least it's not the ocelot." And went on to other things.

Though nothing changed within these walls, the world was temporal and things changed. The books lining the wall of the abbess's office were not about adoration of the Sacred Heart but law pertaining to worldly aspects of religious life: administration, acquiring and disposal of property. Perhaps they were no longer valid, even if she could understand them. She could show the priest one of the books and demand to know what legitimate authority he had to come here and announce dissolution. But how would she know, with his self-interest, if he was telling the truth? She needed legal advice of her own.

Banks. It was Banks, something and something. Iphigenia tried to recall the letterhead glimpsed so long ago. Banks, then a longer name starting with . . . C. Something odd about the spelling, a group of letters in the middle that you didn't pronounce. She tried and tried to recall it but she was thinking too hard and it wasn't letting the name come. A name from so long ago needed to arrive at its leisure.

Perhaps she could write a letter to Banks, something and something. But how would it be delivered? And how would she get a reply? Perhaps make a journey into the world to look for them. But of course she couldn't leave the monastery, not now.

C. What were some names that started with C? Christopher, Cyril, Casimir, Catherine. Iphigenia could only think of saints. She was still trying too hard, pushing the name away.

She made her way to the abbess's cell and started browsing through the car relics again. *Negotiation Skills*. A big book with a picture on the cover of a lot of people sitting around a table talking. Women wearing the same sort of suits as men. Iphigenia flicked through it. Here was a whole new set of phrases: non-verbal alert, personal space, persuasive strategy, synergy, bottom lines, worst-case scenario, teleconferencing.

It was a whole new world, a whole new vocabulary. Iphigenia examined all the relics. When she came across the battery in its plastic casing her nose started quivering. Not all the relics were here, there was one that he brought himself, in his pocket. The telephone! There was no need to write a letter, no need to make a journey. All she had to do was place a telephone call. Banks, C . . . and . . . Collard. No, not quite. Her mind was circling around it now, she was quite close. She picked up a pencil and started writing on a piece of paper. The C first, as if she had found the end of the thread and all she had to do was to tweak it out of the tangle for the rest to unravel. Col . . . Collins.

No. Callaghan. No. But it was like this. Letters in the middle that you didn't pronounce. COLQUHOUN. Yes! This was it. Banks, Colquhoun and Andrews. The Andrews came quickly. ABC but not in that order. She saw the copperplate letterhead in her mind as clearly as if it were printed on paper. Iphigenia was filled with a rush of exhilaration. She didn't think about the fact that Banks, Colquhoun and Andrews were all probably dead, that the man's phone didn't work and she didn't even know where it was. At the moment her exhilaration was such that she could overcome any hurdle.

As he ate his dinner that night, Ignatius savored thoughts of his rescue. They had come looking, they would continue to look. It vindicated him that the Bishop knew his secretary hadn't just run off like Brother Terry. He wondered how widespread the search was, whether he was in the paper. "Priest Missing," no, "Bishop's Right-Hand Man Missing." "Hopes Fade in Search For Missing Priest." No, not that.

Though he wanted desperately to be found he did not relish the thought of being found in plaster, eating dinner with his hands tied together. Everyone would be concerned for a while, then the whispers and sniggering would start, he'd be the butt of presbytery jokes for weeks. He shoveled a piece of turnip into his mouth. There was an air of excitement at the dinner table, as if they were giving him a birthday party; his captors racing through the paltry meal, eager to get started on the new project.

Ignatius wondered what sort of garment they were concocting for him. He didn't care. As long as he could walk out of here in it. He could be out tomorrow if they just gave back his clerical clothes. Obviously that wasn't an option. He was on trial, some sort of test. "The time it takes to make the garment."

Dinner finished, they cleared off the table and went through the preliminary prayers and chants. His legs were itching like Hades. He had a terrible vision of his pale atrophied limbs crawling with maggots. So damned itchy, but he couldn't get down into the plaster. He scratched his stomach instead, reaping the benefit of his growing nails. He normally kept them short and clipped so he'd never noticed before how they curved like bird claws. The thumb and forefinger of his left hand seemed to be thickening, going brown. Probably a vitamin deficiency or a fungal infection.

Margarita was staring at him, making him feel self-conscious. What was wrong with her? It wasn't as if they had any qualms about scratching themselves.

He offered his knitting services. An excuse to get those hands free, to spirit away a needle to reach in and scratch. He might find a knitting needle useful in other ways, too.

"Oh no," said Margarita, "this is our gift to you." She smiled, offering her charity. It was the tone of voice the man imagined the thirteenth fairy used at Sleeping Beauty's christening.

"Tell a story," said Iphigenia.

That was his role in the piece, a story. For the laying of the foundation stone of his garment, the story should be carefully chosen. Something with significance. They were fond of fairy stories but the occasion demanded something with a little more weight and substance. Something biblical would be appropriate. He could hardly go wrong with a Bible story. Something that would find its way into the fabric of the garment, an invisible thread, a prayer. His contribution. Not the life of a saint or martyr, they always came to a sticky end. A story with a happy ending, as he still hoped his was.

They were waiting, poised like musicians in an orchestra,

instruments in hand, waiting for the conductor. The skeins of wool were all lined up and in front of them was the basket of his own black curly hair. It still gave him an odd feeling. His hair over there, away from his body.

He began his story.

"There was once a man who had several sons and the youngest son, knowing that he would inherit a portion of his father's wealth, asked that he could have his share now." The clicking began and took up the rhythm. Despite his itchy, itchy legs he was overcome with a feeling of pleasant coziness such as a winter fire induces. He thought of winter fires at the presbytery with the Bishop and the other priests drinking port, being offered cigarettes from the Bishop's slim gold box, a gift from a parishioner. Ignatius had not been a smoker till he had become the Bishop's secretary.

In the refectory after dinner, the priests would stand with their backs to the fire warming their buttocks or sit in comfortable leather chairs that squeaked when you changed position. They talked of politics—Church and world—or, more to the point, of politicians and those of their brethren who had cases of sexual abuse pending. Sometimes when the Bishop was absent there'd be jokes about it. "An After-Eight or an Under-Eight?" Ignatius felt somewhat uncomfortable when talk turned this way. He wondered if, as a child, he may have been, well, not exactly abused but whether the brothers had been overfamiliar with him and he hadn't recognized it. "More port, Ignatius?" The After-Eights were on a silver tray left by Mrs. Grogan. He liked the chocolate-brown envelopes they came in, the wafer-thin squares of chocolate and the cool penetration of the mint when he bit into it. But he always felt that it was a guilty pleasure, especially after the jokes. He chuckled sometimes but never offered any jokes himself. Sometimes he suspected he laughed in the wrong places. Ignatius had his sights set on higher things. He would be one of the brethren but he would not be reduced to smut. Another sip of port to get over his unease.

"Make a holiday of it. Remember, even God took a break," the Bishop said with a twinkle in his eye. A pity there weren't more young men like Ignatius entering the priesthood. Initiative, meticulousness, ambition, and strength of will, yet deferential to his superiors. "Hire a car, take the mobile phone. Take your bathers. The sea will be brisk but it's good for the soul."

"And so, not many days after, the youngest son gathered his things together and began his journey to a far country. It was on the other side of the sea, a strange land with strange creatures. But this was the place he had chosen to make his fortune. The land offered many diversions and he lingered, enjoying its pleasant fruits. But he found, when the time came, that he couldn't leave, and he lost the things of his father and he was reduced to nothing, lower than the animals of the field where he was obliged to sleep while they looked on. And he would fain have filled his belly with the husks that the swine did eat: and no man gave unto him.

"But by and by the people of that land saw his plight and they fed him with their food and clad him in their clothes and let him return to his father's country. And when he approached his father's house the servants said, 'Sire, there is a beggar on the road.' And the father came to the door in his robes and he saw his son in his strange new apparel and came out to greet him. The son knelt before him and asked his forgiveness.

" 'Father, I have been wayward, I went into the world and across the sea and I have lost the things you have given unto me. But I have completed my task and I am returned to be your faithful servant always. If you will not have me in your house, lodge me with your animals.'

"But the father was joyous to see him and he said to his servants, 'Bring forth the best robe, and put it on him; and put a ring on his hand and shoes on his feet: And bring forth the fatted calf, and kill it: he was lost and now is found.' And they began to be merry.

"Now the other sons heard the festivities and one of these called the housekeeper and asked what these things meant. And she said, 'Thy brother is come and thy father hath killed the fatted calf, because he hath receiveth him safe and sound.' These other brothers were stern and angry, they who had tended the father's flock all the time the youngest son was absent. They knew that the father had given him special things, things that belonged to all of them. But the father said unto them, 'Sons, thou are ever with me and all that I have is thine. It was meet that we should make merry and be glad, for this thy brother was dead, and is alive again, and was lost, and is found.' "

Clickety click.

And again this time, once started on the journey Ignatius found himself going along with the story, entering into it and being mesmerized by it, oblivious to the knitters. It was only when the clickety click stopped that he became aware of them again. Knitting was hanging down from their needles. It was still too early to tell what the final shape would be but he was thankful that they had chosen black. He didn't want to go back to the presbytery looking like Joseph in his coat of many colors. Who knows, perhaps they would knit him fine woolen trousers and a worsted jacket very similar to his original clerical clothes.

Margarita, usually the most furious knitter, had done the least work. "A wasteful, willful child," she said without looking up, "he should have been punished. Punished! Wasteful philanderer." She kept her head down, closely examining an imaginary speck in the wool.

"Lord, who shall abode in thy tabernacle? Who shall dwell in thy holy hill? He that walketh, and worketh righteousness and speaketh the truth in his heart. He that back biteth not with his tongue nor doeth evil to his neighbor, nor taketh up a reproach against his neighbor." The words were out of Iphigenia's mouth before she knew it. Admonishing Margarita with the words of God. She had meant to hold her tongue. She had to be careful with Margarita, she did not mean to chastise her in front of the priest. But the words rumbled and rolled out of her like an unsuspected burp.

It caught him up hearing the ancient tongue of the Lord. It was a sign, God had spoken to him through the nun. God had not forsaken this Prodigal Son and though he was still captive in a strange land, he would return to his father's house and be welcomed with fatted calf. God had looked favorably on his story.

Ignatius saw himself as both the Prodigal Son and the one who stayed by his father's side. He was punctilious and keen, worked to the best of his abilities, courteously trying to preempt the Bishop and carry out orders before they were even given. He was a man who always crossed his t's and dotted his i's. A man who tried to stay above criticism. As far as he could see there was nothing about his behavior or personality that others could find fault with, although he supposed at times he was a little humorless. If he came into a burst of laughter in the common room the atmosphere would change as if he'd brought a clammy mist in with him.

He had always wanted to ask one of the others why he wasn't more . . . popular, but somehow the fact that he needed to ask only contributed to the problem. Anyway, he counted his blessings—the Bishop appeared to be pleased with his efforts, giving him more and more responsibility. "You know, I believe that boy is after my job," he'd joke with the priests. They would laugh politely and shift uncomfortably.

If Ignatius had a fault, apart from being humorless, and that was hardly a fault in the Christian sense, it was that he found it difficult to extend indiscriminately the compassion of Christ. He found it much easier to align himself with the just and fair God of the Old Testament. His traditional point of view on the Prodigal Son was in fact not too different from the one Margarita had so vigorously expressed. He did consider the youngest son to be a waster. Squandering his father's resources, an addict of instant gratification. The other brothers had stayed at home and worked. They deserved their inheritance, the youngest one plainly did not. It simply wasn't fair that the youngest son should go off, squander his inheritance, have the hide to come back with not a penny to bless himself and be taken in again to the bosom of the family. Not only taken in but positively regaled.

Ignatius wondered what fatted calf tasted like in the mouths of the other brothers and whether they were biding their time till the old man died or turned his back before they delivered to the favored brother his just deserts.

But his current predicament was showing him a more charitable view of the Prodigal Son. Perhaps the things that had happened to the Prodigal Son were not entirely his fault. He may well have set out with the intention of increasing his father's fortunes, as Ignatius had when setting out for this place. He had fallen into bad company, much against his will. He was naive and unwary but dedicated to his purpose. He had come back to his father eventually, hadn't he? Crawled back in strange apparel, with nothing to show, needing his wounds licked. He was prodigal, wasteful, and extravagant, but his father had forgiven him. Utterly and completely.

His legs itched in their plaster cast. The room was cold and dank, he could feel fog and mist rolling in off the fields. He couldn't even conjure up the glow of the presbytery hearth, the sweet warm taste of port. There was no justice or fairness about being kept a prisoner when he'd done nothing wrong. Fairness no longer entered into it. Ignatius would have to go back wearing the rags of humility and in full view of the others ask for his father's forgiveness.

Carla was planting seeds. She drilled a hole with her finger and dropped one in. She liked sticking her fingers in the ground and putting things in. To let them be nurtured in the quiet dark place. Things happened to seeds in the ground. They would stay the same for a while, then by and by something would break out, a tiny baby yawning and stretching its body. Its roots pushing farther into the earth and its head popping up above the surface, finding the sun and turning its face to it. Once she put a seed inside herself and waited for it to sprout. She waited and waited. It was a moist dark place, like soil, but nothing came forth. Some seeds can lie dormant for years.

Carla loved the way plants could change shape. This little seed she was planting now would turn from a tiny hard brown dot to a big leafy green. She especially loved how potatoes grew. From one piece of potato would come a whole plant—dark spreading leaves on top and under the earth, crisp new baby potatoes. Where did those leaves come from, were they hiding in the piece of potato? That piece did not look at all like leaves, it wasn't even green. At harvest time Carla liked to dig her hands in, find the baby, and brush the dirt away from it the way the

Agnes sisters licked their newborn babies clean. She wondered if she would ever have a baby to lick clean. Her tummy felt a bit funny, maybe there was a baby in there now. She pushed a little. She brought her legs apart to have a look and when she did, she saw on the ground a fresh glob of dark-red blood. Miraculous. She felt so happy to see it. There hadn't been any blood since the winter. Maybe if she felt around she would find a spring lamb in there as well!

No lamb, just soft squishy blood. But that was good. So many things to do with blood. First she licked it off her fingers. The Agnes sisters always ate the big glob of blood that came after the newborn lamb. She reached in for some more and spread it on the garden to make the plants grow. Then she took a spare piece of fleece from her pocket and put it inside herself. When it had absorbed all the blood she would take it out and watch the newly dyed fleece change from bright red to rusty brown.

Blood wasn't the only thing that changed. Grubs went into cocoons and came out again as butterflies. The spirit of the Lord descended to Earth and was born as Baby Jesus. Who in turn became Christ Our Lord. Once upon a time plants and gods and people and animals readily slipped from shape to shape. Gods became bulls, eagles, flowers, and swans. Athena turned Arachne into a spider. You just had to be careful that a witch didn't curse you and trap you in the same skin forever.

Carla could change skin. In her escapecoat she could be anything, become any shape she wanted. Dead sisters slipped into the skin of sheep. The live sisters took the wool off the sheep and knitted it into skins for themselves. And now they were knitting the man a skin to change him from a fish into a legged creature.

After the Prodigal Son story last night she had held up her work to show him. To show how she had flecked his little tiny hairs into the knitting. It was all going to be knitted in, she wasn't going to keep any for her escapecoat. He seemed quite pleased when she showed him, he smiled. It was time to do the next step in taming.

A treasure. What taming treasure could she give him? His old skin? No, that would spoil the gift of the new one. One of his car relics? That didn't seem right either. Iphigenia might get cross. What about something that he'd brought, his new friend Carla bringing him one of his old friends. The cigarette packet? Carla couldn't remember what happened to that. The phone? But she'd buried that a long way off. Then Carla thought of it. The battery. That was his true treasure. On the first day he didn't leave it on the table with the phone, he put it in a special place.

The battery burial place was not far. By the garden wall near a dried brown clump of ferns that had died off over the winter. Live fronds were so delicate and soft but in death they were dry and brittle, like a hedgehog. She tamped it down with her hand, breaking the fronds into a short crop. Now it was like a thick dense forest. She peered at it closely, looking for any little creature that might have been disturbed when her big hand boomed down. No little creatures but ah, hidden in the forest were two tiny shoots—delicate, pale transparent green like insect wings. On top was a leaf curled as tight as tight could be. Spring had come to the fern after all. Soon it would be Easter, when everything that had died off would rise again. Maybe even the battery had sprouted a green shoot. She started digging.

It was marvelous the way shoots would push up through almost anything—gaps in rocks, between the stones of the chapel, this garden wall. Vines were spreading out over the garden wall too, rampant with spring.

Spring had brought the man crashing through the thickets and brambles. He had unfurled like the fern's green shoot and stood up. She was so pleased he had come. Sometimes Carla felt sad. When she heard the cry of a lone gull she felt as if the sound was coming out of her. She had the sisters, the sheep and birds and plants and God, Jesus and all the saints, but there were no other Carlas. The little hedgehog must have felt like that too—the only hedgehog in the world. It had run away. Now God had sent the man. She would tame him, make sweet noises and hold out grain to him. She would be so nice to him he would never want to go.

In the black earth she felt the hardness of the battery. She smoothed away the soil and was a bit disappointed to find that it hadn't grown roots or any green shoots. She put her finger out to the baby fern frond. It was so small and delicate she could hardly feel it. She could stop the spring right now if she wanted, scrunch those fronds around and break them off. But that wouldn't be nice. Such a dear little baby thing, she would let it grow and grow. And maybe one would grow inside of her as well.

Iphigenia turned away but the picture remained clear in her mind, clearer in her mind than the blurred version her eyes saw. Carla squatting on the ground, prodding around inside herself, almost toppling over in her effort to see inside. "Kiri, kiri." She signaled her impending arrival. But Carla was absorbed. "Ho there, Carla." Iphigenia tried again, using the greeting of Carla's childhood. Iphigenia was quite close now, looking down on Carla, who had at least raised her head.

"Firewood?" queried Carla, wondering what Iphigenia was

doing out here. She and Margarita came out to collect firewood, work in the garden, attend to the sheep but rarely did they just wander.

"Game." Iphigenia squatted down to her level. The black curls of Carla's hair had started sprouting again. They looked so springy that Iphigenia wanted to touch them. She didn't.

Game! Carla was surprised but pleased. Iphigenia rarely played games with her, even when she was little.

"Guessing game."

"Rumpelstiltskin?"

"No."

Ah, the game had already begun.

"Animal, vegetable, or mineral?" asked Carla.

The simple question flummoxed Iphigenia. She did not know what it was made of. "Not animal or vegetable," she decided.

"Found indoors or outdoors?" was Carla's next question.

"Both."

"Something you can carry?"

"Yes." Iphigenia's answer was quick and encouraging.

"Bigger or smaller than a missal?"

Iphigenia drew her mind back to the day she first saw it. It loomed importantly in her mind and yet it seemed implausibly small. "About the same."

"Bible?"

"Not a book."

"Clue."

Iphigenia thought about what clue she could give. "Black and squarish."

Oh no. Not black and squarish. She didn't want this to be the thing in the guessing game, not the treasure for the man.

She hadn't even given it to him yet. Carla tamped it back into the ground.

"Don't know."

"Black and squarish," Iphigenia repeated.

"Don't know." Carla had begun to look sullen.

"It's the man's."

Iphigenia wasn't playing properly. Carla hadn't even asked for a clue.

"Don't know."

"It fits in a pocket." Iphigenia waited a little while longer but Carla appeared to have stopped guessing. "Give up?"

Carla hated giving up but she thought for this game it was the best thing to do. She nodded her head, eyes looking to the ground.

"It's the phone," Iphigenia announced.

The phone! Not the battery after all. She started grinning.

"Do you know where the phone is?" asked Iphigenia.

Oh yes, oh yes, Carla knew. She stood up and grabbed Iphigenia's hand, pulling her away from the battery burial place. "I'll take you."

She ran, with Iphigenia in tow.

"Carla, Carla," breathed Iphigenia, "slow down." She was panting and her cheeks were flushed. She didn't want to dampen Carla's enthusiasm but she could hardly keep up.

Carla slowed to a trot. She was feeling so happy. Two playmates! Iphigenia and soon she'd have the man as well. She was very pleased that she'd been able to guard the battery treasure and Iphigenia hadn't even guessed it was there.

They had to slow anyway because they were coming to the brambles. Carla found the tunnel that had been made before, by the man, by the sisters when they had gone outside. It looked equally overgrown as everywhere else to Iphigenia but there was an invisible path that Carla knew. The brambles that had reached out to fill the gaps were green, sappy and pliant. With fresh sharp thorns nevertheless.

Carla let go of Iphigenia's hand and pushed her way in, taking hold of the new growth and plaiting it back into the old so that it made a tunnel. She made her way to the place where she'd buried it, the childhood hole that the man had fallen into, and started digging like a dog, sending a flurry of soil behind her.

"There!" She beamed. She rubbed the soil off as if it was Aladdin's lamp and held it up triumphantly.

Such a dull ugly black thing. Yet like the tarnished lamp that Aladdin found, Iphigenia was sure it had a genie in it. As Carla held it high against the infinite blue, Iphigenia smelled the bewitching tang of the sea, heard the diving and dipping of seabirds. This was the very place from which they had set out on their journey down to the world. Iphigenia needed no clearer indication that her course of action was the right one.

Carla held out a fist concealing something. "Play?" she invited, putting her head to one side and giving the man her sweetest smile.

At least they had good teeth, yellowish but all intact. They never appeared to clean them. He ran his tongue around his own teeth. Mossy. He supposed his breath smelled as well. He'd almost forgotten the feel of polished mint-tasting teeth. He looked at the soil-encrusted fist. "What?" he asked.

She came right up to him and opened her hand. The

echo of the shouting voice was barely more than a whisper now.

Well wasn't that dandy. Lost but now is found. She'd dug it up from somewhere. Literally dug up, he surmised from her hands and fingernails.

"Your treasure." She gently nudged his memory.

OK, OK. She didn't need to rub it in. The phone battery. The battery he'd gone looking for among the sheep turds. How embarrassed he'd felt to stoop to such a furtive activity. He had no idea then how much further he would stoop. "Low enough to slither under a snake's belly," he said out loud, in an American cowboy voice. Completely useless, that thing in her hand, but she was only trying to be friendly. He must be magnanimous. Suffer the little children, little dirty-faced, middle-aged children. She had pretty hair, now that it had grown a little, lustrous curls like his mother's. Why had he not noticed it before? "Thank you," he said graciously.

"Play?"

"Play what?" he asked.

"Your game?"

"My game?"

"You choose," explained Carla.

He had never been one for playing games, chess yes, ones where the gray matter got a bit of exercise, but not impromptu "made-up" games. He didn't have the imagination for it. But a game, any game, was better than lying here on the bed wondering what was on the menu for dinner. With no chores to do all he had to look forward to were the meager meals. Sometimes they carried him out to sit in the sun for a few hours, sometimes they left him in his room all day. Carla seemed not to notice the crispness in the air but Ignatius found that his plaster tail, rather than providing insulation, proved to be cold and clammy. It was all right when the sun shone into the room but toward evening a chill came down.

"Play?" Like an eager puppy, putting a stick down in front of him and waiting for him to throw it. Running in a little bit to let him get the hang of it.

Ah, but he did have a game he wanted to play with her. I spy with my little eye something beginning with C. Not courtyard. Not cloister. It's car. You can't see it? Let me show you. It's outside. Let's play follow the leader. I'll follow you out to the world. It's a big black thing, can you see it? Well, let's go a little farther. There it is. Now it's my turn. A car can go faster than anyone can run, can go faster than birds can fly, fish can swim. Watch me, I'll show you. Watch me, Carla. The tide is down, the strand is up, watch how far I go. You can run but I am too fast for you. My magnificent black steed. You are just a tiny speck, tinier and tinier till I am on the mainland, the tide is up and you have disappeared.

Oh, but it would be a while before he could play that. Legs back first. If they wanted him to come up with interesting games, they'd have to feed him on something more sustaining than nettles and turnips. He needed protein, a nice piece of haddock with tarragon sauce, a good roast with rich gravy and lots of potatoes. He couldn't see how they survived on their meager fare. He was sure dietary deficiency was the explanation for their peculiarities. Some of them at least.

He was not a very good playmate even though she was giving him every opportunity. She didn't know what game was played with the battery, it was up to him to tell her. He didn't even seem very pleased to see it. She put her finger on her chin and turned her head to one side, as if an idea had just occurred to her. "Name." She knew very well what the name of it was but she wanted to get him started.

"Name?"

"This."

"It's a battery. A dead battery."

She held it up to her nose. "Dead?" It was stiff like a dead thing but there was no smell and no maggots.

He sighed, capitulated, took the thing in his limited hands and started hitting it against his plaster, making a rhythm. She listened to the percussive sound for a bit, then imitated it, making a clicking noise with her tongue and teeth. Then he stopped, interest lost. She would have to give him further instruction. Carla used to instruct the hedgehog over and over but it never learned a thing. "Your treasure," she repeated emphatically, coming right up to his face.

It was a cruelty, didn't she know that? To display, flaunt in front of him his impotent "treasure." He moved it up and down the bed as if it was a toy car, gave it a final push in her direction. She pushed it over to him again. Back and forth it went.

It was not a very interesting game. It had seemed so important to him the first day. She felt sure that there was a special game he played with it. Had he forgotten or was he just not sharing? When he appeared to grow tired of pushing it back and forward, she picked it up, rubbed it in her hands, and held it to his cheek to feel the warmth.

Instinctively he moved his head away. "I know a game," he said brightly, "a treasure hunt. Hunt the battery."

Hunt the battery? But it was here.

He read the quizzical look on her face.

"A new battery, one that works. In the glove compartment

of the car. We could go down and get it. This could be our special game, just you and me."

Oh, she was so pleased to hear the man talk about special games, but the car. The car had disappeared. She carved a slow arc in the air, miming the demise of the car. Step by step, finishing with her hands exploding in a splash. Then she shook her head as if it was a terrible tragedy.

Great. They'd rolled the car into the sea. The helicopter wouldn't have spotted the car because there was no car to spot. There was nothing for the helicopter to see, nothing at all to indicate his presence here. Great. He clenched his teeth and sniffed back the tears. He was sick of it. When were they going to bring him his dinner?

Car relics, car relics. Carla loved best of all the box of soft, apricot-colored papers. When you pulled out one, another arose to take its place. But that wasn't what she was going to fetch. The thing that the man liked best was the battery. The car relics were kept in the abbess's room. The abbess hadn't played with her the way the sisters did. Sometimes the abbess would smile down at her if she passed by, but she never played games like Round and Round the Garden, or This Little Piggy, where the nuns touched Carla's fingers and toes, tickled her under the arm, and made her squeal with delight. For a long time Carla thought Iphigenia was an abbess too.

As Carla put her hand on the door, she heard noises, a soft grunting. Imagine her surprise when she peeped through and saw Iphigenia at play! Playing with the phone. "Ho there, Iphigenia," said Carla, flinging the door wide open.

Iphigenia was so engrossed that she hadn't smelled Carla coming. And so startled to hear her voice that she dropped the phone. She hoped no damage had been done. Not that she could get it working.

Carla and Iphigenia looked at each other, both wondering

whether explanations were necessary. They knew they had caught each other out in a private thing.

Iphigenia was the first to recover. "Looking for something?"

A broad smile spread across Carla's face. "Small and black."

Two games with Iphigenia in the one day. Iphigenia was normally not keen on games although she had once described the game of dominoes. Carla had even made a set of dominoes, cutting squares out of pastry, putting little dots on them. Carla and Sister Cook had baked them in the oven and when Carla presented them to her, tears had welled into Iphigenia's eyes. Carla couldn't understand, she thought Iphigenia would be pleased with the gift. Carla's lip started to quiver and her face wrinkled up. She buried her head in Sister Cook's warm crusty smell. Sister Cook's big hand patted her head and assured her that Iphigenia really was pleased. It was the surprise of it that caught her unawares. Buried in Sister Cook's skirts Carla hadn't seen the question mark ripple from one black habit to the other.

Now, in the small and black game, Iphigenia seemed a bit too bright and gay. But playing was easy. Carla knew that if Iphigenia practiced, she would relax and get better at it.

They were coming at him, almost galloping. Ignatius felt his heart quicken and a sweaty prickly sensation burst out all over him. He had gone too far with Carla and retribution was running to meet him head on. He started working out a story for Iphigenia, the way he had done for his mother when he was a small boy and late home from school. He wouldn't mention the special game of going down to the car. They were just chatting, moving the battery backward and forward when all of a sudden, off she went. Would Carla concur, to keep her playmate? Not by the look of them hastening toward him.

Carla and Iphigenia loomed over him. Iphigenia shoved her hand in her front pocket and pulled out . . . Ignatius blinked. His mobile. "Play," she commanded. Mother Superior wanting to play? Was this part the first of many tests he would have to undergo to see if he was fit to wear the garment?

"Play what?" he said dumbly. The mobile sat in the middle of them, a mouse with nowhere to run.

"Telephones," said Iphigenia. Simply, softly. Like he had no choice.

He was able to pick the thing up but his bound hands didn't give him room to move his fingers. "Untie?" suggested Carla, seeing his difficulty. Iphigenia nodded her head. Carla grunted a bit, stuck out her tongue in concentration but it didn't take long for her to free his hands. He rubbed circulation into his wrists, moved his fingers like a spider walking up an invisible wall. When he was ready, Iphigenia handed him the phone again.

They were up to something. Important enough for them to unbind his hands. Not that there was any danger of him running amok. What could he do, throw the phone at them? He put it up to his ear. "Hello?" Carla put her hand up to her ear and did the same. Iphigenia let it go on for a minute, then she said, "Make it work."

Another game entirely. It wasn't a toy to Iphigenia, she wanted to use it. Who did she have in mind to call? The Bishop? The Rescue Squad? he mused. "It won't work without a battery. A live battery."

"Live?" Iphigenia repeated, imagining an animal or plant.

"Charged battery." He looked at her evenly. "In the glove compartment of the car."

"Show us with this one," Iphigenia said. She gave him the one he and Carla had just been playing with.

"It won't work," he promised.

"Show."

He loaded it.

The spare battery hadn't gone down with the car, they must have it up here with them. But they weren't being foolish enough to let him play with it, just in case he got a message out to someone. "It's very simple." And he showed her. She took the phone from him and pressed the small button at the base, then tapped her fingers over the numbers and finally held the phone to her ear. She went through the routine a few more times, memorizing the actions.

"My soul doth magnify the Lord, and my spirit hath rejoiced in God my Savior. For He hath regarded the low estate of his handmaiden: for, behold, from henceforth all generations shall call me blessed." All contradictions of the day dissolve in the approach of evening. The cool healing balm of evening. The wind has calmed and insects chirrup their tiny song. Margarita kneels in the chapel going through the motions of Vespers. Even without opening her eyes she knows that her sisters have not joined her.

For the first time the words that Mary spoke to her cousin Elisabeth feel like chaff in Margarita's mouth. Both pregnant with the holy children that they would bring forth. Elisabeth pregnant in her old age. Margarita's body feels dry and hollow. Her old age would never be blessed with Elisabeth's fecundity.

She remains a lonely sentinel the whole of Vespers. She takes the aching cold into her knees and spreads it through her body.

Carla and Iphigenia are absent, there is not even an Agnes sister for company, common though it was for them to wander in at the sound of chanting. Margarita has to carry Vespers all by herself. It does not sit lightly on her shoulders.

She hurries over the last part. There is no calm in Vespers this evening, no healing of contradictions. In her heart worms are flipping and squiggling, trying to find their way back into the moist secure darkness of undisturbed soil. She pushes herself up heavily from the kneeling position, her hip bone gnashing in its socket.

Not in the courtyard either. Margarita was alone in its yellow light. She began kneading bread for supper. Kneading, pushing, and shoving. Slapping it loudly on the table but still no one came. Carla no doubt would be off on an exploration, visiting her plants and insects, a hospital sister doing the rounds of her wards. But Iphigenia? Afternoons found her sitting in the light of the Lord, drinking sage tea, sniffing the wind. Like Carla, doing her rounds but without getting up and moving about. She punched the dough into a second kneading, then threw it into the pan. Why should she stay and watch over it, no one else seemed to be bothered about dinner. Too bad if the bread burned. Perhaps the smell of it would bring Iphigenia out from wherever she was.

"Hello, hello?"

Voices down the corridor. Margarita swished her way along, heading for the fish's room. The occupants all looked up as Margarita's shape blocked the mote-filled beams of light coming in through the open door. Carla's face was flushed with excitement.

"Ho there, Carla. A game?" Margarita couldn't even bring herself to acknowledge Iphigenia's presence.

"Play?" Carla invited, unaware of the tight anger in Margarita's voice.

"Play, Carla? But it's time for Vespers," her voice dripped. Too late for Vespers, actually. She cast a grazing glance at Iphigenia and was pleased to see the look of dismay. Iphigenia had missed Vespers. Iphigenia, who never missed a trick.

Margarita was so big she filled the whole doorway, could feel it framing her like a regal cloak. She sniffed the air, jutting her nose into it the way Iphigenia did. "Bread burning," she said. Iphigenia's nose twitched but she could not pick up the smell of burning bread. Margarita continued on down the corridor, leaving Iphigenia to flounder in her wake.

She went to her cell and stood at the window, elated and angry at the same time. They had not changed him one iota. Instead, he was changing them, turning them away from the Lord. Playing frivolous games with him when they should have been at Vespers. Gushing with conversation and chat. Let the bread burn, let them go without dinner, she was sick of being the handmaiden.

She looked at the sheep grazing, the Agnes sisters oblivious to the dark clouds swirling in the cloisters. If only they were human again, Teresa, Assumpta, Sister Cook, all the others. They were her true community. She chanted softly, her special little lamb chant, and occasionally the breath of her voice would flow into an ovine ear and one of them would look up and bleat.

She would be magnanimous when Iphigenia came to apologize, she would resist the urge to point out the evil influence of the visitor who had introduced Devil and Damn into their lives, who was disrupting even their service to God. A bit more time, a bit more rope to hang himself and Iphigenia would see. Then she would beg her sister's forgiveness as well as the Lord's.

For quite a while Margarita watched the Agnes sisters tearing at the grass, occasionally flicking a buzzing evening insect off their ears. They looked so blissful. She wished that God would speed her death so that she too could become a blissful Agnes sister. She watched the sun sink lower, heard small birds twitter and flit about. But she did not hear Iphigenia's footsteps making their way to her cell. Perhaps instead of asking Margarita for forgiveness, Iphigenia was asking God.

Margarita swished back along the cloisters. The chapel was empty. The Blessed Virgin and her mother stood in the same stony attitude as when she had left them. She went farther on, slipping from archway to archway so as not to be observed, till she had a good view of the courtyard.

There they were, carrying on the meal preparations as if everything was normal. Her bread was out of the pan and sitting on the table, its crust a perfect golden brown. Margarita was not pleased.

It was not till the third night after the missed Vespers that Iphigenia noticed the unraveling. She knitted a slight imperfection into her work, a tidal mark to make sure. On the next night she saw that the imperfection was gone and her work was only two rows more advanced than when she'd started the night before. The priest's garment was being unraveled.

Yes, she had forgotten Vespers, but it hardly warranted Margarita appearing at the door like an avenging angel. It was an impressive sight, Margarita silhouetted against the light, wings out like a bat. Had she been wearing her night cloak? Iphigenia was perturbed by missing Vespers but her excitement at watching the phone demonstration far surpassed it. This disturbance was only for a little while, then they would all resume their life.

She must keep Margarita appeased, however. She could see that in the sabotage to the knitting. Iphigenia vowed to be more alert to the movement of the day, the journey of the sun across the sky, the changes in light and temperature that signaled the various offices.

Meanwhile, she would continue with her plan. Unfortunately it now appeared that she would have to do it in secret. If Margarita took such exception to missing Vespers, Heaven knows what she would think of Iphigenia's great and daring plan to contact the world. Margarita's mind was far too choppy at the moment to see it as anything but a threat. Better that Iphigenia wait till she had some positive news to tell.

Banks, Colquhoun and Andrews, a trinity of names. She said them over and over, her private prayer and chant.

She waits at the door, nosing the place like a cat sniffing the air. She hesitates a moment, then when she knows, approaches. Even though his back is to her and he is replicating the deep breath of sleep, he is awake. Does she sense his flickering eyelids? The silence, now that she has entered it, has thickened. He can feel her getting ready to speak.

"Doesn't work."

It is a moment before Ignatius realized what she was referring to. She couldn't get the phone to work. But ah, the thought struck him like lightning, much better if she could. "Have you installed the new battery?" A touch of smugness, just to let her know he knew she had it.

There was a pause, then in the darkness he felt the phone in his hands. The battery was perfectly in place. "That's fine," he said. The phone disappeared from his hands.

"Tell again how to phone."

"It's simple. Press the ON button, then dial the number. Would you like me to do it for you?" What a gallant fox.

He heard the faint sound as she tapped out three or four numbers. Not enough. "Most telephone numbers have seven digits," he said.

"Seven?" Iphigenia couldn't see clearly the Banks, Colquhoun and Andrews letterhead, but she was sure there were fewer than seven numbers.

"Plus the area code, if you're phoning long distance."

"Area code?"

He explains what it is. "Where are you phoning?"

The world. Iphigenia is trying to phone the world. Then she remembers something else Grandmother used to say about the solicitor. Mr. Banks is coming down from the city today. "The city," she says.

He tells her the area code.

She goes over to the window and tries the phone. She must have made it through because she seems startled and almost drops it. Excellent, thinks Ignatius.

She returns to the bed, the phone in her pocket and composure regained. "Is ours the only monastery the Bishop wishes to sell?"

He has heard the question but doesn't answer straightway. Of all of them, she seems to be the only one aware that there is a world outside these walls and that they are part of it. This is the first time she has broached the subject. Is she reconsidering? Does it have something to do with the phone? He must answer carefully, thinking of his goal. "It is happening all over the country, even nuns who own their properties are selling. There are so few of you. So few of us." He includes himself, all those in religious orders.

"So few?" she repeats. The words float in the air, seeking further consolidation before they can come to ground.

"Well, yes," he says. And he shifts position, turns to face her now that he is speaking in general and doesn't need to protect himself. "So few young people are joining orders. Religious houses are communities of old people. They die and are not replaced."

"All the more reason for us to stay here."

The cut and thrust. The parry. He recognizes in her an intelligence that has rarely been exercised. Where would she find reasoned debate, the flexing of logic, in this environment? With training Iphigenia could hold her own in the fireside debates at the presbytery. He grins at the thought of her, shabby clothes and horny feet, in such company.

Ignatius remembers how edifying it felt to have theological debates and what an excellent tool logic was for arguing faith. Ritual and ceremony uplifted the spirit of the masses but a priest needed answers. Once you accepted the initial leap of faith, the rest of it was simply a question of logic.

"We need to take a more hands-on approach. The problems of the world are many: unemployment, youth homelessness . . . The Church . . ." The Church is in crisis, parishioners practicing birth control in spite of the Pope's edicts, brothers falling down like dominoes as more and more cases of sexual abuse become known, the authority of the priests crumbling.

The Church with its direct links to Jesus Christ across the millennia. There had been tough moments before, inquisitions and challenges, but the Church had survived. Critics accused the Church of being rigid, unchanging, but it had lasted for two thousand years and had spread to every part of the globe. It did not achieve that by being rigid and unchanging. The Church's future was Ignatius's future. Admittedly, there were better decades, better centuries to have been a priest. He could not bear to entertain the thought that he had entered a career, dedicated his life, to a body which was already past its use-by date.

"The Church must adapt to the modern world."

"We pray for the world but are not part of it. There are no other people here. Does the Bishop want to build houses and hospitals where there are no people?"

"No."

"Then what?"

There is confusion in the air, an electric hum. He turns his back to her before answering. And what he says is not really an answer. He knows this but he is the Bishop's secretary, schooled in discretion and diplomacy. "Most communities of small numbers realize the selflessness of giving to those in need. It is contrary to the vow of poverty that such communities be surrounded by such wealth."

"But not contrary to the vow of poverty that the monastery become a resort for the wealthy."

She had been through his papers. Is she wanting to ring Connoisseur Resorts, trying to sabotage his project? "The rich also need spiritual sustenance."

A sigh, a heartbeat. "What happens to sisters when their home is sold?"

He wishes she would not use words like "home." He feels much more comfortable discussing it in terms of real estate.

"They are well looked after." He is about to say they go to a more comfortable existence, running hot water, central heating, etc. but remembers how she reacted the first time. "As much as possible, we endeavor to give their lives continuity." He pauses, then adds, "Continuity in another house, with sisters of the same order."

He doesn't understand. It hangs together as delicately as a spider web. Once the fabric is touched the whole unravels. It is not just the three of them, it is the Agnes sisters, St. Anne, and the Blessed Virgin, every prayer, every chant that has seeped into the stones, every private thought and contemplation, each birdsong, blade of grass, worm and insect. The earth itself. It is the place and everything in it, the light and the dark, the day and the night, the generations of sisters, everlasting life, all this contained in the egg of the monastery.

How much longer did Iphigenia, Margarita, and Carla have in their present form? Before their eternal souls were lifted up to the light of the Lord, their decomposing bodies became part of the soil, their spirits reemerged as *Agni Dei*? Lambs of God.

"If many properties are being sold, why does the Bishop need this one?"

It wasn't so much the Bishop, it was Ignatius. This one was his. He'd found it, he was going to see it through.

"It is entirely up to the Bishop. I am his secretary, a mere servant. Sister, these nights . . . Could I have a candle and some reading material? Please?"

The silence roars like a hard wind in his ears. She could be a statue and her voice a figment of his imagination. Perhaps he is dreaming the conversation. The voice is a tide, an ebb and flow. Through the high window the stars are disappearing and the sky grows light. How long has she been here? A second or all night? Something heaves and sighs like water being displaced and she moves.

Her shadow falls over him. "Margarita says if we give you legs you will run."

He can hear his own breathing and the first bird twittering. He does not want to talk about the promise of legs, does not want to expose himself to the danger of tripping. Much better to concentrate on what he is good at. He says, "I would like us to negotiate an equitable arrangement concerning the future of the monastery." He imagines this slithering into her mind like a snake.

"A win-win situation."

He is surprised by her turn of phrase, as if hearing a foreigner misuse English. But she is talking his language, this is a good sign. He is convincing her and she will convince the others. "Win-win. Yes, that's it."

Smiling smugly, Ignatius watched the last few shreds of night disappear. The phone. Such a delicious thought. He sucked on it, rolled it around in his brain, savoring all the implications. An active phone on the premises. He scratched his stomach, thinking up little ways of getting hold of it. But of course he didn't even have to do that.

Oh, such exquisite pleasure, just thinking about it. Ignatius didn't have to do a thing, she would do it for him. What a perfect irony. If she used the mobile, the call would be charged to the Bishop's account.

He prayed there'd be someone at the presbytery as diligent and scrupulous as himself, who would check the account when it came in. The number of whomever she called would be on the account. But that was less important than the fact that a call had been made. From the mobile. The phone was still being used. They would make inquiries, start the search up again.

He would wait a day or two. Then he would work out ways to gain access to the phone. Use Carla. Think up a game.

Establish and build rapport, obtain information, test ideas, simpler and cheaper than traveling to a meeting, one can take notes without appearing rude. Iphigenia had read the page on conducting business by phone and had practiced her telephone manner. She didn't realize there were so many different types of questions—rhetorical, straightforward, hypothetical, testing, softening up, open, closed, leading. The morning birds were in full chirp and Iphigenia had made several calls before somebody suggested she try directory assistance.

She wondered whether the priest had been trying to trick her because directory assistance had only three numbers. But when she asked for Banks, Colquhoun and Andrews, sure enough, she was given seven numbers. Iphigenia said them over and over till they were in her heart, then she tapped them out.

"You've reached Banks, Colquhoun and Andrews," a young woman's voice informed her. "Please call back during office hours, nine to five-thirty. Thank you."

She asked for Mr. Banks but there was no response. "Hello, hello?" she said. The voice ignored her. Iphigenia spoke more loudly into the phone but still there was no response. She turned the phone off. She was tired, perhaps she wasn't doing it properly. She would try again later.

She waited till after Terce. She remembered that Mr. Banks

never came before breakfast or after supper. Usually it was morning-tea time. She remembered that Mr. Banks had a way of stirring the sugar into his tea, holding the spoon by its very end, moving it round in a circle like a hypnotist.

Margarita had stayed in the chapel, Carla was off in the fields. Iphigenia went to the abbess's room to make the call. She sat surrounded by the things of the world, the car relics, *Negotiation Skills* in case she needed them.

"Banks, Colquhoun and Andrews, may I help you?"

"Mr. Banks, please," Iphigenia said in a steady voice.

After a pause the young woman said, "There is no longer a Mr. Banks. Can I be of assistance?"

Iphigenia had thought a lot about Mr. Banks before making the call, she knew that young Mr. Banks would probably by now be old Mr. Banks. But evidently he had passed on. "Mr. Banks's son?"

"It's the name of the firm, there is no Mr. Banks. What is it in regard to?"

Iphigenia went on to the next name. "I will speak to Mr. Colquhoun." An authoritative voice will inspire confidence and get things done.

"One moment, please."

Iphigenia heard some string instruments, then, "James Colquhoun." A gentleman's voice with the roll of thunder in it. The sort of voice she imagined God having.

"Mrs. Featheringale here. There is a matter I wish to discuss with you." Though she had gone over this many times in her mind, Iphigenia was still surprised to hear Grandmother's voice coming out of her mouth.

"Mrs. Featheringale!"

Oh, how she loved that fluffy feather-duster name, a feather-in-your-cap name. A name as long as a whole sentence. "Mrs. Featheringale's granddaughter," Iphigenia explained.

"Yes. Yes, of course," he said. "Would you like to make an appointment to come into the office or would you prefer I come to see you?" It was very strange. She had never had correspondence with Mr. Colquhoun, yet he seemed to know her.

"Our correspondence will be by telephone. It can establish and build rapport, one can take notes without appearing rude, and it is simpler and cheaper than traveling to a meeting."

"Yes, of course, Miss Featheringale. Or do you prefer Ms.?"

Featheringale was Grandmother's name. On Iphigenia it felt odd, like a hat. "I am Sister Iphigenia."

"Yes. Yes, of course."

It was very peculiar. It was as if he knew her but she didn't know him at all. She didn't even have a picture of him the way she had a picture of Mr. Banks. It was very difficult trying to get an impression from a disembodied voice, although, she reflected, it didn't seem to pose a problem when she was talking to God.

"What is your smell, Mr. Colquhoun?"

"My what?"

"How do you smell?"

"I beg your pardon, I do not smell!"

She couldn't understand why he was so indignant, everyone had a smell. But, she recalled, people didn't like talking about it. Even when it was a very strong flatulent smell that made people turn their noses up, they still didn't say anything.

"I didn't mean to offend," she said in a contrite voice. "It's just that . . . Are your clothes made of wool?"

"The suit's a wool blend and the shirt polyester. The bow tie is made of silk. Dark red, if you really want to know."

A dark red silk bow tie. A good head of gray hair with a

part at the side and curls combed back behind the ears. Well groomed. The tangy floral fragrance of cologne. And now leather and pear. Iphigenia saw him sitting at his desk, a big desk with a mahogany smell.

"Sister, exactly what is it you wish to discuss?"

Iphigenia had thought much in the Great Silence about what she was going to say, she had even asked the Lord's advice. The Lord had answered her thus—even if, and this was a big if, even if news of a missing priest and the helicopter search had found its way into the newspapers, and even if Banks, Colquhoun and Andrews had read this news, there was probably no mention of either his destination or the Church's intention. To support this theory God had pointed out that no one had followed in the wake of the helicopter and the matter had probably been laid to rest. So it was with confidence that she said, "It is in regard to the sale of our property."

"Ah, you wish to sell your property?" He seemed quite eager.

"That is precisely what we do not wish. It has come to my notice that the Church, the Bishop, that is, wishes to sell our home. What can we do?"

"Sister . . ." He hesitated. "Surely you must have an advisor on such matters. The Mother General of your order?"

"Mr. Colquhoun, we are an isolated community. We have no other contact but Banks, Colquhoun and Andrews. I would be pleased if you would be our advisor in this matter. Gather the information if it is not at your immediate disposal. I will telephone tomorrow. Good-bye." Iphigenia turned the phone off. She had hurried through the last part. So much talking. It was exhausting doing Grandmother's voice. She had to go and lie down, something she rarely did during the daylight but she was feeling quite dizzy.

She could hear chanting. Sext. Commitment and fervor. The hour when the sun was at its highest, the peak of the day. Noon. A time equidistant from the fresh hopeful start of dawn and the sense of completion that evening brought. The time when the temptation to give up was greatest.

She couldn't miss Sext. Despite the jabbing stars before her eyes, Iphigenia stumbled down the corridor to the chapel. She knelt beside Margarita and Carla, and as she bent her head in prayer, she toppled over into a night full of stars.

Fresh, full, round. Warm. Beads of soft green bursting on her lips, her nose. She moved her head. Her eyes were open but she could see only blurs. At her back she could feel the stony skirt of the Blessed Virgin. "And the angel came unto her, and said, Hail, thou art highly favored, the Lord is with thee, blessed art thou among women."

Margarita came into focus, holding up a mug of tea which Iphigenia wrapped her hands around and drank. Liquid dribbled down her chin. Through the refreshing antiseptic green of sage she smelled blood. Her forehead was sticky with it. Her ears were ringing with an aural version of the tiny stars she'd seen earlier.

Her sisters rippled in the steam rising from the tea. She heard bleating and in the light and shadow of the chapel saw that a couple of the Agnes sisters had come to pay their respects. Iphigenia felt like Baby Jesus in the manger.

She put the mug down and made an effort to get up, leaning heavily on Margarita and Carla. They led her out to the courtyard where she sat in the sunlight, the flagstones warm under her feet.

"Sick?" There was a great disturbance in the voice that landed on Iphigenia's ears. Was Margarita concerned or gloating? Iphigenia could smell both. She looked up. Margarita loomed ominous as she had appeared that night in the doorway. Iphigenia blinked. The smell of gloat faded. She looked again. It was just the way Margarita was standing, with the sun at her back.

"It will pass," said Iphigenia. She was taking too much upon herself. Not only did she have to make a conscious effort to remember to attend chapel, but she was being Grandmother on the phone. She spent half the night talking to the priest and the other half doing the work Margarita was undoing. She had to . . . what was the word in the book? . . . delegate.

Iphigenia was so lovely in these moments when she was sick, her nose quivering like a little gray mouse. Carla could pat her, treat her like a pet. "Ecstasy?" she whispered softly onto Iphigenia's cheek. Iphigenia normally frowned sternly at Carla's ecstasies, but this time she smiled. "Did you see the Blessed Virgin?"

Not the Blessed Virgin, but Iphigenia had seen something. "And the eyes of them both were opened, and they knew that they were naked, and they sewed fig leaves together, and made themselves aprons." Perhaps it was talking to Mr. Colquhoun, but it seemed to Iphigenia that she was seeing for the first time what they had done to the priest.

It was a terrible thing, imprisoning him in plaster, putting him in the holding pen and leaving him there. They never made the Agnes sisters stay in the holding pen overnight. Iphigenia wanted to go to the brambles and hide herself from the presence of the Lord. They had to right the wrong they had done. They had to make the garment that would free him from his plaster, turn him into their brother in Christ. Only then would they regain their former shapes.

Hadn't things improved now that he had a candle and reading material? In *Lives of Saints and Martyrs* was a picture of St. Agnes with a lamb by her side, the sword of martyrdom at her throat, virginal hair cascading like a bridal train. Arrested as a Christian at the age of twelve, chaste Agnes endured martyrdom rather than renounce her faith. She underwent many trials and tortures with pincers, shears, and other instruments. Finally, holding fast to her faith, she is executed. Various accounts have her being beheaded, burned to death, pierced through the throat, or a combination of all three.

Such gory deaths they suffered. He had not taken particular notice of it before but Christianity seemed to be splattered with persecution, described in such detail that it was almost . . . well, pornographic. Gory bloody deaths involving desecration of the body: decapitation, hearts pulled out of living bodies, bones smashed till the marrow spurted, dressed in animal skins and torn to pieces by dogs, used as human torches. Even his namesake, Ignatius, Bishop of Antioch, facing execution, ecstasied, "I am the wheat of God; and I must be ground by the teeth of wild beasts to become the pure bread of God." Such willing victims.

Ignatius shifted uncomfortably on the bed and wondered whether it was possible to be itched to death. He tried to turn it into exquisite pleasure. It was a different matter during Roman times when Christians were persecuted. It was their enemies who inflicted the persecution. It solidified and strengthened the early Church. As their holy reward, the martyrs were welcomed with Heaven's open arms. Go right on up, no hanging around in Purgatory for martyrs. But self-inflicted pain and martyrdom, in light of contemporary psychology, made Ignatius feel uncomfortable. It could all so easily get out of control. Those clandestine clubs with whips and harnesses and fancy dress. He had heard that some of them dressed up as nuns and bishops and inflicted punishments on themselves and each other.

He tried to make his legs comfortable. He had not succeeded in transforming this torture into pleasure. Perhaps he was being impatient, but progress on the garment was interminably slow, each night's work seemed to have advanced only a minuscule amount from the night before. For some reason they were spinning it out. He did not smile at his little joke.

The candle cast a warm light in the room. Though of course smaller and made of unlined stone blocks, without central heating or glass in the window, the cell was not unlike his room at the presbytery. He almost felt at home. He took one last look, then blew the candle out.

There had been moments when he had felt desperate loneliness, he remembered this all too well. Lonely because God had forsaken him, lonely in the midst of these creatures who didn't even belong to the same species as he. But they were human, as he was, they shared a common destiny. He snuggled down under the blanket as best he could. They had become more bearable, companionable even.

When they had gone to their cells that night Iphigenia had come by, a thing she hardly did, and said, "Let's play Shoemaker and the Elves."

Carla was only too pleased to have a game but, "We have no shoes," she pointed out.

"We have knitting. We can be knitting elves. Who work away all night, knitting and knitting. We can have the garment finished in two shakes of a lamb's tail and then it will be Robing Day." Then Iphigenia did a thing she had never ever done before. She tousled Carla's hair. It made Carla feel warm and cozy. Iphigenia was becoming so nice. The more she practiced playing, the more she seemed to enjoy herself. And fancy playing at night.

So if Carla had expected to see anyone in the knitting room it was Iphigenia, not Margarita.

She sat down beside Margarita and picked up some work, turning her head and smiling. Margarita was so grumpy nowadays. Carla wished the sheep's wool would grow quickly so that she would have something to shear. Margarita sang such a nice soft song on those days and she was happy. Carla listened for Margarita's clickety-click so that she could join in. But she did not hear anything. When she looked at Margarita's work she saw that it was all unraveled. Margarita was threading it back onto the needles, her head bowed as if in prayer.

Ah well. Carla started up her own clicking. Knitting away merrily, nimble fingers dancing along the needles, her little elves at work, knitting and knitting. A row of plain, a row of purl, a pattern of feather stitch and two of moss. Her finger elves bending and straightening as they looped wool around the needles, transferring the stitches from one needle to the other.

"Shoemaker's elves, eh, Margarita?" It was not good to break the Great Silence with idle conversation but Carla wanted to bring Margarita out of her own little silence. She always used to play games with Carla. Carla wanted her to know she was still her friend.

Margarita said nothing.

"The shoemaker cuts out the leather and in the morning there's a beautiful pair of shoes already made up. What a surprise, eh, Margarita?"

Margarita grunted.

It was not a very exciting story, there were no spells, no wicked stepmothers, but Carla enjoyed it all the same. She bunched the stitches up to the front of the needle and began a new row. She liked to feel the way the work grew under her hands, in the web between her thumb and forefinger, how the residue of lanolin made her fingers soft and shiny.

Carla's elfin fingers knitted on. Margarita had all the work back on the needles but she was knitting so slowly. Pulling the wool, stretching it. Carla began to hum a little nursery rhyme, a fast one to hurry Margarita along. Humming wasn't the same as singing. In singing the sound came out of her mouth. Carla had her mouth closed but the sound was still coming out. She put a hand up to her face to find where. Her nose, of course. Under her nose she felt the warm hummed air.

She had turned the needles perhaps a dozen times or so when Iphigenia entered the knitting room. Softly, gently, barely creating a ripple. She sat down and picked up Carla's rhythm. Carla hummed away merrily. Wasn't it nice for them all to be here together, three shoemaker's elves working the night away.

Iphigenia tried, Carla tried, but Margarita was growing more and more taciturn. She answered only when necessary but the answers were so brief and curt that the others were reluctant to speak to her at all. She had immured herself in silence, was so far inside its walls that she regarded any attempt at communication as an intrusion. She was punctual, she never missed chapel, she attended to her chores. She knelt when they knelt, stood when they stood, but she did not acknowledge their presence. She was not with them. It was only God that Margarita allowed into herself and so Iphigenia prayed to God to guide and care for Margarita and bring her back to the community.

Lauds. Out of the darkness and into the light. Lauds heralds the gift of a new day, even a day shrouded in mist. Lauds was Carla's favorite office. The chapel would start dark and echoing, and gradually while she watched, light would come streaming through the stained-glass saints, through what was left of the rosette. St. Anne, Margarita, Iphigenia, the Agnes sisters, the leaves on the floor, the Blessed Virgin's viny hair, all would be caressed with the light of the Lord. The spirit that breathed in every living thing. Lift up your hearts and sing.

Some days, after Lauds, after Prime, Carla ran to the wild places, lay on the grass with her skirt up, knees apart, waiting for the light of the Lord to come tumbling down. Oh how Carla loved those days when the sun shone and there was not a cloud in the sky, oh how the Lord loved Carla on those days. She had secret places all over the monastery grounds where the angel of the Lord touched her, different places for different times of day. The sweet moist grass beneath her, the shaft of light entering her body, the way it entered the Blessed Virgin. She felt His warmth quiver on her. On such days God's favorite angel shone in the firmament. He was made of light and fire. Lucifer. Such a bright and dazzling angel that he outshone all the others: the seraphim, cherubim, and thrones; dominations, principalities, and powers; virtues, angels, and archangels. When Carla gazed at him, her eyes would fill with his radiance till she saw nothing but light.

It was afternoon now and Carla was lying on the grass having a little think. Phone, phone, phone. Where could it be? She had the dead battery but apart from making a noise when you banged it, it didn't do anything. Didn't move and didn't change. At least a properly dead thing developed a smell or had maggots, its skin turned papery thin. A little dead bird, for example, would change every day you looked at it, its feathers, then its skin would disappear, till finally all that was left was its fragile cage of bones.

Carla had been so excited when the man, all by himself and without any prodding, had suggested a game. "Do you like secrets, Carla?" Yes, oh yes. "This is a secret game," he said. "A game for you and me. We won't tell a soul, will we?"

She looked in the abbess's room, through all the car relics, but it wasn't there. She looked at the people in the picture, the man's people, to see if they had the phone but they didn't. She went back to the place where she had first buried the phone but it wasn't there either.

Could it possibly be outside? She stood up and pushed open the door to the infinite blue. Such a wind, such a wind! Blowing hard in her face, pushing her lips back, making her eyes screw up tight. It pushed her clothes against her body and she could see outlined her breasts, the round of her stomach, her thighs. The wind even blew through the hairs on her legs. They rippled in waves like wind through grass.

When she got brave enough she took another step and looked down those giddying heights. Her heart beat fast. The sea below was crashing, sending up white foam. She leaned forward, trying to see where the foam landed in case it was a soul being born.

It would be easy to keep going, to bow her head and fall. She could lift her arms and the wind would buffer her up again. She came back in, the wind pushing her inside the ancient door. The phone was not outside.

She went back to the man's room. "Can't find," she said, disappointed.

"There is one place we haven't thought of." She liked it when he said "we."

"Tell."

Was it buried beneath Iphigenia's voluminous clothes? Did she carry it around with her or was it hidden somewhere? If only he knew when she was going to pay him a visit. If only he could say now Carla, go now. Search her room. There seemed to be a lot of nocturnal comings and goings of late. Ignatius recognized their different footfalls. The heavy then light tread of Margarita, the gait that protected her hip. The scurrying of Carla. And the silence of Iphigenia. He hardly heard her at all.

The jailer's privilege of dropping in on the prisoner wherever and whenever she wanted. He would not be aware of her till she was right there in his room, had tucked in her wings and settled.

Carla was looking at him expectantly, waiting for him to tell.

He felt almost triumphant. "Iphigenia."

"Iphigenia?"

"Her cell."

This is not a place on Carla's map. She knows every nook and cranny, every tree, plant, and stone, but Iphigenia's cell is just a door. It is like the abbess's office. She shakes her head. She cannot go there.

Oh God, don't stop. Not now. He only needed five minutes with the phone. Not even that. Day or night, it wouldn't matter. "But, Carla, I will show you how to speak to the world and the world will speak to you. I promise." He watches her closely, smiling all the while. She likes it when he smiles. She is thinking about it, tempted. But not enough.

He leans toward her, as if he's telling her a secret. "At night Iphigenia leaves her cell. You could go then."

"Night knitting," she says, explaining why Iphigenia leaves her cell.

Iphigenia is a bigger block than Ignatius imagined.

"But before the knitting, Iphigenia comes here."

Comes here, to the man's room? Iphigenia? Iphigenia did not come straightaway to be a knitting elf as Carla had done.

Doubt has been cast. The block will crumble. They took his legs, they took his arms, so he will slither on his belly like a snake. He slides into her mind and bites. "She comes here and asks many questions about the phone. Iphigenia has it, that's why you can't find it. I want you to have this treasure,

Carla. Iphigenia is not your friend. She tricked you. She tricked you into getting the phone and now she's keeping it all to herself."

No, no, no. Her baby fists pound the air. No, no, no. She does not want to hear it. Carla runs from the man, runs to her room. Iphigenia tricked her. She tricked her into handing over the phone, she tricked her into night knitting. Just when Carla thought she had become her friend. Iphigenia was a witch. She offered Carla the sweet rosy red apple of a game. Carla should have remembered that it was poisonous.

She gets out her escapecoat. It is a long time since she has seen all the tight little knots of Iphigenia's hurts. She throws it aside, a dusty old cobwebby thing. She runs into the fields. Running running running. But no matter how fast she goes the trick thing follows. She feels her face twisting up, her body shaking. She hears a strange windy sound, like the coming of a storm. It is howling through the trees, coming closer and closer. She is shaking so much her leaves are falling off.

She drops to the ground, scrambling through the brambles. She is outside now, running down the hill, into a sunset the color of blood. When she stops running, she will stop being Carla. She will become a speck of foam, splashed up on a rock in a place that Iphigenia will never find her.

"What man of you, having a hundred sheep, if he lose one of them, doth not leave the ninety-nine in the wilderness, and go after that which is lost, until he find it? And when he hath found it, he layeth it on his shoulders, rejoicing."

The sun was almost down when Iphigenia realized Carla

was missing. She had seen her run past, smelled her turmoil. She had not come to Vespers. Sometimes Carla played games by herself, put herself into a story. She would be Hansel and Gretel, she would be Goldilocks shrieking through the forest with bears running after her. Then she would become Carla again and help them get the dinner ready. It was different this time.

She was not in her cell, she was not in the chapel, she was not in the courtyard. Iphigenia walked into the fields, her nose jutting in the air. No brightly colored clots of Carla. She thought she could detect her faintly but wasn't sure if it was a real smell or the indelible memory of it.

A tunnel had recently been cleared through the brambles and the door to outside was open. Iphigenia followed where the scent led her, sniffing for Carla, trying to get her nose above the smell of her own anxiety.

Iphigenia looked down to the sea below, straining her eyes for sight, straining her ears for sound. There was nothing to see but the sea, nothing to hear but the wind and squawking birds. Carla. Carla.

"Kiri, kiri. Carla?" The wind ripped Carla's name right out of her mouth.

Iphigenia starts to descend. She will find Carla. She will not come back without her.

It was so quiet. Even the Agnes sisters were hushed. Margarita was sitting in the courtyard staring at the fire. Vespers had long been over. She was not going to make bread this evening, she was not going to open her mouth, even to eat dinner. The sun had gone from the sky and still no one came. She threw little sticks into the fire, saw devils jump up. She closed her eyes and prayed, seeking the comfort of the Lord. "Blessed be God, the Father of Our Lord Jesus Christ, the Father of mercies, and the God of all comfort." The words have become dry as dust, there is no spirit moving in them. Her immurement was complete. She is totally and utterly alone.

"Hello? Hello?" His voice. They were in his room again, playing games. Too engrossed in them even to come out for dinner. "Hello? Anyone there?" She took a candle and went along the cloisters.

She wasn't going to say anything, just stand in the doorway.

But there was no one in the room. Except for him.

He bares his teeth. "I wondered if everything was all right." Margarita doesn't say anything. "I mean, would you like a hand with dinner?"

"No dinner."

"Oh well, I'm not that hungry."

They have stopped feeding him. Ignatius is aware that something has happened. He suspects Carla has told Iphigenia about the special phone game and they are discussing what should be done. He is trying to put a brave face on it, but he suspects it will be a long time before he wears that garment. All of it unraveled in one stupid game.

"Looks like an early night, eh? I'll read a few pages, then nod off. Thanks for bringing the candle."

She comes into the room, right up to the bed. It would be so easy, he would not be able to stop her. His mustache is getting brushy, he has hair all around his mouth, down his neck. It is sprouting on his shoulders and back. She is staring at his hands, at the brown claws.

"They need cutting, I'm afraid."

"No!" Margarita does not trust herself with the candle. She leaves it behind and runs out.

She gropes her way along the corridor, she has to get back to her cell. There is no one else here. They have left her in the house alone with him. She needs to be in a very small space.

She clutches at the wall, scraping her nails on the stone trying to get a hold. The corridor goes on forever. She wades on through the darkness till she finds her cell. She closes the door behind her, then crawls to her bed. She can do nothing now but wait. She knows he is going to come for her. She cannot forget the nails, the buffed nails and the black hairs coming out of the starched white cuffs.

He is primped and preened for the occasion. She smells the hair oil and eau de cologne lying heavily on top of sweat. She clipped his nails for him, as instructed, so that he would not claw her fine white skin. It was she who had put the oil into his hair, the cologne, starched the cuffs. She had done all these things because she belonged to him and this is what he wanted.

"Beauty, my Beauty."

She remembered the crystals of the chandelier, the way her tears made them kaleidoscope. How could her father trade her for a promise between men? How could a gentleman's agreement be worth more than a father's love? She lay on the bed like a single white rose, in the white dress with the blue sash, her best white stockings and shoes. A little doll in a big coffin, trying to imagine she was back in her childhood, her mother alive and her father still Daddy.

They had a hot meal at an inn. The man winked at the innkeeper who led them to a booth behind heavy red curtains.

Dinner was a stew of some kind and the man offered her red wine. It started as an offering but soon became an insistence. He smiling with his wine-stained teeth and purple tongue, she with her hand on the crucifix, a keepsake from her mother. His paw passed over her heart as he removed her hand. He squeezed her budding breasts, feeling for ripeness. Then he curled her fingers around the wineglass.

"Drink, Beauty, drink."

Her nose drew back at the dull sour smell of it and he laughed at her childish game. He dipped his finger into the wine and worked it into her mouth.

"Drink, my Beauty, drink. It will give you an appetite."

Now that he had made an opening between her lips, he introduced the wine. The cheap glass chipped against her teeth. Wine and blood came tumbling down. He admonished her till tears came tumbling down as well, admonished her for being a child and what would her father say? But in truth it was the child he wanted.

He smiled his wine-dark smile, thinking of the sweet plum that would burst forth its juices. Yes, it was the child that he wanted. Another year or two and she would be a fat pig. He knew this type, a brief blooming. "There, there." He produced an enormous checked handkerchief, dipped the corner of it in a glass of water, and dabbed at the stain, spreading it even further. "We will have to get baby a bib next time," he joked. She felt the stain grow cold on her chest, sitting impassively in the stuffy smoky atmosphere, her back as straight and wooden as a chair.

He finished his stew, wiping the plate clean with a crust of bread, then dabbed at the corners of his mouth with the soiled napkin. He ignored her while he picked bits of stringy meat from his teeth and swallowed them. When he was through they left the inn and mounted once again in the horse and carriage.

Had anyone given her a look of kindness, of pity even, she might have flung herself at their mercy, but no one did. "My niece," said the man, as he paid the bill. The innkeeper smiled, said something, and both men laughed. It was an inn where uncles often brought their nieces. As Beauty jolted along the potholed road she held tight the crucifix around her neck. Oh Father, why hast thou forsaken me?

In her memory the house was brown and heavy with furniture. As the horse and carriage pulled up a thin-lipped woman in drab colors was leaving the house. "Mrs. James," he said without lifting his hat. "Sir." She nodded. She cast a sideways glance at Beauty and her lips tightened even further. She mounted her bicycle and trundled off down the road without looking back.

He told her first that she would get to like it, then that it was her duty and what her father wanted. The chandelier so grand in this dull brown room, the faceted surfaces of the drops glistening like a glass palace. Oh for a message from her father, his face in the looking glass, that he was sick and needed her. If only the man would let her go. Just for a few days. But there was no message, nothing to move her from this bed.

"Beauty, my Beauty." He unbuttoned his jacket, took off his cufflinks, and lay them carefully on the dresser. Undid the straps of her shoes, peeled her stockings down, ran his hands down those young legs as if planing wood. She kept her eyes on the chandelier, saw her own reflection in the crystals, a fly trapped in amber. She felt the cold air on her thighs and belly as he lifted the white lace skirt. She was as he had instructed—bathed, dressed but without bloomers or any undergarment, except the stockings. He crouched at the end of the bed holding her skirt up, examining.

She tried to tug the skirt down but he held firm. Then he flung it up so that she was entirely exposed. "Such a pretty Beauty," he said. He parted her legs as if arranging a knife and a fork. Her body rolled a little as he brought his elbows down on the bed, making a place for himself between the arranged legs. The chandelier sparkled and shone, a fairy palace. A palace of ice. Cold hands on her, parting her, stroking the quivering young folds. A finger introduced to open her lips. Poke, prod, a magical ice cave, each crystal a heavenly angel. She lay there stranded, her skin peeled off. Hosts of angels in their glass gowns.

The rustle of clothes, the sharp buckle of a belt pressing into the leg, then a shaft of pain as her body was torn apart. She wanted to remain lifeless but the pain pushed a gasp out of her. His hand came up to her mouth, a hand that smelled of blood. Chandelier swaying madly now, a city of glass, its angels beckoning to her, their voices tiny splinters. His body heavy on her, the sick smell of his pomade greasing her dress. The bristles of his mustache rasping against her neck and the angels giddy. If she kept them in view, never blinking, she would not die. His thrusts pushed her up the bed, her head banging against the iron bars. Then the fast breath, the pigsty grunt, the dribble of saliva in her ear as he squeezed the breath out of her, squashing her so tight she thought she would suffocate.

Then it was finished. Everything went limp, the animal spent. The chandelier was still, the room shocked into silence, not even a clock ticked. Beauty did not even feel the weight lift off her.

"Wash." The word came from far away. She flinched as a

wet cloth hit her belly. "Wash," he ordered. She douched herself with the vinegary water, the sop stinging her. He left the room.

She climbed into bed and pulled the blanket up over her head. Her mother was in the room now, cooing and comforting, but she did not want her mother to see her like this.

There were more nights, she did not know how many, when he would come into the room, carrying a candle and whispering, "Beauty, my Beauty," and it would begin all over again. One night she carried the candle to his room, crept in silently, not even a whisper. She trailed the candle under the curtains, around the perimeter of the bed. When it was good and crackling she ran through the flames and into the arms of the nuns.

She can smell the fire and hear the terrible, terrible screaming. Margarita runs and runs.

The moon is huge, almost full. Iphigenia has gone right down to the village, following the smell trail, before she sees Carla. On the rocks where the car had disappeared, playing with the seals. Those smooth heads silhouetted against the silver moonlight, Carla's crinkly one. "Carla!" Iphigenia cries with relief, making her way toward her. On hearing the interruption the flippered creatures plop into the ocean. And before Iphigenia can reach her, Carla plops into the ocean as well.

"Carla!" But the scream does not stop her. She passes by Iphigenia's vision intent on one thing only. Down she goes. She doesn't roll over as the car had done but still the white foam dances up to meet her as she hits the water. A shout comes out of her, her body so surprised by contact with the cold wet black. The water fills her open mouth, then she disappears.

It was so slow. Iphigenia saw every detail. "Carla!" Every instinct in her rushed to the child. Iphigenia was airborne, flying into the sea. It hit her with its cold wet slap and she instinctively moved her arms and legs to stop from sinking. She looked and looked but could not see Carla. Where was she? Where was she? She could feel the icy water rippling past her. Iphigenia swam back to the edge and hauled herself up on a rock to have a better view. She looked in the direction the sea was moving, the way Carla would be drifting. Why didn't she surface, come up for air? Iphigenia waited, keening. It was too long. Iphigenia had lost Carla's smell. But she saw the face in the water and dived into the sea again.

The water was flooding down Iphigenia's legs, a great mystery occurring beneath her clothes. She could no longer recall the pain, as if her mind had anaesthetized her against it. She remembered weeping in her exhaustion, weeping for love of the baby she held in the darkness. She buried the afterbirth, surprised by its delivery, as if this lump of flesh was the baby's twin. She buried it, wrapped in the cloth on which she had lain.

She lay in the field, the baby on her breast like a small marsupial. The sheep nuzzled at them both, in awe and empathy. Iphigenia prayed to God and the Virgin Mary and thanked them for the divine gift of a child. Love poured out of her.

Very very early in the morning, before the first office, Iphigenia kissed the baby's dear little forehead, swaddled her well, and took her to the gatehouse.

Empty yourself so that you can fill with God. Iphigenia had severed the flesh-and-blood cord with her own teeth but she had never been able to sever the spirit cord to Carla. Through sternness and distance she had managed to keep it coiled up in the pit of her stomach like a sleeping snake. When she saw

Carla fall into the sea the cord had unraveled and shot into the sea after her. Iphigenia felt it as it snaked its way up inside her.

The islanders said that saving a drowning person was difficult, they panicked and fought with you and tried to scramble up your body to the highest point, like seals clambering out of the water onto a rock. But Carla had not struggled and Iphigenia feared she had found her too late. She held Carla to her the way animals held their dead babies, knowing the soul has already floated away but needing to hold onto something.

She kissed her forehead, kissed her blue lips. Iphigenia was breathing in short sharp bursts, not only from exertion. For so many years she had turned longing and yearning into prayers, had given the love to God and to the community, had not gone near the baby though her breasts wept milk for her.

It happened in chapel, she smelled it, her downcast eyes saw the stain. It was Assumpta who came that night. She touched Iphigenia on the forehead, surrounding her in softness. "Fear not. It is the miracle of Magdalene. God has given you milk for the baby, you are blessed, Sister Iphigenia." Then she cast aside her walking stick and showed Iphigenia how to milk herself. Expressing, she called it. Then took it away in a cup.

Let her go to God. But Iphigenia could not. Holding the child to her breast, her head and knees supported, Carla's arm loosely out to the side, her face toward Heaven, a look of utter peace. Pietà. Iphigenia's tears rained down on Carla.

Let go. She lay the body down and felt around for the heart the way they did with lambs who had a difficult birth. Faint, irregular, but still beating. She pressed on the lungs. Breathed in and exhaled as her hands pressed down on Carla, showing her how to do it, breathing her breath and her prayers into Carla's body. She sang the lamb song to coax Carla's spirit out of the dark corner where it lay small and limp. "Lamb of God, oh blessed lamb of God." Filling the air with sweet noises that couldn't help but enter into Carla.

Carla's mouth opened and a greenish liquid spewed forth. Iphigenia's tears fell in warm wet splashes on Carla's face. Carla coughed and more liquid streamed from her mouth. Her eyes flew open. She turned on her side and vomited once more, letting the water flow down the rock and back into the sea.

Iphigenia rubbed Carla's cold hands, her cold feet, Iphigenia shivering too, the tears still streaming down her face, a whole accumulated dam of them. Carla was filled with awe at the sight of Iphigenia's watery face. She reached out and touched it.

"Behold my hands and my feet, that it is I myself; handle me, and see, for a spirit hath nor flesh and bones, as ye see me have."

It was midmorning when Iphigenia and Carla got back. It had rained in the night and they had sheltered together in the ruins of the village. The monastery was quiet. Too quiet. The very air itself was hanging in shreds. Something terrible had happened.

"Fox?" suggested Carla.

Iphigenia remembered the time a fox took one of the Agnes sisters.

"A fox," announced Sister Cook, who knew the habit of foxes. Stealth in the night. Iphigenia knew the habit of foxes too. On Sundays after mass there was the hunt. She had never thought of the fox as the predator. It was the one that was chased. The dogs bayed, cornered, and slavered over the fox. The people came on their horses and bagged it. One particularly handsome red fox had ended up around Grandmother's neck.

What had greeted them all that morning was a scene of carnage. Carnage was the word the abbess had used to describe the shocked stillness, the sight of two inert bloodied sheep, one a lamb with its head torn off, bits of its wool everywhere, a trail of blood leading into the bushes. The rest of the flock cowering, fleeces trembling with more knowledge of what had happened than the sisters. "Sheer carnage," said the abbess, looking to the sky for an explanation.

Iphigenia sniffed the air. "Not a fox." It was a different stench that hung over the monastery. It was fire and smoke. It was burned flesh.

They hurried to the buildings. There was no one in the courtyard, no one in the chapel. Margarita's cell was empty.

The smell was coming from the priest's room, so strong that Iphigenia thought she was going to be sick. Near the doorway lay a smoldering blanket. An overturned candle on the floor. *Lives of Saints and Martyrs* was no more than a pile of black, flecky ash. The body of the priest lay uncovered on the bed. Most remarkably, his hands were bandaged in wads of fleece big as boxing gloves.

Carla stomped the remaining smolders out of the blanket while Iphigenia examined the priest. He was still breathing, there was movement under his eyelids. Beside the bed was a bowl with the remnants of a sweet-smelling, green unction. "Carla?" Carla came and sniffed at it too. It smelled like the mixture she had applied the first time to his burned hand.

In the courtyard the fire was still going, a wisp of steam coming from the kettle. Margarita had attended to everything.

"Kiri, kiri." Carla and Iphigenia walked through the overgrown lanes of crosses beneath which lay the earthly bodies of deceased sisters. Everything was wet with last night's rain. "Kiri, kiri."

In a far field by the brambles, they espied a clot of sheep. "Kiri, kiri."

The sheep looked up and bleated in response but were

hesitant to move. Iphigenia and Carla approached, their feet squelching through the spongy grass. Why were they huddled like this? On the air Iphigenia could discern only sheep and the aftermath of rain. No, there was something else. A faint trace of blood? Was one of their number injured or was it another creature? "Baa," bleated Sister Agnes Teresa. "Baa," bleated Assumpta.

Iphigenia parted the flock, laying a hand on each head as she came to it. She gasped when she saw what was in their midst. Fat hind legs, forelegs out at each side forming a cross, the bedraggled fleece on its back. The distinctive Margarita smell was lost in grass and wet wool. But it was Margarita, transforming into an Agnes sister.

She was lying so still, soaked into the grass. Iphigenia and Carla got down on all fours and sniffed at their sister, touched her skin. There were faint little words coming out of Margarita, the lips barely moving. "I acknowledge my sin unto thee, and mine iniquity have I not hid. I acknowledge my sin unto thee, and mine iniquity have I not hid." Her soul, spirit, heart, blood, liver, muscles, everything, all had forsaken their familiar places and were gathered at her mouth in service of these words.

"Kiri." They whispered their warm breath onto her cheek.

She kept on with her litany, oblivious to her sisters.

"Margarita." They touched her hair, her arms, held her hands in theirs.

"Lamb of God, oh blessed lamb Margarita." Whispered it into her ears.

"I acknowledge my . . . my . . ." The litany dwindled away to silence. Their whispers had altered the rhythm, broken the trance. One eye blinked open. She took in an audible breath of air, made a snuffling sound, as if rousing from sleep.

Iphigenia and Carla gently rubbed her arms, massaged her legs. She tried to move but she wasn't ready. The Agnes sisters gathered around and nudged her, breathing their warm lamby breath onto her. Iphigenia and Carla set about lifting her, the weight of the wet wool making the task even more difficult. Eventually they got her to her feet, then Margarita, Iphigenia, Carla, and the flock of Agnes sisters made a long slow procession back to the courtyard.

Carla dropped some restorative herbs into the pot. Special tea was made but none of them was able to drink more than a few sips.

"I'm tired," said Margarita.

"God knows, Margarita, we're all tired."

And so, in the middle of the day, in the middle of spring, the three sisters all took to their beds.

There were no Lauds celebrated, no Prime, Terce, Sext, None, Vespers, or Compline. The life of the monastery, each round fitting exactly into the path made by the round before, the globe that spun with such perfect equilibrium it appeared to be still, had lost its balance and wobbled to a halt. It lay inert, discarded like a child's toy.

They had laid down the burden of community. The chapel was empty, the only movement the uncurling of the Blessed Virgin's viny hair. A veil of mist descended and in the midst of spring the monastery slept, every creature in it hibernating.

Even Ignatius was in a cocoon. There were moments in his soft ecstasy when he would stir, almost float up to the surface, then drop down again.

He was in a taxi, being driven through a street that was golden, brilliant as light bouncing off metal. Indeed, the sky was a canopy of gleaming metal sheeting. Neat verdant trees lined the street, the houses had a somewhat Germanic quality with fretwork on the eaves. Clones of gingerbread houses. The street was wide, deserted, and the taxi driver, who never turned around, kept saying, "I want to show you something," as they drove farther and farther away from the priest's destination. It was not till he saw a clock in a tower with big Roman numerals that Ignatius realized he was twenty minutes late for his appointment, though what the appointment was he couldn't remember. He found it not at all surprising that the taxi driver was wearing big white boxing gloves and had a tail like a fish. Each time he woke, Ignatius felt compelled to sleep again, at least till he'd finished his journey.

"There is no remembrance of former things; neither shall there be any remembrance of things that are to come with those that shall come after."

Iphigenia arose to a fresh breeze and sunlight streaming in the window. The pall of smoke was gone. The air was pure and the birds were singing again. There was a flutter and a plop at the window. A gull had landed, white and plump and neat with its gray trim. It had a piece of food in its mouth. Dry food.

Iphigenia went into the courtyard. The fire was out and the kettle had boiled dry. How long had she been asleep? One day, two? She went into the chapel. The everlasting candle was almost burned down to a stump. Three days?

She fetched a new candle from the stock they had made over the winter, and lit it on the old one, the fresh candle almost as tall as St. Anne herself. She chumped her chops, ran her tongue around her mouth, growled in her throat to release the morning phlegm. Iphigenia was thirsty. She drank rainwater from a bucket. All the buckets were full and overflowing. It must have rained so softly in her sleep, she didn't even hear it. She scrounged around in her pocket looking for a crust of bread and found the phone. She sniffed at the air, saw where the sun was. Yes, in the world it was close to morning-tea time. Time to give Banks, Colquhoun and Andrews a call.

Her fingers tapped out the number. "Mr. Colquhoun, please," she said, clearing her throat once again.

"Sister. How are you?" He was greeting her like a long-lost friend. "I have made some investigations."

"Is it morning tea?" asked Iphigenia.

"I beg your pardon?"

"Cakes and tea. Wide china cups with curved handles. Saucers."

"Well, actually I usually work through till lunch. My secretary will make me a cup of coffee occasionally."

"Are you drinking coffee now?"

"If you really want to know, I am drawing circles and filling them in. An old habit, it helps me concentrate." Iphigenia drew circles on the table with her finger, to get the feel of it. "I have made investigations on your behalf, Sister. If the Bishop owns the property, he can dispose of it at his will. However," he added quickly, his tone brightening, "we have a few options available to us. You could lodge a complaint, I could write to the Bishop on your behalf. We could find grounds. Is it an historic building? We might be able to apply for a heritage order."

"Heritage order?"

"Of course it would take some time, we would have to approach the appropriate bodies, there would probably be some press coverage." He explains to Iphigenia what this means. She understands. People would come, photographers. One visitor is bad enough.

"What are the other options?"

"There may be a legal loophole. Could you send me a copy of the lease?"

"Lease?"

. . .

Iphigenia had already broken the seal of the abbess's office but still she felt as if she was breaking something else by going through the abbess's papers. Lease. A contract by which a property is conveyed to a person for a specified period, usually for rent; to grant possession of lands, buildings, etc., is what Mr. Colquhoun had said. Such a document would have to be in the abbess's desk. The desk wasn't locked. No need. No sister would dare to do what Iphigenia was now doing. Even all these years after, the last abbess long dead, even though she had recently taken a book off the shelf, Iphigenia still felt sly and secretive about going through the abbess's drawers. Nevertheless, she parted the cobwebs and pulled open the first drawer, letting out the odor of old glue and ink, the hempen smell of paper.

There had been three abbess deaths in Iphigenia's lifetime. She hadn't really thought of it before, but she wondered what form abbesses took after their human death. They never seemed to come back as sheep. At least, none of the Agnes sisters ever displayed the strong qualities of leadership that characterized an abbess.

It was in the course of searching for the lease that Iphigenia came across something curious. A letter bearing the copperplate letterhead of Banks, Colquhoun and Andrews. She stared at it. How had Banks, Colquhoun and Andrews ended up in the abbess's drawer? She thought at first her mind was playing tricks, that she only imagined the letterhead, so recently after the phone call. But no, she was feeling remarkably well after her long sleep, a little hungry perhaps, but quite clear-headed.

It was even more curious to find the name Featheringale in the letter. Featheringale Trust. The letter was addressed to the abbess but the subject of it was the late Mrs. Featheringale and her granddaughter.

"According to her will, lodged with our firm, Mrs. Featheringale has instructed us to act as trustees for her estate, with the authority and power to invest monies as we see fit. Her granddaughter, Sister Iphigenia of St. Agnes Monastery, is entitled to take her share under the will absolutely or any proportion thereof at her instruction to us. Yours faithfully, Richard Banks."

The ink had faded, dust had gathered in the folds of the letter but it seemed to vibrate with life in Iphigenia's hand. Of course Iphigenia knew what trust was but the Featheringale Trust, with a capital T, seemed to have a meaning all its own. She did not fully understand, but discovery of this letter seemed as important as the discovery of the head of St. Agnes, a weeping Virgin, Christ's shroud. Iphigenia left the abbess's office, taking the letter with her.

She sat in the courtyard eating an apple, chewing slowly, trying to digest the meaning of the correspondence. Margarita and Carla had still not appeared, but Iphigenia didn't think they could understand this letter any more than she could. Yet still she sensed the weight of it.

She took it to her cell and lay with it on her chest. The words were dense and colorless but beneath the dust and faded ink of the letter was a bright and shining thing. Her nose quivered as she traced the scent. She felt that same exhilaration she'd felt when she first decided to use the phone.

"Mr. Colquhoun."

"I'm not sure that he's still here. Who shall I say is calling?"

It was the same girl she'd spoken to this morning. Iphigenia knew her voice, didn't she recognize Iphigenia's?

"Good afternoon, Sister."

"Mr. Colquhoun, I have found a letter."

"The lease."

"No. A letter from you. At least, correspondence from Banks, Colquhoun and Andrews. Concerning . . ." Iphigenia put her finger under the words and read them out, to make sure there was no mistake, ". . . the Featheringale Trust."

"Ye—s," he said carefully.

"What is Trust with a capital T?"

"It is an arrangement whereby a person or persons to whom the legal title to property is conveyed, holds such property for the benefit of those entitled to the beneficial interest."

"I am still no wiser. Please make yourself clear," she chided him.

"Sister, I'm not sure exactly what you wish to be made clear. The Featheringale Trust is your inheritance. You would have been informed of the details of the Trust and our position as trustees when Mrs. Featheringale passed away. I assumed that it was in full knowledge of this that you had telephoned in the first place."

"I have only now come across this letter. It is addressed to the abbess."

"As would have been the custom," he said. "But did she not explain it to you?"

It was Epiphany when the letter came telling her that Grandmother had passed away. After morning mass the abbess had called Iphigenia to her office and said that while she was permitted to attend the funeral the abbess strongly advised against it. "The journey would be long and upsetting. I think it would be wiser if you paid your respects to your grandmother here." The memory of Midsummer Night was only six months old, for Iphigenia and the abbess. It was not Iphigenia's fault that she had to go to the mainland looking for the bonesetter, not her fault that it had taken so long. The abbess had not made her do penance but she knew something had happened to bring Iphigenia back wild-eyed, her habit in disarray. She did not want the girl going out again.

A few days after Grandmother's funeral a letter came announcing that apart from the house, which had been left to the faithful Taylor, Iphigenia was Grandmother's sole heir. They held a special mass for Iphigenia's grandmother and the abbess offered to write to Grandmother's solicitor to regulate the legal affairs.

Iphigenia remembered that meeting with the abbess, the strained circumstances. She remembered the word "wealth" but what was its context? You are a wealthy woman. Your grandmother died a wealthy woman. Did the abbess say something like this? Did she mean the richness of their spiritual life? In the vow of poverty with day-to-day needs taken care of by the community, freedom from the responsibility of ownership, worldly wealth had no place. Iphigenia had tried to concentrate on what the abbess was saying but she was too full of grief for Grandmother's passing to have taken it in properly.

"Exactly what is my inheritance?" Iphigenia ventured.

"Well, exactly, I'd have to go to the files to find out," replied Mr. Colquhoun. "But I'd say that roughly, you'd be worth a few million pounds."

"Is that a lot?"

He laughed. "Sister, you are a very wealthy woman."

No, she couldn't be. She was a nun, with a vow of poverty, she couldn't be wealthy.

"Sister, are you still there?"

"Yes."

"Give me a call on Tuesday if you find the lease. We're closing early today for the break."

"The break?"

"Easter. Though I suppose it's not a break for you," he joked.

Easter? Mr. Colquhoun in the world was telling her it was Easter? Iphigenia let the phone fall to the ground. How could it be so suddenly? How could they have missed the subtle indications that the days were growing longer, the pattern of the moon? Iphigenia recalled now the fullness of it when she'd gone after Carla. Was it just the disturbance to their routine since the priest had come, or had they been out of kilter for years? They hadn't even started Lent yet. The more she thought the more frantic she became. To find out not only that she was wealthy but that Easter had crept up unawares. Was it already Lent when the priest had arrived, when they had eaten meat?

She calmed her breath. God would understand. She had eaten nothing at all during her long sleep. This total abstinence would make up for Lent. Easter. It was not too late. They could start afresh. Iphigenia began preparations.

When Margarita awoke she found herself lying in a sunbeam. The room seemed different. Lighter, sparser. It had a pulse, like the quiet, slow tick of a grandfather clock. On Sundays after dinner they would all have an afternoon nap. Mummy and Daddy, her brother Tom, all scattered around the house in their favorite nap spots. Margarita would put an angel on either side of her, close their eyes, and sing them a little song. Then it would go very quiet and all you could hear was the big clock. Tick tock, tick tock.

Carla rubbed her eyes and stretched. She could smell dough and currants. She hurried into the courtyard. Margarita and Iphigenia were there, arms floury like Sister Cook's. On the table was a tray full of gingerbread men.

"Easter!" exclaimed Carla. What a long time she'd slept, the whole of Lent. "Sunday?" she asked, worried that she might have missed the Passion and the Vigil. Then she saw the bucket and the sop ready for the washing of the feet. Lovely. She'd woken up right at the beginning.

At Matins bound; at Prime reviled
Condemned to death at Tierce;
Nailed to the Cross at Sext; at None
His blessed side they pierce.
They take him down at Vesper-time
In grave at Compline lay,
Who henceforth bids his Church observe
The sevenfold hours alway.

Ignatius was fully awake now, with a slight headache and a dry mouth. Even the delicious smell of baking wasn't enough to get the saliva working. He moved his jaw from side to side, swallowed a few times, trying for some moisture. How long had he slept? It felt like several days judging by his powerful hunger. Yet he had no sense of time passing, just a journey in a taxi and being late for some fading appointment.

He heard chanting, his jailers were at prayer. It was getting dark outside. Vespers. But what day?

He looked at his wadded hands, saw a flicker of flame. But the memory receded when he tried to look at it straight on. The taxi ride and his lateness for the appointment were much more firmly imprinted. Annoyance at being late on the one hand, and marvel at the shining canopy and gingerbread houses on the other.

The Vespers songs were sweet but the rhyme that had jingled through his head as he had woken left a sour taste. He had been bound and reviled. Now it was Vespers, time to take him down. And at Compline? His hands had been bandaged, there was an ointment of some kind by the bed. They had at least tended to his wounds. They were good at tending to his wounds, he reminded himself grimly.

Another whiff of baking. Were they ever going to come and feed him? What was on the menu? He wished for meat. They would come soon, with a big plate of lamb, roast potatoes and onions, green beans, and gravy. A pudding to follow with brandy butter, coffee, and after-dinner mints. Silver platters with silver dome covers, carried by rosy-cheeked butlers singing a little song. Merry nursery-rhyme butlers, stockinged legs, checkered waistcoats, and shoes with silver buckles.

He looked around the room. His wounds had been attended to but that was all. There was a burned blanket in the corner, a pile of ashes on the floor. There'd been a fire in here and they hadn't even bothered moving him or bringing a new blanket. It simply wasn't good enough.

. . .

"*I give you* a new commandment: love one another as I have loved you."

Margarita was wiggling her clean new toes and chanting the antiphon, Iphigenia kneeling in front of Carla with the sop, when the washing of feet was interrupted with, "Hello, hello?"

Everything stopped. They looked from one to the other, wondering at this strange yet familiar voice.

"Father John!" exclaimed Carla. They had all forgotten about him. "A priest for Easter!"

The halo of light that had surrounded Margarita when she'd awoken, that had lasted all through the preparations and the washing of the feet, now evaporated. It all came back to her, the fire, the penance in the grass. She had not meant to do it, the flame had leaped from her memory and spread out of control. "There's been . . . I . . ." The sop in Iphigenia's hand was dripping on the ground. "There was an accident. He. The . . . priest got burned."

"Only his hands," said Carla. "You took care of him. We have seen. Come."

They took Margarita along to his room, stood at the doorway, and looked into the place where he lay.

"I was just wondering about dinner," he said.

Margarita thought she had killed him. Here he was, resurrected. She was filled with wonder. She looked at his bandaged hands. But surely that would have been Carla. Carla shook her head. You, Margarita.

They lifted the priest off his bed, brought him out into their company, and fed him with their hands. Then Iphigenia knelt before him. She couldn't very well wash his feet, encased as they were in plaster, so she washed his face instead. Dipped the sop in the water, squeezed it out, and gently wiped his brow, around his eyes and down his cheeks. "Faith, hope and love, let these endure among you; and the greatest of these is love."

It didn't matter that they had missed Lent, that they had not noticed the days growing longer. It was Easter and for the first time in many years they had a priest in their midst.

Friday. The altar was bare, the cross removed from the chapel, and the everlasting candle placed in an alcove, out of view. The priest was propped up at the altar, celebrating the passion of Christ. Ignatius had spent the day reading the missal, going over the words he would have to say. It was not a knitting story this time, they had asked him to celebrate Easter.

With his eyes closed he could be anywhere. During his training at the seminary he had often thought about his first Easter mass as principal celebrant. A grand mass in a grand cathedral, haloes of real gold around the statues, cloths of the finest linen. Bishops, cardinals, perhaps even the Pope himself present while Ignatius presided. His brethren prostrate at the altar in their red vestments, the rich tones of a full choir, each member holding a candle, and on the last note of the chant, the last candle being snuffed out and the grand cathedral hushed.

Father Ignatius opened his eyes to his flock—three barefoot old nuns and a gathering of sheep. As the nuns knelt in prayer he caught sight of their white ankles. The soles of their washed feet were already dirty again. This crumbling drafty chapel, this motley congregation, he had never imagined that he would be celebrating mass in a place like this. Nevertheless. "Where two or three of you gather to pray in my name, there you will find me." The words he was saying in this remote outpost were the same holy words being repeated in the ornate cathedrals of the world. At this very moment, throughout Christendom, every church, be it lofty or lowly, resounded with the passion of Christ.

"Jesus went forth with his disciples over the brook Cedron, where was a garden, into which he entered, and his disciples. And Judas also, which betrayed him, knew the place: for Jesus ofttimes resorted thither with his disciples." Father Ignatius took his congregation along the path that Christ had taken, from Gethsemane to Calvary. The nuns, who knew the way very well, took up the refrain. So that when the priest asked, "Who are you looking for?" the nuns became the guards sent by the Pharisees with lanterns and torches and weapons, and they answered, "Jesus the Nazarene."

And when Pilate asked, "What accusation bring ye against this man?" the nuns said, "If he were not a malefactor, we would not have delivered him up unto thee." And when Pilate gave them the choice, the nuns became the crowd that cried, "Not this man, but Barabbas." When Jesus came forth wearing the crown of thorns and purple robe, the nuns cried, "Crucify him, crucify him."

And they crucified him.

The chapel fell silent, the priest, Iphigenia, Margarita, Carla, the Agnes sisters, St. Anne, and the Blessed Virgin, everyone and everything in that gathering darkness reflecting on Christ's suffering.

Saturday. They cleared away the ash of the old fire and prepared a new one, gathering apple branches and throwing sweet-smelling herbs onto the stacked wood. Then they waited in silent contemplation.

The moon was high in the sky when Iphigenia determined it was time to light the fire signaling the start of the Easter Vigil. Ignatius watched her bring the small flicker of candle flame to it. The others bowed their heads solemnly and breathed in the aromatic smoke. Then they lifted their heads again, faces soft with fire glow.

Iphigenia handed the candle to Carla, who led the procession. Margarita and Iphigenia lifted Ignatius into the sedan chair of their arms and carried him like a comical king into the darkened womb of the chapel. They deposited him in front of the altar. In this familiar place, Ignatius took up once again his priestly role.

"May the light of Christ, rising in glory, dispel the darkness of our hearts and minds."

His voice echoed right to the vaulted ceilings of the chapel and out through the holes into the night. As he said, "Christ our light," and they responded, "Thanks be to God," Carla lit the candles clustered round St. Anne and the Blessed Virgin, then the candles all around the chapel. Soon the darkness was filled with flickering light. The stained-glass saints came alive and the angels danced and voices rang out.

Rejoice, heavenly powers! Sing, choirs of angels!
Exult, all creation around God's throne!

On went the *Exsultet* until Ignatius felt his song lift and soar with the congregation. A white dove opened its wings and his spirit was airborne. Alleluia. Alleluia. Alleluia. The breath started deep within him, aaaaaaaaaah, rose in his throat and up

into his mouth where he lapped at it with his tongue, ll llelu. Then out it came, warm, resounding, shaped into winging its way back to God. Alleluia.

Sunday. It was just before dawn when chanting ceased the nuns came to stand before the priest.

"And when the Sabbath was past, Mary Magdalene, a Mary the mother of James, and Salome, had brought sw spices, that they might come and anoint him. And very ear in the morning the first day of the week, they came unto th sepulcher at the rising of the sun. And entering into the sepul cher, they saw a young man sitting on the right side, clothed in a long white garment."

Margarita stepped forward from the three, and picked up his hands. Gone was the ghoulish scowl she wore last time she had stood so close to him. Now her face was placid, almost beatific. She unwound and unwound the wool skeined around him, unwrapping the shroud of fleece. Ignatius kept his gaze on the faces of the other two nuns, not sure if he wanted to see what Margarita would reveal.

He'd been reading about a saint, he couldn't remember which one, who'd been burned at the stake. He'd woken with a jolt to find his binds on fire, his hands circled in flame. He must have dozed off and knocked over the candle.

He felt the slight touch of her hand against his. The bandages were off. He watched as awe filled the faces of the nuns. And now Ignatius looked at his hands. They were pink and new as baby mice. It was as if they didn't belong to him. But of course they did. He stretched his smooth pink fingers, feeling the pull of new skin. He wriggled them, moved his hands as if wearing

in a new pair of gloves. When he made a fist, his knuckles became shiny and the backs of his hands as smooth as soft kid leather.

His nails were still long and curved but the fungal infection causing the discoloration had cleared and his nails were pink and shiny too. Margarita held the hands, turning them over in hers, gazing at them in wonder.

The whole fire episode might have been a dream were it not for the faint mark where the binds had been. Ignatius had once seen the photo of a Hiroshima victim and vividly recalled the floral pattern of the dress the woman was wearing burned into her arm like a tattoo. In the rings around his wrists were the imprints of his binds.

Alleluia.

The Lord's right hand has triumphed;
his right hand raised me up.
I shall not die, I shall live
and recount his deeds.

Ignatius broke down and wept. He became every fluid thing, ebbed and flowed. The stilted fish he had been for so long now swam and rippled in the tide. He brought his new hands up to his face. Tears baptized them. For the first time as a priest, for the first time ever, he understood the meaning of resurrection, the eternal renewal of life.

There was marinated cheese and toasted bread, potatoes and boiled nettles. A bottle of wine and gingerbread men.

Ignatius wondered about the lack of paschal lamb, then thought it was just as well. He felt a little squeamish at the idea of eating an animal he'd just said Easter prayers with. He seemed to have no need of fleshly sustenance. It was all he could do to manage a small mouthful of nettles.

There was a lightness at the dinner table, a daintiness in the way they ate compared to the shoveling-in that had disgusted him at the first meal. Perhaps it was simply that they were all so tired. They had eaten little over the Eastertide, although there had been plenty of spiritual nourishment. Tired but happy. Ignatius smiled to himself, recalling the concluding phrase of school compositions about what he'd done during the holidays.

And he noticed that Margarita was smiling too. A tentative fluttery little smile like a shy young child. As she lowered her eyes and reached for a gingerbread man Carla exclaimed, "Present!" She got up and left the table.

In less than the time it took Margarita to bite the arm off her gingerbread man, Carla had returned, with something hidden behind her back.

"Eastre's egg," she announced.

He blinked. Surely she meant Easter egg.

"Eastre's egg," she repeated.

No, he'd heard right the first time. Oestrus egg. She'd definitely said it. Ignatius wondered if he was blushing. He took a gulp of wine. He could always blame the blush on that. Oestrus was one of those words, along with gonad and uterus, that he and a group of boys had looked up in the dictionary one afternoon when they were supposed to be working on a science project. He particularly remembered oestrus because it was a difficult one to find. They'd looked first under "e," then under "a," and only as a last resort had they tried "o." "A regularly occurring period of sexual receptivity in most female mammals, except humans, during which ovulation occurs and copulation can take place." The definition had engendered a whole new string of words that they were in the process of looking up when Brother Carmody had walked in, pleased to see them working so furiously and not making paper planes.

Carla appeared to be telling a story. He'd missed the first part and had no inclination to ask her to repeat it. Something about a goddess who'd coupled with a serpent and produced the golden egg from which the world hatched. "And the people honored Eastre in the month when spring returns to the world and the resurrection of the Lord Jesus Christ is named after her."

Ignatius had a niggling suspicion that what she was saying was true. Easter was not of Greek or Latin origin, like paschal. He had always assumed that it had something to do with the East, recollecting perhaps the Magi who had come from the East. But then that was another story. The most important event in the Christian calendar and it was named after a pagan goddess. He gulped his wine, even though he was already feeling quite lightheaded.

She brought her hand out of hiding and there cupped in the palm was an Easter egg, dyed red like the ones the Easter Bunny brought him and his sister. Ignatius laughed with relief, glad to be back in familiar territory. He thanked her for the gift.

Perhaps it was because his new hands were so smooth and even but the egg felt oddly bumpy. He looked more closely and saw that he was holding a potato. Then he caught a whiff of blood. It was not red dye at all. He did not want to even begin to imagine the source of that blood.

Now they entered the time between Easter Sunday and Pentecost. They sang alleluia and in the octave of days after Easter celebrated the solemnities.

It had been such a beautiful Easter, the priest leading them in the mass, all tension dissolved, Iphigenia, Carla, and Margarita a community again, that Iphigenia had kept her burden to herself. But now it started to weigh heavily on her. Easier for a camel to pass through the eye of the needle than a rich man to enter Heaven.

It was midmorning, the monastery was at peace. The little assembly was in the courtyard, Margarita having a quiet chat to Agnes Teresa; the priest with yarn around his hands, Carla winding it into skeins. Iphigenia took herself off to the abbess's office. The most appropriate place to think about her unwanted wealth.

There was another reason as well. Though the priest had entered into the spirit of Easter, Iphigenia doubted whether he would give up so easily the sale of the monastery. Though she had come across the fateful letter announcing her inheritance, she still hadn't found the lease. In the world the

Easter break would be over and Mr. Colquhoun back at work.

Iphigenia was back at work too. She sneezed. It was so dreadfully dusty in the abbess's office. There was no reason why she shouldn't at least clean the cobwebs away. Whereas on her previous visit, she had gingerly pulled the cobwebs aside to reach the handle of the drawer, this time she gave one broad sweep with her hand and pulled a whole section of sticky grayness away. She wiped it off on her skirt.

She had already looked through the top drawer and had been halfway through the contents of the second when she had found the Trust letter. She picked up where she had left off. Was she still a real nun if she had wealth, even if she had never seen it and it was a long way away, in several—what had Mr. Colquhoun said—portfolios?

She continued through the drawer, paying special attention every time she found a letter from the Bishop of Ferns and Manner. But it was usually something about repairs, although she did come across a note in response to the abbess's inquiry concerning a gift of specially spun wool from the St. Agnes convent in Rome. Iphigenia remembered the abbess's announcement that they were receiving yarn from the very sheep who produced the wool for the Pope's pallia.

But it had never arrived. The abbess had said she would make inquiries. And now Iphigenia was reading the Bishop's reply saying the matter was being looked into.

No lease in the second drawer. Iphigenia went to the drawers on the other side. If she just ignored the wealth would that be all right? If the wealth remained out there in the world she could still maintain her vow of poverty in here. More letters about repairs. She had stopped looking at handwritten letters now, the lease must surely have been typed. Iphigenia wondered what a loophole looked like and whether she'd recognize it if she came across it.

It was in the bottom drawer that Iphigenia came across something that wasn't a letter at all. Not even paper. A short leather-bound handle with several pieces of leather thonging attached. She puzzled over it. Then amid the leather smell of it she picked up traces of blood. The ends of the thonging were discolored with it. She knew now what the thing in her hand was—a whip for ritual flagellation. She dropped it back in the drawer. She had looked far enough into the abbess's things.

With another sweep she wiped the cobwebs and dust from the top of the desk. For how many years had dust been misting down, so quietly and softly that no one had ever noticed? Perhaps the lease wasn't here at all, perhaps only the Bishop had a copy. What were the other options, a heritage order? But that would bring people. Someone would have to come to estimate the value of the monastery. The worth of it. The wealth. Her nose was quivering. It was coming again. The same feeling she had when she decided to use the phone, when she first saw the Trust letter. Two birds with one stone. It was monumental. She hoped her quivering nose had not made a mistake.

"*Did you have* a pleasant Easter, Sister?"

"Yes, thank you, Mr. Colquhoun. And you?"

"Very pleasant indeed. I went to my country house. Too early for salmon, but we took some nice walks along the river. I presume by your phone call that you have found the lease?"

"No. But I think I have found a legal loophole."

"Yes?"

"Please remind me, how much money is my inheritance?"

"A few million."

"Is that enough to buy the monastery?"

He laughed. "Enough to buy the whole island, I would say."

"The monastery will suffice. Mr. Colquhoun, I wish to make a purchase, I wish to buy the monastery. Please arrange this at your earliest convenience."

Mr. Colquhoun's laughter was replaced by shocked silence.

"Are you there, Mr. Colquhoun, can you hear me?"

"Yes, Sister." She imagined him touching his bow tie, pulling it away from his neck.

"Is there a problem?"

"No, it's just that, well . . . You certainly have found yourself one hell of a loophole, Sister." His voice became more businesslike. "Do you know which agent is handling the sale?"

"Make discreet inquiries with the Bishop. The Bishop of Ferns and Manner. And please, Mr. Colquhoun, I would like to buy it anonymously. Would that be possible?"

"Of course. The Featheringale Trust is a legal entity, we would purchase it as trustees. We would simply approach the vendor on behalf of an undisclosed principal. We sign the contract to purchase the property. In any case, the Bishop might never see the name on the contract. The Bishop would probably not concern himself with such detail. It is an agreement between us and the Bishop's solicitor. Now, if I am to proceed, there are a few things we need to clarify."

. . .

They had just finished lunch. Carla and Margarita and especially the priest himself thought it odd that Iphigenia considered that he needed to have an afternoon nap. "I know you are feeling well now but sometimes after burns there can be a . . . delayed reaction." It didn't sound very convincing but Carla and Margarita started to see that Iphigenia must have a very good reason for wanting him to have a nap.

Once the priest was dispatched, Iphigenia brought her sisters out into the courtyard again. They sat waiting for her to tell.

"She considereth a field and buyeth it," Iphigenia announced.

They looked at her expectantly, waiting for more. "She seeketh wool, and flax, and worketh willingly with her hands." They recognized the precepts for a virtuous woman. Proverbs 31. But it was hardly portentous enough to warrant the trouble of carrying the priest back to bed.

"My grandmother is buying the monastery," Iphigenia said finally.

It made less sense than the first thing. Margarita was beginning to worry about Iphigenia. Many unusual things had happened of late. Perhaps they were all losing their marbles. How could Iphigenia's grandmother still be alive? Margarita was sure she remembered them saying a requiem mass for Iphigenia's grandmother, many many years ago.

"A grandmother?" said Carla. She never imagined Iphigenia or any of the nuns having mothers and fathers and grandmothers. They never talked about them, not to Carla anyway. She assumed the sisters were all gifts from God, foundlings like herself who had just turned up on the doorstep of the monastery.

"My grandmother was called to God many years ago. But she left money behind."

"Where?" asked Margarita, imagining it was in a jar or a sock. How had Iphigenia come across it, was it somewhere in the monastery?

"With her solicitor."

"Solicitor?"

The more Iphigenia said the less her sisters seemed to understand. She stopped. Took some breaths. She was going too fast. How could they be expected to understand straightaway? They knew nothing about the phone calls to Mr. Colquhoun, nothing about the Trust letter.

She gathered it all together and tried as best she could to tell the story. It seemed to take ages because every time she explained one thing ten other things sprang up that needed explaining as well. But eventually she finished. "And we can stay here and nobody can make us move, not even the Pope himself."

Carla was amazed. All of this had been accomplished through black and squarish. Carla watched as Iphigenia produced the phone. Here it was, after all this time. Carla crept her hand around it. She pushed up the aerial and prodded the buttons. She knew just how to do it. "Hello, hello?" But she heard nothing. "Seven buttons," said Iphigenia.

Ring, ring. Ring, ring. What a sound it made, like a thrush in the apple trees calling to its mate.

"Hello?"

"Hello? Hello?" she chirruped.

"Who is this?" It was a gruff, grumpy voice.

"Hello? Hello?"

Then the voice stopped and was replaced by an unpleasant noise similar to the one the car had made.

"Hello? Hello?"

But the voice had gone. Carla was disappointed with the voice from the world. She hadn't expected such gruff grumpiness. Still, she wasn't going to let that spoil her good mood. She was part of a secret, she and Iphigenia and Margarita. She put a finger up to her lips and looked in the direction of the priest's room. "Secret, eh, Iphigenia?"

"Yes," smiled Iphigenia, "we mustn't tell."

"What will become of him?" asked Margarita.

He was to be their guest till they heard from Mr. Colquhoun that the sale had been transacted. "Then we let him go."

A splendid idea, thought Margarita.

They took up their ancient rhythm. The Blessed Virgin, St. Anne, and the stained-glass saints enjoyed the company of the nuns, the vibration of their voices and their holy words seven times the next day and the next. But although observation of the canonical hours returned life at the monastery to its eternal circularity, there was a meteor on a trajectory heading straight for it.

"Do you have news, Mr. Colquhoun?"

"I have made a phone call. Rather curious in fact."

"Curious?" What could be curious?

"They asked where I had heard of the sale. It seems it has not yet been advertised. Considering your desire for anonymity, I could hardly give you as the source." Iphigenia started to get a tingling warning knot in her chest. "I simply said that I had received an expression of interest in the property. And then I was told a rather curious tale. About a priest, the Bishop's secretary actually, who had set out to examine this property and never returned. Did you receive a visit from this priest?" The knot in Iphigenia's chest grew tighter and tighter. She tried to calm herself by remembering that in the book they said the disadvantage of the telephone was that you couldn't see the person's "body language." It was an advantage now. She was extremely grateful that Mr. Colquhoun could not see her. "Hello. Sister, are you there?" She must have made some sort of noise because he continued. "They viewed my inquiry with a certain amount of suspicion. Banks, Colquhoun and Andrews is a highly respected firm of solicitors, of long, long standing. Never in all its history has even the slightest shadow of doubt been cast on any of its dealings. If I am to represent you, Sister, you must be perfectly frank with me."

"Of course, Mr. Colquhoun."

"I am informed that the Bishop wishes to rationalize the Church's assets but needs his secretary's assessment before the sale can proceed on this property. They sent out a search party for the priest but found no trace of him. But in view of my inquiry they are considering mounting the search afresh. If you have had any contact with this person, or any information pertaining to this matter, I believe it is in everyone's interest that you let me know."

Iphigenia found herself gaping like a fish. "Of course, Mr. Colquhoun." She briskly terminated the call.

She went to lie down in her cell, leaving the phone on the courtyard table in case it still had some residual power and could convey a message to Mr. Colquhoun. Her heart was beating fast and she could smell her sweat, a gingery odor.

She lay on the bed, breathing in and out, her hands crossed over her heart, willing it to calm. After all that had happened, after the fire, the breaking apart of the community and its coming together again, the knitting together of its bones, her announcement to her sisters that they would buy the monastery and everything would be all right. Now this. The balance of life seemed very fragile indeed if it could be upset so easily.

They would not be able to hold the priest till the sale was assured. A second search party would be more thorough. They would land, they would look. The community couldn't hide forever. And they couldn't hide him forever. The priest who had disappeared would have to reappear.

She rested on the bed, watching the sky. It would be Sext soon. She would discuss the matter with her sisters and together they would concoct a plan.

She came to Ignatius's room carrying bread, cheese, and apple chutney.

"Are you enjoying your stay with us?" she asked.

To tell the truth, right now he was feeling a bit miffed. They left him alone in his room for long periods while they all sat in the courtyard enjoying each other's company and doing their chores. He was the priest who had celebrated Easter for them, yet now they treated him like a child, a pet, carrying him back in here for an afternoon nap, as if he wasn't capable of staying awake all day. But it was better than before. "It has been . . . interesting."

His response seemed to please her. She gave him the plate of food. He dipped the cheese in the chutney, put it on the hunk of bread, and wolfed it down. Enjoy, no. But at least he was being fed.

The knitting that had been suspended resumed in earnest and once again the priest was back in the role of storyteller.

"Gingerbread Man!" shouted Carla. They had finished the last man off at dinner and it was fresh in her memory. She could still taste him. "Run, run as fast as you can, you can't catch me I'm the gingerbread man," Carla gurgled to remind him.

Yes, yes, he remembered the refrain but how did the story start? He was being chased by . . . a farmer's wife?

"Once upon a time there was a gingerbread man who was being chased . . ."

"No, no, no," roared Carla. How could he get it so wrong? "Once upon a time Sister Cook baked a batch of gingerbread men." Having started him off, Carla settled into the knitting, a happy smile on her face.

"Yes, right," said Ignatius. "When it came time to take them out, she opened the oven door and one of them leaped out and ran from the kitchen. 'You can't catch me I'm the gingerbread man,' he shouted back to her. He knocked over a pot of beans on his way . . ."

"Bucket of water," corrected Carla.

He glared at her. "Perhaps you would like to tell the story?"

He was looking cross. It was wrong to interrupt. She put her head down and concentrated on the knitting.

"He knocked over a bucket of water," he said emphatically, "and ran out of the kitchen. Then he came across a sheep. He ran up and butted into the sheep's back legs. The sheep was very annoyed at this interruption to her grass eating and started to chase him. 'Run, run as fast as you can, you can't catch me I'm the gingerbread man.' Now he had the farmer's wife, sorry, Sister Cook, and the sheep after him. He ran over the fields and down the hill, leading them in a merry chase. Halfway down the hill he met a rabbit. 'What a silly tail,' he said to the rabbit and off he went. The rabbit ran after him. He came to a body of water, big and wide. He could not go in the water because he would go all soggy.

"Just then a wily fox appeared. 'Quickly, gingerbread man, hop on my back and I will take you across the water.' The gingerbread man looked around. His pursuers were very close. He hopped onto the fox's back.

"Halfway across the water the gingerbread man had forgotten all about the danger and boldly picked up his old refrain, 'Run, run as fast as you can, you can't catch me I'm the gingerbread man.'

" 'What's that you say, gingerbread man? I can't hear you. Creep closer.' The gingerbread man crept higher up the fox's back and repeated it.

" 'What's that you say, gingerbread man? Creep closer to my ear so that I can hear you.' The gingerbread man crept up even closer to the fox's pointy ears.

" 'Run, run as fast as you can, you can't catch me I'm the gingerbread man.' But still the fox seemed not to hear. Silly old deaf fox. Now the gingerbread man got up so close he could see right inside the fox's ear. 'Run, run as fast as you can,' he shouted into that strange labyrinth of curls and folds, 'you can't catch me I'm the gingerbread ma—' The fox snapped his jaws and the gingerbread man disappeared in one gulp. And that was the end of the gingerbread man." Ignatius settled back.

But they seemed to be waiting for more. "And . . ." Carla encouraged him.

"And . . ." He tried to think of something. "And the fox got to the other shore and lived happily ever after?"

"No, no, no," said Carla in the voice she used to admonish the hedgehog. "After eating the gingerbread man, the fox came back. Because he remembered the sheep. And where there are sheep there are lambs. He quietly followed the sheep and Sister Cook back up the hill, and waited till night. He ravaged a lamb and left a scene of sheer carnage. So the nuns had to kill the fox. Then all the Agnes sisters lived happily ever after." She smiled merrily at him. They put their knitting down and sighed. A story well told.

They had done a lot of work to his nice, fast rhythm. They brought the knitting over and held it up against him. It was getting quite long. "Robing Day soon," they announced.

They carried him back to his bed. Though his legs were still encased his new hands had remained unbound. Still, the candle was not replaced and he thought it was probably better not to ask for another one. He put his hands behind his head. Robing Day soon. Legs. And then he would go.

The darkness thickened and he knew Iphigenia had entered. It had been some time since she had paid a nocturnal visit.

"So much to do to turn this into a resort," she said.

He shifted slightly. He said nothing but he had heard.

"Cut back the brambles. Mark out the path. Swimming pool. Golf course."

She had hardly touched the surface. There was a lot to do but it would be worth it. The location was too good to be true. Playground of the rich and famous.

"And then there is us. We could become difficult. 'Church turns three elderly nuns out of their home,' " she quoted imaginary headlines. Mr. Colquhoun had given her the idea about the newspapers.

Ignatius had imagined similar headlines but he wished she hadn't brought it up.

"We have been making inquiries. You have come here to assess the property. There is no committed buyer for it." He felt annoyed. It was none of her business. It was his project, he was in charge. "This is true, is it not, Father Ignatius?" He felt his face flush in the dark. It was true, damn it, but how did she find out? Had she actually phoned the Bishop and spun him some story? Worse, had the Bishop actually listened to her! He noticed that for the first time she had addressed him as Father Ignatius. But rather than showing respect, it somehow seemed to erode his authority even further. He felt as if she'd caught him playing with himself.

Uninvited, she plopped herself down on his bed. He had to steady himself with his hand to stop from rolling in her direction. "Not very talkative this evening, are we?" She leaned over and picked a bit of lint off his arm, tucked the blanket around him. Good grief! "A story?"

He opened his mouth, his response to the request almost automatic. But no, it was Iphigenia who was going to tell him a story.

"Once upon a time there were three sisters who lived in a big house high on a hill. The seasons turned, they prayed to God, tended their sheep, and knitted their wool. One day a visitor arrived. Visitors had not come for many years and they were quite surprised. Nevertheless, they welcomed him as an honored guest.

"When he had eaten of their meat and drunk of their wine, he announced that the house was being sold and they would have to leave. Leave? It was preposterous.

" 'Cut out his heart and bury him in the forest.' 'Fatten him up and eat him.' But none of these things seemed quite right. He tried to trick them and run away. He hurt himself, they brought him back and attended to his wounds. They tethered him to quieten his savage spirit. They prayed and prayed.

"And by and by one of the sisters remembered that her fairy grandmother had a helper. All they had to do was call him. But this was not an easy thing. Although their voices reached God, they did not reach as far as Grandmother's helper. But there was a way. Something the visitor had brought from his world. They learned its magic, put their voice into it, and this time the fairy grandmother's helper heard them.

"This helper was a very, very good elf and the fairy grandmother was a very, very wise woman. She had left a pot of gold in the elf's care. He was to mind the gold until such time as it was needed. And now was the time. The solution was plain as the nose on your face. If the house was for sale then it must be bought. And the sisters would be the ones to buy it!"

Iphigenia walked to the window and looked into the night. The Easter moon was waning, almost half of it in shadow now. She turned to face him. "This is the happy ending for the sisters but the man is in the story too. What is the happy ending for the man?"

He waited, expecting her to reveal it.

But it was Iphigenia who was waiting.

"They give the man a new set of clothes and send him on his way?"

"A good idea, but there is still a loose end. Does the man recommend that the monastery become a playground for the rich?"

"No," he murmured.

"Pardon? I didn't hear you."

He sighed and said it louder.

"But ah," said Iphigenia, pointing her finger in the air, "that will never do. Because the man will have failed in his mission. And so his ending is not happy. How can he accomplish his mission so that the ending is happy for everyone?"

It was late, he wasn't in the mood for riddle solving. He was not Oedipus, even if Iphigenia thought she was the Sphinx. "I don't know," he said. He wishes she would leave now, he just wants to go to sleep.

"It may not be an answer you can think of immediately, yet there is a way. Just as the sisters' solution was in the story all the time, so is the man's. I will give you until tomorrow morning." And with that she disappeared.

He was overtired, he could not sleep. She had gone but she had left behind a conundrum. He could almost see it sitting there in the room, a lump with glowing eyes. If he didn't think of something it would grow out of control. What had she said? Help from an unexpected source. Where was his unexpected help going to come from? The solid stone walls remained mute. When he looked out the window the moon hid behind a cloud.

Although Ignatius recognized familiar patterns in the story it had not soothed him. Perhaps it was the way she told it. Ignatius reflected that though she had become more and more voluble, this was the first time he had heard Iphigenia tell a story.

The loose end dangled in front of him. He adjusted his position. Was she honestly trying to tell him they had money stashed away, enough to buy the monastery? It was all bluff. This farce had gone on long enough. He was well within his rights to have them all charged. Despite the détente that Easter had brought he had not lost sight of the fact that they were keeping him here against his will. He was the prisoner, but they were the ones that needed locking up.

But he wouldn't be pressing charges. He wouldn't be telling anyone that three old nuns had managed to keep him prisoner all this time.

He had till morning. Then what? Was she going to have him put to death, like the sultan and Scheherazade? That is what Ignatius had become, a Scheherazade entertaining them nightly. And also, like Scheherazade, trying to stay alive, to keep his audience in his thrall.

She was giving him the chance for his own happy ending. He went over the story bit by bit. By morning, when Iphigenia appeared, he hadn't slept a wink and he didn't have a solution. "I don't know," he cried.

She didn't seem to mind at all. "It's simple." She beamed.

It was simple. Simple, outlandish, impossible, absurd. Nevertheless, here he was out in the courtyard, a party to it. That's when he realized how truly exhausted he was. He had brain fatigue, the filter needed changing.

It was a foggy cold morning. They had eaten breakfast but the dampness hadn't yet lifted. The sisters, the sheep, the trees, the fields, the buildings were swallowed up in fog.

"I believe you wanted this?" Iphigenia came into focus, laying the phone on the table. He stared at it dumbly. It seemed so long ago that he'd played his clever games with Carla. And now here was the phone that his cleverness had failed to produce. For some reason the mere sight of it made him want to burst into hysterical laughter. He tried to compose himself. He bit the inside of his lip and pictured the Bishop and the other priests around the presbytery fireplace. Even that seemed hilarious. He cleared his throat, picked up the phone, and prepared to be businesslike.

"The Bishop, please." He was told that the Bishop was unavailable. "It's . . . it's Father Ignatius." He dropped his bombshell.

"Ignatius? Where are you, what the hell happened? The old man had a chopper out looking." It was Dominic, one of the ones who told the jokes about boys. The three sisters loomed, so close he could feel their breath.

"It's a long story. I'd better speak to the Bishop."

The unavailable Bishop suddenly became available. "Yes?" he said. As soon as Ignatius heard the Bishop's voice he saw him. Pink skin like Ignatius's new hands, thin white hair with his scalp shining through like a baby's. The Bishop looked as if he had spent his entire life swaddled. So much at odds with that clear-spoken authoritative voice. Dominic wouldn't have been able to stop himself telling the Bishop that it was Ignatius on the phone but until he had personal confirmation the Bishop wouldn't assume a thing.

"It's Father Ignatius, My Lord."

"Where are you? Are you all right?"

Ignatius looked up again. How could he tell the Bishop he had a tail instead of legs, that three mad women were breathing down his neck.

"Yes, yes," sputtered Ignatius, biting his lip. The nuns were looking at him so earnestly. He couldn't help himself, he was shuddering with the effort of holding the laughter in.

"Excuse me, My Lord, there's some interference. I'll call back immediately." He put the phone down, shooed the nuns away, and laughed till tears ran from his eyes. The nuns looked from one to the other. Not even Carla found this amusing. The sight of them so stern-faced made him laugh even more. "I can't," he managed to get out between sobs.

"Perhaps the chapel will cure you," said Iphigenia.

They sat him down in front of the altar, where he had celebrated mass. It worked. His giggles disappeared and he merely felt tired. He turned away from the Blessed Virgin in case her ludicrous hair set him off again and phoned the Bishop back. "Sorry about that, My Lord. Yes, perfectly all right. Well, not perfectly." It was a little easier now that the nuns had left a space around him and no longer had their ears glued to the phone.

"I had an accident, I'm afraid, lucky to get out of it alive. I . . . I was unconscious. Broke my leg. Legs," he added, looking down at himself. "This is the first chance I've had to phone. I'm sorry to say that the car ended up in the sea." That bit at least was true.

Now that he was calm, Ignatius was amazed at the ease with which it all came out. "Fortunately the accident happened on my way back, so I was able to have a good look at the monastery. Or at least the ruins of it," he embellished. "I don't really think it's suitable. In my opinion, the initial outlay would be enormous, a road would have to be built, the buildings are in great disrepair, there's a small graveyard—that would be a problem. Consecrated ground. The remains would have to be removed. There appears to be a seal colony on the cliffs at the base of the island. There would be all sorts of environmental objections. If the media got wind of it . . . However, I do have good news. I struck up conversation with a chap in a pub, a rather eccentric gentleman." Ignatius cleared his throat and gulped. There were parts of the story that even he was having trouble swallowing. He saw himself floundering in water, trying to touch the bottom. But if he stopped swimming now he'd drown. "We had a drink or two. It seems he was down this way looking for a property to purchase. A property away from it all, is what he said. Well, naturally I mentioned I had come from just such a place and we got talking. He seemed quite interested and said he would go and have a look."

The expression on Ignatius's face changed as he heard what the Bishop had to say. He looked over at Iphigenia, his eyes wide open in surprise. "Is that so? He has moved quickly, hasn't he? . . . Featheringale Trust?" A look of disbelief came over him. What had Iphigenia been up to? How could the Bishop have fallen for a ludicrous name like Featheringale? "No, I'm not familiar with it . . . Well"—he tried to quiet his voice so the nuns couldn't hear—"there was no firm commitment to the development company but I'm sure if we tell the representatives of the"—he could hardly bring himself to say it—"Featheringale Trust that there is another buyer interested we can get a very healthy price. And with the minimum of fuss."

It was the Bishop's turn to speak.

"I'm not sure," Ignatius answered. "Soon. No, no, no. I wouldn't hear of it. It's all right, my sister will drive me." He looked up at the nuns. When? "When I'm fully recovered. I'll let you know." Ignatius switched off the phone. "He wanted to send a car to pick me up."

"You have a very caring Bishop," remarked Iphigenia.

"A Bishop who will become very suspicious if I don't go back soon."

 She had known that once contact had been made between

the Bishop and his priest, it wouldn't stop there. How much time did she need to be assured that the sale had progressed so far it was irrevocable? Iphigenia picked up the phone and tapped out Mr. Colquhoun's number.

"Mr. Colquhoun? You may expect a call from the Bishop or his representative. Do not be surprised if they have the impression that you are acting on behalf of an eccentric old millionaire."

Mr. Colquhoun laughed. "Oh, but I am, Sister, I am."

There was a puzzled silence. "I don't understand."

He seemed on the point of explaining something, then changed his mind. "I'm sorry, Sister, please continue."

"I wish the sale to proceed as quickly as possible and for anonymity to be preserved at all times. How long is it likely to take?"

"You are going too fast," he laughed. "In the normal course of events, there is a settlement period, during which vendor or vendee can change their minds. I will have to liquidate some of your assets but I shouldn't imagine that would take too long." He paused. "However, I am a little concerned about the other matter. It may drag out the affair."

"The other matter?"

"The case of the disappearing priest. As I mentioned, they were not moving on the sale till that had been cleared up."

Iphigenia looked at the priest. "I think you will find that problem has solved itself."

"You seem to be very well informed, Sister."

She felt as if Taylor had caught her doing something naughty and Grandmother had to pretend she was chastising her. Grandmother never got angry with Iphigenia but she did enjoy watching her squirm with embarrassment. "In Church matters. In other matters, Mr. Colquhoun, I rely on you. If you do not hear from the Bishop, please telephone him. I will . . ." There it was again, a sudden silence, like a missed heartbeat. "Mr. Colquhoun?"

"Yes."

"I will call you again soon. Good-bye."

There was a flurry of activity that the monastery hadn't seen for years. Cleaning and polishing, dusting and spitting, as if they were preparing for a great event. And indeed they were. But it was an event that would take place far away, that would be represented on a piece of paper they would never see. Margarita and Iphigenia picked up their skirts and dusted St. Anne and the Blessed Virgin. Carla climbed up and delicately washed the stained glass, a bit of spit on a page of Bible, lovingly wiping the grime from the corner of the saints' eyes, dust from the angels' wings. The Agnes sisters rubbed their woolly bodies along walls and pews in an attempt to polish and shine, leaving tufts of wool behind all the while. They even let the priest help, polishing smaller items with his new pink hands. The table was scrubbed of sacrificial blood and spilled things, the Agnes sisters' droppings were picked up and spread on the garden. Carla even put her head in the trough, rubbed her fingers through to loosen the new curls, and shook like a dog, spraying water everywhere.

She was living in something great and momentous. Though she couldn't see it, she felt it everywhere like the breath of God.

Iphigenia had explained "sale" to her but there was nothing in monastery life remotely resembling "sale" and she still found it difficult to grasp. Nevertheless, she threw herself wholeheartedly into the sale preparations. It was like the Christmases of her childhood when they had pageants. Every year Carla would be Baby Jesus. She would lie very still in the manger, smell the sweet straw.

There were too few of them now. They would have to keep swapping around, just the three of them, to be Mary and Joseph, Baby Jesus, the Magi, the midwives, the oxen. Carla had tried to get the Agnes sisters to play the parts but they quickly lost interest and wandered away to eat grass. But now it felt like Christmas again and they'd only just had Easter!

Best of all in the cleaning was the abbess's office. It was such a long time since anybody had been in there apart from Iphigenia. They got wads of fleece and wiped away all the cobwebs. Such a lot of books, all dark red with pretty gold lettering on the spines. Carla was disappointed that the books had no pictures. But she was pleased to discover a small Blessed Virgin hidden behind a veil of web. When the abbess's office was finished they stood back and looked at it. A new room. It wasn't a bedroom, it wasn't a bakehouse. But although she didn't properly understand it, Carla thought it was just the right room for the thing that Iphigenia had done. "Flowers on the table!" Carla remembered one more detail of cleaning. She went to pick some buttercups.

No one was coming but Iphigenia said they would know when the "sale had gone through." What was it going through, the eye of a needle? Everything was mysterious and wonderful—new words, new ideas, excitement over things she couldn't see. The man's garment was finished, they were just waiting for the right time for the Robing.

When the scrubbing and spitting and polishing were done Iphigenia returned to the office to make another phone call to Mr. Colquhoun. She sat at the abbess's desk, imagining Mr. Colquhoun at his as he told her that steps had been taken, but that the Bishop was awaiting the return of his secretary before any sale could be finalized.

"And when does the Bishop think that will be?" probed Iphigenia.

"Soon. He seems to be a very popular young man, everyone is awaiting his return. Including the car-rental firm. They have lost a vehicle. In the ocean apparently. Their insurance company is anxious to talk to the priest. They may get impatient enough to start investigating without him." Iphigenia heard her heart pounding. "Are you sure, Sister, you have no information that can shed light on this matter?"

"We pray for the priest's safe return," Iphigenia managed to say. "Meanwhile, please progress as far as you can with the sale."

There was a crackle and the line went dead. She was consciously taking large gulps of air, as if her lungs were too tired to do it of their own accord. It had been difficult to hear everything Mr. Colquhoun said, the fuzzy prickles in her chest had moved into her ear and into the phone. Sometimes Mr. Colquhoun's voice was blocked out altogether.

They couldn't wait till the sale was secured, they would have to set the priest free now. She gathered the sisters together.

"It is time for Robing Day."

It was such a long time since there had been a Robing Day in the monastery. Carla loved the beautiful white wedding dresses the nuns wore before donning the black habits. Kneeling in front of the prelate in their flowing gowns, the matrons of honor removing the veil and the Bishop snipping off a lock of hair with his small silver scissors. Carla remembered too that on Robing Day they had biscuits made with honey. She reminded Iphigenia, in case she had forgotten. Iphigenia smiled tiredly. She was more concerned that they could still remember the words.

The nuns have come into the Knitting Room to fetch the priest's new garment. Carla opens the cupboard and everything tumbles out. Aprons, vests, skirts, blankets. All the knitting they have ever done, the pure white garments, the multicolored ones. Carla laughs, bowled over by the avalanche of wool, enough to outfit every sister in Christendom. She picks out the priest's garment. "Straw that broke the camel's back." She grins to Margarita and Iphigenia.

Iphigenia stares. At the millions and millions of tiny stitches, row upon row upon row. She hears the quiet click of needles, their voices chanting and telling stories before the Great Silence descends. Carla and Margarita begin to put everything back. But Iphigenia is still staring. At their own threadbare garments while scattered all around are the things they have made, of every hue and pattern. All this in the service of God yet stuck in a cupboard where God can't see.

They brought Ignatius into the courtyard and stood before him, a trinity of prelates. They had discarded their old garments and donned fluffy new white ones.

All morning he had been thinking about it. With the plaster off he would be free to leave. But instead of exhilaration he felt apprehension. Now that the moment he had so long awaited had finally arrived, he wasn't sure he was ready. He took a deep breath and put his trust in his Heavenly Father.

The nuns didn't know the words to robe a priest so they used the words to robe a sister instead.

"What do you ask?" they said.

"The mercy of God and the grace of the holy habit."

"Do you ask it with your whole heart?"

"Yes, my Lords, I do."

Ignatius kept his eyes to the ground, trying for the solemnity worthy of the true occasion.

"God grant you perseverance, my daughter," they said to him.

"My son," Ignatius murmured under his breath.

Now it was time for him to take off his white gown and don the black.

It was Margarita who was going to divest him. She approached with the shearing shears, smiling benignly. He turned his head to avoid the flash of sunlight bouncing off the blades.

She stood in front of his feet and looked at the white plaster, somewhat less white and pristine than when it had been applied. Margarita remembered applying the cast, wrapping the bandages round and round to keep the legs together, slapping the plaster on thickly, trying to immure him at it. And now she was going to let him out.

She walked around the plaster, assessing the task at hand. The best way in, of course, was at the top. She came up level with his hip. Ignatius noticed her hands tremble a little. Instinctively his hands made a cover for his penis. She came down to the feet again, tapping at the plaster, feeling for the hollow space between the feet. But she had done too good a job in the first place, inside the fishtail the feet were welded together like Siamese twins.

She decided to make the first cut at the side. She stuck one blade in between the plaster and his skin.

He flinched at the coldness of the metal. He must remain perfectly calm and still, so that she can do the job with no mistakes. This is the moment he has hoped and waited for. He knows it must happen but he feels as if he is being skinned alive. The plaster cast has become so much a part of him that he has to bite down on his lip to prevent himself from screaming out stop!

Iphigenia and Carla are watching, hands together over their stomachs.

Snip. The blade cuts into the plaster with a rough unpleasant sound, like metal being scraped over rock. Margarita's hand is steadied by the contact and she soon is absorbed in her task. She has even started humming the shearing chant. Carla and Iphigenia start humming too. The Agnes sisters come for a look. Snip. The incision reaches knee level.

Ignatius feels the coolness of air on his thigh. Without disturbing his pose, he stretches his neck a little to peer into the gap being created. Snip. And now he feels the blade along the outside of his calf. Snip, the ankle. Across the feet and up the other side. She stands back. It is done.

The priest lay perfectly still while Carla and Iphigenia lifted the dirty white carapace to free his legs. They stood gazing at those white legs with their brushing of black hairs so flattened down they looked as if they had been etched on. The pattern of hairs on his big toes made a sea anemone.

His legs were thinner, much thinner than Ignatius remembered. They were strange unfamiliar creatures. He tried to wiggle his toes but nothing happened, the nerves and the ganglions in that area were not receiving the message his brain was sending. Carla's hand hovered over his leg, checking with him to see whether he minded.

It was the lightest of touches but it shot through him like an electric charge. Nevertheless he bore with it. She gave a few more tentative strokes, delighted at the way the hairs sprang away from the soft moist skin.

The hairs weren't the only thing to spring. The charge that had jolted his legs also jolted his penis. His cupped hands proved to be poor covering indeed. Carla's eyes were round as saucers, yet she had learned not to touch Baby Moses in the bulrushes.

Her attention was diverted by Iphigenia. "The garment, Carla." The garment was neatly folded on the table. Carla took one more look, then picked the garment up and let it fall to its full length.

"Here," Carla said breathlessly. Without too much ceremony they placed the garment over his head and smoothed it down the length of his body. He was clad again, his body covered in fine wool that did not scratch. Margarita approached with the shears and snipped off some of his hair.

"He shall receive a blessing from the Lord, and mercy from God the Savior."

They had robed him, he had repeated the words of Simple Profession. He had become a nun.

He did not join in the nuns' prayer but fell to the prayer of St. Ignatius Loyola.

Soul of Christ, sanctify me.
Body of Christ, save me.
Blood of Christ, inebriate me.
Water out of the side of Christ, wash me.
O good Jesus, hear me;
Hide me within Thy wounds;
Suffer me...

Ignatius could not continue. How had he ever found those words edifying or uplifting? Suffering and hurts and blood and oozing wounds. This was not the prayer for a man who had just regained his human form, his dignity.

Ignatius sat with them for the evening meal, straight-backed, his feet touching the ground. He felt tall and elegant in his new robes. The garment resembled a cassock, and it was only when you took a closer look, at the warp and weft of it, did the nuns' designs become visible. There was no knitting and no stories this night, and immediately when supper was over, the four of them fell into the Great Silence.

In the days that followed a new set of preparations began—preparing the priest's legs for his return to the world. They took him for walks in the fields, at first with two of them supporting him, then eventually just Carla accompanying him.

"This is where I first saw you," she said, taking him to the spot in the brambles. "Down on all fours," she added, wondering if she reminded him, whether he'd do it again. "You said damn," she told him, whispering the word. But he wanted to move on. She told him the story of his stay at the monastery, took him to every place he had left a trace, showed him where he'd first put the battery, the hollow he had fallen in, the holding pen, everything.

They sat down in the grass, the sun catching all the different patterns in his cassock. Carla named all the stitches, taking him on a journey around the garment as she'd taken him around the monastery. "Purl and plain, feather and fan, moss, honeycomb, hunter's stitch, chevron, sand stitch, caterpillar, basket, embossed leaf, swarm, starfish, bobble, chalice, tassel, chain, eye of partridge, horizontal bat, plaited cord, knotted, St. John's wort, snaky cable. And fisherman's rib," she said finally.

She offered to show him how to do them all but he said he was feeling a bit tired and might go and lie down. Of his own accord, in the middle of the afternoon.

Before he left, Ignatius had to make one more phone call. The call to let the Bishop know he was coming back, to let him know it was time to put the fatted calf on to cook.

But what was to be a simple announcement became much more complicated. Now that he had had time to reflect, the Bishop had more probing questions for his secretary, questions that Iphigenia couldn't always preempt. Why hadn't he been taken to a hospital? What was the exact location of the accident? Had it been reported? More ominously, the Bishop had phoned Ignatius's sister to find out when she'd be driving him back. "She seems not to have heard from you, Father."

Ignatius gulped. "Yes, well, I did try to phone. She must have been doing the shopping." Ignatius was certain that the Bishop thought he was up to no good. He closed his eyes, dreading the thought of them all sipping port and joking about him the way they'd joked about Brother Terry.

"Does someone else have access to the phone?" asked the Bishop.

No. Yes. What should he say?

"A bill has come in. A call has been made from the mobile. Dominic has been very thorough. He rang the number but nobody knew you."

The thing he had hoped for, the thought he had savored on the other side of Easter had come to pass. Only now it was the last thing Ignatius wanted.

A call? One? The one she dialed in his room? "Perhaps the child of the family," Ignatius invented. He had to get back and intercept the next bill, the one that would show calls made to the Featheringale Trust people. Dominic would be sure to check. Trying to ingratiate himself with the Bishop, take over Ignatius's job.

He steered the Bishop away from the phone bill. "My Lord, my saviors are simple fisherfolk. They have no vehicle apart from their boat. As for the accident . . ." He looked at Iphigenia. The story had to convince her as much as the Bishop. "I cannot tell precisely. A narrow road around cliffs, there was mist and rain. I went straight over." The bishop asked him to give an approximate location, the name of a church, a village, town, anything. "Neenish." Ignatius named the last village he'd passed through. Or at least he thought that was what it was called. The name sounded odd to him. He could say any name and it wouldn't make any difference. Places in the world were just words.

The conversation was difficult for another reason. The

Bishop's voice kept dropping out, there was a background fuzz. The battery was going. Still, he could recharge it once he was back. Electricity! TV, computers, calculators, central heating, traffic lights, cars, buses, trains, satellites, cinemas, power tools. Oh, he could hardly wait.

"*I'd like* to have a wash," Ignatius said on the eve of his departure. They looked up from their kneading and chopping. He had thought that perhaps they would fill a basin with hot water for him, there was a kettle boiling on the fire, but instead they pointed to the trough. He sighed and walked over to it. Cold water but it was better than nothing. He wet a sop of fleece and squeezed it out. No. This warranted more than a dab wash. Tomorrow he was going back.

He took the bucket and sop out of the courtyard, away from the meal preparations. He gazed into the infinite pale sky wondering how far he could actually see. One mile, ten? What was the limit of his vision in the limitless sky?

Some of the Agnes sisters had gathered round. To them he smelled just like the others now. On his garment they picked up their own scent, his hair mingled with their stranded fleece.

He took the garment off and laid it over a bush. Then he tipped the bucket high over his head and water cascaded down. Sheep scattered everywhere. Bracing! His body came alive, hardened. He stood firm and was not moved by the force of water or the cool prickling breeze on his skin. He wiped himself down with the fleece and stood a minute longer, letting the elements play on his body. Then he donned his priest's garment again.

As he picked up the bucket and fleece he saw Carla, garment off, bucket above her head, grinning in his direction. He

quickly turned away, but the image had already been recorded. He wished he hadn't seen it. Not through a sense of propriety but because it was such an unwitting parody of himself.

As he shoveled handfuls of turnip into his mouth he looked from one to the other. Already their fresh white clothes were getting grubby. How similar they appeared. What was the expression they all wore as their jaws worked the food around their mouths—wariness, watchfulness? He couldn't tell.

Although the meal had been subdued Ignatius was not. He was so full of anticipation he could hardly lie still. The last night in this austere stone cell, the last sleep on this hard narrow bed. Tomorrow he would be out. He lay in the dark trying not to have too great expectations. He wouldn't relax fully till he was off the island. There would still be a long way to go after that before he was safely back in the presbytery, but all he could think of now was having the sea between him and the nuns. They would stay on the shore, they would not follow.

How much of the real story would he tell the Bishop? The last thing he remembered thinking was that he could tell the Bishop whatever he liked.

He drifted off. There was a soft amber blur, then the picture became clear and distinct, illuminated with evening light. Full-breasted, her arms raised, nipples erect under the sparkle of water as it cascaded over the mound of her belly, her thatch of curly hair, her sturdy legs strong and firmly planted. Her dark eyes glistening through the drops of water, acknowledging him,

playing a game with the water as if her nakedness didn't exist. An image of wanton voluptuousness.

He woke up with a jolt, his hands tightly round his penis as if trying to strangle it. He had only caught a glimpse of Carla before averting his eyes but apparently it had been enough. He wrenched his hands away and put them in the safety of the cold night air outside the warm cozy blanket. Tomorrow. He transferred this pounding desire into strength for his journey.

He became aware of noise. Footfall and whispering. They were moving up and down the corridor. Ignatius was fully alert now, waiting for them to come. Then the footsteps stopped and a faint chanting began. They were in the chapel. It was nearly morning. There was time. He brought his hands under the blanket again. "Soul of Christ, sanctify me. Body of Christ, save me. Blood of Christ, inebriate me. Water out of the side of Christ, wash me." Wash me, wash me, wash me. Faster and faster now, till he felt the rush and sweet release as he dedicated his seed to the Lord.

Iphigenia winced. The sudden smell clogged her nose like a lump of old cheese. She could hardly drag her breath up past it. She gazed at the adoring eyes of the Blessed Virgin, breathed in the freshness of her green coils till the smell settled into place and became one of many. Since he had his legs back he had taken to coming to chapel. He usually waited till they were here before he entered. He stayed at the back, never came and knelt with them.

After Lauds there was a flurry of activity—a picnic hamper prepared, things fetched. Ignatius stood in the cloisters watching. All the preparations were for his departure, yet no one asked him to do anything or what he needed. And only when they were ready did they bid him into their midst.

There on the table beside the basket he saw a pair of shoes, his shoes, and his priest's collar. Oh wondrous, wondrous. He almost cried at the sight of them, as if they were long-lost friends, they who were dead and had risen again. He reached out to embrace them but they were placed in the basket.

"Food for our journey and clothes for your world."

He wondered whatever had happened to his socks.

It was midday by the time the four had fully descended. The mist had lifted but the strand was still under water. With no way of knowing the tides, they determined to wait.

Ignatius was too restless to sit and look at the sea, much as he wanted that causeway to appear. He walked away from the group and went up the hill on the opposite side. Something had led him to this spot. It was the place where the car had gotten stuck. No trace of it now. He looked back at the sisters and for a moment he thought they were a stone formation, so still were they. He had left the car, activated the alarm, and climbed up the hill. He was only going to be an hour or two, then back to the mainland.

He looked up to the summit. The monastery was not visible from here. The entire island seemed to be covered in gorse. It was only when you got up close did you see patches of other colors, wildflowers and different shades of green, lusher where the stream ran, sparser and more hardy near the cliffs. He sat and looked over at the mainland. He could make out the deserted tavern, other buildings. Soon.

Then he saw it, the water a paler color, the path of sand just below the surface. The more the tide ebbed the more distinct the causeway became, like watching a photo develop. It was clearly out of the water now, stretching right across to the mainland. His way home. He ran toward it.

The sisters stood on the brink of the white sand and offered him farewell gifts. Ignatius had the absurd impression of streamers, crowds of people, as if he was about to go off on a big ocean liner.

They put the collar, stiff and tight, around his neck. They gave him his shoes, with new knitted laces. Instead of putting the shoes on his feet he tied the shoelaces together and slung them over his shoulder. They gave him the rest of the honey biscuits, a bottle of water, bread, cold cooked turnips, all wrapped in fleece. He put them into the pocket they had thoughtfully knitted into his cassock. Everything was done, all he had to do was depart.

Should he shake hands, thank them for having him? Nothing seemed appropriate. Once more he looked up, thinking perhaps his eyes had deceived him, trying to discern the shape of the monastery in the vegetation.

"I will lift up mine eyes unto the hills, from whence cometh my help.
He will not suffer thy foot to be moved: he that keepeth thee will not slumber.
The sun shall not smite thee by day, nor the moon by night.
The Lord shall preserve thee from all evil: he shall preserve thy soul.
The Lord shall preserve thy going out and thy coming in from this time forth, and even for evermore."

There was nothing more to say.

Iphigenia and Margarita watched the figure walk the path

across the water. But Carla was looking at the footprints that he'd left behind. She put her own foot in the first shoe of sand. Then the next and the next and the next till she too was walking out onto the strand.

Iphigenia felt a tugging at the cord as Carla went farther and farther out. A pliant cord, it stretched but would never break. She found that there was a cord attached to the man as well. How far would that one stretch? They had placed food and drink in his pocket, surrounded by the fleece of their prayers. She hoped he would not discard their prayers, once across the water and back in the world.

The sun was well into the west by the time two tiny figures, first one and then the other, reached the other side. Iphigenia sat looking out to the world but it was Margarita who had to tell her what she could see.

"Will she go with him?" she asked.

Iphigenia seemed not to hear. She was gazing out to the world but she was seeing something else. A young girl who lived with her sisters in a big house on top of the hill.

One day, one Midsummer Day, one of the sisters took ill and the girl had to fetch someone to attend to her. Down the hill she went, running fast, to bring help to her sister, and for the sheer joy of running through that bright summer day.

When she got to the village she met a fisherman mending his nets. His skin was smooth and brown as eggshell, his eyes like dark plums. His hair fell down in black waves. She watched his quick fingers, the slide of his arm, the curve of his glistening chest. He smiled at her, his teeth polished as ivory. Behind him the sea was silver and his skin glowed in the late afternoon sun. She told him what her task was.

"Sure, there's no one here," he said, "they're all over yonder." So dazzled was she by the comeliness of the fisherman she had not noticed the sound of merriment across the sea, but now she heard it. Between her island home and the mainland lay a strand of sand and when the tide was down you could walk across, but it was covered now. "Tide won't be down till tonight," said the young man. "I'm rowing across presently, I can take you if you like." She hesitated. She hadn't expected to go that far. But he was respectful and meant no harm. He did not even see the beautiful girl inside the clothes that hid her shape.

She waited till he had finished his mending, then, picking up her skirts, got into the boat. She sat with her back straight and her eyes downcast, unfamiliar as she was with being at such close quarters to a young man. And this is how she came to notice the way his feet held firm to the bottom of the boat and that they were curiously splayed, with webs of skin between the toes.

She heard the lap and pull of the oars and a faint music all around, as if the water itself was singing the boat across. She dared not look at his lips, the beads of salt on his cheek. Now the music of the sea was joined by the music and merriment from the land, rumble of voices, instruments, poem, and song and soon she felt a soft bump as the boat came to the shore. She had been away for hours but time seemed suspended, as if the muted light of Midsummer would last forever. She did not even know it was Midsummer Day till the fisherman told her. In her house this was the day of St. Aloysius Gonzaga. In three days they would celebrate the birth of John the Baptist.

The fisherman knew that the tavern was no place for a girl

who covered herself in such clothes and bid her wait by the boat. "I will go and fetch the bonesetter," he said. And so she waited a long time by the boat and on the sand and near the water till finally night came and the merriment showed no sign of dwindling. Twice she went and looked in the misted window of the tavern but she could not see her fisherman. She asked a man rolling out of the tavern where the bonesetter was. "He'd be in there," he said, and nearly toppled over a keg by the door.

She had never been into a tavern before but she had crossed the water, come this far, and she could not go back now. She pushed her way through the crowd. People offered her drinks. There was a fishy oily smell in here, mingled with ale. The talk and the merriment were very loud. "I'm looking for the bonesetter," she said. "He'd be here," was the reply when she finally made herself heard. But she didn't find him. Nor did she find the fisherman. When she asked after him nobody knew him.

The girl went back to where the strand would appear when it was time. She had drunk a glass of wine in the tavern and carried the sound of merrymaking in her ears. She wanted to dance on the sand. The air was such that her skin felt neither hot nor cold. The sea gently lapped the shore. On such a night as this the door between the worlds opens. The girl looked up and saw the milky smattering of stars and the crisp crescent of moon. When she looked for the strand she saw the sea too, smattered with stars.

She put her toes in. The water felt like champagne that she had drunk once in her grandmother's house, cold and bubbly on her skin. And now she wanted to immerse her whole body in the sparkling darkness. So she peeled off her skins, one by one, and left them on the shore. She felt no shame or embarrassment and she went in deeper and deeper. First her toes disappeared, then her knees, her belly, her breasts, her arms, and finally her head.

When she came up to breathe in the soft velvet night she spied on the shore another pile of discarded skins and heard the plop of a creature diving under the water. She put her head under to look for him, so enchanted and bewitched that she had no care for whether she would be able to see anything in that deep blue. How cold and invigorating the water was as it closed over her head, how alive she felt, how every pore of her body tingled.

And she could see beneath the surface. See the shape of the creature gently making his way toward her. Her hands came out to meet him and she felt his hair trailing like seaweed and then his mouth upon hers, surprised by its warmth and moisture. How quickly her arms moved to him, how smooth was his body. Soon she felt his lips, the gentle suck of a sea anemone, a necklace of kisses, her whole body decked in the treasures of his mouth, fastening onto the tips of her breasts, coaxing them.

She must have come to the surface for breath but she had no memory of it. The sea contained them, held them like a bed. She returned his kisses, swum in his mouth, his hands cupping her like shells. Then she felt him, an oar through the water, he entered her and she closed around him the soft suck of the anemone, to hold her captured creature. She marveled that he could fill her, that she had a space inside herself for this. She feels the rapture, she calls and is called, she seeks and is sought, she lifts and is lifted up, she clasps and is closely embraced. She gives him her breasts and receives unto herself his spurting milk.

When they were spent he kissed her tenderly, holding her

face in his hands, a kiss for remembrance. Iphigenia carried the seed inside her, a grain of sand that became a pearl.

"I don't know if she will be back," she said.

"Should we wait?"

"We will leave the fleece. If she is coming back, she will find the way. God keep her from harm," she whispered so that only God could hear.

"And he?" ventured Margarita.

"Would you like him to come?"

"He could visit from time to time. Like the priests of old."

They made their way home. It was a fair evening with no rain. Iphigenia stayed all night in the chapel praying with Mary, the Mother of God, and St. Anne her mother.

"Gabriel, Uriel, Michael . . ." Carla fairly ran up the hill, gathering the angels on the way. What a night, what a night, what a night! She had been to the world. She brought back with her a brown bottle and a weathered oar. By the time she had reached the island again the water had lapped up behind and covered her trace. But she knew where the strand was and how it appeared and disappeared. She could go across to the world any time she liked, she just had to wait till the path became visible.

She came in through the biscuity door, through the brambles, across the fields sparkling with dew and the courtyard smelling of bread. She knelt beside her sisters in the chapel, bursting with stories, bursting to tell.

. . .

In the days to come Iphigenia phoned Mr. Colquhoun once again. "The Bishop has not changed his mind?"

"Not so far."

"Thank you for everything you have done. Mr. Colquhoun," said Iphigenia. "If you would like to visit us sometime, we would be pleased to see you." She couldn't tell what Mr. Colquhoun's response was, so many crackles and gaps as the battery moved fitfully in and out of consciousness. When it wound down completely the phone became a relic to spend the rest of its days on the abbess's desk.

They knitted the story of the priest, each working on her own piece, then stitching them together till the story was complete.

Brambles grew over the door and soon it was winter again. A sudden sound, a buffeting of wind, the crack of a twig, would cause prayer to swell in their chests. In spring they set the table with forks, sat facing outward, watching and waiting for visitors in the vast blue emptiness.

Father Ignatius was appointed undersecretary to the Congregation for Bishops and the following Easter joined his brethren in their red vestments, so close to the Holy Father he could have reached out and touched him. In the darkened church he feels the texture of the garment fashioned from his hair and their fleece, the round of days in the monastery, the pattern of their lives. And as the candles are lit and the *Exsultet* begins, he sees Carla walking toward him on the ribbon of light. And now Iphigenia and Margarita, the Agnes sisters, the Blessed Virgin,

St. Anne and the stained-glass saints, the worms and the birds. Shimmering.

That which was from the beginning, which we have seen with our eyes, which we have looked upon, and our hands have handled, of the Word of life;
That which we have seen and heard declare we unto you, that ye also may have fellowship with us:
And these things write we unto you, that your joy may be full.